COMPROMISE with SIN

Leanna Englert

ENCHANTED INDIE PRESS

Austin

They enslave their children's children who

make compromise with sin.

—Helen Keller
(quoting James Russell Lowell)

PUBLISHER'S NOTE

Although this story was inspired by actual historical events, it is a product of the author's imagination. With the exception of several historical figures, any resemblance of characters to actual persons, living or dead, is purely coincidental. Helen Keller and Edward Bok are sometimes portrayed in a fictitious manner but always in a way that remains true to who they were. The description of the Nebraska campaign for "babies' sore eyes" legislation and workings of the Nebraska State Legislature are fictitious.

Copyright © 2017 by Leanna Englert
Cover design by Kristin Bryant of 99designs
Additional cover design and interior design for print and digital editions by Tosh McIntosh
Author photo by Timothy Englert
Editing by Susan Mayson and Patsy Shepherd

**Published in the United States of America
by Enchanted Indie Press**

ISBN-13: 978-1-938749-36-0
ISBN-10: 1-938749-36-0

Also Available in Digital Format

ISBN-13: 978-1-938749-37-7
ISBN-10: 1-938749-37-5

Praise for Leanna Englert's
COMPROMISE with SIN

Kirkus Reviews Starred Review

"Englert's novel intriguingly mixes fiction and real-life history. . . . A recommended historical novel that almost perfectly captures its time and place."

—Kirkus Reviews

"The quality of writing is outstanding; much historical information is conveyed within the context of a fascinating story. . . . The book is truly a page-turner."

—Readers' Favorite 5-Star Review

Dedicated to all who make the journey

in spite of the dark

COMPROMISE with SIN

PART 1

Chapter 1

December 1894

Slumped on the toilet after her nausea subsided, Louise Morrissey pressed a wet handkerchief against her forehead and made no effort to stop the cool rivulets trickling down her wrist. She could hold her breath only so long; then the foul smell of the public comfort station above Anderson's Seed and Feed assaulted her, and she reached for the atomizer of lavender water.

As Louise sprayed the cloying fragrance about the cramped room, she longed to be back in her own pristine water closet. Home. What was it she needed to tell Frank? Then she remembered. As she was leaving Riverview Inn, the hotel they owned and called home, a guest had stopped her to complain that his room was as cold and drafty as an old castle. Frank could be so exasperating. He had promised weeks before to seal the room's ill-fitting storm window, but he frittered away hours in his workshop with their friend Yonder LaFontaine, tinkering—she stopped mid-thought and set down the atomizer. What did she care about the Inn, the thankless job of the innkeeper's wife? Her future was with Doc.

In a matter of minutes she would hear the words that would launch her new life. Benjamin Dewitt Foster, M.D., expected to be named to the faculty of Washington University School of

Medicine in St. Louis. As his wife, she would accompany him, her arm in his, to the theater and charity balls, indulge her love of classical studies, and champion worthy causes. And bear his children.

Feeling stronger, she stood and studied her face in the crazed mirror that hung askew from a rusty nail. In the miserly light from a bare overhead bulb she looked all of her thirty-one years. With a trembling hand she dabbed powder to conceal dark circles under her eyes and blotted perspiration that made flaxen curls cling to her forehead.

The sound of the doorknob turning startled her. It turned again, accompanied by insistent knocking.

"One moment, please." She composed herself with a deep breath that she exhaled slowly, picked up her handbag and hat, and unlocked the door.

A farmer in ragged overalls looked down at his boots. "Pardon, missus."

Louise stepped out into the empty hallway. Few people would have reason to come to the second floor today, as the professionals who had offices there took Wednesday afternoons off and the Riverbend Ladies Lending Library, which Louise had founded and now operated with the help of other volunteers, was closed.

She walked down the hall past the lawyer's office and, without pausing, as though the space were nothing out of the ordinary, past Doc's surgery. When she reached the library, she picked up three books from the wicker table that sat in the hall for the after-hours convenience of patrons. Unlocking the door she made a mental note to post a fresh sign to replace the tattered one that read, "Open Monday and Thursday all day, and Saturday morning. Adult Literacy Class, Tuesday night."

On Wednesday afternoons the library belonged to her. She went there alone to order materials, keep financial records, shelve returned items, and, in recent months, to meet her lover.

She set her hat and handbag on a shelf in the library workroom. She was shivering in spite of her coat but lacked the strength to get a fire going just yet. Instead she reclined on the green sofa in the social corner. Her swelling breasts and expanding midsection pushed against her shirtwaist. Should she have told Doc earlier? No, she had done the right thing in not forcing his hand.

With one finger she traced the upholstery pattern of raised ivy vines. Her thoughts drifted to the forbidden pleasures she had known here. Doc's words that she had recalled so many times thrilled her anew: "Wild horses could not keep us apart." She smiled and forgave him the cliché.

She watched as dust moved from shadow to become illuminated in shafts of sunlight streaming through the windows. Her finger traveled along the upholstery pattern and idled on its misaligned seam where leaves and vines failed to connect. A glimpse of her emerald-and-pearl ring broke her reverie. Frank had presented it to her for their tenth anniversary two years ago in a sudden and gushing display of affection so sentimental it made Louise squirm. What had possessed him to disturb the superficial calm which they both had accommodated? If he had intended it to be a pivotal moment, an attempt to rekindle what they had lost, it failed. They were estranged within the confines of a marriage, and that was that. If he had intended the ring to be a public show of his modest wealth—but no, in all fairness that was not his nature. Now the ring fit snugly on her swollen finger. Her throat tightened. She had become the thing Pa had called her.

As the moments dragged by, her eyes went often to the Regulator wall clock, an ornately carved cherrywood timepiece donated to the library by a grateful patron. Louise wanted to speed up its swaying pendulum and silence its incessant ticking. Marking time until the moment of truth. What if Doc didn't come? What if he didn't get the faculty position? What if he had a change of heart?

In spite of still feeling weak, she could sit no longer. Her restless mind and nervous energy forced her to get up. She moved the loaded shelving cart a safe distance from the wood stove and gathered small logs and kindling from the wood box.

The stove being cold, it resisted supporting a fire. After a considerable passage of time, Louise succeeded in coaxing a log to flare and was prodding it with the poker when she heard the sound of the door opening and the words: "Allow me."

In Doc's full, baritone voice Louise heard everything that her husband was not. A man in charge, a refined and serious man who admired her abilities and ambitions, a man who awakened her passion when she had assumed that part of her life was over. She had loved Frank once. Gentle, charming, a good provider. An engaging crooked grin. He had taught her to laugh. But he was a dreamer, and to her dismay she'd become a nag, ever reminding him to look after business. Six years after their marriage vows he became impotent. And with his impotence came thinly veiled resentment of her ambition and achievements, little jabs that taken singularly amounted to nothing but collectively could open old wounds if she let them. Instead she kept her dreams and accomplishments to herself, found safety in silence or in words that passed for communication, but just barely: *I saw a flock of geese flying south today; do you think we'll have an early winter?. . . Gunter and Alice finally got a telephone. . . . Anderson's delivered your order today.*

Louise turned toward Doc's voice. Usually when he came through the door, his professional look and bearing softened. Not today. He seemed aloof, or perhaps she was looking too hard for signs that their future together was assured.

He reached for the poker. She straightened and caught the familiar, maple-syrup scent of pipe smoke that clung to his jacket. The fragrance, which she loved, belonged singularly to him. But today it made her queasy.

When he knelt to tend the fire, Louise noticed the spot where his thick raven hair was thinning. As he prodded the wood, flames sprang from the flickering embers.

"That will do," Louise said. "It will get going of its own accord."

But he continued to jab the wood with the poker until flames swelled to fill the stove's belly.

Her breaths grew shallow. Did he think her incapable of building a fire? Or was this a delaying tactic?

The stove door squealed shut.

He stood. "Where is your oilcan?"

"It's—I don't know. I shall tend to it later."

He replaced the poker in its stand. Then his dark brown eyes took on the same admiring look that months earlier had set her moral compass spinning, had defined the moment she knew herself vulnerable—not just vulnerable—but *destined*.

"Now." He softly exhaled the word.

Louise braced for the words she could scarcely wait to hear.

His gaze steady, he reached out and took both her hands. Then he leaned down and let his tongue tease around her lips before parting them, exciting her in all the wrong places. His hand slipped inside her coat and gently but deliberately glided over her breast as he felt for a button on her shirtwaist. She pulled away.

He gave her a quizzical look. "You look peaked. Have you taken ill?"

"No, not exactly. Please tell me you bring good news."

He frowned.

"About the faculty position. You said you expected confirmation this week."

"You are mistaken, my dear."

No. For weeks his exact words had been her last thought before falling asleep and the first upon awakening. Now addled by his condescension, she questioned her own memory. "If not this week, when?"

"I expected to learn *if* I'd been confirmed. I was not." His voice was matter-of-fact, as though he were reporting that the greengrocer was out of apples.

Louise gasped. She strained to believe that even without the faculty position Doc would take her away and make her his wife. *His cool manner is a man's way of expressing disappointment. He needs comforting.* "I'm so sorry. I know it's a cruel blow after you were promised the position."

"So I had been led to believe."

"We'll go somewhere else, perhaps the mountains of Colorado. You said you loved it there, and I suppose I could adapt to the lack of cultural opportunities. I could start another library."

He shook his head. "It would be impractical to give up a good practice here to start over again." His words seemed to be coming from a distance. "Only a first-rate faculty position could lure me away."

Louise pressed a hand to her chest, as though to stop the expanding void inside. What had been vaguely unsettling was becoming crystal clear. The void was where her future had resided, a future slipping away. *Such a fool.* Respectable, rational Louise Morrissey had toyed with temptation like a giddy shop girl. She had fallen in love, and now she faced ruin. "What about us? You said yourself your wife would be better off without you, and you all but begged me to divorce Frank and go away with you. you're not thinking we'll divorce and remain in Riverbend . . ."

"This is difficult for me as well, my dear. If I could follow my heart, I would take you away this minute. We shall continue to have our afternoons—"

"Our afternoons? No. I refuse to continue like this." The shrill audacity in her voice surprised her. "You vowed that you loved me, that you couldn't wait to end your wretched marriage."

"All true, my dear. But leaving is financially out of the question. Besides why would you want to leave Riverbend? Life is comfortable, you have your friends, and one day you will be its most prominent civic leader."

Her voice quivered. "I would go anywhere to be with you, to become your wife . . . and bear your children."

"Perhaps another opportunity will arise. Meanwhile—" He reached for her.

She sidestepped to avoid his hand and positioned herself next to the shelving cart, which she gripped with both hands. "Your pledge to me meant nothing. Listen to yourself. How can you be so cavalier . . ."

A sound like a muffled gunshot gave her a start. She jerked the shelving cart. "Just a log popping," Doc said. "You're certainly jumpy today."

"My world has been turned upside down, and you, our future—"

"It's my future, too, Louise. You say I am cavalier, but you are mistaken. I am not a demonstrative man, not one to wear disappointment on my sleeve. I am a realist, and it would be foolish for us to go away together at this time. Be patient."

"Patient? I'll show you *patient.*" With a fury she had felt only once in her life, she plucked a book from the cart and hurled it across the room, and before it hit the floor she launched a second book. As she reached for a third, Doc's hand stopped her.

"You're getting hysterical! Pull yourself together."

She glared at him. "I am not hysterical." Her breaths came hard. *How can I say it? My next words will either win him over or drive him off.* "I am in the family way."

He backed away. "You cannot mean it."

"I am certain of it."

"Just because your monthly is late . . ."

As the heat of a blush crept up her neck, she looked away and struggled to regain composure. "I waited to be absolutely certain before telling you." She approached him. "This could be the son who will carry on your name." She placed his hand on her belly.

He yanked it away. "Is this a trap?"

A side of Doc that Louise had never seen emerged, accusing eyes and curled lip that made her cringe. She tried to damn him with her next words, but her trembling voice, barely more than a whisper, betrayed her. "How . . . dare . . . you?"

"What makes you so sure it's mine?"

Shallow, ragged breaths frustrated her efforts to appear calm. "I told you that Frank had lost his ability to perform."

Doc reacted with a bemused expression. "Married to a Jezebel such as yourself? Highly doubtful."

"Jezebel? Is that all I am to you?" Now she was shouting.

Doc's look and voice sobered. "Or have you been consorting with that halfbreed?"

"With Yonder?" Light-headed and wobbly, Louise steadied herself on the shelving cart. "How could you—"

He grabbed her wrist and pulled her toward the door. "We'll fix this. No one will know."

"Stop! What are you—? No!" She kicked at his ankle, striking his boot.

When he turned toward her, she struck a backhanded blow to his chin. She clutched her throbbing knuckles and watched blood trickle from his chin, scratched by her ring.

"Damn you," his guttural words came out almost as a growl.

"Get out!"

His face relaxed into a self-satisfied expression as he dabbed at his chin with a handkerchief. "This will heal in a few days. But that . . ." He pointed at her belly.

Fear seized Louise with a sensation that her skin was shrinking. She was about to slam the door behind Doc when a fresh stack of books on the wicker table outside the door caught her attention. She flipped open the book on top of the stack, but there was no check-out slip on the inside cover. Frantic to know who left the books, she examined the three that remained. None belonged to the library. Someone had donated them, but who? If some gossip had overheard her fighting with Doc, she would become the laughingstock of Riverbend, Nebraska.

She collapsed on the sofa, her hand over her eyes as though she could shield herself from the thoughts that assaulted her. What would make Doc change his mind? Threaten to tell his wife? She couldn't. Withdrawing her affection might work, not that she even wanted his affection any longer. But a baby needed a father. God pity the bastard child. And her reputation was at stake.

A thought she hadn't dared to consider presented itself. Maybe she would lose this baby, like the others. Tears began to flow, and soon the sound of her own racking sobs assailed her ears, alien sounds that seemed to belong to someone else. And when the tears were spent, the darkest self-loathing followed. "Daughter of the devil." Betraying a husband who had been more than just a good provider. Frank awakening her in the night to go outside and see the magical northern lights. Sitting at her sickbed and telling stories to cheer her. He had never raised a hand to her except on one occasion when he was drunk. And when he learned the next day that her bruises had been caused by his hand, he was genuinely remorseful. No marriage was perfect. Would he let her bear another man's child and raise it as his own? What if he threw her out? The home for unwed mothers in Omaha—she could go there to have the baby. But they would make her give it up. No, better to go somewhere and pretend to be a widow. Her rainy day fund would provide support for the duration of her confinement but not much longer. Such thoughts had presented themselves before, but she banished them. Now their gravity held her in its gray stillness long after the fire sputtered its last.

It was getting dark. Frank would worry if she did not arrive home soon. *Home,* a place she'd come to think of as temporary. She stood and shook off pins and needles in limbs that had gone to sleep.

She collected her hat and handbag and began buttoning her coat, one she had worn against her better judgment. The red, fitted coat, her favorite, had a curly black lamb collar and cuffs, and solid brass buttons. One of the buttons loosened when she tugged it to meet the buttonhole over her bosom. *I waited too long to tell Doc.*

It was futile to dwell on what might have been. She directed her thoughts to the practical matter of the button. It would need reinforcing before she wore the coat again. But then it occurred to her that, given her expanding figure and the necessity of going into her confinement, she would have to put the coat away until next year. Next year? Would she actually have a baby? Would she be with Doc? Or with Frank? Alone?

She was out in the hall and locking the door when she heard Doc approach.

His voice was velvet, the tone that had always signaled the preamble to lovemaking. "Louise, my dear, I am so sorry."

He placed his hand over hers and unlocked the door. With a hand on the small of her back, he guided her into the library.

Did she dare to hope he had changed his mind? She saw the scratch on his chin.

He frowned. "How long has the fire been out? You must be chilled to the bone."

His concern touched and confounded her. It was so like him to soften her in this way. "Why did you come back?"

"I lashed out in anger, said some things I wish I could take back. Please, my dear, may we sit down?"

Louise presumed he meant the sofa, but instead he guided her to the large reading table, seated her, and took the chair across from her.

"Have you considered what you will do?" he asked.

He sat less than an arm's length away, yet she felt stranded alone with the baby—*their* baby. The table dividing them might as well have been a chasm. *Does he care if I fall . . . and the baby?*

"I'm at a loss," she said. "What I believed turned out to be a myth." She fingered the loose button on her coat. "You're not the man I thought I knew." She paused, knowing what she was about to say was false, but she was grasping for an accusation, some way to strike back. Her breathing grew shallow. "I question if there even was a faculty position. Perhaps it was just a ploy to keep me from ending our affair."

He took her hand. "Of course it was real. I had every intention of taking the position, getting a divorce, and having you with me as my wife."

Louise heard a plea in his voice. Had he not said those words—"my wife"—she might have been able to hold back tears. She retrieved her handbag and fumbled for her handkerchief, forgetting until her hand touched it that it was wet. She slammed her handbag on the reading table. The loose button fell to the floor.

Doc seemed not to notice. He stood. "I found you irresistible because you were a strong, rational woman, my dear, not like most of your sex. Face the facts. You are in a predicament, and . . ." he paused, seemingly reluctant to go on.

You are in a predicament. Now it flashed before her, all the object lessons of women in life and literature who had fallen prey to a man's charms only to be left alone with their "predicament."

"Louise, there's a risk, a strong possibility of a medical complication. There's no good way out. Come, we shall dispose of this burden—"

She stood, her hands on the table, and leaned toward him. "So now, it's a 'medical complication,' is it? This 'burden' you speak of is a child. Do you know how I've longed to have a child?"

"A child you cannot explain to an impotent husband? Possibly a child who's impaired? Summon your wits, woman."

"Impaired? Now you're sounding desperate."

"Have it your way." Doc walked toward her, bent down, and picked up the button. He gave it to her, letting his hand linger so that for a moment they held it together. He didn't speak, but his eyes said it all: *time was running out.*

He gestured toward the stove. "Oil those hinges."

Chapter 2

The night after the confrontation with Doc, Louise became a woman on a mission.

As was their custom after supper Frank retreated to his cluttered den to work on his latest obsession, a contraption he called the Whirlwind Maid. On its top would be compartments to hold various cleaning supplies, and underneath, a motorized canister with a hose for collecting dirt. He would harness electricity so that one maid could do the housekeeping chores of two, rendering the sweeper, broom, and rug beater obsolete.

"Poetry in motion" was how Frank envisioned vacuuming with his Whirlwind Maid, a product that would outperform and outclass the Hoover, a noisy, ugly bag-on-a-stick with a trailing power cord that could trip its operator.

The scene in the back parlor, Louise's domain, was one of domestic tranquility. Walnut beadboard wainscoting with blue toile-patterned wallpaper above. Grandfather clock in one corner, upright piano in another. Under the glow of an electric lamp, Louise sat wrapped in a crocheted afghan in her upholstered chair, her feet propped on an ottoman. Holding a pillowcase clamped in an embroidery hoop, she worked a needle threaded with orange floss in and out, laying down back stitches for the outline of a butterfly.

The clock chimed, and she flinched. She'd always wanted to

silence that clock, which Frank's father had named "Goliath." Silence its nagging—*hurry, wait, too late, get caught up, kill time, time is running out.*

She took some deep breaths, stuck her needle in the arm of the chair, flexed her fingers, and examined her progress. The daisy and back stitches passed inspection, but she ripped out the satin-stitched leaves. To produce perfectly aligned stitches required a tranquil mind and steady hand, a state she might never know again.

Most nights, Frank would have begun drinking by now. But sometimes when he lost himself in a project he might abstain for a week or more, as though intoxicated by the project itself. Perversely, tonight, she worried that her husband's ebullient mood could work to her disadvantage.

Butterflies were taking shape on the pillowcase, but eventually even the daisy and back stitches went awry. To kill some more time she cut enough workable lengths of embroidery floss to finish the pillowcases and threaded several needles. As Frank would say, "Fish or cut bait."

The clock chimed ten-thirty, and Frank had not yet ventured to the liquor cabinet, so she got up and poured a glass of brandy. As she approached the den, her breathing grew shallow.

He sat at his desk, his back to the door. There was a reason he called this room "The Repository of Everything." So naming it might elevate its status in *his* mind, but to Louise it was a dump. She threaded her way through the maze of tools that had migrated from the workshop, rolls of linoleum, stacks of *National Geographic Magazine,* and chests stuffed so full of goodness-knows-what that their lids wouldn't close.

He looked up and smiled.

His lopsided smile, the look of innocence, caused Louise to waver. Could she really follow through with her plan? "Here." She handed him the brandy. "You need to relax. You'll work yourself to exhaustion."

He took the glass. "What a welcome surprise. I'd have thought you'd be in bed by now."

"I'm too engrossed in my needlework. I can't rest until I get it just right."

It was very late when Louise delivered the fourth brandy. She leaned over to set the snifter on his desk, hesitated, then deliberately and brazenly brushed her breast against his cheek. "Mmm." She had never before played the seductress. The boldness of it frightened her, but the thought of failure frightened her even more. She pressed against him, played with his ear, and caressed his sandy-colored hair.

He set down his pencil and turned in his chair toward her. In reaching for her, his hand hit the snifter, which Louise managed to keep from toppling. Breathing heavily, he pulled her onto his lap and made a droning noise as he nuzzled her neck. "Aren't you the vixen tonight?" His words were garbled.

Finally he led her by the hand to their bed. Any other night she would have resisted his drunken passion, his sloppy wet kisses, and pawing hands. But tonight she held her breath and hoped she could arouse him and he could perform.

He rubbed himself against her, then rose on his knees and probed and thrust. He repeated the action several times, grunting with the effort. Louise even tried to guide his flaccid member, but he never got hard enough to penetrate her. He pushed himself off and fell to the floor.

Moonlight illuminated his clumsy effort to get to his feet and find his balance. Suddenly he lunged forward and threw his fist against the wall.

He weaved back toward the bed. "You're not half the woman you used to be." His slurred speech sounded more pathetic than damning. "Don't start what you can't finish."

Louise longed to escape in sleep but lay trapped next to the leaden, snoring presence of her husband. She should have bought one of the potions advertised to restore a man's vigor. Any further attempt to seduce him would be futile, for he had been sufficiently sober to remember failing.

She ached to have this baby. Maybe it would fill the hollow she carried from her childhood. In a home without love, she had experienced the emotion for the first time after the birth of her baby brother, Malachi. The hollow was left after a part of her stayed in the makeshift grave where she helped bury him. And then her mother gave her two more babies to care for and love. And bury.

Frank had wanted children as much as she. The first time she was with child, he had dropped everything and built an oak rocking chair. But one day not long after her condition was beginning to show, she lost the baby. That night, awakened by a creaking sound, she had reached for her husband, but her hand fell on the rumpled quilt where he should have lain. When fully awake she heard the creak of the rocker and his muffled weeping.

The second time, he fussed over her, patting her knee and issuing sweet reprimands to stay put while he fetched her book or embroidery hoop or shawl. The loss of that baby drove them inconsolably into one another's arms. In the space that remained once they parted hung lingering, unspoken questions, heavy as a broken promise.

* * *

IN THE GRAY DAWN, THE day after Louise's failed attempt to seduce her husband, desperation drove her to a decision. Abhorrent as it was, she would go to Doc and have him "dispose of this burden." Once the queasiness subsided, she would get up to put on her robe, but for now she sat on the edge of the bed. Fully awake, she noticed a tinkling on the windowpanes. Sleet? Not today. But the staccato on the windows intensified, announcing a crippling storm. She went to the window and looked at the ice-glazed trees. Only a fool would venture out.

Louise was a practical woman, not one to look for omens, much less be swayed by them. But once again, weather was determining her destiny. Had it not been for a deadly tornado, she and Doc would not have been thrust into each other's lives. And had it not been for this winter storm, she would have single-mindedly pursued her plan. Instead, the storm knocked her off course, so that in place of a mental roadmap there was now a blank space for her mind to wander, and the wandering led to a new plan. It would require some preparation.

* * *

AS IT HAPPENED, THAT NIGHT Frank wanted to retire early, exhausted from a day spent dealing with the ice storm's aftermath. Louise turned back the bed covers and placed two flannel-wrapped hot bricks at the foot of the bed. Feeling responsible for last night's failed lovemaking, she could not look at him directly but watched from the corner of her eye as he unbuttoned his shirt. He avoided looking at her as well, and she regretted having set him up for what must have been a terrible blow to his manhood.

Tonight going through the motions of her bedtime ritual felt unfamiliar and awkward. As she pulled the bench out from her dressing table, its screech on the wood floor seemed unusually shrill. Before sitting down she neglected to hike up her nightgown so that when she sat its high collar nearly choked her, and she squirmed to free it. Looking at herself in the mirror, she felt her mouth fill with excess saliva. She swallowed, reminded herself that everything was in place, and picked up her hairbrush. But tonight she began brushing without counting.

In the mirror she watched Frank take his nightshirt from its hook on the closet door. Willing herself to keep the gravity of the moment out of her voice, she said, "Do you remember the night a few months ago when you played poker at J.D.'s?"

Frank answered without looking her way. "Those horse-thieves cleaned me out."

"Yonder brought you home." She made a face. "You smelled of beer and sardines."

Frank slipped the nightshirt over his head. "I remember the next morning. Figured you had hit me with a sledgehammer, and I passed out."

Louise noticed his bruised knuckles, injured from hitting the wall the night before. Would his memory of failure thwart her plan tonight? "You didn't pass out immediately."

He looked sideways at her mirror image and shrugged. "I was three sheets to the wind. What a man does when he's drinking—"

"Don't be sorry." Louise set her carved ivory hairbrush on the dresser and smiled into the mirror. "We've always wanted a child."

Midway toward joining a button and buttonhole of his nightshirt, Frank's hands froze. "That can't be, I . . ."

Still looking at his mirrored image, Louise said, "You were crazed with passion."

He looked away, then back again, his gaze thoughtful. He took a little breath as though about to speak but remained silent.

So as not to appear overly anxious, Louise rearranged her brush, comb, and hand mirror on the dressing table before placing a hand on her bodice. "You even tore my nightgown."

He looked at her reflected hand. "I'm sorry. I hope—"

"Not this one. My favorite baby-blue one."

Louise went to him and buttoned the open placket of his nightshirt, a simple act that felt awkwardly intimate. She smiled. "I hope you're as happy as I am."

Unable to still her fluttering eyelids, she turned from him to plump their pillows. Frank had learned long ago to read her telltale eyes. "It's that thing you do with your eyelids," he had said the day he challenged her story about growing up rich and losing her family and fortune in a prairie fire.

As they lay in bed in a spooned embrace, Louise sought with her feet the comfort of a hot brick. Her breathing eased, the knots in her shoulders relaxed, and her head settled into the pillow. Frank's callused hand slipped between her breast and arm. What had once been their customary way of lying together now felt almost like a violation, as though his were the hands of a stranger. Too many of the ways of knowing one another had withered from neglect.

He nuzzled her neck. "Francis Joseph Morrissey Jr."

* * *

At the breakfast table the next morning, Louise picked at the pork chop, applesauce, and fried potatoes on her plate. Now that Frank knew of her condition she could tell Henryetta, her cook and housekeeper, to prepare lighter fare.

Louise sat across from Frank, or rather across from the newspaper he held like a shield, dropping it only to pluck sugar cubes from the bowl and stir them into his coffee. Slurping sounds and the clink of the Blue Willow china cup against saucer interrupted the rhythmic taps of fork against plate.

When she had said the night before that he had been crazed with passion, a hint of recognition had come over his face suggesting he might believe her, but today he hid behind his newspaper, and that set Louise on edge.

Henryetta brought in a platter of hot biscuits, flanked by a mound of butter and pitcher of molasses. On the pudgy hand that held the plate, two fingers had strings tied around them. Although Henryetta had learned to read and write after Louise urged her to attend the Riverbend Ladies Lending Library's literacy classes, she was not inclined to surrender her habitual method for remembering things.

Frank reached for a biscuit and thanked her without looking up. Henryetta glanced at Louise with a little scowl and shook her head.

Normally Frank's energy filled the breakfast room as his head fairly exploded with random ideas that fomented while he slept. He might announce a design to make crutches more comfortable, or a promotion to entice tourists to Nebraska, or a device for clearing snow from brick walks and streets. Henryetta would shake a finger at him and scold him for letting his breakfast get cold. He would pause long enough to tease her about the strings on her fingers, then he would be back to reciting his schemes. But not this morning.

*   *   *

RIVERVIEW INN, A HANDSOME H-SHAPED building, sat atop a bluff. It might have looked imposing, except its brown-shingled façade and landscaping gave it a cozy lodge feeling. The spacious front lawn held maple and blue spruce trees and flower gardens with stone paths. A comic feeling emanated from Frank's grand lawn ornament, a sunken Missouri River paddlewheeler he had lovingly restored. River traffic was all but gone, overtaken by the railroad, a circumstance that made Frank's paddlewheeler even dearer to him. He often said that Riverbend had become a river town that didn't know it had a river except in name—Riverview Inn, Steamboat Café, River Rat Saloon, Barge Inn—and in the rusty recollections of old codgers. As names went, his paddlewheeler's christened name, *The Blanchard,* had been all but forgotten the first time someone called her "Morrissey's Folly."

The hotel entrance and east-facing rooms had a view of the gray, untamed river. A drive on the south side led to a porte cochère and a second hotel entrance. Spring would bring the fragrance of honeysuckle growing along the drive, which continued to a parking area and carriage house. Beyond the honeysuckle the bluff became a wooded plateau, its paths popular with Inn guests for their morning and evening constitutionals. At the north edge of the Inn property, the land dropped like an apron toward town and in winter provided a popular sledding hill for youngsters from the houses below.

Frank had become an indifferent innkeeper. It was Louise, behind the scenes, who tended to essential details. At the time she met and married Frank, he was a more-or-less aspiring banker, a career for which he was equally ill-suited. His father had made the banking career a condition of Frank's considerable inheritance. Frank's brother, Aidan, had inherited the Inn, but upon his sudden death, thrown drunk from a horse, the Inn passed to Frank.

The Morrisseys' apartment occupied the entire southwest wing of the second floor and was relatively private. Frank had been born in that apartment, and Louise feared, in spite of his promises to build their dream house, it was where they both would die, as his parents had, of old age in their sleep. Probably one of the last things she would lay her eyes on would be her mother-in-law's knickknack shelf, framed cross-stitch sampler, and reproduction of Gainsborough's "Blue Boy." She'd have removed them years ago, hiding the faded rectangles they'd leave on the wallpaper, but to do so would feel like her dream house would ever remain a dream. Or so she had thought until the day she began checking her sanitary pad for stains that never materialized.

*   *   *

IN THE AFTERNOON LOUISE STOOD at the kitchen sink polishing silver and taking in the view outside her window. Icicles on the neighbors' pasture fence sparkled in the sun, and the horses' breath fogged the air.

Gunter Dietz owned the riding stable, where he boarded those horses, gave riding lessons, and bred American Paint horses. He also operated the town's coach service, which transported visitors to and from the Burlington depot to Riverview Inn and other destinations. In a longstanding agreement, the Morrissey family boarded their horses and kept their carriages and wagons at Dietz's.

The whistle of a freight train passing through town meant that Gunter's wife, Alice, would soon emerge from the house to feed her two dogs. She appeared, bundled in a heavy coat, a scarf wrapped around her face, and food bowls in her hand. She dodged the dogs' excited leaps, teetering to keep her balance until she set their bowls down. It amused Louise that her good friend, whose life revolved around her husband's horses, had never sat in a saddle and never intended to.

Watching a colt frolic, a brown and white patchwork on four legs, Louise recalled a fond childhood memory of sitting on a tall Arabian with Pa, who had worked as a trainer on a private estate. That memory, so fleeting—if only she could isolate it and stop the images that would follow.

The sound of the front door opening and closing heightened her senses. Then silence. Frank usually called out to her when he came in. Moreover, when he was wearing work clothes his practice was to enter the apartment from the back stairs which led into the kitchen, rather than walk through the lobby and up the front stairs. Louise stood perfectly still, listening. After hearing soft footfalls apparently heading toward the hallway to the bedrooms, she waited another moment, then inched down the hallway toward the master bedroom. She stopped outside the bedroom door. Her eyes lingered on the small of his back where in happier times she had placed her hands to pull him close. Frank eased open the top drawer of her chest of drawers. He lifted the sapphire blue nightgown.

Not that one. Louise dared not breathe. She pushed back the image that had haunted her for days, that of living alone in some garret, stuffing newspaper in cracks around windows against the cold, the pitiful "widow" alone in her confinement. Her deception had to work.

He turned the gown over and over in his hands. Dropping the nightgown, he rummaged in the drawer. This time he picked up the baby-blue nightgown. After a close examination he nodded and let out a sigh that relaxed his whole body. Louise exhaled. Frank had almost certainly seen the stitching, which she had taken care to make obvious.

Louise retreated down the hall, then turned. "Frank, where are you? Did you come in?" She heard a drawer close, then, unexpectedly, another slide open and slam shut.

Frank rushed from the bedroom and waved a pair of work gloves. "Had to get these. Got a crew weather-stripping storm windows." He threw his arms around Louise, pressed his cold cheek against hers, and rocked her from side to side. "How's the little mother?"

Chapter 3

June 1895

Frank traced the rim of his coffee cup and watched the early morning sunlight play on its now-cold contents. In recent months he had tried to stay out of the way as Dovie Henkleman led the other "biddies," as he called them, who took over his home in frenzied preparation for the baby. They bustled about making curtains, rag rugs, blankets, and lord knew what else.

Now he had reached the height of redundancy. A new life was coming into the world, but he was barred from the inner sanctum, a man of action condemned to sit in the breakfast room and twiddle his thumbs. To his fatigue-addled mind, the moans coming from the bedroom were escalating to guttural wails that could only issue from the depths of hell. Finally silence suggested that his all-night vigil was about to end. He went weak with the realization that silence could mean good news or bad.

Hearing heavy footfalls, he went to meet the midwife, who carried a tiny bundle from which protruded a mop of black hair.

"You got yourself a fine baby girl, Mr. Morrissey."

In that instant Francis Joseph Morrissey Jr. vanished, and in his place was a creature Frank was at a loss to fathom. He could only stare.

"You can go to your wife," the midwife said.

Entering the bedroom he caught a whiff of blood from the pile of stained bed linens sitting next to the door. He kissed Louise's forehead, wet with perspiration, and fingered the damp tendrils that curled around her face. She had never looked more beautiful.

"Thought of a girl's name?" Louise's voice was weak.

Frank was taken aback by her weak voice. He shook his head. He looked at the four-poster bed in which he had been born. The very place he'd pictured his son being born.

"I do believe you're sulking."

Off the top of his head he linked the month of the baby's birth and Louise's middle name. "June Elizabeth."

Louise's grimace told him it would not do.

He pondered it. Finally a name presented itself from a forgotten corner of his mind. He and Louise had honeymooned in Kansas City, a time when he took his masculine prowess for granted, never imagining he would lose his virility a few years later. Louise was the properly modest bride, but to his surprise and delight, on the third night of their honeymoon she responded with passion. He suspected her awakening was no accident, for that night they had attended a risqué operetta in which a woman, scorned by her suitor, seduces his brother. Later that night, basking in the afterglow of lovemaking, Frank had determined that his first daughter should be named for the actress.

"Marie Alouette," he said. "It has a musical ring, don't you think?"

Before Louise could answer, the midwife entered and placed the baby in her arms. Looking at the baby, stroking her black hair and silky skin, nearly took her breath away.

The midwife said, "Looks like a little papoose."

Louise's hand stopped on a rosy cheek, the tender moment broken. The black hair had come as no surprise, something Louise was prepared to explain. Still, the midwife's remark caught her off guard. Before her fluttering eyelids could betray her, she lifted the baby and held her in front of her face. She spoke to no one in particular. "Whenever you lift her, you must support her head with your hand." She closed her eyes, kissed the baby's head, and breathed deeply. Except for the baby's fair skin, there was nothing to suggest she would ever look like Frank with his sandy hair, blue eyes, and crooked grin.

Frank said, "There's no black hair in my family."

The midwife was gathering up her supplies, preparing to leave. "She could end up a little towhead. I seen a baby's hair go from black to spun gold."

Her eyes still closed and nuzzling the baby's neck, Louise said, "Black hair like my Indian grandmother. She was part Sioux, belonged to the Ioway tribe." She cuddled her daughter against her breast, and looked at Frank. "That's the Morrissey complexion if I ever saw it. Ivory skin, once the pink goes away. And she has your nose." Louise touched Marie's chin. "And where did you get that dimple, Miss Marie Alouette Morrissey?"

As she unwrapped the receiving blanket, Louise swelled with maternal relief to see the perfect little body, ten toes, ten long fingers. But into the midst of the joyful first moments with her daughter came the fears that had dogged her for nine months. Fear that Frank would discover her infidelity. Fear that her infidelity would become public, she and her daughter would be shunned and Frank, the cuckolded husband, ridiculed.

* * *

Frank dropped into bed at the end of the day, exhausted as though he, not Henryetta, had bustled about all day caring for Louise and Marie. He kissed Louise on the cheek, inhaled the fragrance of clothesline-fresh sheets, and fell into a deep sleep.

Marie's cries awakened him from a dream about duck hunting with Francis Joseph Morrissey Jr. He got up, turned on a light, roused Louise, and propped pillows behind her before bringing her the baby.

Louise bared her breast, gleaming white in the lamplight, and guided the nipple into Marie's little mouth. Frank wondered at the strangeness of it. How his own mouth used to delight in Louise's breasts and her undulating response. Now little more than a bystander, he turned away from mother and babe, black hair against white breast. Complete unto themselves.

The next day, Frank felt like a visitor, popping into the bedroom now and then to see how the little mother was doing.

On the third morning, he entered the bedroom as Louise was nursing Marie. They were sitting in the oak rocker that Frank had built the first time Louise was with child.

"Can I bring you anything?" he asked, knowing full well that Henryetta supplied everything Louise might need.

The baby finished suckling and appeared to be drifting to sleep. Louise settled Marie in her lap.

"Yes. Bring me a clean washrag."

Frank returned with the washrag and handed it to Louise. He could not take his eyes off the breast that was still fully exposed.

Then Louise wiped Marie's right eye with the washrag, lifted the eyelid, and squirted milk from her nipple into the eye. "See how red the lids are? Henryetta says Marie has a cold in her eye." She wiped the baby's cheek. "The remedy is mother's milk."

* * *

THAT NIGHT FRANK WAS AWAKENED by a blow to his cheek. Louise was thrashing about, heat radiating from her body. He got a basin of cold water and a washrag and bathed her face and neck. In just a few moments the rag became warm. He wet it again and wiped her face, actions he repeated until the water itself grew warm, and he replaced it with cold. He persisted until at last the fever subsided. The emergency over, he went weak thinking his beloved wife could have succumbed to one of the deadly consequences of childbirth.

Mid-morning Louise shuddered with chills. Frank and Henryetta rounded up blankets which they piled on top of her. The day was turning out to be unseasonably hot, and Frank wiped sweat from his brow with his shirtsleeve. "How can she be cold?"

Henryetta rubbed Louise's arm vigorously. "She needs a doctor."

Frank hastened to his den where he shoved past boxes to reach the phone. He shouted at the telephone operator to connect him to Doc Foster, who said he would come immediately. Frank dropped into his chair.

He wanted to return to Louise's bedside, but hearing Marie's faint cries, he went instead to the nursery. Marie's cry was feeble, not the hearty cry of a baby demanding to be fed. A thick discharge came from her reddened right eye, and now her left eyelid appeared red. With Henryetta tending Louise, he was left alone to comfort Marie.

He lifted her and placed her on a shoulder, careful to support her head. He paced the length of the hall, back and forth, patting her little back until she settled down. Almost surprised at his ability to calm her, he placed her back in the bassinet and watched her sleep. "There, now. That's my girl."

When Frank went back to the bedroom, Louise's fever had returned. Curls, damp with perspiration, clung to her forehead, and she was writhing and becoming tangled in bedclothes.

Frank answered the knock at the door. "Doc, you're not a minute too soon."

Doc reached inside his leather bag for a handkerchief and blotted perspiration from his forehead. "I shall need to wash my hands first."

Frank led the way to the water closet and paced outside the door as he waited for the doctor to wash up. When Doc went to the bedroom to examine Louise, Frank stayed in the hallway, shifting from one foot to the other. He withdrew a pad and pencil from his shirt pocket, intending to sketch a schematic for his Whirlwind Maid cart, but his shaking hand drew scribbled lines instead. He jammed the pad and pencil back in his pocket.

Eventually Doc emerged from the bedroom. "Puerperal sepsis. Whoever attended the delivery knows nothing about hygiene."

"What's she got?"

"Childbed fever. From dirty hands or instruments. Used to be much more prevalent, but the knowledgeable physician practices modern methods of sanitation."

"Will she get well?"

"Who is caring for your wife? I have some instructions for her."

"Our housekeeper, Henryetta. She's in the kitchen."

"Your wife will recover. I know you're worried. She's very sick now, but that's her body fighting off the infection." He was trying to latch his bag as he spoke. "Now, if you'll direct me to your housekeeper."

"The baby is doing poorly. I hope you can do something."

Doc stopped fumbling with the latch. He looked hard at Frank. "After I wash my hands."

When Doc returned from the water closet, Frank led him to the nursery.

Doc leaned over the bassinet where Marie slept.

"Henryetta says it's a cold in her eyes," Frank said, "but she gets weaker by the day."

With a trembling hand, Doc pried open one eye. It was red, and the pus was so profuse Frank had to look away. Marie whimpered, a pitiful little sound.

The doctor's voice was somber. "Babies' sore eyes."

"Hurts a lot, I suppose," Frank said.

"This is a serious infection. I'm sorry to have to tell you this, but it has the potential to blind her. I shall put some drops in her eyes that might arrest the infection if it's not too late."

"She could go blind?"

Doc spoke with a catch in his voice. "Yes."

Frank shook his head and waved his hand as though he might whisk away the news. He felt the same sense of nowhere to turn he'd experienced after his brother died. He looked at Marie, realized how attached he'd become to this little creature, and rebuked himself for having felt cheated out of a son.

At the doctor's request, Frank had Henryetta bring some boiled water, a clean rag, and a small bowl. Doc wet the rag, let it cool, and wiped Marie's eyes. Then he took a bottle and a glass rod from his bag. He opened the bottle and inserted the rod. "This will sting." He held one of Marie's lids open with his thumb, and with the other hand held the rod over her eye until a drop fell.

She let out a faint, shrill cry and flailed her little arms.

"Hold her, please," Doc said.

Frank's heart ached to see his baby girl suffer, but he held her still while Doc instilled a drop in her other eye.

Doc took a pad and pencil from his bag and talked as he wrote. "Wipe her eyes with a clean rag and flush them with boric acid at least once every hour. Follow the treatments with ice packs. She won't like it, but it's very important as germs tend to thrive at higher temperatures. Wash your hands before and after handling her, and give her fresh bedding twice a day. Keep her swaddled so she doesn't touch her eyes."

Marie continued to cry, softly, and her arms flailed about. Frank wrapped the blanket about her.

Doc picked up his bag. "Direct me to the woman caring for your wife and baby."

Frank pointed. "That would be Henryetta."

Doc seemed to ignore him. He was looking at the baby and setting down his bag. "Newborns need proper swaddling. It comforts them, makes them feel safe like they did in the womb." He picked Marie up and held her to his chest. With one hand he smoothed wrinkles from the blanket, then placed her on it, held down her arms and wrapped the blanket snugly around her. Her cries subsided. He patted her gently. "There,

there, now. That's better."

Once again Frank waited as Doc went through the ritual of washing his hands, then directed Doc to the kitchen. "You'll find Henryetta there. Thank you for coming. She'll see you out. I'm going to be with my wife."

* * *

For the rest of the day Louise either slept or wrestled with hot and cold fits. During the night she awakened, sufficiently lucid to notice the clammy sheets and nightgown and to remember throwing off the covers earlier in a feverish spell. Exhausted, but calm and coherent, she felt better than she had in days. She vaguely recalled having nursed Marie. A longing washed over her, a desire to be fully aware of her precious daughter, to cuddle her, caress her silky skin, and smell her baby breath.

Miraculously absent was the self-loathing that had consumed her in the months leading up to Marie's birth. Never mind that Marie had been conceived illicitly. This baby was God's mercy made manifest, the fulfillment of an abandoned dream.

In the morning, with Frank's coaxing, Louise took tea and a few bites of toast. As he was removing the bed tray, she asked him to bring her the baby.

As she reached for Marie she said, "How are her eyes today?"

Frank's hesitation alarmed her. She looked at Marie's eyes and gasped at seeing how much worse the swollen eyelids had become. She lifted first one reddened lid, then the other. A thick, yellow secretion coated the eyeballs. "Call Dr. Harrison."

Frank attempted to straighten the tangled sheet dragging

the floor. "Doc Foster says they're infected."

Frank's words—Doc Foster, infection—played tricks with her mind. Perhaps they were remnants of her delirium. "How would Dr. Foster know?"

"I had him look at you and the baby. She's very sick, Louise. She may lose her sight."

"No, no. It can't be." With one finger Louise wiped matter from the corner of Marie's right eye. "It's just a cold in her eyes." Holding Marie's eye open, she reached for her breast and squirted milk in it.

Frank patted her arm. "We're following the doctor's orders to a T, Louise."

She shifted away from him, as though to distance herself might make his news less real. "Please, I need time alone with her." Dismissing him deepened the anguish in his eyes and made her look away.

He left.

She settled Marie to nurse, which she did fitfully, alternately suckling and making pitiful mewing sounds. Louise found herself clutching the baby close and swaying, murmuring over and over, "Take my strength. Take my strength." Perhaps the incantation would work this time.

Louise had been six years old when one afternoon she heard Ma screaming from behind the curtain that hid her and Pa's bed. Screaming for no apparent reason—Pa was at work. From that mysterious dark place came a wet, homely little creature Ma named Malachi Jacob.

At first Louise resented the extra chores that fell to her, especially having to clean the baby's stinky bottom. But the first time he reached out his arms for her to take him, she surrendered her heart, and when he took his first steps, she swelled with pride. Loving him as completely as she did, she sometimes fell blissfully to sleep at night without fearing what the next day would bring.

But it was she who awakened one night to hold him as a coughing fit wracked his little body. The next night, desperate to relieve his suffering, she cooed, "Take my strength. Take my strength." And she imagined a transfer of healing spirit from her body to his. When he died of the croup, something inside Louise died, and when Joshua David was born she vowed she would not lose her heart. But he stole it nevertheless before succumbing to scarlet fever. A third baby was simply called "Baby" because he was born sickly and Ma had already wasted two favorite names. Louise had grown wiser. She bargained with God: give Baby my strength and I shall be your righteous servant forevermore. Baby died in Louise's arms without a name.

Now holding her own frail infant, all Louise knew to do was to rock back and forth and murmur, "Take my strength." Louise spoke softly so as not to disturb Marie Alouette who was sleeping now. The years of longing for a baby had come to this. All her fears about the possible consequences of her infidelity had been misplaced. If Marie went blind, such retribution would be cruel beyond imagining.

A phrase lodged in Louise's mind. It came from a long poem she'd memorized in school: "They enslave their children's children who make compromise with sin." Marie, the little innocent, paying for my sin.

Self-loathing rose as did her fever. She called to Frank. He came and scooped Marie from her arms. Louise hovered at the threshold of delirium, grateful for its asylum.

* * *

THE NEXT NIGHT A STIFF, cool breeze from the den's window fluttered the house plans Frank had unrolled with the best intentions. Time to build the house he had promised Louise. But after a cursory review, he yielded to the beckoning of his Whirlwind Maid. There was nothing more irresistible than a design problem.

Late June was Frank's favorite time of year, when hot days gave way to pleasant nights. He was lost in his work in the den when he looked up to see Henryetta standing quietly in the doorway.

"Look at this." Frank jumped up, weaved his way through the clutter, and thrust the schematic at her. "No one wants a vacuum sweeper that trails great lengths of electrical cord. A woman has to keep gathering up the cord so as not to trip over it. So I've got this recoiling device that will let out as much cord as you need when you push forward and take up the slack when you pull backward."

Henryetta looked blankly at the drawing. "Mr. Morrissey, it's going on midnight. I got to get home to my family."

In the moments after Henryetta left, Frank took stock and realized how inconsiderate he had been. The faithful housekeeper had cared for Louise and Marie for nearly a week without complaint.

Beginning the next day, he adopted a routine of sending Henryetta home after supper to her husband, a railroad worker, and daughter in Cindertown and tending his wife and baby himself. When Louise broke out in a sweat, Frank removed the bed covers, mopped her brow, and turned on the electric fan he had bought to keep her comfortable. When she shuddered with chills, he filled hot water bottles, placed them all around her, and piled on blankets.

He faithfully treated Marie's eyes with boric acid and ice packs. And when she finished nursing, he held her in Louise's rocking chair. Grasping her little hand, he sang to her the only song he knew, softly and off-key, "She'll be coming 'round the mountain when she comes, she'll be coming 'round the mountain when she comes . . ."

He prayed for the first time in years.

PART 2

Chapter 4

May 1904

Riverbend's Main Street was a north-south thoroughfare on a modern macadam highway that ran parallel to the Missouri River, leading up to Omaha and down to Kansas City and points beyond. Missouri Avenue was the principal east-west street. Outside of town the dirt country roads criss-crossed in near-perfect grids. These roads were traveled mostly by farmers who hauled wagonloads of grain and livestock to market and swapped lies at Anderson's Seed and Feed while their womenfolk and daughters shopped and their sons sneaked off to the livery stable to play mumbledy-peg, shoot at mice with slingshots, and pick up other rough habits from boys who never went to Sunday school. Since the turn of the new century, it was not uncommon for the quiet of a country drive to be broken by engine racket that signaled the presence of a horseless carriage moving at several times the speed of a wagon. Voluminous dust clouds hovered long after the intruder had passed.

Such an encounter took place on an otherwise tranquil Saturday morning when a Buick Model B touring car, a flashy open-air vehicle with an indigo blue body and bright yellow wheels, shattered the fragile peace and caused a pair of horses pulling an oncoming buckboard wagon to shy. The buckboard driver jerked his team to a halt. His passengers gripped seats and one another to keep from pitching forward. The driver cried out, "Lord, help us! That blind Morrissey child is driving!"

The automobile slowed to a crawl, and a grinning Frank Morrissey, wearing driving goggles, popped up like a Jack-in-the-box and waved.

He dropped into the passenger seat and shouted over the engine racket. "That was the Sawyers, probably headed to the tent revival. You should have seen their faces, Junior. They were so scared their pants will never get dry."

His humor hit the mark with Marie, who was now nearly nine. She squealed with laughter.

Yonder LaFontaine sat in the back seat grinning. "Seeing us probably did them more good than a revival meeting."

Frank took the steering wheel, and Marie pleaded, "One more time."

"Not now, Junior. Your mother told us to kill time, not annihilate it."

"What's 'an eye—'"

"Never mind. Get in the back seat. We need to pick up your mother and then take you to your piano lesson."

"Okay, but please tell me what you see." Holding her beloved Dolly close, Marie climbed over the front seat and settled in the back next to Yonder.

Marie was totally blind in her right eye but, under ideal conditions, could make out shadowy images with her left. Infection had left her right eye looking like a fried egg white shot with blood and the left eye similarly but only partially occluded. Both eyes jerked from side to side. Their appearance caused most observers to recoil and look away.

Frank said, "Now here's a picture for you. There's a little

brown calf grazing in the buttercups, and its mama is lying there chewing her cud." Frank continued a running description of the scenery for Marie. "And here's something you don't see every day. A coyote running into the trees by the river."

"Tell me if he turns into a man," Marie said.

"Indian folklore?" Frank asked.

"Coyote often appears as a man in Sioux stories," Yonder said.

"Coyote is clever and smart," Marie said, "but he makes a big mess of everything he does. Uncle Yonder's stories always end, 'Don't be like Coyote.'"

* * *

LOUISE HAD CHANGED BACK INTO her everyday clothes after a fitting for the new dress she would wear for The Twister Tenth Anniversary Observance. From a shelf in the dressmaker's sewing room, she selected silk ribbons in pink, yellow, and mint green with which to decorate the collar and peplum of the dress she had ordered for Marie. She had taught herself ribbon embroidery for Marie's benefit. "A yard of each, please, Sylvia."

The dressmaker held the spool of pink ribbon up to her face and reeled off a length of ribbon from her nose to the end of her extended arm. Then she coiled the ribbon and secured it with a straight pin. She did the same with the remaining colors.

Louise followed Sylvia from the sewing room to the kitchen, where the dressmaker ignored the wailing of her three-year-old getting pummeled by his older brother and gestured for Louise to take a seat at the kitchen table to wait for Frank.

The boys' faces were smeared with prune filling from kolaches that Louise had brought. The small room reeked from a pile of rotting potato peels that should have been thrown to the pigs days ago. Louise considered that the dressmaker's childhood had probably been no worse than her own, so what twists of fate had condemned Sylvia to this gritty existence and favored Louise with relative luxury?

The dressmaker set her Coleman iron and its protective plate on an ironing board that stood near a wall where several scorched areas attested to probably more than one occasion when flames flared from her iron. She lifted the iron, gave it a shake, and seemed satisfied there was fuel in its attached tank. She struck a match, adjusted the air and gasoline mix, and lit the iron, jerking her hand away from the hissing flames.

Louise flinched. Flaming irons had become the stuff of nightmares when she was a young housekeeper tasked with caring for her employer's clothes. Marrying Frank had freed her from washing and ironing, chores that were handled by the Inn's hired girls.

She held her breath while Sylvia lowered the setting. The flame backed down and settled into a quiet hiss, and the iron was ready to press the diaphanous pastel aqua fabric Louise had chosen.

The dressmaker removed straight pins from a temporary hem and held them in a row between her teeth. Then she adjusted the hem where she'd marked it with chalk, pressed it, and repinned it. She talked while her teeth held the pins. "Wait till you get a look-see of Mrs. Henkleman's dress. The neckline's cut all the way down to here." She pointed to her bosom.

"She is nothing if not bold," Louise said.

"Well, if you ask me, a lady ought to dress modestly, like you. Look too provocative and you never know what can happen."

Barking dogs announced the automobile's arrival, and Louise stood. She placed the ribbons in her handbag, then put on her hat and tied it down.

"Stay inside," Sylvia said. "Some fool turned the dogs loose." She grabbed a stick propped by the door and ran out.

But hearing screams that could only come from Marie, Louise dashed outside and ran toward the automobile where three dogs were jumping. One came face-to-face with Marie. Frank twisted around from the driver's seat and punched its nose, which sent it reeling so fast its landing raised a dust cloud. Yonder leaped from the automobile and charged, shouting, his arms flailing, to drive off the remaining dogs.

Marie kept screaming and crouched down on the floor. No wonder, Louise thought, trying to imagine facing danger as a blind child. Even though Marie no longer felt the dog's hot breath on her face, no longer smelled its rancid breath, she couldn't know the beast had been driven off. From the fainter, more distant barking, she could tell the pack had run away, but for all she knew they might turn to charge again

The dressmaker yelled and waved her stick, and the dogs retreated under the porch.

"You're safe, Marie." Louise gestured to Yonder to take the front seat. "I shall join Marie in the back."

With Yonder's hand to steady her, she stepped onto the running board and into the car. His touch brought the warmth of a blush, something she hoped Frank wouldn't turn and see. She took pains to avoid the slightest appearance of impropriety—pretending not to notice the butcher's generous weighing of beef, the taciturn bank teller's nervous smile,

Yonder's helpful hand on her arm. Such actions broke the calm surface she strived to maintain.

For nearly ten years she had endeavored to live her life beyond reproach. Sometimes she went for long periods of time feeling secure in the role as devoted wife and loving mother. But the coming of The Twister anniversary nudged her off balance and heightened her sense that the past was out there somewhere gathering strength in the shadows.

*   *   *

Sitting in the back seat behind Yonder as the four of them drove from the dressmaker's, Louise recalled that when he'd showed up in town a dozen years earlier his presence had initially brought out the best in Frank and the worst in her. The man she judged to be about five years older than she had been dressed well enough. He wore a working man's shirt, pressed trousers, and expensive pigskin boots. And his hair was cut in the fashion of up-to-date white men. Although his calloused hands hinted at hard work, his speech was that of an educated man. But fresh facial cuts and bruises suggested a barroom fight. He had come to Riverbend from St. Deroin, located forty miles south on the edge of the vanishing Halfbreed Tract, the place where his mother and he had gone after his father moved on.

Louise had objected when Frank agreed to let a room to this stranger who handed over a full month's rent in cash. Why not direct the man downtown to the Whistle Stop Hotel instead of jeopardizing the Inn's reputation? Lodging a halfbreed would drive away Inn patrons, and she would not be able to hold her head up in town. Her position seemed too obvious to need an explanation, and Frank's failure to understand exasperated her no end. Everyone knew that Indians and halfbreeds were not to be trusted. Even so, she stirred up a mixture of lard and salt in a small glass jar that had once held solid fragrance and gave it to Frank. "Tell him to apply this to the bruises but avoid the cuts because it has salt in it."

It wasn't long before Louise warmed to Yonder's polite manner and serene good looks. Most endearing were his dark brown eyes, framed by high cheekbones and crow's feet that made them always appear to be smiling. He had the dark skin and coal black hair from his Santee Sioux mother and almost delicate facial structure which she presumed came from his father, who had been among the last of the French fur trappers. He had left Yonder's mother while she was pregnant with her only child. Louise had heard that trappers married Indian women to gain favor with a tribe so they could trap game on tribal lands. But often their offspring ended up outcasts, shunned by whites and Indians alike.

Turned out Yonder was an ardent "assimilationist," whose views on helping Indians adapt to white society awakened Louise to a neglected social problem in her own back yard. He believed that so-called "blanket Indians" must change their ways or get left behind, and he spent most of his time writing tracts and articles for the assimilation movement and traveling to conferences and meetings with the movement's tribal and white leaders.

Eventually the town gave him grudging acceptance, a nod here and a "good morning" there. People began to refer to him among themselves as "our halfbreed." His standing in the small community escalated about a year after he'd come to town when he appeared at Henkleman County Bank, presented a satchel with a large sum of money, the bills arranged by denomination with all the faces pointed in the same direction, and opened an account. Ever since, he had been greeted at the bank with, "Good morning, Mr. LaFontaine. What can we do for you today?"

*   *   *

LOUISE PICKED UP DOLLY OFF the floor of the Buick and handed her to Marie, whose cries had settled into muffled sobs. "Dolly is safe, too." She lifted Marie's braids in order to take her into her arms without pulling her hair. "There, there now." She regretted having let guilt and fear crowd out, if only momentarily, her maternal concern. She pulled Marie close with a silent promise to keep her safe forever.

Once on the road, Marie's mood brightened. "We scared the Sawyers so bad their pants will never get dry."

"For heaven's sake, Frank, what possessed you to teach our daughter such vulgarity?" Louise's tone of voice was that of a scolding parent, something she couldn't help when Frank behaved so childishly.

Before Frank could respond, Marie said, "We were playing Blind Girl's Bluff. Father gets down on the floor and operates the pedals, I place my hands at ten and two o'clock on the steering wheel, and Uncle Yonder sits in back and says, 'Now, right hand to three o'clock, Marie.'"

Marie's approximation of Yonder's voice had Frank and Yonder chuckling.

"'Now back to two o'clock,' or 'left hand to nine o'clock,' and so on. And he tells Father, 'Ease up on the gas, Frank, not that much,' and so on. So it looks like I'm driving the automobile."

Louise glared at the back of Frank's head. "Frank, you should be ashamed of yourself. You're supposed to set an example for Marie. And did you even once consider that your shenanigans reflect on us all, not just on yourself?"

She had married Frank having had little experience with men. Most made her wary. In Frank, a man who was kind and charming, she found a haven. He had inherited his standing in the community but was not particularly civic- or business-minded, a likeable companion but a feckless Irish dreamer not to be taken seriously. Louise once thought this characterization of her husband unfair, but as the years passed she could not ignore the mounting boneyard of failed ideas. But where would she be without him? Living in a garret with a leaky roof, pretending to be a widow, doing piecework to feed herself and her child? No, she was fortunate to be Mrs. Francis Morrissey. And fortunate that Frank and Marie adored each other.

"Shenanigans, you say. Well, at least Marie has never hit anything, which is more than I can say for someone I know."

As much for herself as for him, she let his words melt her icy mood. She forced a smile, knowing he would hear it in her voice. "Well, someone *I* know should have provided proper training."

Marie giggled, and Louise gave her a squeeze. For everyone's sake, she willed herself to remain congenial, knowing that her irritation with Frank had nothing to do with him and everything to do with The Twister Tenth Anniversary Observance, for it would bring her face to face with Doc.

CHAPTER 5

May 1904

The following Tuesday morning, Louise was dressing for breakfast when there came a knock on the bedroom door.

"Yes?"

"Cook says two people didn't show up." It was Henryetta's voice.

"You go on. I'll join you shortly."

Louise was not above working in the Inn's kitchen or dining room now and then. Or occasionally assuming the duties of Mr. and Mrs. Monfort, the resident front desk managers. These tasks came with being the innkeeper's wife. Frank drew the line at cleaning rooms.

Louise went to the bedroom where Marie sat playing with Dolly. "Get dressed and come downstairs with your father to have breakfast." She pushed hair away from Marie's face. There was no time to re-do her braids.

"May I work in the kitchen?"

Louise sometimes let her daughter grind coffee or help the dishwasher by putting away cups and saucers. "After you eat breakfast."

* * *

THE AIR IN THE STAIRWELL was thick with the aroma of pork

chops and sausage. Louise entered the dining room, filled with an eclectic mix of patrons that, this morning, included traveling salesmen wearing shoes polished to a mirror finish, overalls-clad laborers from the highway construction crew, and retired farmers. J.D. Henkleman, husband of Louise's best friend, Dovie, and owner of the *Riverbend Nonpareil* newspaper, held up his end of a fault-finding discussion among the group that called themselves the Roundtable Regulars: the banker, school superintendent, Methodist minister, railroad district supervisor, and owners of the cigar factory, chicken processing plant, bicycle shop, and mercantile company. The town's boosters, they had promoted early adoption of electricity and telephones, something neighboring Smithville had only recently embraced. Today's heated discussion was in response to word that Union College, in spite of Riverbend's long courtship, would locate in Smithville.

Frank, trailed by Marie, entered the dining room through the swinging doors from the kitchen and took a table. Louise delivered their standard dining room breakfast. Steak, hash browns, eggs over easy, and coffee for Frank. Oatmeal with cream for Marie. And kolaches for both. "Here's a hearty meal. It'll give you the pep and energy you need for your work." Louise enjoyed seeing Marie happy to "go to work."

As Louise was clearing tables, she noticed the different habits of people eating kolaches, which had become a specialty of the Inn. Some ate the doughy perimeter and saved the fruity or sweet cheesy center for a climax. Others spread the filling evenly over the dough, making each bite a marriage of sweetness and dough. Her own experience was that usually the first bite was sheer perfection against which the remaining pastry, being slightly too doughy or sweet for her taste, could not measure up. But there was always the promise of next time.

From the corner of her eye Louise saw Marie make her way toward the kitchen, touching chairs in her path. Frank should have insisted she bring her cane to navigate the dimly lit dining room. As she neared the kitchen, the swinging doors opened.

"Look out!" Louise yelled.

Marie collided with Mrs. Jelinek, the plump baker, whose platter of kolaches crashed to the floor. Mrs. Jelinek clasped a hand over her mouth as a flush crept from her neck to her cheeks. She appeared to be on the verge of tears. Marie looked stunned

Louise clutched her daughter and moved her away from the scattered pastries. "It's all right. No one's hurt. A few kolaches got spilled is all."

"May I still go to work?"

"Of course." Louise wanted to take Marie's hand and guide her to the kitchen, but she helped her daughter only when asked. She held her breath as Marie took tentative steps toward the swinging door.

The cook rushed out of the kitchen toting rags and a bucket. She nodded toward Mrs. Jelinek, who stood by, wringing her hands, being too fat to bend over. "That one's trouble. Eats like a field hand, she don't speak English, and I plain don't trust her."

From the look on Mrs. Jelinek's face, she appeared to grasp the cook's meaning, if not her words.

"It's just her Old Country ways." Louise gestured and smiled to let Mrs. Jelinek know she was not in trouble. Louise pitied the woman whom she had hired six months earlier. She might have been no older than Louise, but her haggard face suggested a hard life.

"Besides," Louise said to the cook, "how would you get by without her kolaches?"

The Bohemian baker had introduced the rich, sweet pastries to the breakfast menu and almost overnight they became the talk of the town. That she usually made more than enough for the breakfast crowd was her one saving grace with fellow workers.

Now that things were under control, Louise carried a coffee pot to the table of three old-timers, who worked at the Burlington yards, where trains were serviced and repaired. Caught up in conversation, they seemingly hadn't noticed the commotion. They went on talking as she refilled their cups.

"Before The Twister women knew how to act like ladies," the man wearing a railroad cap said.

"Have you noticed they's been more two-headed calves borned?" The oldest of the trio poured coffee into his saucer and back into his cup, then repeated the ritual.

"By golly, now you mention it, more folks come down with the consumption," the red-haired man said.

Overhearing their talk reminded Louise how recollections of events had organized themselves neatly into two categories: before and after The Twister. "The storm of the century," people called it. J.D., always a stickler for correct spelling and punctuation in his newspaper, had proclaimed The Twister to be a storm of such magnitude that it merited capitalizing to distinguish it from lesser tornadoes.

While dismissing the old-timers' superstitions, Louise could not shake her belief that the storm had possessed magical powers. Otherwise how had she been transformed from one person before The Twister to someone she scarcely recognized after?

* * *

After a quick sponge bath that afternoon, Louise put on a flowery print dress that flattered her wasp waist, an illusion achieved with a painfully cinched corset. The dress was a favorite. It transported her to a setting in a photograph she had once seen: the white veranda of a Kentucky horse farm where ladies of impeccable breeding sipped mint juleps from silver cups.

Looking in the mirror, she tamed the rogue strands of hair that escaped her otherwise well-mannered coiffure. Lamenting the streaks of gray and the tendency of her flaxen hair to resemble excelsior in the humidity, she carried on the long-standing debate with herself about whether to abandon her Gibson Girl hairstyle for the neat Marcel wave like Dovie wore.

She noticed her hands, which Dovie always called her "signature." They compensated for the flaws the mirror revealed—hazel eyes set a bit too wide, a somewhat determined jaw. Next she applied just enough face powder and rouge to create a look of glowing health. Then the finishing touches: beige pumps, hat, lace gloves, and parasol.

With one last, studied look at her mirrored reflection, she was satisfied that the fluid motion with which she picked up her handbag and the book she had intended to finish reading that morning exhibited refinement. Graceful gestures anchored her in the role and elevated other behaviors so that her voice would be well-modulated, her words well-chosen, and her posture erect but not ramrod stiff. Silly, she knew, but after all these years she still sought the mirror's assurance that she would not slip with an "ain't" or a careless wipe of her nose with a sleeve. A cultivated lady gazed back.

It being a mild, sunny day, Louise enjoyed her walk to the Tuesday Bibliophiles meeting. Entering Anderson's Seed and Feed, she paused to close her parasol and let her eyes adjust to the dim light. She walked the stairs to the second floor through a cloud of seed and feed dust. When she entered the library, the musty odor of books thrust her back, as it always did, to her Wednesday afternoons with Doc. She nudged him out of her mind and recalled the private library of the Logans, her first employer. There she had discovered great literature.

Louise joined the four women Frank called "the biddies," a collection of individuals united in their love of literature and literacy. Dolores "Dovie" Henkleman, her sister-in-law Gertrude Gottschalk, and Madge Anderson stood fanning themselves with cardboard fans, courtesy of Ludwig's Furniture Store and Undertaking Parlor. Louise's neighbor, Alice Dietz, plump and asthmatic, sat in the wingback chair in the social corner, still gulping breath after having climbed the stairs. She clutched a package of Potter's Asthma Cigarettes in one hand and an ashtray with a spent cigarette in the other. Smoking in what was undoubtedly a firetrap made Louise nervous.

Alice's wheezing eased somewhat, her face slack as though she'd just survived a battle for her life. Louise ached for her and remembered having led the Bibliophiles in a failed effort ten years earlier to get a Carnegie library in Riverbend, a clean space that would be free from feed dust that hung in the air and clogged lungs. And there would be a first-floor meeting room.

It would be worth trying again, but now her duties as Marie's mother came first. Louise had become consumed with teaching her daughter to read and write Braille and do sums, and with grooming her for a career as a concert pianist. Marie's welfare meant everything. The fires of personal ambition burned no more.

Louise and Dovie took seats on the sofa while Madge and Gertrude took the remaining upholstered chairs.

"I don't believe a man could have written *The Trojan Women,*" Dovie said. She was a tiny woman and voracious reader whose nickname reflected her bird-like energy. "I think *Mrs.* Euripides wrote it."

Madge, a former schoolteacher who late in life had married widower Andy Anderson, corrected her. "Euripedes' wife would not have been referred to as *Mrs. Euripides.* The ancient Greeks did not use those forms of address."

The insult appeared to escape Dovie.

Dovie's comments often exasperated Madge, who now taught the library's Adult Literacy Class. Madge, who had a square, no-nonsense jaw and wore her hair in a bun, might have been more tolerant if Dovie would dress properly for their meetings instead of wearing bloomers, attire the high school girls had taken to wearing to the ice cream parlor. Dovie also enjoyed the notoriety of being the first woman in town to drive an automobile and didn't care that people snickered at seeing her crank the engine. And everyone knew that in the privacy of her home she smoked the occasional cigar. Louise envied her friend's ability to bend rules and get away with it, one privilege of having been born well and marrying one of the most influential men in Riverbend.

"Well, I still think she wrote it," Dovie said, the rapid flutter of her fan reminding Louise of a hummingbird. "It wouldn't be the first time a man took credit for a woman's work."

Madge said, "You have a point there."

Alice nodded as she removed her crocheting from a bag. She was making antimacassars for the threadbare arms of the library's sofa and three upholstered chairs. When not in the throes of an asthma attack, she was inscrutably beautiful, like a porcelain doll.

Gertrude, today's discussion leader, looked at the Regulator wall clock, then at the watch pinned to her shirtwaist pocket. Her stalwart black eyebrows met in a frown. "My watch says it's time to begin. Louise, it appears the library clock is nearly three minutes slow."

"I shall have it checked." Louise had long ago gotten over letting Gertrude's nitpicking annoy her, and now she found it amusing. Gertrude was the younger sister of J.D., Dovie's husband. She always carried her Bible, which she might pull from her purse and read during a meeting, particularly if she didn't like the turn a discussion had taken. Three years earlier, Gertrude had lost her husband. Louise felt sorry for her, a woman in the prime of life made a misfit for lack of a husband. She now lived with her mother, a woman who was much lighter-hearted than her two children. The Henkleman matriarch was also Marie's beloved piano teacher.

"I won't be able to join you in the discussion," Louise said. "To tell you the truth, I didn't finish reading today's selection. I apologize."

"That's not like you." Dovie set her fan in her lap. "Usually I'm the scatterbrain. I forget which of the dozen books lying around my house is the one we're reading."

Louise marveled at how her good friend could appear to be moving even when sitting still.

"Oh, and Louise, everyone in town is talking about that trick Frank played on the poor Sawyer family. Have you heard what he did?"

Louise felt a flush rising in her face. "I'm afraid so. It's a game he likes to call 'Blind Girl's Bluff.' Believe me, I'd put a stop to it if I could."

Alice had been sitting quietly, crocheting and just listening until her wheezing subsided sufficiently for her to talk. "Speaking of books lying around . . . I have some I've been meaning to donate to the library."

Louise's pulse quickened. But Alice's expression was without guile. There was not the slightest knowing twitch in Louise's direction, nothing to suggest she might have been the one who had left books on the wicker table that long-ago December day. Deciding that anxiety over The Twister anniversary had her on edge, Louise took slow breaths to calm herself. There was no reason to believe her reputation might be in jeopardy.

During the discussion of Euripides' play, Louise's mind drifted back to her tentative first days as the twelve-year-old housekeeper for Mr. and Mrs. Logan. One day while dusting books in their cavernous library, she had sneaked a look at *Jane Eyre* and discovered a girl whose loneliness and yearnings resembled her own. Hearing Mrs. Logan's voice, Louise steeled herself for a reprimand, but instead her employer, with no children of her own to fuss over, welcomed Louise's interest in books and set up a course of reading for her to follow after her day's work was done. A favorite memory was the occasional winter afternoon when she and Mrs. Logan would sit over hot chocolate and discuss books. Louise dreamed then of one day having children of her own and greeting them with steaming mugs of hot chocolate when they came home from school.

"Time's up," Gertrude said. "Madge will present the word for the day."

"Today's word is *progeny*." Madge said. "It is a noun that means 'direct descendents.' It derives from the Latin verb *progignere* which means 'to beget.' Synonyms include 'children' and 'offspring.' I shall use it in a sentence: The Trojan women's progeny suffered at the hands of the Greek conquerors."

"Is the word related to 'prodigy?' Dovie asked.

"No," Madge said.

"Louise is related to a prodigy," Alice said. "Her progeny is a piano prodigy."

"Thank you." Louise appreciated Alice's remark, especially given that she knew the reason Alice's daughter quit taking piano lessons was because Mrs. Henkleman had told Alice not to waste her money.

"That's clever," Dovie said, twirling a lock of hair on the back of her head. "Not gloomy like Madge's sentence. And it's true, Marie is a prodigy."

Louise could not have asked for a more perfect opening. "Thank you. I don't know if Marie is a prodigy, but I've just been bursting to tell you that J.D. asked her to play the piano for The Twister anniversary."

"I wouldn't miss it for the world," Alice said. "Now let's have refreshments."

While the others adjourned to seats at the large reading table, Louise went to the kitchen and returned with hot tea and kolaches and took the seat next to Dovie.

Dovie took a bite of her apricot-filled kolache and licked her fingers. "Positively sinful."

Gertrude scowled. "I'll tell you what's sinful. It's the latest *Ladies' Home Journal* . . ."

Madge interrupted. "I thought you cancelled your subscription long ago."

"I did, but Mother bought a copy on the newsstand. Anyway, you'd think that magazine would know women won't tolerate such filth in their homes. Whatever you do, don't leave that magazine lying about where children might see it."

"My copy of the *Journal* has not arrived yet," Madge said. "What makes it unsuitable for children?"

Gertrude's black eyebrows arched over eyes that flashed in anger. "An article about venereal disease. My church circle was fit to be tied yesterday."

"I saw it," Dovie said.

Louise had received the magazine but hadn't read it yet. As Dovie began to speak, Louise wondered if she'd express her own opinion or channel one of J.D.'s self-righteous rants.

Dovie said, "The editor says the magazine will continue to educate women about an epidemic that threatens to destroy the home, that wives need to know they might unwittingly become infected with gonorrhea that can make them sterile or even kill them. He goes on to say that seventy percent of special surgeries on women are for complications of gonorrhea."

Louise recalled the surgery she had required the year after Marie was born. "Pelvic inflammatory disease," the gynecologist had called it, a complication of childbed fever.

"They can't be talking about *respectable* women," Gertrude

said. "It's those immigrants."

Madge chastised Gertrude with the practiced look of a woman who had taught high school for many years. "Let me give you a bit of advice. You're sadly mistaken if you think respectable women don't get gonorrhea. They get it from husbands who have visited brothels. The article makes the point that some men can carry the germ for years after they were afflicted."

"I liked the magazine better when they stuck to housekeeping matters and recipes and raising children," Dovie said.

Louise noticed Gertrude's neck and cheeks had turned bright red. "Gertrude, are you all right? Do you need to lie down?"

"No, I'm fine." Gertrude fanned herself with a napkin. "It's the world that isn't fine. When good people allow that godforsaken magazine into their homes." Her mouth tensed, and her voice grew strident. "There's a breakdown of morality in this country. Satan has a hold."

Louise took the teapot to the kitchen, refilled it, and returned. She sat down next to Dovie, who was fanning herself.

"No more tea for me, please. It's way too hot."

"Let me give you a bit of advice," Madge said.

Louise anticipated—and received—a light kick directed at her ankle by Dovie. She managed to hold a stoic expression even while thinking of what Frank had to say about Madge: "If she were in a burning building, instead of yelling 'Fire,' she would command, 'Render aid forthwith as this structure is being immolated by a conflagration.'"

"Hot tea, without sugar of course," Madge said, "is more conducive to a healthy constitution than iced drinks, which are a shock to the system."

"Speaking of a healthy constitution," Louise said, "Gertrude, did you find your visit to the hot springs revitalizing?"

Gertrude dabbed at her lips with her napkin. "Truth to tell, I only go for Mother's benefit. I'm not particularly fond of the springs myself. Well, as you all know, Mother is always chatting up strangers, and she got to talking to an eye doctor from Philadelphia. Mother is convinced he took a shine to me." A hint of a self-conscious smile appeared, then Gertrude looked at Louise. "Mother told him about Marie's eyes, and he said he might could help her."

"Thank you, Gertrude," Louise said, "but we've been to the best ophthalmologists in the Midwest—Omaha, Chicago, Rochester. They all say the same thing, that there's nothing that can be done to restore her sight."

"Oh, but this doctor isn't an ophthalmologist. His specialty is natural vision correction. When Mother told him Marie can tell night from day and not much else, he said he could teach her to do eye exercises to strengthen muscles that focus images on the brain or some such thing."

"You're so kind," Louise said. "But I'm skeptical. I just can't get Marie's hopes up again only to see them dashed."

CHAPTER 6

In Philadelphia Louise carried Marie's satchel and helped her daughter board a streetcar outside their hotel. Then she followed Marie, who used her cane to get down the aisle until Louise indicated two available seats.

Marie wore her navy blue sailor dress and straw hat. In the barren years before Marie's birth, Louise had dreamed of having a daughter to dress up, one whose beauty, manners, and fine apparel would bring approving looks from the matrons of society's highest echelons. Every garment in Marie's wardrobe was top quality, and her raven braids shone like her patent leather boots. But it was her eyes that commanded attention.

A little boy and his mother got on the streetcar. The boy pointed to Marie and said, "Lookity. What's wrong with her eyes?"

Louise gave the mother a look that said, "Teach that little savage some manners."

The woman slapped the boy's pointing hand.

Marie whimpered. "I want to go home. I miss Father."

Louise patted her arm. If only Frank had come along, he would have handled the situation. Originally Frank had planned to accompany them, but a "pressing business matter" came up. She knew better than to ask for particulars. He urged Louise to postpone the trip, not wanting her to travel alone, but she explained it had been fortunate that Dr. Mayhew, the eye doctor Gertrude had told her about, had had an immediate opening. No telling how long it could take to secure another appointment.

Frank had been skeptical. Louise argued that the fact Marie's left eye registered images as faint shadows in strong light could mean there would be something Dr. Mayhew could work with. This would be the last time she would chase a cure. She meant it. Most likely, nothing could be done. She had steeled herself against that outcome but didn't know how she'd react if he said, "I could have restored her sight had you brought her to me sooner."

"This won't hurt, will it?" Marie asked.

"No. We hope that Dr. Mayhew might be able to help you see some things that you can only feel now."

"Like Braille dots?"

"No, sighted people don't read raised dots."

"Will I be like other children?"

"No matter what happens, you will always be your own, special self."

"If I could be like other children, that would be the best birthday present in the world."

Louise so wanted to promise her daughter a miracle, wanted to believe it herself. A lump formed in her throat. Better to say nothing,

The streetcar left the city's bustling commercial center, where sidewalks swarmed with purposeful men and women who seemingly had no time to waste, and passed into a grimy district where men idled on street corners, and women toted bundles and children. Louise double-checked the address. It would be in the vicinity of the next stop.

The foolishness of her expedition gripped her. A woman alone in a strange city trying to safeguard a blind child. She should have waited for Frank.

But she had not come this far to quit. With all the bravado she could muster, she guided Marie off the streetcar, around the street's loose bricks and potholes and, wishing she and her daughter were not so conspicuously well dressed, past characters she suspected of being pickpockets or worse. At the place where Dr. Mayhew's office should have been was a boarded-up storefront flanked by a barbershop and dentist's office. Louise stopped and scanned the buildings on both sides of the block.

"What's wrong?" Marie asked.

"I'm not finding the doctor's office. Perhaps the dentist can direct us."

Louise opened the door to a small, dimly lit room, which smelled unmistakably of cloves. The dentist, his jacket spattered with blood, and a patient stood shouting at each other, the patient disputing the fee for a simple extraction.

"Pardon me," Louise said, "but will you please tell me where I might find Dr. Mayhew?"

"No idea." The dentist glanced at Marie and looked away. "You just missed him. Got evicted last week."

Her hopes dashed, she felt weak. What now? Frank would have known what to do.

"You're not looking well, ma'am," the dentist said. "I'll fetch you some water."

Louise took a deep breath and straightened. "No thank you. But we came all the way from Nebraska just to see Dr.

Mayhew."

"Would've been a waste of your time either way," the dentist said. "He was a quack."

The patient nodded toward Marie. His jaw was swollen and his speech slurred. "You might could take her to see Dr. Vandegrift. Don't know the man personally, but he's famous."

"That's true," the dentist said.

* * *

That afternoon Louise and Marie joined other patients in the tastefully appointed parlor of Dr. Durwood Vandegrift's home, located in a leafy neighborhood of grand estates with vast, manicured lawns and ornate wrought iron fences. Normally it would have taken several months to get an appointment, but when Louise had appeared and pleaded her case, the doctor agreed to see Marie on short notice.

Louise guided her daughter to an overstuffed sofa where they could avoid the curious glances of other patients in the waiting room. Even the woman with a badly aligned glass eye, no doubt the object of rude looks herself, craned her neck to see Marie's affliction.

Once seated, Louise patted Marie. "You're quite the little trooper. It's been a hard day, and I know you must be hungry, but you haven't complained one bit. After we see Dr. Vandegrift, we'll go to the restaurant I saw nearby."

Marie pulled a cumbersome Braille book from her satchel, an installment of *Swiss Family Robinson*. She turned to the middle of the book, glided her fingers over a line of raised dots, flipped some more pages, and stopped, visibly distressed. "I've lost my place. I already read this part. I forgot the page number."

It was not like Marie to forget or give up. Louise felt her frustration. "I can help. What was happening?"

"The family had just made it onto the lifeboat."

Able to read Braille by sight, Louise scanned pages until she found the word "lifeboat," then looked ahead to the part Marie had indicated. "Here it is, the middle of this page."

She handed the book to Marie, thinking how unfair it was that Marie's fingers could never glance at a book or a page and know what it's about. At the same time she admired Marie's capacity to read with her fingers and to "write" Braille using a slate and stylus.

The woman who beckoned them from a doorway looked from Marie to Louise with raised eyebrows. Louise's neck and shoulders tightened. Perhaps her attire, modish by Midwestern standards, did not measure up.

When they entered the drab windowless room, Dr. Vandegrift stood to greet them. Louise had envisioned him to be a portly man with graying hair, but he was young, perhaps thirty-five.

He invited Louise and Marie to sit, then took a seat on a low, rolling stool across from them. Instead of immediately beginning his examination, he said, "Miss Marie, I understand you traveled a great distance to Philadelphia. What did you like best about your trip?"

"I can't decide. Maybe eating beer cheese soup for the first time. No, wait, my most favorite thing was getting to sleep in a berth with my mother and having the train rock me to sleep."

As he listened to Marie's response, he did not act preoccupied or bury himself in note-taking but gave her his full attention.

Louise liked his manner, but her heart raced as she waited to learn what, if anything, he could do for her daughter.

"What a wonderful trip." When he pushed his stool back the casters squealed, and Louise flinched. He gave her a sympathetic look. "I understand you've had a trying day, Mrs. Morrissey."

He moved the stool until he sat about five feet from Marie. He reached for a glass jar, removed a lemon candy straw, and held it at Marie's eye-level. "I have something for you in my right hand. Can you point to it?"

Marie started towards him.

"Stop there, please. Can you point to it without coming closer?"

Louise leaned forward and held her breath. If Marie demonstrated that she could make out his hand, perhaps this doctor could do what others could not.

Marie shook her head.

Louise hastened to justify Marie's performance. "The light in here is too low. In bright light she sees people and large objects well enough to keep from bumping into them."

"What about now, Marie?" Dr. Vandegrift said. He waved the candy from side to side, then held it still.

Marie pointed, and the doctor gave her the candy.

Louise's heart made a little leap. Marie had outdone herself.

"You're a clever little rascal." He turned to Louise. "She detected the sound of my arm moving and the 'acoustic shadow' left by my arm where it stopped. In other words, my arm and hand blocked the background sound waves that you and I scarcely notice."

Louise scowled. It hardly seemed a fair test.

Marie giggled. "Thank you. Lemon straws are my most favorite."

He moved closer to her, lifting her eyelids with his thumbs and giving each eye a cursory glance. "There, now. That didn't hurt, did it? Come with me, and we'll get one of my helpers to read you a story while I visit with your mother."

He took Marie's hand and led her from the room.

In his absence Louise reflected on his cursory examination of Marie, straining to recall anything hopeful in his voice or manner. But he had given no clues one way or the other.

When he returned he moved the stool closer and sat across from her. "Mrs. Morrissey, I wish I could offer encouragement, but Marie's corneas are too severely damaged. The best I can offer you is that she will not lose what little perception she has now. It may not seem like much, but it's vastly preferable to total darkness. You can help her by providing ample lighting."

The words taxed Louise's resolve to be strong, whatever the outcome. She covered her face. She had been foolish to make this trip. Dr. Vandegrift's opinion echoed that of every other doctor who had looked at Marie.

He tilted his head and raised his eyebrows. "Do you have any children other than Marie?"

"No, she's our only child." A curious question.

"Are you able to bear more children?"

Such impertinence. He did not need to know of the female troubles that followed Marie's birth and the complications that necessitated surgery. "I fail to see what this has to do with Marie's eyesight."

"Please, bear with me. Now will you describe the condition of her eyes in infancy?"

"She was born with perfectly healthy eyes. But three days later, her right eyelid turned red, and a watery discharge appeared, which soon turned to pus. And the symptoms appeared in her left eye as well. She was very fretful."

"Did she receive treatment?"

"At first our housekeeper said to treat her eyes with mother's milk. By the time the doctor saw her, her eyes oozed copious amounts of pus. He put drops in them and advised us to bathe her eyes with a boric acid solution every hour and apply ice packs." Louise bit her lower lip. Finally, she knew she must ask. "Could you have helped her if I had brought her to you before now?"

The doctor shook his head. "No. Had treatment been administered at the first sign of infection, the damage could have been mitigated. It's possible that mother's milk, along with boric acid and ice packs, served to retard the damage in her left eye. But, and I know this will be difficult for you to hear, had a prophylactic been administered at birth, there would have been no infection." He sighed. "Mrs. Morrissey, your daughter is needlessly blind."

It seemed the air had been sucked from the room and the walls were closing in. Louise could only look at him, her hand covering her mouth, and shake her head. When she was able to speak her words came out soft and measured. "Am I to understand that with proper medical care she would not have lost her sight?"

"Almost certainly if the doctor had instilled drops of dilute silver nitrate in her eyes immediately after birth."

"She was delivered by a midwife. And her eyes appeared healthy at birth."

"Doctor, midwife, I don't know about Nebraska, but here in the East we struggle in vain to make them understand the importance of instilling drops immediately after birth to prevent blindness. Unfortunately most fail to practice it. Should you give birth to another child, you must insist on prophylaxis. It's a delicate subject that physicians don't want to broach lest they turn wives against husbands."

This doctor made no sense.

"Let me explain something to you that other doctors obviously have not. They see that you're a lady, so they tell you the infection resulted from certain micro-organisms that entered Marie's eyes during birth."

"Yes," Louise said. "A bacterial infection. I've been told that many women harbor bacteria, but it doesn't usually infect the baby."

"Several organisms, such as *pneumococcus, bacillus coli*, and Koch-Weeks *bacillus* can cause mild *ophthalmia* and even scar the corneas sufficiently to impair sight."

"*Pneumococcus?* I once had pneumonia. Might the germ have remained in my body?"

"None of the micro-organisms I mentioned is likely to result in the extreme damage I'm seeing in Marie's eyes. She has *gonococcal ophthalmia neonatorum,* or 'babies' sore eyes.' That's the work of *Neisseria gonorrheae,* a germ transmitted when the baby passes through the birth canal of a mother who has— there's no way to put this delicately—gonorrhea."

Louise jumped to her feet. "You have your nerve speaking such filth to a lady. Just because you're a big city doctor gives you no right . . . Where I come from your kind would get run out of town on a rail."

She whirled about. She would collect Marie and they would return to the safety of Riverbend. Philadelphia had been a nightmare. But as she reached for the doorknob, the door opened and sent her staggering backward.

The nurse caught Louise's arm and kept her from falling. "I am so sorry."

"Miss Hitchcock," Dr. Vandegrift said, "I think Mrs. Morrissey would be more at ease if you remained here."

Louise reached for the door. "I have heard quite enough,"

"Please, Mrs. Morrissey," the doctor said. "You made a long journey here on your daughter's behalf, and I am truly sorry that I've not only disappointed you but made matters worse." He gestured toward the chair.

She hesitated, her mind reeling. Finally, she realized the only way to convince him he was wrong was to stand her ground. She sat. "There must have been another source of infection."

The nurse, who had begun gathering instruments, lifted the lid from a metal tray, and Louise caught the scent of alcohol.

"Next to impossible," Dr. Vandegrift said. "Transmission sometimes occurs in a hospital setting when a nurse fails to use proper hygiene after handling an infected baby. But even then the germ cannot thrive for long in air. Modern medicine has yet to unravel the mysterious workings of most germs and infections, but I can tell you with certainty that the link between gonorrhea and your daughter's blindness is irrefutable."

Louise jumped at the clatter of the tray full of instruments hitting the floor.

The nurse clasped a hand to her mouth. "I'm so sorry." She grabbed a towel, squatted down, and began placing the instruments in the tray and wiping up the alcohol.

"Not to worry, Miss Hitchcock," the doctor said. "Mrs. Morrissey, I don't want you to leave here without understanding what almost certainly happened to you and your daughter. The unfortunate truth is that most men contract gonorrhea at some point in their lives. You're a proper lady, and to learn that your husband gave you gonorrhea is unthinkable. In his defense, he probably contracted it before marriage, went to a doctor and got relief for the symptoms, thought he was cured, and didn't realize he was still a carrier. I saw one case in which a man carried the germ for fifteen years."

Louise buried her face in her hands and shook her head. Impossible.

"Your husband will be as devastated as you by this news," Dr. Vandegrift said.

Now Louise understood why the nurse had raised her eyebrows when she first saw Marie. It had nothing to do with Louise's attire. "How widely known is this type of blindness?"

"Unfortunately it's almost unknown outside the medical community."

"Why *unfortunately?*"

"We know that one-fourth to one-third of all children admitted to schools for the blind are needlessly blind because of babies' sore eyes. We have statistical evidence—some of it going back twenty-five years—from lying-in hospitals in the British Isles, France, Boston, New York City, and here in Philadelphia, where universal application of dilute silver nitrate drops almost totally eradicated the disease. Yet, as much as I am loath to speak against my medical colleagues, it is shameful that babies are being blinded because physicians fail to act on what they know. In fairness to them, part of the problem is that medicine is a culture of healing, not preventing."

As he spoke, Louise only half listened. Why believe him? No other doctor had told her about gonorrhea. What if gonorrhea had been the true cause of her pelvic inflammatory disease? If so, who was the carrier, Frank or Doc?

"Forgive my lecture," Dr. Vandegrift said, "but greater public awareness will bring pressure to bear on lawmakers to mandate prophylactic drops in every newborn baby's eyes. Getting that legislation will come about through grassroots movements in each state. We need courageous people to educate the public and their legislators plainly about what causes babies' sore eyes and how it can be prevented. Respected people, like yourself."

"Me?" Louise asked. "What respectable woman talks about an unspeakable disease?"

"One with courage and determination." He looked at her as if she were that woman. "One willing to risk her reputation to save the sight of innocent babies."

"I beg your pardon, but you cannot know what it means to be a mother. No mother would publicly expose her daughter to the ridicule that would follow if it were believed she had been blinded by . . . " She couldn't bring herself to say the word. "Besides, you are wrong. My husband and I do not have what you said we have."

"I know this is difficult for you." His expression and voice seemed sincere. "But please consider this: imagine that ten or twenty years ago, a courageous mother had pressed your state legislature to mandate drops, and a law was passed. Because that didn't happen, Marie is needlessly blind."

No, it wasn't for lack of a law that Marie was needlessly blinded. It was my own selfish compromise with sin.

Louise was shaking when she and Marie left Dr. Vandegrift's office. They walked to the Olde English House where they ate in the courtyard. She allowed Marie to order dessert even though she had not finished her meal.

Marie mashed her vanilla ice cream against the sides of the silver bowl with her spoon. "This bowl is very cold. Touch it."

Louise touched the bowl, an object that was just one more topic in a stream of chatter in which Marie flitted from the fragrance of roses to the sounds of birds at their feet searching for crumbs to anything else that struck her fancy.

Marie held her spoon suspended. "Listen."

"What is it? I don't hear anything."

"Music."

"I hear it now. It's coming closer."

"Accordian music. It would be fun to play the accordion. What's your favorite instrument?"

Louise could wait no longer. "Marie, I don't know how to—I'm afraid Dr. Vandegrift can't help you." Her voice broke and the tears flowed.

Marie pawed the table until she touched her mother's hand. She grasped it tightly. "Don't cry, Mother. I knew he would say that."

"But I wanted so much . . ." What Louise had wanted was to be a good mother, to give her daughter the comforts and advantages she never had, yet what she had given her was eternal darkness. "I am so sorry!"

Marie appeared to be holding back tears herself. She patted Louise's hand. "It's not your fault."

*   *   *

The flickering hope Louise had brought to Philadelphia had been extinguished. One more expert had decreed that Marie would be permanently, irrevocably blind.

Nothing had changed, except that in place of the flickering hope was a new horror. What if he were correct, that public attention was being called to the condition he said Marie had, "babies' sore eyes?" What if it became common knowledge that children whose eyes looked like Marie's were infected by gonorrhea? Would Frank suspect that she had betrayed him? On the other hand, was it he who had infected her or had Doc? Marie must never know. *God, heap all the punishment you want on me, but spare Marie the shame.*

Through the train's window Louise saw Frank waiting on the platform. Her body ached from sitting too many hours, and her head throbbed from the Pullman car's smoke-filled air, but she almost wished she and Marie could stay on the train, escape to a new life where she would no longer have to worry about a husband finding out her secret.

Frank helped first Marie, then Louise off the train. They went inside the depot to await a porter with their bags. Frank gave Marie a penny to buy French roasted peanuts, her usual treat when they went to the depot.

Marie walked assuredly with her cane to the row of candy dispensers, located the one on the far left, and counted over three to her right.

"No, Marie," Louise called. "Your peanuts have been moved to the dispenser on your left." Such was Marie's reality today, tomorrow, and forever.

Louise told Frank about discovering that Dr. Mayhew was a quack and about meeting with Dr. Vandegrift. "Frank, he can't—"

"I know. I saw it in your face when you stepped off the train. Now you've heard it from a big specialist in the East. You're not a quitter, but it's time to give up. You've done everything humanly possible."

"He said she was blinded by *pneumococcus*." Louise buried her head in his shoulder to hide her fluttering eyelids.

CHAPTER 7

May 1904

Louise sat stiffly in the assigned wooden folding chair on the stage of the high school gymnasium, which doubled as an auditorium. The large mother-of-pearl buttons on her new dress dug into her back. Doc sat just a whisper away on her right, looking smart as ever in a handsome suit. Seeing the man who had wronged her, called her a "Jezebel," accused her of consorting with "that halfbreed," and, even worse, probably carried the gonorrhea that caused Marie's blindness, roused loathing like she'd never felt for another living soul. Yet she could not help remembering the power of his velvety voice and sweet, smoky aroma.

She had come to the ceremony with an agenda. Not the full agenda she desired. That would have meant facing Doc and demanding answers. Did he have gonorrhea? Why had he not warned her that her baby might be blinded? Why had he not intervened and instilled sight-saving drops when Marie was born, not when it was too late? Demanding answers was not possible in this public setting. The most she could hope for was to wound him with words that would indicate she knew the cause of Marie's blindness—not that she had fully admitted it to herself—and, if he had any conscience at all, perhaps he would suffer.

In front of the stage, Marie sat on the piano stool, swinging her legs and waiting for the signal to begin playing. Looking angelic in her new dress, she ran her fingers over the peplum's ribbon embroidery flowers and leaves whose colors she had memorized. The embroidery served more than a decorative function. To a bystander, Marie's actions would seem pointless, but Louise knew she was calming herself.

As people were taking their seats, J.D. approached Marie and touched her shoulder. Marie extended her hands to find the ends of the keyboard, then her fingers found the keys, and she began to play Sinding's "Rustles of Spring." She swayed with the music's rhythm, a habit Louise hoped she would eventually overcome.

Curly Ambrose was bent over, his head under the hood covering his camera. He lifted the hood, stood, and limped as he moved the tripod a couple of feet forward. The photos he was taking today would appear in a commemorative book that would include his pictures of the actual tornado. He had gotten so caught up in photographing the storm that he hadn't seen a flying board headed his direction, hence the limp. Now his camera was positioned to get a picture of Marie.

The piano was set at an angle so that Marie's face was visible to people on stage but not to the audience. Louise sensed that Doc was watching Marie. Did he see himself in her, the raven hair and dimpled chin? So undeniably his child. Was he consumed with guilt? Louise shifted in her seat, took a handkerchief from her pocket, and blotted her perspiring forehead.

Doc's attention was on Mrs. Graves, seated to his right, the civic leader Louise had once hoped to succeed. The matriarch kept him engaged in conversation, or more accurately, riveted him in place with a relentless monologue.

Louise scanned the audience, wondering if she would recognize anyone she had aided after The Twister. But other thoughts kept intruding. Doc wasn't the one who shielded Marie from thoughtless and downright cruel people. Doc wasn't the one who worried about her future, a day when, as a blind, disfigured spinster, she would have no one to shield her. Doc was the one for whom a handful of Wednesday afternoons were a lark and nothing more.

A woman's voice said, "Mrs. Morrissey."

Louise had to incline her body in Doc's direction to look at Irina Taylor seated behind him. She held her breath as though to numb herself against Doc's closeness, but the moment was heavy with the sense that in another lifetime she would have quivered in anticipation of his lips on her neck.

"Your daughter is a brilliant pianist."

"Thank you." Feeling the enchantment of Irina's misty blue-violet eyes, Louise wondered how such a beauty was still single at what must be nearly thirty years of age. She was employed as a visiting nurse, and no doubt her path and Doc's sometimes crossed. She was far more attractive than Dr. Foster's wife who, according to rumor, had been reduced to a brooding homebody by the "change of life." Had Irina known him as well?

Marie was nearing the end of a medley from Mussorgsky's "Pictures at an Exhibition." Louise held her breath waiting for a passage where Marie's fingers sometimes stumbled in practice. But Marie executed it flawlessly. Louise exhaled.

The next song, a new ragtime composition by Debussy, would set folks to tapping their feet, the senior Mrs. Henkleman had said at Marie's most recent piano lesson, a song perfectly suited to the tinny-sounding school upright. Indeed, when Marie began playing "Golliwogg's Cakewalk" it so captivated the audience that they stopped talking.

Louise closed her eyes and listened. Though not a musician herself, she had a good ear. She assisted Marie in daily practice, tending the Victrola when Marie was learning a new piece. Louise would set the needle on a recording and let it play through a phrase of music, then lift the needle. Marie would attempt the passage, then Louise would play the same passage on the recording and Marie would try it once again. Mother and daughter repeated this musical dialogue until both agreed Marie had it right. Then they moved to the next passage.

Now with her eyes closed, just listening, Louise reveled in her daughter's command of the difficult piece. Anticipating her favorite part, she opened her eyes to see Marie's right and left hands play syncopated octaves. *Good restraint, Marie, not overstating the rising volume.* Just then Marie stumbled over the notes.

Louise held her breath. *Just keep going, Marie.*

Marie stopped, then went back to the bass octaves and attacked them with determination. She stumbled, but this time she kept going and played the rest of the song with joy that was contagious. Now she wasn't just providing background music, she was an admired soloist who finished to a standing ovation. She rose, turned toward the audience, and responded with a curtsy, a move she had delighted in practicing over and over at home.

As the applause continued, Doc said, "Remarkable how she recovered. Such poise. You must be very proud." With his chin tilted up and eyebrows raised, his look felt like that of a master taking the trouble to compliment a servant.

Louise wanted to spit words at him but instead affected a civil tone: "Remarkable, yes. One wonders what she might accomplish were she not needlessly blind."

His face sagged. Caught without words he shifted his eyes away from Louise's determined gaze. She had expected to feel satisfied, but anger stiffened her neck and squeezed her head, signaling the onset of a headache.

When the high school choir began to sing "Nearer My God to Thee," Frank, as planned, appeared and guided Marie toward the seat he'd saved between him and Yonder, who had just arrived home hours earlier, having cut short a trip to San Diego so he could see Marie's performance. Louise watched as Frank and Marie walked past the rows of people in the audience. Seeing some people recoil at the sight of Marie's eyes was an affront Louise had experienced often but never got used to. She covered her mouth with a balled fist. Her breaths came hard, and her head throbbed.

A long, rambling prayer followed the music. No doubt the twenty-seven victims of The Twister had prayed, too, and for what? To no more avail than her prayers over her baby brothers or her prayers for deliverance from her father or her prayers that Marie's sight be saved.

J.D. presided as Master of Ceremonies. He looked the part, being a man who carried his ample corseted physique with an air of success. He gestured with pink, manicured hands that had never known the stain of printer's ink. As publisher of *The Riverbend Nonpareil* he enjoyed the comfort of a private office where he spent as much time acquiring and managing real estate as running the newspaper.

In the oratorical tones of the politician he aspired to be, J.D. began: "Welcome. There could be no more fitting location for The Twister Tenth Anniversary ceremony than this, the high school gymnasium. Where you are sitting now was the infirmary after The Twister of 1894, just as it was following the blizzard of 1888, the flood of 1892, and the train derailment of 1893."

Next he introduced the honorees seated on the stage and presented each with a plaque. The last of these he invited to come forward together: Dr. Benjamin DeWitt Foster, Mrs. Francis Joseph Morrissey, and Miss Irina Lee Taylor.

Louise felt her face flush. With the eyes of several hundred people on her, she took self-conscious steps, as though walking were a new endeavor. Standing between Doc and Irina, she hoped the audience would not notice her trembling, or if they did they would attribute it to stage fright, which would be partially true. She strained to fix her attention on J.D.'s words.

"The Twister would have claimed more souls had it not been for Dr. Foster's lifesaving efforts and the assistance of these two civic-minded women," J.D. said. "No sooner had the furious storm left town than the good doctor appeared on these premises and set up his infirmary. Moreover in the weeks following the storm he provided treatment without a fee to the injured. Dr. Foster, for the generous gift of your expertise and medical supplies, the citizens of Riverbend thank you."

J.D. presented plaques and shook hands with the honorees, who took a moment to acknowledge the applause. Then they turned to file back to their seats. Conscious of Doc's looming presence behind her, Louise was still tense, her head still aching, but at least she had been spared from speaking.

J.D. then read an account of the storm that he had written for the newspaper. He allowed that his writing represented only a fraction of the story, that many a citizen of Riverbend had a story worthy of being told. He invited people to share their experiences. Louise only half-listened, her mind taken over by her own story.

Chapter 8

May 1894

When swaying trees blocked Louise's view of the black cloud slab skidding closer, she dragged a chair over to where the balcony railing abutted the wall. She had been seduced onto the balcony—the roof of the porte cochère—by the ghostly green sky that brought welcome but uneasy relief from stifling afternoon heat. With one hand hoisting her skirt and the other pressed against the wall for balance, she stepped onto the chair and from there onto the railing where she teetered for a moment, then steadied herself.

She stood transfixed by the advancing black cloud that thrust and retracted little twister fingers, teasing the way a bully jabs his victim's chest before striking the blows that will flatten him. Louise had grown up in Nebraska where talk of twisters and tornadoes and funnel clouds heralded spring, but in her thirty-one years she had never witnessed one of the magnificent storms. And now she had a front-row balcony vantage point. "Come on!"

No sooner had the words escaped than she clapped a hand over her mouth to censor herself. *Perish the thought.*

A downward glance. Her body stiffened. A misstep and she would end up splattered on the brick drive two stories below. Gone was the exhilaration of climbing up. Coming down left her quaking.

Then came rain. She lifted her face and threw her arms wide. She remembered the old-timers who seemed wise in the vagaries of weather always said tornadoes did not strike when it was raining.

Soon the sting of wind-whipped rain on her face forced her inside where she peered through the French doors, unable to see anything beyond a shimmering curtain of rain. From a distance came a rumbling like a train derailing, except the Burlington tracks lay to the north, and this sound came from the southwest.

"Louise! Louise!" Frank's alarmed voice came from the kitchen. He raced toward her, his eyes blazing. "Are you addled, woman? We got everyone to the basement, and here you are!"

She knew her husband scolded out of fear, not anger. "It's raining," she protested. "Tornadoes don't hit when it's raining." But he acted with such conviction that what she thought she knew about tornadoes vanished, and she chided herself for a ridiculous display of bravado which she hoped no one had witnessed.

When he grabbed her hand, she tensed with the fear communicated through his grip. He led her on a frantic dash through the kitchen to the back stairway.

Hissing from the stove caused Louise to turn around and see boiling water cascading from a pot. "Potatoes!" She darted to the stove and turned off the fire under the pot Henryetta had abandoned.

She followed her husband down the stairs in darkness relieved only by the greenish-gray light from the window at the first floor landing. Animated voices drifted from the basement storm shelter.

Suddenly the building shuddered and windowpanes rattled against a thunderous roar. Terror, Louise discovered, is textured with little hollows of pure calm. Out of one of those hollows came a fit of insight and clarity. The phrase her mind had labored many times to knit together, never to her satisfaction, now presented itself wholly constructed. "Devoted Wife and Civic Leader." The perfect epitaph.

Frank turned and pressed her into a crouch against the stairs. His chest heaving against her back, the scent of his sweat and bay rum aftershave, his breath on her neck, calmed her. Sheltered in this strange bubble, a place where the storm seemed of no consequence, she succumbed to the intimacy of the moment, a respite from the state of loneliness that had come to define her marriage.

The roar swelled, and Frank's arms around her tightened. Louise curled her body against the stairs and braced for the storm, imagining a shower of glass. But the roar faded and passed.

"Straight line winds." Frank released her and continued down the stairs.

How he knew the tornado had missed them Louise didn't know. She could hear him assuring Inn guests that the storm had passed. So had the illusion of intimacy.

Louise comforted guests, some of whom were most agitated, and invited them to the dining room for coffee and kolaches. Meanwhile, Frank, Yonder, and Buster, the Inn's building superintendent, boarded up the half dozen windows that had been broken.

It was assumed that the high school gymnasium would serve as an infirmary, so Yonder hitched a team and carriage and Louise and Frank joined him. Their drive to the high school was interrupted several times by the need to stop and remove tree limbs and other debris that littered the streets. By the time they arrived at the high school, the afternoon sun cast a benign light from a washed-out blue sky. Louise marveled at the capriciousness of Nature, behaving like a two-year-old who kicks his sister one minute and blows kisses the next.

Frank halted the wagon, and Louise stepped down and followed a path strewn with fallen branches, puddles, and tangles of nightcrawlers flushed from the earth. Wailing and moaning drifted from the gymnasium's open windows. Nature's tantrum had been anything but innocent.

From behind Louise came a man's voice. "Beg your pardon, ma'am."

She moved aside to let a rain-drenched trio—two men supporting the underarms of a stumbling and bleeding woman—precede her up the steps.

Inside, the floor was littered with the badly injured covered with mud and debris. Their cries reverberated off the concrete block walls. A few souls milled about, navigating the maze of victims.

The gymnasium smell of ancient sweat mingled with other human odors to foul the hot, still air. Louise took the arm of a staggering, glassy-eyed woman and guided her to an area where people were scattered like driftwood. "Sit here, and someone will attend to you soon." But would she get noticed, with so many seriously injured people needing care?

"Out of the way, lady," a man called from behind.

Louise stepped aside and watched as he and another man rushed by carrying folded-up cots. She looked about for a canteen area where most likely Mrs. Graves would have an assignment for her. She spotted the woman on the far side of a badminton net, appearing to be barking orders to a crew setting up tables and chairs and unpacking food.

The path to Mrs. Graves led past a kneeling woman sponging mud and blood from a man's head, and toward a table where a woman lay screaming while above her a man's hand moved in and out of the shadow of a railroad lantern hanging from a nearby stand. Louise recognized the tall and commanding presence of Doc Foster.

As Louise came closer, she cupped a hand over her nose and mouth to block the stench of burning flesh. The woman bucked against the hands of a burly man and straps that secured her to the table while Dr. Foster held a cauterizing iron against her partial leg. His sleeves rolled up, his brow furrowed, the doctor appeared far different from the smartly dressed man who occasionally visited the library.

Nearby some rescuers gestured wildly and argued over which streets had already been searched.

Like an officer in charge of the infirmary, Doc called out commands, all the while working on the woman's leg. "You with the beard, you be the dispatcher."

The man nodded.

"You, make a map for these men," said Doc.

Louise passed by him without looking.

"Mrs. Morrissey, I mean you!" He waved the cauterizing iron in her direction. "Do you know Cindertown?"

"Yes." She looked sideways at him so as to avoid seeing his patient's bloody leg.

His voice moderated. "Make a map so these men can keep

track of the areas that have been searched."

Mrs. Graves could wait. Louise dashed from the gymnasium to a classroom to find poster paper and something to write with. No luck in the first classroom. From a drawer in the second classroom she grabbed three pieces of colored chalk and hastened back to the gymnasium without wasting time looking for paper.

Louise scrawled a map with green chalk directly on the wall and planned to color in the blocks in red as they were searched. Above the background noise of victims' moans and volunteers' verbal exchanges, a shrill voice called over and over, "Where's my dog?"

"No point writing street names," the dispatcher said.

"Of course." With that she drew crosses where the two churches were located, and indicated Cindertown's half dozen taverns, such as the Caboose and the Wild Boar, which were easy to represent as they had been named with signs in mind so a thirsty man did not have to know his letters to find his friends.

"Did the tornado hit anywhere but Cindertown?" Louise asked as she wrote.

The dispatcher, who looked like a railroad man himself, shook his head. "Ain't that always the way? Poor people can't win for losing."

Louise hoped Henryetta's house had been spared. Most likely her husband and grown daughter had been safe at work when the storm hit. "Was the Dempseys' house hit?"

"Don't know."

She looked up as she completed the map, and Doc seemed to sense her readiness. "Get a bucket of water, soap, and sponge!"

She handed off the chalk to the dispatcher, then located the custodian's closet and retrieved a bucket, soap, water, and sponges which she set on the floor within Doc's reach. She turned to leave, intending to go help out in the canteen.

"Mrs. Morrissey, I need you here." Doc pointed to a sobbing child lying on her stomach. "Clean her up."

She wanted to protest that surely there were others more qualified. But Doc had turned away, and the little girl, about four or five years old, needed help. Louise rolled up her sleeves and knelt beside the small body from which shards of glass protruded like pins in a pincushion. She reached for a piece of glass, reluctant to grip it for fear of causing the child even greater pain as glass was moving this way and that with the undulating sobs. Louise gritted her teeth, and when she yanked out the shard the girl shrieked. Louise patted her shoulder. "Shh, shh. We have to do this. We're going to play a little game. I will count to three, then you hold your breath and get still as a mouse, and I'll pull out the glass. If you're very still, it won't hurt so bad."

The girl sniffled, turned her head to look at Louise, and nodded.

"Now, one, two, three." The child lay still, and Louise yanked out a piece of glass. "You can breathe now." To Louise's surprise and relief, this time the child let out a gasp, not a shriek. They played the "game" until the last piece was removed.

Louise sat on the floor and scooped the child into her lap, never mind the blood stains. She rocked her from side to side. "There, there, now. Hush, little baby, don't you cry," she sang softly. She wanted to hold the girl and comfort her until parents came looking for her, wanted to be assured that the parents survived, but Doc called out an order to help another victim. Reluctantly she placed the child back on the floor.

From then on Louise moved from one victim to another. Just when she thought the worst must be over, rescuers brought in workers who had been cleaning and gutting chickens when the tornado cut a swath through the poultry processing plant. The influx of these badly injured workers strained the ability of volunteers to keep up.

"More water," she shouted, but no one responded. Plunging the sponge into bloody water where chicken flesh and feathers floated set her stomach churning. *I've got to get out of here.* But she could not leave the wretched man lying at her knees. With one hand he lifted his other arm. A bloody rag had come undone, revealing two dangling fingers, nearly severed. Louise looked for help, knowing the futility of it, that surrounding her were more people needing care and others like herself working at capacity. She ripped the man's work shirt to make a fresh rag and, fighting back vomit that rose in her throat, wrapped his mangled hand tightly.

Louise noticed Frank and Yonder carrying a woman into the gymnasium on a screen door turned makeshift stretcher. Yonder happened to look in her direction, and they exchanged weary glances.

Another movement caught her eye, and Louise saw Irina stand and heard her tell a screaming patient she would get some morphine. She dashed over to Doc who handed her several glass ampoules of morphine, showed her how to inject it, and gave her a look which might have been appreciative, but then again could have been an admiring look a married man gives a woman only furtively. Following Irina's lead, Louise asked Doc for morphine for her patient, watched carefully as he demonstrated how to inject it, and scolded herself for not thinking of it sooner.

Later when the flow of wounded into the gymnasium subsided, Doc summoned Louise to relieve his assistant.

"Scrub your hands over there." He nodded toward a basin.

After washing up she stood across from Doc and held a woman's hand while he sutured a gash on her chin. Doc's brown eyes, so bright earlier, looked dull. Blood splatters dotted his expensive shirt and vest. He smelled of pipe smoke, a sweet fragrance, something like maple syrup.

She knew him only casually. She had never gone to a doctor, and the Fosters and Morrisseys traveled in different social circles. He always said hello when they passed in the hallway as he went to his surgery and she to the Riverbend Ladies Lending Library. An occasional library patron, he dressed in the finest tailored suits that complemented a cosmopolitan air seldom seen in small-town Nebraska. What distinguished him most was his deep, resonant voice. He was always courteous but not particularly communicative. If Louise had to sum him up in one word, she would say he had "presence."

"Scissors, Mrs. Morrissey," he said without looking at her.

His voice conveyed fatigue. She realized exhaustion had taken a toll on her as well. As she handed him the scissors, they slipped from her hand. She lunged to catch them and set a lantern swinging.

Doc jerked the suture. "Damnation!"

His patient screamed.

Louise hurried to stabilize the lantern. She steeled herself against a thorough bawling out, but Doc said nothing more. She waited, scissors in her trembling hand, until he reached for them. He carried on without remarking, and she exhaled her held breath.

The incident gave her a second wind. She began to pay close attention, not just to Doc's instructions but also to his every move. Eventually she felt surprisingly confident acting as another set of hands for Dr. Foster.

Something strange happened as they worked through the night. They spoke sparingly. But they eased into a rhythm so that meanings passed between them without words. She sensed whether to clean an instrument or hold onto it until he needed it again. Emboldened, she ignored her own censoring thoughts and took to mopping perspiration from his brow as he worked. She wondered if he thought her brazen.

They finished with the first light of dawn seeping through the windows. His parting words would nourish her for days: "You performed your duties as skillfully as a trained nurse."

*   *   *

THE NIGHT FOLLOWING THE STORM, Louise, in spite of being overcome with fatigue, slept fitfully. When the grandfather clock struck four, she remembered that at this hour the night before she had been standing across from Doc. Thoughts unfit for a respectable married woman surfaced again, thoughts she had tried to push down all day. But Doc would not go away.

Her reality was here in this bed, lying back to back with Frank. How long since they'd been intimate? Since they'd given up hope of having a child? Was she to blame for his impotence?

Finally daylight jarred her out of reverie and into action.

Victims of the storm would be needing relief. She got up and began planning. She enlisted Henryetta, whose house had been spared, to help pack up boxes of food, clothing, and other supplies which they later delivered to storm victims.

That night she slept undisturbed until morning. Undisturbed except for a dream in which she stood on a seaside cliff watching Doc and Irina hand in hand, laughing and twirling, carefree as tumbleweeds. With each rotation, the woman with the blue-violet eyes danced closer to the edge. Doc let go of her hand, sending her still-twirling body slowly to the sea. Louise felt a surge of delight that intensified when Doc turned and gave her the admiring look he'd given Irina in the infirmary.

Louise awakened. Little ripples of desire collided with Frank's cheery "Time to get up" and swelled to giant waves of guilt.

Once the immediate needs of The Twister victims passed and relief efforts slowed down, Louise willed herself to resume her normal life. But in spite of good intentions, she faltered, unable to inhabit the routine that once had been second nature. Responding to the emergency in the infirmary had challenged her to perform beyond her own expectations. She had risen to the occasion and never felt more alive. By contrast her everyday life left her numb, there being nothing to excite her senses or test her mettle.

* * *

TWO WEEKS LATER, A THURSDAY, Louise was working her regular library shift when the door opened. It was nearly closing time. From her position on the ladder where she stood dusting shelves, she saw it was Doc who had entered. Being alone with him set her skin tingling and cheeks burning. She ran her dustcloth over the same shelf repeatedly, lingering there in order to avoid him as he browsed in the fiction stacks.

She finished dusting and was straightening the newspaper shelf when he approached. "I seem unable to locate Jules Verne's *Journey to the Center of the Earth.*"

"Perhaps it's over here." A glance at the shelving cart told her it wasn't there, so she led him to the shelves. His scent took her for an instant to the night in the infirmary, the moments they had worked together in harmony without words.

"Have you read it?" he asked.

"I have."

"I am revisiting the story. I enjoy being transported to its fantastical world."

She stopped at the "J's," ran her hand along the books, and scanned the titles.

He said, "Verne."

"Of course." *He'll think I'm a fool.* Turning to the shelves behind her, there sat the book right where it belonged.

"I somehow overlooked it." He reached past her and took down the book. He smiled.

His intense brown eyes aroused feelings unsuitable for a sensible, married woman. She lowered her gaze.

"I'm as taken with your flightiness here as with your competence in the infirmary. What a charming combination of virtues in a woman."

She wanted to protest that being momentarily distracted hardly constituted flightiness, and who would ever think flightiness a virtue? But his look struck her speechless. It was the look he had given her in the dream.

* * *

SO IT HAD BEGUN WITH The Twister. No divine power controlled people's lives and events like a cosmic puppeteer, so why had events conspired to throw her and Doc together? For no apparent reason the volunteer who ordered books and supplies for the library quit. Louise offered to take on the additional job. And decided to work on Wednesday afternoons, a time the library and all the second floor offices were closed.

On one such Wednesday afternoon, Louise was unlocking the library door when Doc's voice startled her.

"Is the library open today?"

She turned the doorknob, but she had inadvertently relocked the door or hadn't locked it in the first place, she couldn't recall which.

"Here," he said.

He sidled close, his arm brushing hers. Was that deliberate? She stepped aside, and he unlocked the door.

"It's officially closed." Her breath caught in her throat. "But I shall be working every Wednesday afternoon."

"Mind if I return some books later?"

"Yes, I mean, no, I don't mind." She hoped he didn't notice the flush creeping up to her cheeks.

"Until later then." He spoke softly, holding her gaze a bit too long.

Shaken by that look without fully understanding why, Louise closed the door behind him and retreated to the library's kitchen where she busied herself rearranging drawers and shelves. Not until she was satisfied that spoons and forks were properly nested and cups turned so their handles all pointed in the same direction did she allow herself to look in the small mirror. She pushed at tendrils that framed her face and undermined her efforts to present herself as a serious-minded woman.

Louise felt anew the shame of being female. It was her duty, as it was that of all respectable women, to cultivate a pleasing appearance while masking the temptress that was her true nature as a descendant of Eve. She jabbed at the wayward tendrils, but they sprang back, visible reminders of the lesson drilled into her as a girl: woman is the Biblical embodiment of evil that drives men to commit acts for which they cannot be blamed. "Daughter of the devil," Pa had called her.

Men's lascivious looks and advances frightened her. But what she feared more at this moment was her own sinful longing.

Her passion had once been fulfilled in the marriage bed with Frank Morrissey. Their early years together were glorious, the years before he lost interest and she lost the ability to arouse him. Since then she had held her passion in check. But that was before Doc. Now desire consumed her, crowding out reason. The woman in the mirror looked irretrievably bent on seduction.

She turned away. Idle hands are the devil's workshop. Work would save her from herself. After making a quick mental inventory of the afternoon's tasks, she set about boxing up old magazines, the first item on her list. Next she tackled the shelved books, putting them in their proper order and aligning them just so with the edges of their respective shelves.

When she reached the end of the "Biography" shelves,

she noticed the key resting in the door's lock. She could lock up and leave now and go on with the admirable life she had worked so hard to create. Devoted Wife and Civic Leader. But perhaps she was mistaken, and Doc had merely intended to return books.

She returned to her task, arranging her least favorite shelves, those that housed the "Travel" books. Not that she didn't like the books. It was just that some were too tall and had to be placed out of order on the bottom shelf. She picked up Herman Melville's *Typee: A Peep at Polynesian Life*, to return it to its place. Holding the dog-eared volume brought a lump to her throat. It was a favorite of Frank's. Who had she become to lust after someone other than her husband? To think of violating her own convictions as a morally upright woman? Now she understood. It was destiny she had seen in Doc's parting gaze.

"Satan, get thee behind me," she whispered. She dropped the book on a shelf. Grabbing her handbag and the key, she hastened out the door and down the stairs to the boardwalk. She stopped to catch her breath. The key was in her hand, the door unlocked.

She dashed back upstairs. Her hand shaking, it seemed the key would never find the keyhole, but finally it did and she locked the door. Out on the boardwalk once more, she looked back, her chest heaving. Virtue had triumphed.

* * *

VIRTUE PROVED NO MATCH FOR longing. On the following Wednesday when Louise finished dressing for her afternoon at the library, she removed the stopper from her Muguet perfume and lifted it to dab fragrance behind her ear but caught herself with her hand mid-air and replaced the stopper. To wear her signature perfume would be a mistake, she realized after recalling a story about a philandering man who was caught bearing the scent of his best friend's wife. Looking hard at her image in the dressing table mirror, she recognized the magnitude of this decision, that it set her on an irrevocable course. Turning away from the mirror, she took off her corset and replaced it with silk drawers.

Nearing the library, with her body free of the binding garment, the thought of herself as a "loose" woman almost caused her to turn back. Almost.

Doc did not appear. Nor did he appear the following Wednesday.

He showed up a week later and acted the way she remembered him before they worked together in the infirmary, courteous, but aloof. He greeted her and went to the shelves. While he browsed she dabbed glue on ragged bookbindings and resisted the urge to look in his direction. *Don't be a silly goose. He's just another library patron.*

Out of nowhere Doc suddenly appeared at her elbow. She flinched and nearly toppled the glue pot.

"Didn't mean to frighten you." He handed her six books, and she pulled the cards for him to write his name. She picked up the date stamp and opened the inkpad. She took special care, gently rocking the stamp back and forth to ink it evenly. Then she firmly pressed the stamp on the return slip glued inside the first book. The date was imprinted smartly inside the little rectangle allotted for it, not smudged or sitting at a rakish angle like some of the preceding dates stamped by careless librarians. She sensed his watchful eyes as she methodically stamped each book.

"You were one of the library's founders, were you not?" he asked.

That voice. If he merely recited the alphabet he could mesmerize her. "Yes, along with Dovie Henkleman and Alice Dietz."

He handed her the cards. "I admire your efforts to uplift the citizens of our little town."

His voice touched her like a caress. *Be sensible.* She set the cards on the desk. "Thank you. It's a labor of love. As a young girl I had access to a fine private library. Most people aren't so fortunate, and a public library provides opportunities for them to better themselves."

"You are undoubtedly a lover of books."

"Yes. Like you." She faced him across the desk as she had across that makeshift operating table in the high school gymnasium. She looked down, then up in time to catch his eyes sweeping over her body. With her fingertips touching the desk, she took tentative steps to walk around it, drawn into the space which their eyes electrified. She moved closer to him.

But he held up his hand. She stopped, and her heart stopped as well. *I've misread his intentions. What a fool!*

He smiled. "Better lock the door." He walked over, turned the key, and returned to take her hands in his. She waited for him to come closer. When he did not, she leaned toward him, tilting her head, inviting his lips. As their lips met, he grasped her neck and the small of her back. He smelled of pipe tobacco. As his tender kisses meandered over her face and neck, she dismissed concern that her make-up would stain his white shirt collar. Her breathing quickened, and she yielded to his hand pulling her body into his.

But just as the awakening of pent-up desire urged her on, Doc released his hold and turned her away from him. Surprised by his move, she wondered what she might have done to cool his ardor. Her own mood broken, she heard Pa growling the words "daughter of the devil." She stepped back, but Doc, seemingly amused, moved with her, then picked her up, carried her to the sofa, and placed her in a reclining position. For the moment she inhabited an other-worldly body, one soaring beyond the narrow confines of a proper, small-town existence. Not even the threat of eternal damnation could stop her.

*　*　*

ALL-CONSUMING PASSION MADE THE TIME from one Wednesday to the next almost unbearable. Physically and emotionally her anticipation on Wednesday mornings nearly drove her mad. Days before, she would decide what to wear, but come the appointed day she would change her mind several times, her mood bouncing from exhilaration to dread. What if he didn't come? What if they got caught? What if she should conceive?

As she left the Inn one Wednesday, Louise paused to say good-bye to Frank, who stood on a ladder scraping bird droppings from his treasured paddlewheeler. "While you're at it, she could use a coat of paint," Louise said.

"She's a wreck," Frank said. "Wouldn't do for her to get too prettified. But you look mighty pretty, too pretty to go hiding yourself in a dusty old library."

Her hand went to her earlobe, to the pearl earbobs that had belonged to Frank's mother. *What have I become?* She burst into tears.

He put one hand on her shoulder and lifted her chin with the other so that she had to look at him. "What's wrong, my pet? One minute you're giddy as a schoolgirl in puppy love, and the next you look like you've lost your best friend."

"It's nothing." It had been years since he'd called her "my pet." She leaned away from him and reached in her pocket for a handkerchief, an excuse to avoid the possibility of an embrace.

"A female malaise?"

She nodded as she turned to go.

After an hour or so at the library Louise paced from window to door, checked the time, straightened shelves, emptied ashtrays, paced again. She busied herself with one task and another and yet another without completing any. Alone with the ticking Regulator clock, she brooded. *Doc doesn't want to see me anymore. He has someone else—Irina? How could I be so naive to think I was his only plaything? He's sick. He's dead. His wife found out.* Doc did not come.

On the next Wednesday she was deliberately subdued. Doc might arrive with a perfectly forgivable apology. Still, she wanted him to have suffered as much anguish over their missed meeting as she had.

Seated at her desk in the library she wrote up orders for new books and avoided looking at the clock. But in spite of her effort to concentrate, she couldn't resist thoughts of Doc. Truth to tell, much about his behavior was unsettling. He rarely touched her except in the act of lovemaking. He was secretive. His self-confidence bordered on arrogance.

When at last he arrived, he greeted her as though nothing were different. Looking at him, she saw not the lover she had found fault with in his absence, but the competent and dedicated doctor she had so admired in the infirmary. Only after they had made love did she have the courage to ask him where he had been the previous week. Without apologizing, he said he'd had business to attend to in Chicago. His tone suggested that any woman should understand that a man's business was paramount, and she did.

Placing a finger on her neck, a touch that sent a shiver through her, he said, "Till next time."

Once again her self-imposed yoke of respectability fell away, releasing the passionate woman it had restrained for too many years.

Week by week Louise slid further down the slope until what had been unthinkable seemed inevitable. She would leave Frank to become the wife of Dr. Benjamin Dewitt Foster.

Chapter 9

June 1904

Frank finished helping Buster, the Inn's building superintendent, replace weathered shingles and then called it a day. Although tired, he bounded up the back stairs, his spirits lifted by a fresh scheme. As he entered the kitchen by the back door, he heard Marie's voice from the breakfast room. Stopping in the doorway he watched and listened. She was speaking aloud, apparently composing a poem. Perhaps stuck for a word, she paused, reached till she touched the sugar bowl, and popped a sugar cube in her mouth.

Then she began writing. A piece of stiff paper was clamped in her metal Braille slate, which had rows of rectangular "cells" cut out, one for each letter. Locating the edges of a cell with her Braille stylus, she pushed it against the paper to raise carefully aligned dots—from one to six—to make a letter. Then her stylus moved to the next cell. The first time Frank saw her working in this way, he thought she was doing everything wrong because she was working from right to left. Then he realized that Braille letters had to be made from the back of the paper, the letters reversed so they could be read from the front. Struck by her ability and tenacity, he'd had to fight back tears.

He walked up behind her and kissed her on the head. "Where's your mother?"

Marie continued writing. "Sleeping."

"Well, I have something to tell her that will be worth waking up for."

He found Louise lying on top of the bedspread, still clad in her clothes, her shoes tucked neatly under the bed. She lay perfectly straight and rigid on her back, as though refusing gravity's invitation to relax. Only a fool would try to fathom her mood.

He told himself it would be wise to leave her alone, but his idea spilled forth before he could contain it. "I have a grand idea for Marie's birthday party. What say we hire a pony cart to take her and her little chums for a ride? Yonder met a fellow who works at Dietz's stable. The guy dresses up like Buffalo Bill and entertains the youngsters with Wild West stories."

Louise sat up, and her expression let him know she was not keen on the idea.

"First of all," she said, "Marie has *acquaintances* who play amongst themselves and exclude her. She *has* no 'little chums.' Second, why must you go overboard for her birthday?"

Frank shook his head. "I don't understand you."

"Do you honestly think your efforts will make those children be her friends?"

"I just want to make her happy. You don't seem to care about her birthday. Look at you, moping in bed."

"Nine years ago I gave birth to a beautiful, healthy baby girl, and my heart overflowed with the hope every mother has for a daughter. Then the sight vanished from her eyes, and I had to abandon hope. Yes, I become melancholy as her birthday nears. I always wonder if I could have done something to save her sight."

Frank had heard enough. "You sure know how to rain on

a fellow's parade."

Standing at the water closet basin, he scrubbed his hands, then washed his face with a cool washrag. It reminded him of when Marie was a baby, how he swabbed Louise's feverish body and cleansed Marie's eyes with boric acid.

He vaguely recalled the night Marie must have been conceived or, rather, he recalled the fragmented thoughts that surfaced in his throbbing head the next morning. Struggling to remove his boots. Stumbling into bed. Then oblivion until well after dawn. He remembered his disbelief and joy when Louise told him she was in the family way.

He stared at the washrag in his hand. He had done just what Doc told him, but maybe Marie's eyes did not get washed out often enough. What if he had taken her to an eye doctor in Omaha right then and there; could he have saved his precious daughter's sight? He dried his face and looked in the mirror. There he saw a father who had failed his daughter.

*   *   *

FRANK FINISHED TACKING YELLOW CREPE paper streamers at the corners of the dining room's crown molding and moved the stepladder so he could attach them to the chandelier above the dining room table. Marie, clutching the strings of a half-dozen balloons, followed.

"I'll take those balloons now, Junior." He was tying balloons to the streamers when Henryetta, carrying a birthday cake, came through the door from the kitchen, and what had been the sound of muffled laughter rose.

"What's going on in there?" Frank said.

"Mrs. Morrissey was watching Yonder crank the ice cream

maker and let her fudge sauce boil over." Henryetta set the cake on the table and smoothed the tablecloth where it wanted to wrinkle. "They're laughing because the same thing happened on Marie's birthday last year."

Frank found it heartening to hear Louise finally joining in the spirit of Marie's birthday celebration.

After Marie handed him the last two balloons, she started making a clapping motion.

Frank came down from the ladder. "I'll show you once more. Here's how you make a galloping sound."

Holding her wrists, he clapped her hands together and then one after the other against her thigh.

"Let me." She bit her lower lip and practiced clumsily.

"Faster," Frank said.

She picked up the tempo and found the rhythm.

"You've got it."

Louise peeked in from the kitchen. "Time to get dressed."

Marie stood steadfast, and her hands galloped on.

"Hit the trail, Junior," Frank drawled.

Marie left and a few minutes later returned wearing her new yellow dress with flowers embroidered at the neckline, cuffs, and hem. Carrying Dolly on her back in the cradleboard Yonder had made for her birthday, she shadowed Henryetta, who shooed flies away from the cake and smacked them with a swatter.

"Tell me," Marie said.

"Cake's right pretty. Wish you could see it."

"What's on it?"

"Nine candles in fancy holders—ceramic carousel horses." Henryetta swatted another fly.

"Where are the flowers I pressed?"

"All around the cake."

"Are we using the good dishes?"

"Only the best for you, missy. Haviland china and sterling silver. And table linens too nice for a passel of kids. It'll take the wash girls a pound of elbow grease."

"What's elbow grease?"

"Mercy sakes, I never knew a child had so many questions." Henryetta handed Marie some red party poppers. "Put these above the plates."

"What are they?" Marie asked.

"Party poppers. You hold it real tight at both ends, give it a tug, and it sounds like a firecracker."

The doorbell rang, and Frank opened the door for Curly Ambrose, who held a tripod and large case. Frank took the tripod and led Curly, limping, to the kitchen, then picked up a ruler and returned to the dining room. He waved the ruler like a scepter over the table. "Table's fit for a princess. Now let's see how much the princess has grown."

He placed Marie's hand in the crook of his elbow and escorted her through the kitchen to the back door. Henryetta followed them to the kitchen where Louise and Yonder had stopped what they were doing to observe the annual ceremony while Curly positioned the tripod and mounted his camera to it.

Marie set down the cradleboard and patted Dolly's head. Then standing with her back against the doorframe, she stretched her body to reach the ruler Frank held above her as Louise arranged her long braids over her shoulders. Curly took pictures of Frank holding the ruler on top of Marie's head and making a pencil mark on the doorframe where the ruler indicated.

"Now, Junior, step aside so I can make a notch." He took his pocketknife and cut into the doorframe at the pencil mark. Then he measured the distance between the fresh notch and last year's. "Look. You've grown a full three-quarters of an inch," he said.

"That's good, isn't it?" she asked.

Curly got another picture of Marie feeling the two notches.

"Three-quarters of an inch marks the difference between a little squirt and a budding neophyte," Frank said.

Louise moved to the doorway, hugged Marie, and touched the latest notch. Her baby girl growing up. What was important now was to see to it that her daughter had a wonderful time at her party.

Marie picked up the cradleboard and patted Dolly. "We're having a party." She slipped the carrier on her back.

The party guests arrived—Dovie's twin boys, Paul and John; Madge's step-granddaughter, Ella; and Alice's daughter, Lana. Louise sent the children to play on the balcony.

But no sooner had she returned to the kitchen than Marie came in crying. "John threw Dolly off the balcony."

Louise hastened to the balcony where the children were leaning over the railing and laughing. Dolly flew up from below in a high arc over the railing, and Paul leaped to catch her. Louise looked over the railing and saw John shinnying up a support column. Louise yanked Dolly from Paul's hand. "All of you take your places at the table and sit like young ladies and gentlemen."

Once assured that Dolly was safe, Marie allowed her mother

to place the doll and cradleboard high on a shelf.

Marie sat at the table surrounded by lively chatter but invisible to her guests. Invisible except for the novelty of watching a blind girl eat. When Marie asked for the pitcher of root beer, the children stared as she placed one finger inside her glass and poured with her other hand until the drink reached her finger.

Louise was at a loss as to how to coax children to include Marie in their activities. One time she had Marie play songs they all could sing, but the children broke into laughter when John sang loud and off-key. At Ella's recent birthday party, Marie won a game of Pin the Tail on the Donkey only to have the others accuse her of cheating because she didn't wear a blindfold.

Frank entered as the children finished their cake. "Time for a pony cart ride."

John jumped off his chair.

"Whoa," Frank said. "Pop your poppers first."

"I didn't get one," Lana said.

Henryetta looked at the table and frowned. "I'm sure Marie set out five." She got another one from the buffet drawer for Lana.

Poppers had been Frank's idea, in spite of Louise insisting that loud noises upset Marie.

"Poppers ready," Frank said, "on the count of three. One, two, three!"

The poppers sounded, and the children squealed. Even Marie clapped her hands, and Frank gave Louise an "I told you so" look.

"Let's go." Picking up Curly's tripod, Frank led everyone

outside where Yonder waited with the pony cart and its driver, an old, grizzled imitation of Buffalo Bill.

Louise carried out a bunch of carrots, which the children fed to the friendlier of the two ponies while Frank helped Curly set up the camera.

As the children climbed into the cart, scrambling over one another for the best seats, Yonder set Marie on the bench next to the driver who placed the reins in her hands. Louise remained by the ponies, feeding them the last of the carrots.

Curly was taking his time composing the first shot, alternately ducking under the hood to peer through the viewfinder, then jumping up to move the tripod or to direct youngsters to change places.

Seated in the cart, the driver turned to face the children, the fringe of his buckskin waving in the breeze. His eyes had the faraway look of another place and time. "Drove the Concord stagecoach for Wells Fargo," he drawled. "Finest coach ever built—sturdy enough to handle the meanest, rutted trails you ever seen and gentle enough to rock you to sleep on them very same trails."

He went on talking even while the children fidgeted and ignored him "Don't know what we feared most—robbers or Indians."

The children giggled at John, who was mimicking the driver. Louise was glad to see Frank stride to the cart where he gripped John by the ear until he sat perfectly still, a move that sobered the other children, who listened respectfully as the driver told his story about outsmarting the robber Rattlesnake Calhoun.

Soon after Frank walked away, Paul pointed to one pony's

elevated tail and held his nose. When the children grabbed their noses and laughed, Louise realized the breeze was wafting the odor over the cart. She stepped away from the animals and the aroma and watched Marie laughing along with the others.

She looked past Marie just in time to see John take something from his pocket. *Snap* went the party popper, and the ponies bolted. Shrieking children grabbed the sides of the cart and each other. Marie dropped the reins and held onto her seat. When the driver jerked the reins, bringing the cart to an abrupt halt, Marie lost her grip, and her flailing hands sought another hold without success. She tumbled to the ground.

Yonder rushed to where she lay motionless on her back and scooped her into his arms. Louise ran to them and huddled over her daughter. "She's not breathing." Louise screamed at Yonder. "Do something!"

Frank nearly knocked over Curly's tripod in his haste to join them.

The driver asked Yonder, "Is she okay, Dad?"

"*I'm* her father." Frank snatched Marie from Yonder and jostled her until she gave a little gasp, then gasped and cried at the same time.

"Thank God, she's just winded," Frank said. "You're all right, Junior."

"Are you hurt?" Louise tried to wipe away her daughter's tears, but Frank's jiggling made it difficult.

Choking on little sobs, Marie shook her head.

"You'll be fine," Frank said. "I'll sit next to you in the cart and keep you safe."

"No, no!" She pounded his chest. "Don't make me go. Take me inside."

Curly bobbed up from under the hood and threw up his hands.

"Your mother will hear about this, John Henkleman," Louise said. Then she instructed the pony cart driver to take the party guests for their ride without Marie. If the youngsters' solemn looks were any indication, they felt repentant. But no sooner had the cart left the driveway than she heard boisterous Indian war whoops. She vowed that next year's celebration would be different.

CHAPTER 10

Louise wrapped up the book discussion at the next Tuesday Bibliophiles' meeting and asked Madge to present the word of the day.

"*Portend.* Portend is a verb meaning 'to serve as an omen or warning, to presage.' It comes from the Latin *portendere.* Synonyms include 'bode,' 'foretell,' and 'presage.' I quote from our reading of Shakespeare's *King Lear*: 'These late eclipses in the sun and moon portend no good to us.'"

"I do declare, I hope none of us has occasion to use that word." Alice's asthma was under control so she talked without wheezing.

As the others moved to seats around the reading table, Dovie looked up from pouring glasses of lemonade. "I already know how I'll use it. I'll say to my boys, 'Poor table manners portend no dessert.'"

Madge raised her eyebrows. The others laughed. Looking proud of her witticism, Dovie passed around a plate of frosted sugar cookies.

A welcome rain patted the windows. The library, uncomfortably hot in recent weeks, was now pleasant and cozy, its ceiling fans stirring and lamps glowing. Five umbrellas left open to dry huddled in one corner.

Madge wiped her glass. "I suppose everyone saw Mr. Bok's

editorial in *The Ladies' Home Journal.*"

Everyone except Gertrude nodded.

Dovie licked her fingers. "He thinks mothers should explain the 'mystery of life' to their daughters so they won't get caught unawares on their wedding night."

Gertrude lifted her formidable eyebrows. "It's that kind of indelicate subject that's the reason I cancelled my subscription."

"He evidently writes for urban readers," Madge said. "Girls reared around cows and horses are not likely to get caught unawares."

Dovie fingered a tendril of hair and absently twirled it. "I'm glad I have sons. How about you, Alice? You going to have a little talk with your daughter?"

"Madge is right," Alice said. "I grew up on a farm. Nobody has to tell farm girls how babies are made."

As Louise listened to the conversation, she thought of Marie. At some point, she would have to explain her "monthlies." But she regretted she would probably never have occasion for "the talk," as a blind girl stood little chance of marrying.

"Did you see that other write-up, the one by Helen Keller?" Dovie asked.

"Now *that* was edifying," Madge said. "Just imagine being deaf and blind and working on a college degree."

"What's it about?" Gertrude asked.

"She writes about her life, what it's like to be deaf and blind," Dovie answered. "I always thought she'd been afflicted since birth, but she could hear and see until a fever struck her unconscious sometime before her second birthday."

"Changing the subject," Gertrude said, "Mother asked me to invite all of you to the Hoover party she's holding a week from Thursday."

"I'm dying to see the Hoover," Dovie said. "My sister in Ohio bought one for her maid and raves about it." She looked at Alice. "And they say it's just the thing for asthma."

Louise's thoughts went to Frank and the many hours he was spending on his cleaning invention, the Whirlwind Maid. Would the Hoover dash his dreams?

"Mother is planning games and refreshments after the Hoover man does his demonstration," Gertrude said. "And you know she invites only the best people."

"Please thank your mother for the invitation, but I won't be able to attend," Louise said. "I have a prior commitment." It was not exactly a lie. Her commitment was to Frank.

* * *

CURLS OF PAPER TAPE STREAMED from Frank's adding machine, the product of an afternoon's work. His nimble fingers punched the machine's keys as he worked out the financials of the Whirlwind Maid's business plan.

Louise might think his invention a passing fancy, but what she didn't know was the state of their finances. The "pressing business matter" that had prevented him from accompanying her and Marie to Philadelphia involved his failed attempt to salvage what amounted to worthless railroad investments. That left the Inn as the family's principal source of income. Now it was rumored that Burlington might close its Riverbend depot, leaving only freight service and the yards, a move that would leave the Inn high and dry. There were no two ways about it: the Whirlwind Maid would have to succeed.

Sounds of the adding machine's keys clacking and its handle

grinding prevented Frank from noticing Henryetta's entrance into the den until the yellow- and blue-speckled Whirlwind Maid caught his eye. It was cleaning day, and Frank loved nothing more than to see his beautiful brainchild in operation.

"How's she working for you, Henryetta?"

"Recoiler's stuck again." She untied a string from her finger and tucked it in her apron pocket.

Frank sprang from his chair and saw about three feet of cord behind the cart. He pulled the cord, and it unreeled just as it was meant to. But when he let go, it failed to recoil. "I'll get the boys at the bicycle shop working on it. Other than that, how's she doing?"

"Picks up dirt good."

Frank would have liked for Henryetta to display a little enthusiasm—the Whirlwind Maid should arouse passion in every user—but that was not her way even though she had played a part in the invention's development. For one thing, it had been Henryetta's idea to speckle the cart's lemon yellow and flag blue enamel finish so it would not show wear.

Her major contribution, however, had to do with the size of compartments for holding cleaning supplies. Frank had based his design on products used by the Inn's maids. Henryetta pointed out that not everyone used the same sized products, such as a gallon jug of vinegar or giant box of baking soda. Frank turned the idea over in his mind. Doing away with compartments altogether would not work, as things would shift when the cart was taken up or down stairs. The solution, he realized, was to make the compartment dividers adjustable, instead of fixed.

"Okay to turn it on?" she asked.

"Music to my ears," he said. "What do you think of the adjustable dividers—your idea?"

"Uh-huh." She plugged in the cord and flipped the power switch.

The machine growled, an assuring sound to Frank. He returned to his calculations, fine-tuning his business plan, but it was hard to concentrate with Henryetta vacuuming the rug, drapes, and upholstery. The rattling sound when the machine picked up a foreign object unnerved him. He cringed at the thought of a pen nib puncturing the hose.

After Henryetta wheeled the Whirlwind Maid from the den, Frank spent several more hours reviewing and revising the costs of production materials, labor, marketing, travel, shipping, and repairs. He made a conservative estimate of monthly sales and arrived at a price per unit. Finally he committed the figures to paper in ink.

When he finished he mentally tied a string around his finger to remember to talk to the boys at the bicycle shop about the recoiler. A nagging but minor problem. He was confident they would fix it once and for all. But he had far less confidence about what he needed to do next: tell Louise he was taking to the road to sell the Whirlwind Maid.

* * *

AFTER SUPPER LOUISE WAS SURPRISED by Frank's invitation to take a walk in the woods, something they had not done for many months.

There was a time long before Marie was born when sharing the walk with Frank could transform the experience of the woods. Coming upon a tree once split by lightning, Louise would marvel at how one half thrived while the other stood scorched and lifeless. Frank would marvel along with her, and the moment would become transcendent. Such resonance between them was rare these days.

A walk might do him good. He needed to relax. For weeks he had holed up till all hours in the den, and it was starting to show. His face looked haggard, he showed no interest when she brought home the latest gossip, and he seldom teased Marie and Henryetta anymore.

Exiting the Inn, they exchanged pleasantries with guests who lounged in the Adirondack chairs on the porch. Louise linked arms with her husband as they descended the Inn's front steps. "Those chairs are overdue for a new coat of paint," she said.

"I have more important matters on my mind than a bunch of chairs," he said.

His solemn tone of voice worried Louise. What did he need to tell her that Marie shouldn't hear? Was he ill? Louise knew Frank's fear that, like his father, he would die before his time, before achieving fame and fortune. At forty-three, he carried a cloud over his head, his father having had his first heart attack at that age. The older man lived three more years, a sleepwalking version of his former ambitious self. "Cut down when he still had a chance to conquer the world," Frank used to say.

They entered the woods in silence. The noisy chatter of birds settling among the tree branches for the night was one of Louise's favorite twilight sounds.

Frank looked up at the tree canopy. "They sound like a bunch of convention-goers."

"Frank, forget about the Inn, forget about the Whirlwind Maid, and just enjoy nature. You've been inordinately preoccupied lately."

He kicked a small stone along the path until it skipped into a dense growth of ferns. The path narrowed, and Louise walked ahead. She pointed out a doe and her twins in a clearing.

At the split tree, she turned toward Frank. He looked down at his feet.

"What is it?" she asked.

His hesitation fueled her imagination. Was it illness? Financial ruin? Another woman, one capable of reviving his manliness?

"It's the Whirlwind Maid."

Relief came over her, then irritation at having become alarmed over nothing.

"Louise, there will never be a finer cleaning system." His voice brightened, his eyes nearly sparkled. "I have a foolproof plan—"

Recalling her husband's many abandoned ventures, such as his "foolproof plan" to own a string of hotels or his "foolproof plan" to breed mink, got Louise's blood boiling. But two women were approaching on the path, so she masked her anger with a cordial nod.

"Lovely evening for a stroll, ladies," Frank said.

The taller of the two pointed down the path behind her. "When you get further along, you'll see a baby owl in a cottonwood tree."

Her companion scowled. "They *live* here. Don't you suppose they've seen baby owls before?"

Louise chafed at the intrusion but said sweetly, "I never tire of seeing the owls, especially the babies."

The women passed, and Louise decided to broach a subject she'd been withholding. If Frank had grand plans for his invention, he needed to know that Hoover was far ahead of him. "I didn't tell you this, but I was invited to a Hoover party, but of course—"

"Don't you see, Louise, Hoover is doing me a big favor. The man is a marketing genius. He stirs things up, convinces every woman she needs to own a vacuum cleaner. He creates the market, then I come along with the Whirlwind Maid, which is obviously superior. I've worked it all out. Tom knows the bicycle can't compete with the automobile, and he's got to get into a new line of work or go out of business. Right now he's tickled to have my business to keep his boys busy. Once I get going, we'll expand his shop into a small factory."

Louise thought of Hoover salesmen going door to door or putting on party demonstrations. "Will you hire traveling salesmen?"

"No. They couldn't begin to do her justice. I plan to go on the road and sell her myself."

Louise pictured her husband, a caricature perched expectantly on a doorstep with his Whirlwind Maid. She sensed desperation. Perhaps his string of failed schemes weighed too heavily or he felt he was running out of time to make his mark.

"Door to door?"

"Goodness, no. The Whirlwind Maid has too much class for that. I'll take orders from hardware stores and mercantile stores. Put this baby in a store window, and everybody will want one."

She had to agree it was probably far superior to the Hoover.

She could tolerate—even enjoy—her husband being gone a few days each month. "Where would you go, Omaha? Kansas City?"

"No, Hoover's already in the big city stores. But up-and-coming rural towns that have electricity, why, the Whirlwind Maid will sweep them right off their feet." He grinned at his little joke.

"How are you planning to get to these places?"

"I'll buy a truck. And during the winter months, I'll just take one sample along and ride the train."

"How long would you be gone?"

"Couple of months at a time. Then—"

"You can't mean it. If you think you're going to leave me here to run the Inn alone, you have another think coming—"

"Listen, Louise." Frank looked away, his eyes scanning the trees left of the path. "The hoot owl. There. There's two of them."

"Don't change the subject. Have you given any thought to Marie? How could you abandon her to go off on some lark?"

She could see that her words stung. Accusing this loving father of failing his daughter, calling his beloved project a "lark." She had crossed a line. A woman might confide her husband's failings to her closest friend but should never question his authority to his face. A prudent woman would drop the subject. But if she didn't vent, she could choke on the grievances stuck in her throat. "What about our dream house, a proper house for Marie? Must we remain trapped in this mausoleum all our lives?"

"Mausoleum?"

"I'm sick of living with your parents' ghosts. Everything we own belonged to them. I want my own house, furnished to my taste. And I want a proper porch and garden that I don't have to share with paying guests."

He straightened to his full height and glared at her. "I always admired you as a woman who knew her place. My business is none of your business. I intend to forget this conversation ever occurred."

She strode out of the woods alone. She passed a blur of guests without a word or a nod and headed to the back door. *Let them think what they will.*

*   *   *

THE FOLLOWING MORNING YONDER BROUGHT the last of eight Adirondack chairs to the yard behind the Inn where Louise had begun scraping peeling paint from a chair back. He reached for a scraper and began working on another chair.

"These chairs have seen better days," Louise said.

One of the hired girls, walking by with a basket of laundry, greeted Louise, and gave Yonder a quick, shy glance when he looked up.

After the girl passed, Louise said, "She likes you."

Yonder did not respond.

"Ever been sweet on a girl?" The question slipped out, its boldness catching her by surprise.

Yonder dipped his paintbrush, wiped it against the can's rim, and applied paint to a chair leg with sure, steady strokes. "There was someone in St. Deroin, blonde hair, green eyes, rebellious spirit."

Louise worked on a matching chair, scraping weathered paint that flaked off to expose the wood beneath. "What happened?"

"Nothing out of the ordinary." His sarcastic tone—so uncharacteristic of this gentle man—caused Louise to stop scraping and look up.

He straightened and wiped his forehead with the back of his hand. "I got beat up and left for dead."

"I am so sorry. Is that why you came here?"

"I had to leave town. It was that or get killed." He looked directly at Louise, his eyes cold with resentment. "Know what happens to white men who kill a halfbreed?"

She nodded. She'd made a mistake prying into his past, thinking it just a bit of playful mischief. She hadn't meant to arouse some barely repressed bitterness. Was the anger in his eyes meant for the men who had assaulted him or for all whites? Might it include her? The thought brought on a sensation like her skin was shrinking. She set down her paintbrush and stroked her left arm as though she could comfort herself.

Yonder must have read her thoughts. His eyes, no longer angry, sought connection. "I didn't mean to burden you with this."

Never had Yonder been more dear to her. She grasped for healing words. "I cannot dare to say I've shared anything like your experience. But you were the learned man who wore pigskin boots, and I was the cultivated lady who wore snakeskin pumps. I suspected that, like me, you had known the pinch of hand-me-down shoes, and you seemed to understand that I was an outsider, that like you, I had shed my old skin."

He nodded. "We pay a price for denying our roots, for striving to become someone our ancestors wouldn't recognize."

"Isolation—that's what pretending has cost me. I had grown

numb to it." What she wanted to say was that knowing him, coming to accept him and feel a kinship with him, awakened something real in her. But if she dared to say those words, other words might tumble forth, revealing improper feelings that wanted to surface in spite of her every effort to censor them. Instead she dipped her brush in the can and without wiping off the excess paint slapped the dripping brush onto the raw wood of a chair leg.

Chapter 11

August 1904

Frank winked at the supper guests when he deflected Marie's question. "Chautauqua? It's an Indian word. Tell us what it means, Yonder."

Affecting an authoritative tone, Yonder said, "'Chautauqua' is a very old Iroquois word. It means 'wallowing in culture.' And there's no one who likes to wallow in culture more than your mother." He grinned at Louise.

"I'm not alone." Louise was in her Chautauqua mood, happily anticipating five nights of entertainment, music, and lectures, as well as classes during the day. She still regarded the event with the pride of ownership, having led the campaign to bring the tent Chautauqua to Riverbend, though it had been so many years ago that most people did not know her role or had forgotten. "Chautauqua brings a cultural and educational feast to a starving town."

Inviting J.D. and Dovie, Yonder, and one or two presenters to supper on the eve of Chautauqua was a tradition. As in years past, Bernard Feldman, the Chautauqua's popular Mr. Science, was a guest. A bald, scrappy man with expressive eyebrows that looked like brown woolly caterpillars, he had passed the age when most men retire; however, his eagerness to share his fascination with medicine and science seemed to keep him young. A new supper guest this year, something of a surprise, was Giovanna Sortino who accompanied Yonder.

"I'd like to bring a guest this year," Yonder had said to Louise. "Miss Sortino."

Louise tried not to appear startled. "The Chautauqua soprano?"

"We met last year. I'd very much like for you to meet her."

His face had the bright glow of what could be eagerness or pride . . . or love. The idea of this woman enjoying his affection stirred resentment, which was foolish because he didn't belong to Louise. But she couldn't help herself. "Of course. I'd be honored to have her at our table."

J.D. ladled gravy onto a slice of beef tenderloin until it pooled perilously close to the edge of his plate. "Speaking of feasts, Louise, I do believe you've exceeded your own high standards tonight."

The others murmured agreement. The men raised their cocktail tumblers, and the women, their glasses of champagne and sloe gin.

"Thank you, J.D.," Louise said. "Most of the credit belongs to Henryetta."

"Will someone please pass the corn pudding?" Marie asked.

"That's what's missing," Bernard said. "I had come to think of it as a tradition."

Louise had hoped no one would notice the omission and momentarily wished hers was a household in which children were seen and not heard. "I thought potatoes au gratin might be a welcome change."

Giovanna scowled. "Is corn pudding not a dessert?" Her lyrical voice was quintessentially feminine yet suggested her power to reach an audience in the back rows.

Yonder explained. "It's a savory dish my mother used to make, and when I described it to Louise, she was able to recreate it. As you can tell, it found favor with guests."

It was deliberately omitted tonight because Frank had said to Louise days before the party: "I don't know why everyone makes such a fuss over corn pudding. It tastes like paste with lumps and looks even worse." Knowing him to be anything but a picky eater, Louise found his words disturbing. She had said nothing about the party menu, yet he had been thinking about corn pudding. Was this a sign of jealousy? If so, why now after all these years? Did it have to do with Marie falling from the pony cart? When the driver called Yonder "Dad?"

Following the entrée, Henryetta cleared the table and wheeled in a serving cart bearing Louise's new silverplate chafing dish, an essential item for the up-to-date hostess.

"Can it possibly be peach melba?" Bernard said.

Louise nodded as she assembled the dessert in the chafing dish with practiced flair. She poured brandy in a steady stream to bathe the warmed peaches and raspberry sauce without splashing, then touched a candle flame to the pooled liquid. The resultant spectacle brought the "oohs" and "aahs" she had anticipated.

The room grew still, the only sound that of silver spoons scraping china bowls.

Frank held his spoon aloft, using it to punctuate his slurred words. "Louise, here, deserves credit for the dessert. She's been practicing for weeks. I've got peach melba coming out my ears." He settled back in his chair, a self-satisfied grin on his face.

Giovanna said, "Louise, I have enjoyed peach melba in the finest restaurants in Vancouver and Boston, and I daresay yours is without equal."

Murmurs of approval underscored her praise.

She continued. "I am afraid I could never be as clever as you in the kitchen."

"Thank you, Giovanna. Perhaps you underestimate yourself."

Bernard dabbed his mouth with his napkin and pushed back his chair. "I have some Chautauqua news. I understand that Miss Helen Keller will join the circuit next year."

"As a presenter?" Louise asked.

"Yes. Her topic will be 'My Life.' The public is fascinated with how she manages given her handicaps."

"But can she speak?" Giovanna asked.

"Yes, but most people can't understand her. Her companion and former teacher, Miss Anne Sullivan, will translate."

A lull in the conversation followed. Marie spoke up. "I know something no one else knows. May I tell, Uncle Yonder?"

"Go ahead, Miss Smarty-pants," he said.

"Uncle Yonder and Miss Sortino are going to get married."

Scarcely hearing Frank's call for a toast, Louise was slow to raise her glass. She half-smiled, her eyes drawn to a candle flame's flickering reflection on her crystal wine glass. She tried to feel happy for Yonder, but part of her spirit had been sucked from her body.

Following Frank's toast, Louise, looked at Giovanna. "I'm happy for you both. Have you set a date?"

"I've always dreamed of a wedding on my parents' anniversary, March twenty-fourth." Giovanna smiled at Yonder.

"Does this mean you'll no longer favor Chautauqua audiences with your presence?" J.D. asked.

Giovanna nodded. "I'm weary of living like a gypsy. We plan to settle down in San Diego near my family."

It dawned on Louise that Yonder's trips to California over the past year probably had nothing to do with the assimilation movement.

Giovanna continued. "We both want a place to call home."

Louise bristled at the implication that Yonder had no home. All these years—fifteen at least—Riverview Inn was his home. He was family.

"San Diego will be the perfect place for Yonder to assimilate," Giovanna said. "He has the blessing of my father, and that makes him as good as a full-blooded Italian."

"We haven't told him everything about my heritage," Yonder said. "He doesn't know that I'm half French."

Everyone laughed.

"What do you plan to do in San Diego?" Bernard asked.

"Giovanna's father plans to make me a partner in his construction business, and Giovanna will open a music conservatory."

Frank looked at Bernard. "Yonder came to Riverbend from St. Deroin, hardly famous like your Pompeii, but fascinating nonetheless."

Yonder said, "I never intended to leave St. Deroin. But I saw signs the river was changing its bed and about to take the town."

Giovanna looked at Yonder and placed a hand on his arm. "You're making it sound so matter of fact." She looked at the guests. "When he told me how he watched chunks of earth and houses and stores fall into the river, I could scarcely believe my ears." Excitement shone in her eyes and voice. "And at night it rumbled like thunder. Some people moved up on the bluff, but most people left. Fortunately for me, Yonder decided to come to Riverbend or we probably would never have met."

That Yonder had told Louise of his first love, his real reason for leaving St. Deroin, gave Louise some satisfaction. She and Yonder had a special bond. He might be smitten with the lovely soprano, but she doubted they were kindred spirits.

"Pardon me," Marie said, "may I be excused?"

"Of course," Louise said.

Marie whispered to her mother. "Do you know where I left Dolly?"

"In the back parlor next to the piano."

Marie excused herself from the table and walked a familiar path to the adjacent parlor.

On the threshold of inebriation, Frank nevertheless succeeded in pouring brandy for everyone without spilling a drop. He had begun drinking bourbon before the guests arrived, and no doubt he and Bernard would continue drinking long after the other guests left. In a *non sequitur,* he announced "Ozymandias" and launched into a recitation of his favorite poem.

> I met a traveler from an antique land
> Who said: Two vast and trunkless legs of stone
> Stand in the desert. Near them, on the sand,
> Half sunk, a shattered visage lies, whose frown,
> And wrinkled lip, and sneer of cold command,
> Tell that its sculptor well those passions read
> Which yet survive, stamped on these lifeless things,
> The hand that mocked them, and the heart that fed . . .

When Frank paused to take a drink, the sound of Marie's voice came from the back parlor:

And on the pedestal these words appear:
"My name is Ozymandias, king of kings;
Look on my works, ye Mighty, and despair!"
Nothing beside remains. Round the decay
Of that colossal wreck, boundless and bare
The lone and level sands stretch far away.

Frank gestured toward the parlor. "Ah, but there's *my* immortality; I shall live on through my daughter."

"Come here, child," Bernard called out.

Marie retraced her steps to the dining room and went to Bernard's side.

He took both her hands in his. "The child has a gift."

The way Bernard looked at Marie's eyes, the slight wrinkling of his brow, caused Louise's shoulders and neck to tighten.

"The Chautauqua is looking for a new child elocutionist," Bernard said. "Anna Joy Blake is going on fourteen and won't return to the circuit next year. Seems she pines for a beau back home in Ohio and has not renewed her contract. Just say the word and I'll arrange an audition."

"Please, may I go to the circus?" Marie asked, then shook her head and let out an embarrassed giggle. "I mean *circuit*."

Everyone laughed.

Unless Louise changed the subject fast, Frank would pick up on Bernard's suggestion. "I suggest we retire to the parlor to watch Bernard's Magic Lantern show. And Marie, it's time to say good-night to our guests and your father."

After Marie bid everyone good-night, Louise put her to bed. When she returned to the parlor, she encountered Dovie standing apart from the others.

"She's wearing the S-corset," Dovie whispered. Her eyes were directed toward Giovanna, who was holding up a sheet as Yonder tacked it to a wall. The soprano's bosom and bottom were thrust out, a look that had not yet reached Riverbend. "Isn't it sensational?"

"Do you suppose the stores in Omaha will have them?" Louise asked.

"Let's go shopping as soon as the Chautauqua is over."

When everyone was seated, Frank lit the Magic Lantern's wick. Bernard opened his large case of slides, and Louise turned out the parlor lights.

Projecting pictures of people who appeared to have been sculpted in lava, Bernard said, "Imagine these people some nineteen hundred years ago, going about their everyday lives, caught unawares by the eruption of Mt. Vesuvius."

As he showed the ruins of a bakery, laundry, and the Temple of Jupiter, he held his little audience spellbound with his descriptions of how people lived. When he came to an image of a faded mosaic, he said, "This picture is not one I show Chautauqua audiences. This was the floor of a brothel, one of about thirty brothels in the town. Pompeii was a veritable den of iniquity."

Louise was surprised and dismayed that Bernard would bring up such a vulgar topic with ladies present. Her face must have registered her displeasure because he moved quickly to the next slide.

"This last picture shows the amphitheater, which could hold nearly twenty thousand spectators—approximately six times the number of people in Riverbend. Designed for one purpose only. Do you know what it was?"

"Athletic contests." Frank punctuated his thick-tongued response with a quick nod of self-satisfaction.

"Killing exhibitions," Bernard said. "The Romans had an insatiable appetite for blood sports. Men of wealth and culture took great pride in the gladiators they owned, pitting them against man and beast. For the owners and spectators, it proved a thrilling demonstration of raw power, perhaps the ultimate expression of a human being's power—not the poor gladiator's, mind you, but the owner's, because his wealth and position rendered him capable of sponsoring such a contest."

J.D. removed a silver toothpick case from his pocket and settled back in his chair. Seated next to J.D., Dovie fidgeted more than usual, alternately twisting her wedding band and twirling a lock of hair. Louise reflected on the couple's happier days when J.D. doted on his flighty wife, and Dovie had no cause to worry that he might stray. But recently Dovie had told her of J.D. coming home late with the scent of perfume on his clothes.

His attention fixed on Giovanna, J.D. returned the silver case unopened to his pocket. "They got their just reward, did they not? God caused Vesuvius to belch forth its gases and ash and lava to smite them for their hubris and wickedness. Mind you, it's no coincidence that God led us to discover the buried story in our time. Clearly a warning of what He shall do if we dare to put our love of money and flesh ahead of Him."

"Nonsense," Giovanna said. "What moral lesson is

contained in the deaths of innocent babies and children? If God truly wanted to teach people a lesson, He would single out only the wicked for destruction."

Louise and Dovie exchanged shocked expressions. Giovanna was a woman who didn't know her place.

"Ah, but there's an important lesson we forget at our peril," J.D. said. "Sinners themselves are not the only ones cursed for their sins. No indeed. Like it says in holy scripture: 'I the Lord thy God am a jealous God visiting the iniquity of the fathers on the children to the third and fourth generation of them that hate me; and shewing mercy unto thousands of them that love me and keep my commandments.'" He emphasized the words "keep my commandments."

Louise stiffened, taking the brunt of his words as though they were meant for her.

Giovanna's eyes flashed. "That was written in Biblical times before science provided rational explanations for natural disasters and disease. I cannot accept that Miss Keller was struck blind and deaf because her parents or grandparents brought the wrath of God upon her."

J.D. leaned forward. "Ah, but mind you, God's message has been forgotten in modern times. Miss Keller's affliction is meant to be an object lesson."

To speak up would violate Louise's code of ladylike behavior, but she wanted to say, "God forbid that Marie's blindness is punishment for something her father or I did." But, of course, Marie's blindness *was* God's punishment. She looked at Frank, who was eyeing his snifter and swirling the brandy. Could he not see J.D.'s argument as a personal affront? If he had been sober and half a man, he'd have stood up to J.D.

Instead of holding her ground, Giovanna sat back and looked at the pendant watch that hung from a gold rope around her neck. "The hour is late. I must follow a strict regimen when I'm performing. We must bid adieu to you lovely people."

Grateful to Giovanna for breaking the tension, Louise stood and saw her and Yonder to the door. She watched them walk down the hall to the stairs where they stopped, reluctant to part. Louise had to turn away from their intimate moment, but she couldn't banish the thought of their intimacy.

She closed the door, reminding herself she'd become a sensible matron, one whose contentment was derived from carrying out her duty to family and community. And now there were guests awaiting her return.

As she turned from the door to head back toward the animated voices in the parlor, she stopped as though physically restrained. A curious thought got her attention. She would never serve corn pudding again, and perhaps worse, never experience the anticipation of corn pudding, a loss that left her feeling old.

She took deep breaths to collect herself, hating it when sentiment intruded on her carefully constructed world.

J.D. was speaking as Louise entered the parlor. "Mind you, I am the first to say there are good ones, like Miss Sortino."

J.D. had recently begun writing editorials in *The Riverbend Nonpareil,* exploiting the threat of immigration from Eastern and Southern Europe. It was hard to discern when he sincerely believed something and when he was pandering to the newspaper's readers.

"Her family has probably been here as long as yours," Bernard said. "We're a nation of immigrants, but people get here and want to keep out anyone who isn't their own kind."

Frank spoke up. "Want to hear something funny? When my father came to this country and looked for a boarding house, there was one that had a sign that said, 'No dogs or Irishmen.'" Frank cocked his head, seeming to wait for a big reaction, but it didn't happen. Louise wondered how many times their guests had heard his story.

J.D. got a conspiratorial look in his eye. "Changing the subject, Yonder isn't the first man to whom Miss Sortino has been betrothed." He paused for effect. "I have it on good authority that she joined the Chautauqua—that would have been the season before last—after her fiancé in San Diego got cold feet and called off the wedding just days before."

* * *

UNABLE TO SLEEP, LOUISE SHIFTED her pillow once again. The rough seam of her nightgown was chafing her side so she rolled onto her back, trying not to hear Frank and Bernard's voices which carried from the back parlor where they had settled after Dovie and J.D. left. Whatever they were arguing about would be forgotten tomorrow.

Not until tonight had Louise realized how abrasive J.D. was becoming. Almost everything he said, actually everything he stood for, offended her. From his diatribe about God's punishment, to his seeming enjoyment at revealing Giovanna's troubled romantic past, to his ugly stance on immigration.

She turned from her back to her side and kicked off the sheet, knowing that in minutes she'd pull it back up.

Dovie had been fidgety and unusually quiet throughout the evening. A reaction, no doubt, to J.D.'s behavior. Poor Dovie, as though a corset could help her marriage.

Giovanna's spirited opposition to J.D. had been something to behold. Was it her Italian nature or the West Coast influence? What would it be like to be Giovanna, a worldly woman who spoke her mind, had a glamorous career, and traveled unaccompanied by a husband? Recalling the trip with Marie to Philadelphia, Louise didn't ever again want to juggle train and trolley schedules or deal with strange people and places on her own.

But to be honest, the coming of the Chautauqua aroused nostalgia for a time before Marie was born. Those were the days when the raw drive to establish herself as a civic leader led her to found the library and to campaign for the Chautauqua. She slept well then and bounded out of bed each morning eager to tackle the tasks that would occupy her till nightfall.

Devoting herself to Marie's welfare and piano studies had been a conscious decision, one she didn't regret. But she had never intended to trade her reputation as a civic leader for that of a hostess who dazzled her guests with a flaming peach melba.

And there was the way Bernard, who had once studied medicine, looked at Marie's eyes. Did he know about babies' sore eyes?

Her meandering thoughts turned to Yonder, to the way Giovanna took over his story about St. Deroin, not in the collegial manner of couples who finished each other's sentences, but in a condescending way as though his telling of it wasn't good enough. She couldn't shake the bad feeling she had about their union. If it failed, she hoped he would come back home.

Chapter 12

August 1904

For five days each August a grassy Missouri River flood plain was transformed into a cultural mecca with the coming of the Chautauqua. As the Morrisseys walked through the grounds on opening night, Frank swept his arm wide to indicate the whole scene. "Look what we started, Louise."

Louise didn't take issue with him, but it had been she who had mobilized a group of women fifteen years ago in a campaign to bring the Chautauqua to Riverbend. At the time, Frank had called it her "little project." Only after her efforts had turned local indifference to enthusiastic support did he see the bandwagon and jump on.

A tall tent commanded the temporary, bustling Chautauqua community. A hundred or more small camping tents dotting the grounds were rented by families who came from the countryside and small towns by train, buggy, or the occasional automobile. The campers brought along sleeping bags, which resembled long pillow cases, and stuffed them with straw, provided free by the local Chautauqua Committee, which also maintained outhouses and water wagons.

Outside some of the campers' tents sat little cages with squawking chickens that would end up as stew before the week ended. Families who could afford it ate from the many food concessions operated as fund-raisers by local churches and civic groups. Long lines always formed at the booths of the Methodist Missionary Society, famed for fried chicken, and the Bohemian Society, whose members dressed in colorful folk costumes and served hearty suppers of pork sausage, sauerkraut, dumplings, and kolaches. Other vendors sold lemonade, root beer, ice cream, and corn on the cob slathered with butter.

Absent were the fortune-tellers, hucksters of rheumatism cures, and peddlers of girlie pictures who followed carnivals and other traveling shows. The Chautauqua prided itself on moral purity, and vendors had to meet the organization's standards.

The main tent's vast canvas canopy covered a platform and orderly rows of wood plank seats. The tent remained open on three sides for ventilation unless rain necessitated the lowering of canvas curtains. Families arriving early took seats near the openings so they could send children outside if they became restless during the long show. Older children climbed the steep hill to the south to play in Chautauqua Park, another civic improvement instigated by Louise, or to roll down the hill.

After the mayor took the platform to greet the audience, the Chautauqua manager opened the show with the Alpine Yodelers. Outside the tent several ruffians howled in imitation until a man seated near the tent opening chased them off.

At the end of the act, the audience applauded and waved white handkerchiefs in the "Chautauqua salute," a tradition that had begun when the Chautauqua had a deaf presenter who was unable to hear applause.

When, several acts later, Giovanna Sortino sang selections from "La Boheme," Louise observed Frank looking mesmerized, probably by her rising and falling bosom which was accentuated by her S-corset. Other men seemed transfixed as well, and Louise wondered how they would explain to their wives their sudden passionate interest in opera.

Next came a ventriloquist with his dummy, and the audience strained to catch the man's lips moving. This was the first of several olios, which included a juggler and The Man of a Thousand Bird Songs.

Bernard Feldman was an old favorite. He excited children and adults alike with demonstrations of electrical power and magnetism. Less popular with children was his graphic chalk talk on germs which helped advance the "sanitary revolution" going on in homes across America. Indeed a look at the audience would reveal a testament to this revolution. With growing public awareness that beards and floor-length skirts harbored deadly germs, it was becoming a mark of sophistication for men to be clean-shaven and women to wear skirts with raised hemlines.

When the piano soloist played Debussey's "Claire de Lune," Louise watched with amusement at Marie's hands playing an imaginary piano and pictured her on a concert stage one day.

Among the various acts that followed were the Voices of Beulahland singing Negro spirituals; Anna Joy Blake whistling a patriotic medley and reciting "The Highwayman;" the Children's Chorus; and Bernard's program on Pompeii.

And finally opening night closed with the ever-popular "Acres of Diamonds" motivational speech presented by the Reverend Russell Conwell. His very long speech had been published so widely and delivered so often that Frank and other ambitious men in the audience could mouth significant passages, such as one in which Conwell exhorted men to see it as their Christian duty to acquire wealth which was not to be found in far-off places but in their own back yards if only they would dig there. The end of his speech was met by thunderous applause accompanied by fluttering white handkerchiefs.

When the Morrisseys stood to leave, Frank said, "You see, Louise, Conwell speaks directly to me. My Whirlwind Maid, now if that isn't an invention from my own back yard—why, you know what gave me the idea was watching our hired girls lug around all their cleaning supplies. Mark my words, Louise, we're going to be rich."

*   *   *

LOUISE AND MARIE WERE FINISHING breakfast when Frank charged through the door as though possessed. His face was lathered with shaving soap except for one clean swath.

Eyes flashing, he jabbed at the air with his razor, punctuating his announcement. "I've just been struck with a capital idea. How is it the most wonderful ideas pop into my head when I'm shaving? Remember hearing Anna Joy Blake last night? '*The highwayman came riding—riding—riding—*'" He mocked the girl's sing-song delivery. "'*The highwayman came riding, up to the old inn door.*' That girl sucked all the life out of that magnificent poem. I kept thinking how our Marie Alouette could do better without half trying. It dawned on me this morning. They're looking for a new child elocutionist for next season, so why not take Marie for an audition?"

"You want her to be a presenter with the Chautauqua?" Louise said. Had he been too drunk to recall it was Bernard's idea?

His eyes brightened. "Have you been thinking the same

thing?"

"Marie, go outside and play. I need to have a word with your father."

Louise shook napkin crumbs into the plates, rolled up the napkins, and slipped them in their respective rings. She waited for the sound of Marie's footsteps on the stairs to fade, then turned to face her husband. "Have you given any thought to how disruptive it would be, traveling like gypsies? That's no life for a sighted child, let alone Marie. She depends on familiar surroundings and routines."

"A break from routines, a little adventure would do her good. Untie the apron strings, Louise. They're strangling her."

"Not to mention interrupting her piano studies. And do you think I can just drop everything to accompany her?"

"Here's the beauty of it." His face smeared with shaving soap, his eyes and voice charged with hell-bent enthusiasm, he seemed a comic figure. "*I'll* travel with her and make sales calls along the way."

Far from being appeased, Louise was repulsed by his giddy delight, which was part and parcel of his reckless nature. Struck with an idea, he became oblivious to everything else, and ideas struck often. It would be foolhardy to entrust him with Marie's care. Louise focused on breathing and remaining calm. She stacked the breakfast dishes. She could not bear to look at her husband. "And I suppose you'll braid her hair and iron her dresses."

"We'll cross that bridge when we come to it."

Louise moved the sugar bowl to its proper place where it hid a permanent stain on the tablecloth. "Little things, like the dependable placement of her plate and fork and glass—she needs that stability."

"*You* need for her to have that stability. Marie will have fun."

"What if she auditions and doesn't get selected? I would hate to see her hopes dashed."

"Oh, ye of little faith. You'll see."

Her arguments exhausted, Louise turned back to the table. Nothing she might say or do would stop her husband. But there was something she would not say, and she clung to it as the little remnant of power left to her. She would not aid Frank's scheme by reminding him of Bernard's offer to arrange an audition.

* * *

THE NEXT MORNING IN SPITE of vowing she'd not be a party to Frank's Chautauqua scheme, Louise nevertheless wanted Marie to look her best. She dressed her daughter in her navy blue sailor dress, white stockings, and black patent leather shoes, then took extra pains with her braids to which she attached red ribbons. Beyond that, this was Frank's project.

Frank and Marie headed to the Methodist Church's musty basement where the Chautauqua tour manager had his temporary office. The pair walked down a long hallway lined with posters—Jesus shepherding his flock, Jesus holding the hands of little children, Jesus driving the moneychangers out of the temple.

They entered the office as a young man placed the telephone receiver in its stand and stammered to an impatient-looking older man, "I'm sorry, Mr. Ryder, but Mr. Henkleman won't be in his office until this afternoon."

Ryder mopped his brow with his handkerchief and shook his head.

Frank smelled opportunity. "Perhaps I can help." He introduced himself to the Chautauqua tour manager and handed him a box of kolaches.

Ryder glanced in the box and set it on a table. "Oh, yes, the hotelier." His face was flushed and his speech clipped. "Decent lodging. Mattress could be firmer. This isn't an opportune time to visit. I spent the last hour getting The Man of a Thousand Bird Songs out of jail. Got himself arrested last night for public drunkenness and disturbing the peace. Wasn't too hard to get him sprung—he drove the jailer crazy with his screech owl. But now I would move mountains to see it doesn't end up in the newspaper."

"You'll find J.D. Henkleman at the barbershop at this hour," Frank said.

"Ring the barbershop, Conklin."

"No telephone." Frank relished watching Ryder's color deepen to crimson. "Call over to the River Rat Saloon. They'll fetch him."

Marie tugged on her father's hand.

Frank leaned down. "What is it?"

"What's happening?"

"It's all right, Junior," he whispered. "We'll get you an audition."

When at last the assistant handed the phone to Ryder, Frank listened briefly to the frustrated man plead his case with J.D., then motioned for the receiver.

"J.D., Frank. Look, you know your Bible-beating readers. They get wind of this and they'll raise hell, probably demand a refund of every nickel they spent on the Chautauqua so as not to support the devil's work."

J.D. chuckled. "I have no intention of publishing that item, Frank. But I want our friend Mr. Ryder to squirm and remember the favor when we book the Chautauqua next year. This year the Committee had to personally guarantee so many ticket sales that not a one of us could sleep."

"I see." Frank feigned disappointment. He picked up the slim, black telephone stand and paced until he reached the end of the cord, then turned and paced back. "But you're the publisher, for God's sake. Look, it's too late for this week's paper anyway. What's the point of running it next week after the Chautauqua leaves? It won't be news anymore."

"You rascal," J.D. said. "I don't know what you're up to, but tell Ryder you've convinced me to look the other way."

Frank gave Ryder a smile and an "okay" sign. "I'm sure the Durfee Chautauqua Bureau will be forever indebted to you, J.D."

Even before Frank could hang up the telephone, Ryder grabbed his hand and pumped it excitedly. "I don't know why you're here, but you're the answer to my prayers."

Frank introduced Marie and told Ryder the purpose of their visit.

"Does she know any of the great poems?" Ryder asked. "'Kubla Khan' or 'Charge of the Light Brigade?'"

"I know 'The Swing,' by Robert Louis Stevenson," Marie said.

"Let's see what you can do," Ryder said.

Ryder interrupted her recitation after a few lines. "That's enough." He turned to Frank. "Tell you what. We've met a couple of passable candidates in other towns, but your daughter has a special quality they don't, if you know what I mean. Bring her to Mrs. Ryder's elocution classes each day. Can you make it to her class today?" He looked at his pocektwatch. "Starts in a half hour."

Frank nodded.

"If she measures up by the end of the week, we can talk about a contract."

* * *

FRANK FOUND HIMSELF THE SOLE parent sitting in the dimly lit high school English classroom. He felt cautiously optimistic. In the front row were six children who had eyesight and two days of classes on Marie.

A large American flag hung above Mrs. Ryder's head where she stood at the blackboard writing out "The Owl and the Pussycat," the chalk screeching as she added marks for emphasis and pauses. She turned and picked up the little bell sitting on her desk. Its tinkling silenced the children and stilled their squirming.

"Now I want each child to take a turn reciting." The clicking of ill-fitting dentures punctuated her words. "Thomas?"

The boy walked to the front of the class. He took a deep breath, but before he could begin, Mrs. Ryder rang her bell. "Thomas Seastedt, you have jammed your hands into your pockets with such force as to risk poking holes in them, and mind you, won't your mother be upset?"

Thomas looked at his shoes and eased his hands from his pockets. "Yes, ma'am." He gave a halting recitation and sat down.

Following him, a girl in a pink dress managed to get through the first stanza before Mrs. Ryder slapped the bell. "Amanda Farragut, stop swinging your dress from side to side."

Frank wondered if the woman's sour expression was a matter of uncomfortable dentures or her usual demeanor.

Two more children gave passing recitations, but the next girl had no sooner spoken the title of the poem than Mrs. Ryder's hand went for the bell. "Patricia Blackman, I told you yesterday and the day before that you mustn't be so shrill. I do believe your voice could curdle milk."

A pall fell over the room as Patricia stumbled to her seat in tears.

After the sixth child had recited, or attempted to, Mrs. Ryder began passing out papers. "For tomorrow's assignment—"

Marie interrupted. "Mrs. Ryder, may I please have a go at it?"

Mrs. Ryder looked surprised. "I understood you would just be observing today. But if you're ready, I see no harm in your reciting."

Marie stood and sweeping her cane from side to side took sure steps to the front of the classroom. Frank was glad he'd listened to Louise when she insisted Marie needed her cane in case lighting was poor.

Frank held his breath. Marie must have memorized the poem by hearing others' recitations. He exhaled when she got through it without hesitation. Her competent, if uninspired, presentation brought an inscrutable nod from Mrs. Ryder while classmates glanced sideways at one another.

For the rest of the week, Frank accompanied Marie to class each morning. He carried a leather-bound notebook in which he copied the poems, complete with marks for emphasis. At night he took out his notebook, sat with Marie at the breakfast room table, and coached her on matters like projecting her voice and using pauses and drawn out phrases for dramatic effect, the very qualities Mrs. Ryder had noted in her critiques of Marie.

*   *   *

MR. RYDER'S PRESENCE IN THE classroom on the morning of the audition had a sobering effect on everyone present. Frank wished he'd brought the notebook to occupy his nervous hands as he sat with the hopeful parents of three other children at the audition. At the final class the day before, Amanda Farragut had delivered a polished, even heartfelt, recitation of "The New Colossus." Her childlike, yet dramatic appeal, "Give me your tired, your poor, your huddled masses yearning to breathe free . . ." had moved Frank and dashed his hopes.

He'd doubled his efforts working with Marie that night, and now he worried that he'd pushed too hard. She looked exhausted.

Frank watched Ryder making notes on each child and tried without success to read the man's expression. Marie was last to audition. She walked to the front and faced the class.

Frank leaned forward and brought a clenched fist to his mouth. *Why doesn't she speak?*

"Please begin," Ryder said.

Marie took a deep breath and, to Frank's relief, began reciting "The Raven" just as Mrs. Ryder had instructed. But seeing Ryder stop taking notes after the first few stanzas, Frank imagined the worst.

After Marie finished the poem, Ryder stood before the class. Pressing his hands together in a steeple, he gazed thoughtfully over the children's heads. Gesturing to Mrs. Ryder, he praised her work as evidenced by the superior quality of the morning's audition. Then he proclaimed that the youngsters were fortunate to be learning elocution, a skill they would one day fully appreciate. In his experience, people came to the Chautauqua to be morally and intellectually uplifted, but what moved them beyond anything else was the nostalgia they felt upon hearing a beloved poem, one they themselves might have memorized, rendered masterfully and passionately by a child.

Frank fidgeted, waiting for the man to get to the point.

Finally Ryder said, "I predict," and here he paused for dramatic effect, "that the next time you see and hear your fellow classmate Marie Alouette Morrissey, she will be gracing the Chautauqua platform, and the audience will be waving white handkerchiefs in the Chautauqua salute."

Marie gripped Frank's arm. Amanda Farragut ran crying to her mother while the other children slouched in their chairs and glared at Marie. Frank did not care. Fame would elude him no more. His little girl would be a star. Louise would warm to the idea.

* * *

"When will you leave?" Louise asked her husband, who was sitting on the edge of the bed and buttoning his nightshirt. She picked up his socks where he'd dropped them.

"End of March. We'll report to Lawrence, Kansas, for orientation."

"Promise me you'll go for just one season."

"She'll have three seasons before she's too old."

"Have you considered the consequences?" She turned a sock right side out. "Marie can't afford to take that much time from her piano studies. That's her future. There's no future in reciting poetry."

"This will do her good." Frank swung his feet onto the bed and laid his head on his pillow. "Stage presence. She'll need stage presence for a concert career."

Louise sighed. Frank was making up arguments as he went along. She placed his socks in the clothes chute, then picked up his shoes and deposited them in the closet. Then she sat at her vanity. "Promise me you'll arrange for her to practice the piano. It's her life, Frank."

"Promise." He was already breathing heavily, the sound of a man nearly asleep.

Louise began brushing her hair, which had turned to frizz in the humidity. As she counted strokes, she strived to find merits in Frank's scheme. The Chautauqua would broaden Marie's experiences. She'd be appreciated. And she'd have her father all to herself.

Her hairbrush caught a snarl, stinging her scalp.

Nothing good can come of this.

Chapter 13

August 1904

If the S-corset were available anywhere in Omaha, it would be the ladies' foundations department at Wilson's Mercantile. The week after the Chautauqua left Riverbend, Louise and Dovie pressed through the store's narrow entrance. A barefoot boy in overalls shoved past them. Two stylish matrons, one young and one striving not to be old, strutted and scowled, jostled by some people chattering excitedly in a foreign tongue. A gaggle of giddy young women, no doubt flush with a week's wages in their pockets, scurried toward the perfume counter.

Odors of cheap toilet water hung in the air. Overhead, giant fans hummed, and metal canisters stuffed with shoppers' payments clankety-clanked through a labyrinth of pneumatic tubes to a caged cashier who removed the cash and returned the canisters with change to the clerks.

Louise called Dovie's attention to a girl wearing bloomers. "You never wear bloomers anymore."

"I liked wearing them, if nothing else to needle Madge. But, just between us, J.D. has political ambitions, and my attire mustn't be a distraction."

The women reached the back of the store where a huge wall clock overlooked the natural segregation that occurred beneath it. The masses walked down creaking wooden stairs, wavy from years of being trod upon, to bargains below, and the women of means, or those so aspiring, took elevators to the mezzanine and second floor.

When the elevator doors rattled open the operator cautioned Louise and Dovie to watch their step. Louise remembered Marie's first time riding this very same elevator, asking what keeps the elevator from going through the roof and where would they end up if it did.

Louise and Dovie got off on the mezzanine and went directly to the ladies' foundations where they were greeted by a clerk with a long measuring tape around her neck.

"Please tell us you carry the new S-corset," Dovie said.

"I'm sorry, madame."

"Perhaps you could tell us when you might have them in stock," Louise said.

The clerk looked around, then leaned in and spoke in a conspiratorial voice. "We won't. Mr. Wilson's orders. He told our buyer that the S-corset offends the modesty of our respectable clientele."

Dovie threw back her shoulders and snapped, "Well, I never. Someone needs to inform Mr. Wilson that two respectable ladies are very disappointed."

Louise gave the clerk an apologetic glance. She was actually far less disappointed than Dovie. Wearing the S-corset would probably produce a backache. "Come on, Dovie. Let's go look at shoes."

Dovie's mood brightened.

The two women took the elevator to the second floor where the doors opened to the distant sound of babies crying. One by one people exited and were greeted by the impeccably dressed floorwalker, whose ingratiating welcome suggested nothing was out of the ordinary. But the shoppers ignored him and looked intently toward the crying.

Louise started to go the other way in the direction of the shoe department, but with Dovie's nudging she relented. Nearing the infants department, Louise remembered the time Marie threw a tantrum, thankfully one of the only times she behaved so badly in public, over being fitted for her first hard-soled shoes.

On an easel stood a sign reading: "Baby Giveaway Saturday, sponsored by Wilson's Mercantile and the Good Shepherd Orphans Home." On the floor sat a basket of baby things—bottles, diapers, gowns, and blankets—along with a sign that read "FREE Layette."

Louise looked toward the crying and saw two oversized cribs, each of which held several babies. Blue and pink ribbons festooned the cribs, but there was no hiding their stark institutional design. Next to the cribs, toddlers squirmed on a bench. Behind them sat older children, their stiff comportment suggesting their awareness of being in a competition. A lump arose in Louise's throat, and she choked back tears.

A woman cradling a baby in her arm pushed her way past Louise to get to the free layette display. She stopped every few steps just to look down at the infant. Her face radiated joy.

"Oh, Louise, aren't you glad we came shopping?" Dovie asked. "Getting to see unwanted babies get loving homes? Could anything be more uplifting?"

Two onlookers were leaving, and the opening they left in the throng provided Louise and Dovie a good view of the spectacle. The woman in front of Louise had a bearing that matched the severity of her tailored navy blue suit and cloche.

Her companion, wearing a peach-colored hat bedecked with silk roses and netting, was sniffling.

In the girls' crib two babies stirred without waking while a third—an olive-skinned beauty with curly black hair—amused the crowd by pulling herself up and shaking the crib bars. A dark-skinned woman with black, straggly hair and a soiled gingham dress approached the crib. A tap-tapping sound interrupted the pin-drop hush.

Dovie leaned her head toward Louise. "Look. That's her boot sole flapping. And that hair—why, rats could nest in it."

The baby held out her arms. The nurse plucked the baby from the crib and handed her to the woman.

"I can scarcely believe my eyes," Louise said. "Apparently anyone who wants a baby just points, and it gets wrapped up and handed over like a pot roast at the butcher shop."

The woman in the showy hat standing in front of Louise dabbed her eyes with a handkerchief. "Poor motherless babe."

"Don't you wonder what happened to the mother?" Louise asked Dovie.

"Could be she died in childbirth," Dovie said. "More likely she was an unwed girl who found herself in the family way."

"You look at these little innocents and wish their mothers had exercised restraint instead of yielding to temptation." Suddenly Louise was struck with her own hypocrisy. How could she judge these mothers? She considered the curious workings of her mind. Somehow having been a woman who yielded to temptation had not altered her fundamental convictions.

After a few moments, the nurse took the baby girl back and pushed several papers toward the new mother, who signed them, though she could hardly keep her eyes off the baby.

Dovie glowered with righteous indignation as she whispered, "I hate to think of that cute baby girl going home with that slovenly woman."

"Probably a better home than an orphanage," Louise said. "If there were an abundance of good homes, they wouldn't be giving away babies in a department store. Besides, Dovie, look at that baby's Mediterranean coloring. As cute as she is, what are her chances of getting adopted into a white family?"

The nurse led the new mother to the bench and pointed to a dark-skinned little boy, about three years old, in a corduroy suit. The woman took a couple of steps toward him, and the baby bounced and squealed.

The little boy jumped out of his chair. "Sissie! Sissie!"

The woman stopped. The baby reached out for the little boy, but the woman shook her head and turned away.

When the boy grabbed for the gingham skirt, the nurse pushed him back onto the bench. "Leave Sissie be."

He strained to get away, but the nurse snatched him up by one arm. "Stop crying, Vinnie. Nobody wants a crybaby."

"Oh, my God," Louise said to Dovie. "How can they split them up?"

The stoic woman in front of Louise turned to her companion. "I heard them say no one wants him because he's practically blind. Not much point taking in a young-un and paying for food and clothes if you can't put him to work in a few years."

An angry knot gripped Louise's stomach. "We must go. This is heartbreaking."

When she and Dovie passed the little boy, the knot tightened. He sat bound to the bench with a length of pink ribbon. He had dutifully stopped crying but his nose was running, and he gave it a swipe with his corduroy sleeve. Now it became clear why no one would adopt him—scarring on one eye, like fried egg white streaked with red. Identical to Marie's scars.

Needlessly blind.

"Dovie, may we go home? I haven't the heart to shop."

Louise said little on the way home. "Needlessly blind," Dr. Vandegrift had said. Children like Marie and now this little boy were needlessly blind because babies' sore eyes was preventable. It had been nearly eleven years since Marie was infected at birth, and babies were still being blinded. What had he said? Something about how courageous people must demand a law to require drops in babies' eyes.

Chapter 14

A mild December had many locals warning of a wintry blast come the new year, and January had rewarded them. On one of the colder days, Louise was waiting impatiently in the back parlor for Frank to drive her to the Tuesday Bibliophiles meeting. Amplifying her annoyance was the collar of her wool coat chafing her neck, and she shifted her scarf. Finally she peeked into the den where her husband was in animated conversation on the telephone. When he looked in her direction, she raised her eyebrows in a question.

Frank waved her away and whispered, "Get Yonder to take you."

The wind in her face, she walked with her head down to the carriage house and knocked on Yonder's door.

"Happy to oblige," Yonder said in answer to her request. "Glad to have a chance to drive the new car."

When Cadillac introduced the first closed-body car, the Osceola, Frank had bought one and sold the beautiful but impractical open-air Buick.

The new car lurched a few times as Yonder and Louise drove along the driveway. "My apologies." Yonder shouted over the engine noise. "First time."

The ride didn't get any better going down the hill as Yonder shifted forward, back, and forward again attempting to find the right gear.

When they neared the intersection at the base of the hill, Louise said, "Turn around."

"Was that so much fun you want to do it over again?" Yonder's grin faded when he looked at her face.

"No." Louise pointed to houses on her right. "In the alley there's an old woman scavenging through a trash bin. Go back. I'm going to get her a coat."

Upon returning home, Louise got a coat from her closet, and after getting settled in the car again she took five dollars from her handbag and tucked it in a pocket of the coat.

Before putting the car in gear, Yonder looked at her and said, "You have a good heart, Louise."

At the alley they turned in and searched its length and back again, but the old woman was gone.

"I'll get you to your meeting, then I'll drive around and look for her."

"I want to look with you."

They drove up and down streets and alleys until it finally became obvious they would not find the woman.

Louise tried in vain to hold back tears. "She could have been my mother." Louise remembered a coat from years past, one she'd worn not against the cold but in eager anticipation of it.

* * *

IT WAS THE YEAR BEFORE Louise ran away from home, so she must have been eleven. One day late in the summer, Ma brought home a beautiful fitted green coat given to her by a lady she cleaned house for. Louise tried to imagine being a lady so rich that she could discard a coat only slightly worn at the elbows.

In private moments Louise would slip the coat from its peg, inhale its smell of rich lady's perfume, and run her hand over the silky lining. She'd slide one arm, then the other into the sleeves and finger the black braid trim on the cuffs and collar. At first her hands were awkward on the frog closures, but she practiced until she could manipulate them gracefully.

Posing without benefit of a mirror, which Pa called the devil's contrivance, she dreamed of wearing the coat to school where the snooty girls who made fun of her ragged clothes would admire and envy her. Winter could not come too soon.

At last, wearing the magical coat, Louise practically strutted into the schoolyard. Daisy Friend, a girl with big, wide-set calf eyes, the first girl in her class to sprout breasts, pointed and said, "Look at Lulu all gussied up in my Aunt Mamie's coat."

Her cheeks burning, Louise fled into the schoolhouse, hung the coat on a peg, sat at her desk, and slouched behind a book. She whispered a prayer for deliverance.

Over the next few days the taunts subsided. But then someone spied Ma downtown wearing the coat. Word spread throughout the school like contagion that she and Ma had but one coat between them.

Humiliation was to be her constant companion, rarely far from her consciousness. She accepted that she had brought it on herself. Accepted and repented. God was punishing her for worshipping the coat. But what God let happen to Ma was not fair.

One gray, cold morning Louise dressed for school in the lean-to where she slept. As she carefully removed the coat from its peg, she could hear geese migrating south, their calls signaling urgency. She could also hear Ma and Pa arguing about a trip to town.

Ma begged off going. "It's too cold . . . the rheumatism—"

"Get your coat, woman, 'cuz you're going anyways," Pa said.

Louise rushed to Ma, removed the green coat, and held it out. But she could see on Pa's face that she'd made a mistake, that he knew she and Ma shared the coat. When Ma reached for it Pa slapped her face, knocking her off balance. She grabbed a chair to keep from falling.

"Think I ain't a good enough provider?" he shouted.

Please, Ma, don't let him do that to you.

But Ma cringed and backed away. He lunged, grabbed her hands away from her face, and struck her again.

"Wicked woman!" He shoved Ma out the door and climbed into the wagon.

Louise watched from the doorway. Ma hobbled toward the buckboard wagon. She gripped the handle with one hand and lifted her leg with the other but could not make her foot reach the step. Pa had no patience for stiff knees, and he was mean enough to set the wagon in motion just to teach Ma a lesson.

Louise ran out. She placed Ma's foot on the step, supported her arms, and lifted her into the wagon. She thrust the coat in her lap. "I'll stay home today, Ma."

Pa cracked the whip, and the wagon lurched forward.

*　　＊　＊　＊*

WHEN YONDER PARKED THE CAR, Louise dabbed her eyes with a handkerchief before getting out. She was able to hold back the tears but not the images of the old woman and Ma. Once she walked up the steps to the boardwalk, the wet snow scrunching underfoot, she was jolted back to reality. A black-bordered card was posted on the door of Rich's Ice Cream Parlour. Someone had died.

"Mrs. Benjamin DeWitt Foster has been summoned to her Great Reward," read the first line of the printed notice. Louise clasped a hand over her heart and stepped back, as if putting distance between herself and the words might make them less real. Doc's wife? She could not shake the ludicrous thought that in some way she was responsible. *I wanted her out of the picture. But I never wished her dead.*

She faced the notice again on the door of Anderson's Seed and Feed. Impatient for details, she hastened up the stairs to the library.

The others were already assembled, and they interrupted their conversation to greet Louise. She went to the workroom where she removed her coat and hung it on a peg and set her hat and handbag on a shelf. When she returned to the library, she took a seat on the sofa next to Dovie.

Alice was saying, "I hear it was bladder cancer." It was one of the rare days she could speak without wheezing.

"What a dreadful way to go." Gertrude sat with her Bible in her lap. "How old was she?"

"Forty-two or forty-three," Dovie said. "She was in my sister's class. Teacher's pet."

"Poor Dr. Foster," Gertrude said. "Such a nice man. I remember after The Twister how he set up a hospital in the high school gymnasium and didn't so much as sit a spell until every soul was tended to."

"By the way," Madge said, "did you notice the funeral will be held at Ludwig's Undertaking Parlor?"

"Seems to me the undertaking parlor should be for folks who don't have a decent parlor in which to hold a service," Gertrude said.

"I understand that back East the practice is gaining currency with the upper class," Madge said.

"Well, I don't care what's fashionable, I want to be laid out in my own parlor," Alice said.

"Did you notice *The Ladies' Home Journal* doesn't call it the parlor anymore?" Dovie said. "It's the 'living room.'"

"I do declare," Alice said, "it exhausts a person trying to keep up with all the changes today."

When it was time to start the meeting, Louise opened the discussion of Jane Addams' *Newer Ideals of Peace*. "Miss Addams advocates giving women the franchise and wants women represented in government so as to bring about humanitarian reforms. What do you think?"

"Women should do what they've always done—influence their husbands' vote," Gertrude said.

Dovie scowled. "But you're a widow so your influence isn't felt at all."

Gertrude straightened the antimacassar on the arm of the sofa. "I happen to think the church is more important to the quality of community life than any government, and I have plenty of say in what happens at my church."

"The vote is one change I would welcome," Alice said. "The mister is so contrary that if he thought I wanted him to vote one way he'd be sure to vote the other. And I agree with Miss Addams that running a city government is a lot like housekeeping. If we women were in charge, we would see to it that the streets were kept clean, children wouldn't go hungry, and young boys wouldn't drink and gamble at the livery stable."

Aware she was injecting her own bias, Louise asked, "What do you think, is the housekeeping analogy silly or does it suggest women doing what we've always done, clean up the messes that men make?"

All except Gertrude nodded and chuckled.

"Your thoughts, Gertrude?" Louise asked.

"Men make messes because of their sinful nature. Our place as women is to be helpmates who lead them to righteousness."

"Let me give you a bit of advice," Madge said. "Women will serve in government at the pleasure of men, doing the jobs eschewed by men. I taught high school for twenty-six years, worked as hard as any man, got paid half as much, and never had a say in the school's governance. We are like women from time immemorial. We do what we can with what we have."

"Such as our library and literacy classes," Alice said. "Has it occurred to you that while we women are here on Saturday mornings doing something to enrich the community, our menfolk are out at the town dump shooting rats for sport?"

"Maybe that's their idea of civic duty," Louise said.

Everyone laughed.

"I was talking to J.D. about Miss Adams' book, and he thinks small towns like Riverbend will benefit from Chicago's problems," Dovie said. "He says Chicago has been ruined by industries that brought in a criminal element from Poland and Italy and such to get cheap labor. Now some industries are looking to locate where they can get cheap labor and a wholesome environment at the same time."

"That's our Riverbend," Alice said.

Watching the clock, Louise interrupted the chuckles that followed Alice's comment by asking Madge to present the word of the day."

"The word is *revelation.* It means something revealed or the act of revealing, especially a dramatic disclosure of something not previously known. Used in a sentence, one might say, 'The revelation that Stephen Ambrose sometimes used the writings of others in his own works did not adversely affect his career.' Also," she looked at Gertrude, "for those who are spiritually inclined, the word can mean a message of divine will or truth. Used in a sentence, 'Having been spared by the fire that destroyed her family was a divine revelation that led her to become a nun.' Synonyms for *revelation* include 'discovery,' 'exposure,' and 'manifestation.'"

Watching the others shifting in their seats or fumbling in their pocketbooks, Louise knew the signs they were eager for refreshments. "Alice?"

Louise helped Alice set out cinnamon coffeecake and hot tea.

Dovie pressed her finger into bits of streusel that had fallen on her plate, then licked her finger. "I would give my eye teeth to have this recipe."

"I'll bring it next week," Alice said. "I'll never again give out a recipe over the telephone. My sauerbraten recipe, the one I got from Gunter's mother, has ended up in the St. Paul's cookbook. It had to be somebody on the party line who stole it."

"Changing the subject," Madge said, "the school superintendent approached my husband to see if I might return to the classroom."

"Well, I, for one, think your influence is needed in the classroom," Gertrude said. "Teachers today are far too permissive."

"But we depend on you to conduct our literacy classes," Alice said.

"Don't leave us hanging," Louise said. "Will you do it?"

"I would. I am akin to a horse that was too long in the harness. But my husband told the board precisely what he told me before we married: 'Over my dead body.'"

Dovie, twirling a lock of hair, said, "Speaking of the dead, if you ask me, Dr. Foster could have treated his wife better than he did. That mousy little woman hardly ever left the house. I used to tell him after church that he needed to get her out more, to which he always said she was happy to be a homebody. But it didn't look to me like there was one happy bone in that homebody."

Amid murmurs of agreement, Gertrude spoke up. "We should all be happy for Mrs. Foster now that she's gone to be with our Lord."

After the meeting closed, Louise went to the kitchen where Dovie was stirring soap powder into the dishwashing pan. Louise retrieved a tea towel from a drawer.

Dovie fixed her attention on washing and rinsing a cup and setting it on the drainboard. "There's an indelicate matter I didn't want to bring up in front of the others, about Mrs. Foster."

Louise stopped drying the cup she was holding. Her skin crawled with a sense that her hidden past was stirring there. Wanting Dovie to get on with her news and get it over with, she said, "It's a pity she died, but do tell." She opened the cupboard door, placed the cup on a hook, and rearranged the other cups so they all hung in the same direction.

"J.D. knows the medical director at Immanuel Hospital in Omaha . . . saw him Saturday at his Stockton Military Academy reunion. Anyway Mrs. Foster had been there—in the hospital, that is—for several weeks. He told J.D. that years before the cancer got her she . . ." Dovie scrubbed a stubborn spot on the plate in her hand and studied it. "I can't say it."

Louise sighed and put a hand on her hip. "You know what you tell me won't leave this room."

"That's not it."

"Well?" Louise reached for a plate.

"Some years ago, Mrs. Foster was hospitalized with . . . gonorrhea."

"Dovie Henkleman, did you say what I think you did?"

"I have it on good authority."

"Mrs. Foster? Virtue personified? I can't imagine." As soon as the words escaped, she realized the fallacy of her assumption.

"Come now, Louise, surely you don't think *she* was the promiscuous party in that marriage."

CHAPTER 15

Louise tried to prepare methodically for Frank and Marie's impending departure, needing to learn aspects of running the Inn that were unfamiliar to her. But Frank was anything but methodical. Something would occur to him, such as the fact Louise had never overseen the shutting down of the heating system in the spring, and at that moment he would interrupt whatever she was doing to instruct her.

One mild day he approached her in the back parlor. "Get your coat, Louise. Time for some target practice. "

She sighed and set aside her mending. *This will be fun.*

He helped her with her coat. "You'll be safe with Yonder here, but I wouldn't feel right leaving you without being able to defend yourself."

They followed the stone path behind the Inn that led past dead hollyhock stalks to the clotheslines where sheets flapped in the breeze. Frank guided her to a spot beyond the clotheslines, and she gave him her full attention as he demonstrated how to load, aim, and fire the thirty-eight revolver.

"Don't be afraid of it. Think you're ready to give it a try?"

She nodded. Taking the firearm, she turned it over in her hands, trying to get familiar with the feel of it. She was counting on past experience with Pa's rifle to serve her.

Frank walked to the fence that separated the Inn property

from Dietz's pasture, set a can on a post, and stepped far to one side, wearing his crooked grin. "Whenever you're ready."

Louise gripped the pistol with both hands, sighted on the target, and squeezed the trigger. The bullet grazed the can, which sent it flying in Frank's direction. He dodged it and set up another can. "Beginner's luck. Try again."

The gun's report had set her ears ringing. "Speak up. I can't hear you."

"Try again."

Holding a wet finger in the air, she tested the wind and compensated for its direction when she aimed. This time the bullet hit the can squarely and knocked it off the post. Frank shook his head.

Feigning surprise, she said, "Would you look at that?"

He set up a third can. "All right, step back ten paces, and we'll see what you can do."

Even from the greater distance she hit the target dead on.

He walked to her side. "You've done this before."

Louise grinned as she handed him the pistol. "A rifle, not a pistol. You forget where I came from. Time was my family wouldn't have had any supper if I couldn't have bagged a squirrel or a rabbit."

He patted her on the back. "Good girl. I won't have to worry about you. Just make sure you keep it loaded and on your nightstand."

"I intend to. What about you out on the road?"

"I'll take the rifle along."

"That reminds me, I don't want to make bank deposits alone, and with Yonder leaving soon to get married—"

"I meant to tell you. He won't be leaving. Giovanna has

postponed the wedding."

Louise could hardly believe his words. "What happened?"

"Her Chautauqua contract. She has one more season, and she told Yonder she wouldn't feel right being an absentee bride."

Delighted that Yonder wasn't leaving, at the same time Louise felt badly about the way he was being treated. "That's odd. Surely she knew—"

Frank seemed not to hear. "There's one more thing." He talked as he removed bullets from the pistol's chamber. "You'll have to order dark glasses for Marie."

"What?" Louise's ears were still ringing. Surely he hadn't said what she thought she heard.

"The Chautauqua contract requires Marie to wear dark glasses and use her cane whenever she's in public."

"No. What—"

Frank interrupted. "Ryder says her white bloodshot eyes will repulse people. You have to admit—"

Louise felt the blood rush to her face. "You would handicap her further for the sake of appearances? I've put up with all your cockamamie schemes, but—"

"I signed a contract, Louise."

She was powerless. Poor Marie. She took pride in navigating without her cane whenever possible. Dark glasses would make her totally dependent on it.

As if to underscore Louise's thoughts, Marie approached, walking her familiar path toward the clothesline without a cane. "I heard firecrackers."

"Gunshots, Junior," Frank said. "We were practicing with the pistol. Your mother is a sharpshooter." He patted Louise's shoulder. Turning away he said, "I've seen glasses in the Sears catalog."

The thought she'd had when Marie was selected to be child elocutionist resurfaced: *Nothing good can come of this.*

* * *

IT WAS THE EVE OF Frank and Marie's departure for the Chautauqua. They would report to Lawrence, Kansas, for rehearsals and orientation and begin the circuit the first week in April.

"Not there." Louise stopped Frank from depositing Marie's newly polished shoes on the tissue paper next to the open suitcase on their bed. Louise packed according to her own inviolate system. To avoid creases from folding, she rolled garments in tissue paper, then stacked them in the suitcase in tidy rows that would make a brickmason proud.

Louise stopped momentarily to listen to Pachelbel's "Canon" coming from the back parlor where Marie and the piano had been inseparable since supper. Picking up Marie's candy-striped nightgown, a gown that epitomized childlike innocence, Louise resisted the idea that her daughter might outgrow it before the tour ended in September. She held it to her nose and inhaled its fresh-air fragrance, remembering how Marie used to go to the clothesline and wrap herself in a dried sheet. Louise tried to hold her emotions in check by attending to the details of packing, but tears welled up nevertheless. The child she was sending off would not be the one who returned.

This was not Marie's first time to leave home. When she was six years old, Louise had yielded to pressure to send her to Smithville State Asylum for the Blind, fifteen miles north of Riverbend, only on the condition that she'd return home once she learned Braille and cane travel. But boarding school ravaged the spirits of Marie and her parents alike. When the superintendent reported that Marie was having "accidents," Louise went weak imagining her daughter's ordeal and pulled her from the school immediately.

A different child came home. Her black braids had been cut in an institutional bob, the same cut seen in pictures of children in Indian boarding schools. She craved cuddling, slipped into baby talk when she was tired or upset, and begged Louise to feed her. After many months she began to act her age once more. Louise vowed to never send her away again. But this time Marie was choosing to go.

Louise held up a dress. "Don't let anyone starch Marie's dresses or petticoats unless you want her scratching on stage in front of hundreds of people."

"I'll surely try to remember," Frank said. "And you remember everything I told you. Keep your eye out when those musicians from Texas come through. They'll try to sneak extra people into their rooms. Get Yonder to fix the loose railing on the front porch. Keep the pistol by your bed. And don't ever go to the bank alone. Take Yonder with you."

Frank's allusions in recent weeks to Yonder as her protector affirmed what Louise needed to believe. He trusted her.

After Frank left home for a final poker game, it was Marie's usual bedtime, but tonight was special. Marie clapped her hands when her mother presented the plan: hot chocolate together, then a story, and then Louise would lie down with her until she fell asleep.

Louise made hot chocolate while Marie donned her nightgown, robe and slippers. As they sat together at the breakfast room table, Louise studied her daughter's movements, having vowed that she would commit this evening to memory. It saddened her to think of the everyday things she couldn't recall from Marie's earlier years, such as the name she gave her first teddy bear. Tonight she etched in her mind the manner in which Marie stirred her hot chocolate until the instant she felt the floating marshmallow dissolve into a frothy cloud, and how she slowly licked the spoon.

Louise envied Marie's blissful and total engagement in their simple interlude. By contrast, Louise could not will herself to stay in the present, overcome with the realization that these precious hours were numbered.

When they finished their hot chocolate, they went to the back parlor. Marie said, "Read to me about Chopin and how he fell in love with that lady who smoked cigars and dressed like a man . . . please."

"We've read that part several times." Louise took down the book and leafed through its pages. "Here's a picture of his first love, Konstancja Gladkowska, a most elegant young lady. She has dark hair, like yours, only hers hangs in ringlets. Would you like to hear about her?"

"Yes."

With Marie nestled beside her in her favorite chair, Louise drank in the almond fragrance of her daughter's just-washed hair. A moment not to be forgotten. Marie sat still as a statue as Louise read about how Frederic Chopin loved the beautiful opera singer from a distance and, being too shy to speak, expressed his feelings in romantic letters. "'Finally they proclaimed their love for one another.'"

"Did they get married and live happily ever after?" Marie

asked.

"I think not." She continued reading. "'In spite of his intentions of marriage, he tarried too long and lost his beloved. She wed a merchant and became mistress of his country estate. Heartbroken, Frederic sought comfort in fleeting romances—'"

"What are 'fleeting romances?'"

"That means he courted several women without finding lasting love." She read on. "'Some years later Konstancja began losing her sight, and in spite of the efforts of the most skilled physicians, she went totally blind.'" Thinking fast, Louise had substituted the word *totally* for *hopelessly.* "One wonders . . . " Louise stopped and gasped. The unfinished sentence read: *One wonders if Chopin was relieved that she had become the responsibility of another man.*

"I'll never marry, will I?"

"Don't be silly. You're lovely and talented. Eligible young men will vie for your attention."

"No they won't. No one likes me."

Holding Marie's head against her breast, Louise felt the pulsing of muffled cries and dampness of tears. She stroked her daughter's hair. "Nonsense. I shall tell you a secret. I've been saving all your favorite dresses, and when you turn sixteen, I shall cut out the embroidered parts and make them into a magnificent quilt for your hope chest."

She wiped away Marie's tears. "You're about to embark on a great adventure, and you'll make new friends." Louise hated her falsely cheerful tone.

"Other children won't play with me."

Louise recalled the birthday party. It wasn't fair that blindness hid so much that was beautiful, such as rainbows and sunsets, yet it failed to hide the cruelty. "Of course other children like you."

"Don't lie to me," Marie screamed. She leaped from the chair and pounded her mother with her fists. "I hate you. Just leave me alone . . ."

Louise gripped her daughter's hands and pulled her onto her lap. Marie continued to resist, but Louise held her securely and rocked her from side to side. "I'm sorry that sighted children won't play with you. Children can be very cruel to those who are different. I know, because when I was your age no one would play with me."

Marie sniffled and wiped her nose on her sleeve. "But you weren't blind. Why wouldn't they play with you?"

"Their families were rich, and mine was poor. I wore rags to school and shoes with holes in them. Other children called me a ragamuffin."

"You never told me."

"I never wanted anyone to know I was poor. But I want you to know I sympathize with how you feel, how lonely it is when other children don't like you. When you grow up things will get better. You're beautiful and talented, and people will want to know you."

"But you have friends because you're not poor anymore. I shall always be blind."

Louise had hoped Marie would not detect the flaw in her logic. "That's true. But consider Miss Helen Keller. She grew up with only her family and Miss Sullivan to love her, and now she has many friends."

Louise stood and lifted Marie, almost too big to hold, and carried her to bed. They lay together, Marie on her side facing away from her mother. Louise sought to soothe the tension in the young body next to hers, to ease the rigidity of the child's head resting against her shoulder. She rubbed Marie's back.

"Guessing game, please?" Marie said.

That Marie would request the childish game they hadn't played for several years touched Louise. The game's object was for Marie to guess the object her mother traced on her back.

"Banana," Marie said after Louise traced the first object.

"Good." Louise then made a star, which Marie guessed correctly.

They played their game until finally Marie exhaled a shuddering sigh, went limp, and surrendered to peaceful sleep.

"I shall miss you, my darling."

Perhaps it was the frequent need for pretense, the masking of feelings, that made Louise acutely aware of instances when she was being genuine. She had told Marie she would miss her, and that was the heartfelt truth.

This moment, so precious and transitory, lodged as a lump in Louise's throat. *Daughters have a way of growing up and out of reach of a mother's comforting hand.*

CHAPTER 16

The intoxication of the open road coursed through Frank's veins like a spring tonic. With his new customized Mack Brothers truck, outfitted with a plate glass windshield and side curtains, he and Marie were the envy of many Chautauqua presenters who had to make their way from town to town any way they could.

He needed this break from the Inn. It had been his whole life except for a stint at an Omaha bank as a young man. Learning banking and finance was his father's plan for him, but Frank had chafed at being captive in a gloomy building and having to look busy. How was a man supposed to dream and invent with his mind and body in hock from dawn to dusk? Frank's older brother, Aidan, had been groomed to take over the Inn, but his sudden death from a horseback riding accident thrust Frank in his place.

Frank had gladly left banking and returned to the Inn, where he had worked since he was a child. He could count presidential candidates, captains of industry, and European royalty among the people whose shoes he had shined or trunks he had hauled. Occasionally a head of state from a far-off land swept in with an entourage, stopping en route to the plains to hunt buffalo.

The rooms held stories. One room became forever known

as "the drummer's room," so named for a salesman who was an occasional guest until one Christmas Eve when he took a gun and splattered his brains on the wall and floor. Frank had to help scrape up the mess and replace wallpaper and curtains. To this day, the room gave him cold shivers.

One time Buffalo Bill himself stopped, and after he left Frank helped the hired girls clean the room. At school the next day, he held his chums spellbound as he unfolded a piece of paper to reveal the great showman's beard clippings.

He learned younger than most that people are not what they appear to be. The detritus left in rooms taught him volumes—used condoms left under a bed, blood-drenched pads tossed in a corner, a priest's forgotten collar along with empty whiskey bottles and dirty pictures.

Also at a young age he cultivated a charming manner, partly to boost the size of tips, but mostly to challenge himself to win over strangers in a matter of minutes. What made him irresistible was a spark that said, "I think you are fascinating."

Indeed Frank seldom met anyone he did not find interesting. But owning a hotel eventually proved a poor fit for a man who hated being captive. Taking to the road was just what he needed.

*   *   *

AFTER THREE WEEKS ON THE tour, Frank was having misgivings. When Marie begged him not to make her wear the dark glasses, he spared her the truth. "The glasses are a 'prop' necessary to convince audiences they're seeing a blind child." Louise's angry objection to the glasses resided just below his skin and surfaced whenever Marie put them on.

One of Louise's objections to the Chautauqua Frank had to concede was valid: Marie needed familiarity and routines. While the novelty of living out of a suitcase exhilarated him, it challenged Marie. It meant navigating a new environment every few days. With each move she had to learn the locations of her bed, a chest of drawers, wall pegs for her clothes, and obstacles that could stub toes.

Her distress was affecting her performance. After opening night in Norfolk, Nebraska, Mr. Ryder put it to Frank bluntly, "She's too timid. I overheard a mother in the audience say, 'My little Janie can do better than that.' I'll give her two more weeks to get up to snuff."

Frank went straight to work to salvage Marie's budding career. He arranged for Bernard to coach her. And to help her feel more at home, as well as to appease Louise, he scheduled piano lessons with the Chautauqua accompanist, a man who held a degree from an Austrian conservatory, and vowed he'd see to it she could practice two hours a day.

* * *

After Norfolk, the next tour stop was Sioux City, Iowa. When Mrs. Ryder arrived in the hotel room two hours before the show on opening night, Marie was sitting on a bed composing a letter to her mother with her Braille slate and stylus while Frank lounged on the other bed rubbing Vaseline on a black patent-leather shoe. He employed the matronly woman to personally tend to Marie, aside from her duties policing the appearance and behavior of Chautauqua presenters and teaching elocution.

Mrs. Ryder plugged in the curling iron, placed the hotel

room's lone chair in front of the dressing table, and stacked books on it. Marie climbed up and sat perfectly still so as not to get burned by the hot iron. Mrs. Ryder wound a strand of hair around the iron, slipped the iron out, and repeated the action with another strand of hair, then another.

As she worked, she gave Marie a pep talk, delivered as though she aspired to the platform herself. "Here's what you must remember. Think about the people in your audience. They toil in fields and kitchens day in and day out. Once a year the Chautauqua comes, and they travel for miles and sleep on the ground because they crave a dose of culture. You, my child, are their life raft. You will transport them from their cares, sweeten their lackluster lives, and they will love you for it. Think of the good you are doing."

The incongruity of an elocution teacher with clicking dentures made Frank smile to himself. At the same time, he appreciated the woman's sincere desire to help his daughter. She might be brusque with everyone else, but she adored Marie.

Once Mrs. Ryder finished making coils with the curling iron, she allowed them to cool, then combed each one out and wrapped it around her finger. "Such stubborn hair, child. Doesn't want to hold a curl. Straight as a little Indian's."

"That's because I *am* part Indian," Marie said. "My great-grandmother was an Ioway Indian."

Once every curl met her satisfaction, Mrs. Ryder unplugged the curling iron and eased the yellow dress with brown trim over Marie's head without disturbing the sculpted ringlets. She retrieved a yellow ribbon from a drawer, deftly swept hair away from Marie's face, and tied the ribbon in a bow. Finally she slipped the now-lustrous black shoes on Marie's feet.

Frank handed Marie the glasses, which she put on without a fuss, and her cane. In keeping with routine, the trio went to the Chautauqua tent where Frank and Marie waited backstage while Mrs. Ryder scrutinized the presenters before they went on. "Mr. Whitney," she said to the ventriloquist, "you had best have that suit pressed by tomorrow night or you'll be paying a fine."

"Yes, ma'am," he said.

"And get that shaggy hair of yours cut before decent folks mistake you for a derelict."

Just before Marie's introduction, Frank whispered the magic words: "You are queen of all you survey, and those people are your adoring subjects."

Even behind the dark glasses, Marie's face brightened with self-assurance.

The Master of Ceremonies called out, "And now, The Chautauqua Darling, Marie Alouette Morrissey." Marie picked up her cane and took the stage amid applause that accompanied her confident stride.

Ten days earlier this would have been the moment that set Frank's nerves on edge, not knowing if Marie's delivery would thrill or disappoint the audience. Tonight was different. As much as the coaching had boosted her confidence and piano lessons had helped her adjust, he realized that taking minor roles in other acts had played a big part in her transformation. She sang in the Children's Chorus, assisted Mr. Science in his hand-washing presentation, and sometimes played the part of the patient when the Ballantynes did their first-aid demonstrations.

Tonight she seemed born to present. With her first step

onto the platform, she became The Chautauqua Darling. Frank filled with pride and could not wait to share the wonder of it all with Louise.

"It was the schooner Hesperus that sailed the wintry sea," began Marie' recitation of "The Wreck of the Hesperus," a long, narrative poem about a skipper and his little daughter who sail into a hurricane. Marie milked each poignant phrase, embroidering words with her voice, pausing to build suspense, and clutching her heart at the height of sentiment:

> He wrapped her warm in his seaman's coat
> Against the stinging blast;
> He cut a rope from a broken spar,
> And bound her to the mast.

> "O Father! I hear the church-bells ring,
> Oh say, what may it be?"
> "'T'is a fog-bell on a rock-bound coast!"—
> And he steered for the open sea.

> "O Father! I hear the sound of guns,
> Oh say, what may it be?"
> "Some ship in distress, that cannot live
> In such an angry sea!"

> "O father! I see a gleaming light,
> Oh say, what may it be?"
> But the father answered never a word,
> A frozen corpse was he.

By the twentieth stanza, when at daybreak a fisherman sees a maiden lashed to a drifting mast, Marie owned the audience. When she spoke the final words, a hush followed. Then applause swelled and handkerchiefs waved.

After opening the floodgates of pity with "The Wreck of the Hesperus," she delighted the audience with "An Oversight of Make-up."

Dear God, The baby you brought us
Is awful nice and sweet.
But because you forgot his toofies,
The poor little thing can't eat.
That's why I'm writing this letter,
'A-purpose to let you know,
Please come and finish the baby.
That's all. From Little Flo.

The audience erupted in applause. Marie beamed her brightest smile and curtsied.

After the show admirers lined up to shake her hand.

"You're wonderful."

"You made me weep."

"I used to recite that poem in school."

"I'd be scared to death to get up in front of all those people."

"My Lucinda here can't do half as good as you, and she's got two good eyes."

After the last of the admirers had been greeted, father and daughter followed the crowd down the path beyond the glow of the Chautauqua tent, into the darkness punctuated with stars and cavorting fireflies and toward the lamplit downtown where the ice cream store remained open.

"Got a riddle for you, Junior. What walks all day on its head?"

"I don't know."

"A nail in a horseshoe. Get it?"

Marie laughed. "Okay, I have one for you. What has a tongue, cannot walk, but gets around a lot?"

"I give up."

"A shoe!"

"That's a good one."

It was a glorious night to sit at a sidewalk table sharing a Chautauqua sundae—a scoop of butter-brickle ice cream topped with chocolate sauce and marshmallow creme. Frank enjoyed watching his daughter relish each spoonful. A man shouldn't squander a night like this drinking himself to oblivion in a stinking saloon.

Tonight father and daughter lingered at the sidewalk table until Marie said she was getting sleepy. Frank walked her back to the hotel and tucked her into bed. Then he left in search of Bernard and oblivion.

Chapter 17

April 1905

One bare lightbulb lit the Inn's cavernous kitchen when Mrs. Jelinek arrived at work just before midnight. She plopped her large handbag on the counter and set about her routine. One by one she tugged the chains of the remaining three lights which set them swinging and casting sweeping shadows.

It was Monday night, and she had already put in a shift cleaning the Sokol Hall. Monday was the worst, having to lug cartloads of trash and mop floors sticky with beer after Saturday polka fests.

But now at the Inn, she made two ham sandwiches, which she ate greedily, as it was her first meal of the day. She followed the sandwich with a hardboiled egg and a glass of milk.

Then it was time to make kolaches, and she fell into the familiar routine, her eye telling her just how much sponge, milk, sugar, and butter to use. Counting overflowing scoops of flour was her one concession to measuring.

While stirring she imagined herself standing in her own little kitchen back in Bohemia where her son Miklos would lick his lips and rub his belly as he watched her. When the pans of fragrant pastry came out of the oven, the sixteen-year-old boy would clap his hands and squeal, to the disgust of his father and four siblings. Picturing him now, she wiped copious tears with her apron.

She remembered having to leave her tiny house in Bohemia when her husband was promised a steady job at a cigar factory in Riverbend, where his cousin had worked his way up to supervisor. She had wept often in the days before their departure. Even a final farewell to the pigs and chickens brought sobs, which she had to muffle as the family was sneaking away under the veil of darkness. The pigs would more than pay the landowner the back rent he claimed to be owed.

On board ship it seemed the steerage passengers vied to tell the most outrageous stories about Ellis Island. One rumor Mrs. Jelinek's husband reported to her set her weeping loud and often: "They don't let nobody in what's crazy in the head or deaf, dumb, or blind or got a disease. They send people back for so much as looking dreamy-eyed."

Mrs. Jelinek warned Miklos to say nothing unless someone asked him a question. She drilled him over and over because his head would not hold her words for long. After the ship docked at Ellis Island, a photographer—later Mrs. Jelinek discovered he worked for a Bohemian-American newspaper—shot a picture of the boy in his high-water pants and boots about three sizes too large. He was grinning and holding a little American flag.

Miklos stayed close by his mother on the walk from the ship to the immigration processing center. Standing in an endless line, Mrs. Jelinek prayed Miklos would not attract the attention of the uniformed inspector who carried the dreaded blue chalk to mark the lapel of anyone suspected of carrying disease or becoming a burden to society. Those bearing the blue X were pulled from the line for further examination.

"Stop squirming." Mrs. Jelinek knew the heat of the room

made Miklos' woolen jacket prickly.

He started to scratch, occasionally at first, then in a frenzy that caught the eye of an inspector. Seeing the uniform, Miklos snapped to attention. The inspector looked directly into his eyes and frowned. Miklos looked back and frowned. The inspector's frown deepened. So did Miklos. The inspector scratched his own head. Miklos did the same. The inspector strode toward Miklos, grabbed his lapel with one hand, and brought out a piece of chalk from his pocket with the other. Miklos reached for the inspector's lapel, but the inspector grabbed his arm, whirled him around, and pinned his arms behind his back. Miklos whimpered. The inspector let go of his arms, marked his lapel with an X, and moved on.

Amid the stares and whispers of others waiting in line, Mrs. Jelinek clutched her son, almost as tall as she was, and rocked from side to side until a second inspector wrenched him from her arms and led him away.

After the family completed processing, they were directed to a small, crowded room where they sat waiting to learn of Miklos' fate. It came through a translator: "Your son has failed the simple tests and must be deported. The shipping line will pay for his passage. Who will meet him at the boat?"

Mrs. Jelinek begged the inspector to let her accompany Miklos, but her husband spoke loudly over her objections, naming his brother and sister-in-law, who would almost certainly put Miklos in an institution. Seized by an idea, Mrs. Jelinek threw back her head, thrust out her chest, raised her elbows, and crowed like a rooster. Her husband grabbed her, and the interpreter let her know that no one would fall for her act so she might as well settle down.

Subdued, she went with the family to say good-bye to Miklos. With no idea of what was happening, he mirrored her choking sobs. It was when the men took him away and he looked back over his shoulder at his mother as though she could save him, that she collapsed.

A slap across her face brought her back to consciousness, and she gazed up at the fuzzy image of her husband. He lifted her to her feet, and she followed with a leaden shuffle as he guided the family out of the building to their new life in America, to a home in which any mention of Miklos was forbidden.

In spite of her husband's order, Mrs. Jelinek enlisted her eldest son to write and post letters to Miklos—she dictated them once a week. She wondered if anyone read the letters to him. No one ever wrote back.

Mr. Jelinek's job was not all it was cracked up to be. It could take years to advance from cigar roller to a decent-paying supervisor's job. He took to spending his free time in the saloon. The two oldest children left home. To pay the rent and avoid eviction from the house Mrs. Jelinek's cousin owned, the two remaining children quit school and took jobs, and Mrs. Jelinek went to work at Riverview Inn baking bread, pies, and kolaches. Eventually she hired on at the Sokol Hall as well.

Work offered a refuge from her husband's drunken rampages—they occurred almost nightly—and his flailing fists.

One day Mrs. Jelinek shyly approached the stern-looking man who taught English classes at the Sokol Hall. Learning some English was essential to carrying out the plan in her head. And so she attended classes three evenings a week. Her crying spells became less frequent. To anyone who cared to notice, it seemed she had quit grieving over Miklos and accepted her new home.

But she needed more than English. She needed money. Her husband's drunken sprees became opportunity. On the nights he took off his pants before falling into bed, she pilfered cash from his pockets and stashed it on a shelf under her corsets.

Tonight, once the kolaches were in the oven and emitting their yeasty aroma, Mrs. Jelinek made another sandwich, this time with meatloaf. By skipping meals during the day and eating only as she worked during the night, she was able to squirrel away pennies, nickels, and dimes from her grocery allowance.

In the morning, before the Inn's cook arrived, she stuffed her canvas tote bag with butter, eggs, pork chops, and potatoes.

*　*　*

AWAKENED BEFORE DAWN BY AN insistent knock on the kitchen door, Louise grabbed her robe and stepped into her slippers. She opened the door to see the cook, her chest heaving from climbing the stairs.

"That Mrs. Jelinek," the cook said. "I catched her stealing."

Louise followed the cook to the Inn's kitchen where Mrs. Jelinek stood with her head bowed, her rough, red hands twisting her apron. On the table where she had made kolaches and bread sat her tote, bearing a telltale grease stain, and next to it, all the food she had stuffed in it.

The cook clattered about, hoisting pans, firing up the griddle, and beating batter in preparation for breakfast.

Louise directed Mrs. Jelinek to sit at the desk in the corner of the kitchen. Sitting across from the baker, she nodded toward the evidence. "You've been stealing from me."

"Not you." Mrs. Jelinek shook her head emphatically. "Kitchen."

"When you steal from the kitchen, you steal from me." Louise considered how Frank dealt with pilferers. He fired them on the spot, but before they could leave he made an example of them to other employees.

"I pay you well," Louise said. "Why do you steal?"

"My boy Miklos, Bohemia." She pointed to her head and shook it.

"You left him in Bohemia?"

Mrs. Jelinek nodded.

"You send him money?"

"No."

"Why did you steal?"

"People not want Miklos. People not care Miklos. Miklos big boy," she held her hand above her head, "little child," she pointed to her head. "Miklos need Mama."

"Are you going back to Bohemia?"

Tears welled in the woman's eyes and spilled onto her ruddy cheeks. She wiped her nose and eyes with her apron. Then she reached in her handbag and took out a rumpled newspaper clipping. She laid it on the table and tried to smooth its wrinkles before showing it to her employer.

A boy holding an American flag stood in front of a ship, surrounded by expectant-looking immigrants.

"He came to America?" Louise asked.

Mrs. Jelinek nodded. "No good." She pointed again to her head.

"Did they send him back to Bohemia?"

"Yah."

Louise had a wifely duty to uphold her husband's standards. But Frank was miles away. "Come back to work tonight." From the corner of her eye, Louise noticed the cook's disapproving glance. "Don't steal again."

Mrs. Jelinek looked down, wringing her apron.

"You're free to go now."

Louise reflected on her decision. Frank would be furious if he found out. But firing Mrs. Jelinek would have been foolish, as no one else knew how to make kolaches. Kolaches, Louise realized, were the perfect justification for doing what her heart commanded when she put herself in Mrs. Jelinek's place.

*   *   *

THAT NIGHT LOUISE ENTERED THE kitchen just as Mrs. Jelinek was taking butter from the electric icebox. The woman hastened to drop the butter into a saucepan, causing the heated milk to hiss and spatter when it splashed onto the hot stove.

Louise held up a thick wad of cash. "You teach me how to make kolaches. This should be enough to get you back home to Miklos."

Mrs. Jelinek scowled, and Louise tried again to get her point across. "You go home to Miklos. But first teach me kolaches."

Louise slipped on an apron and wrapped its strings twice around her waist. Then she opened the flour bin and lifted a scoop of flour. "You teach me."

Mrs. Jelinek's eyes brightened. "Ahh."

Louise signaled for the baker to wait while she got a pad and pencil from her desk.

She questioned the wisdom of helping the woman leave, especially given that just this morning Buster, the Inn's building superintendent, had quit. But she resolved to handle matters on her own without bothering Frank.

She watched the baker and wrote down her every move. Sometimes Mrs. Jelinek would gesture for her to help by sifting the flour, forming the dough into balls, and setting them on the baking sheet. Occasionally the baker would try to explain something about the filling or dough. Grating lemon rind for the sweet cottage cheese filling, she pointed to the underlying white rind, made a sour face, and shook her head. Louise already knew what the woman was trying to tell her, that the white rind would make the filling bitter, but nodded appreciatively nevertheless.

As the little balls of dough were rising, Louise helped make the fillings. Tonight's were apricot, poppyseed, and lemon. While mixing sugar, butter, and flour for the topping, she referred to it as *streusel*.

"Not *streusel*," Mrs. Jelinek said firmly. "*Popsika.*"

"Popsika," Louise said.

Louise made the next batch under Mrs. Jelinek's watchful eye. Come time to remove them from the oven, she admired their delicate golden color and uniform size.

Mrs. Jelinek nodded in approval.

Louise handed her the money. "Go ahead, take it with my blessing. This is payment for teaching me."

Holding her apron to her gaping mouth, the baker gushed with "thank-yous."

*   *   *

TWO WEEKS AFTER MRS. JELINEK'S departure, as much as Louise wanted to hire a baker, she was desperate to hire a new building superintendent. In the afternoon a hired girl knocked on her door, coming to tell her a man named Lars was waiting in the dining room.

Louise had already interviewed two men. One seemed earnest and reliable enough but lacked experience. The other impressed her with his experience, but he changed jobs frequently, and when asked why said he just got restless to move on. Perhaps the third would be a charm.

She went into the dining room, empty except for a wiry man with hair that resembled straw she mucked in the horse barns as a girl. He sat at a table and dug at his fingernails with a pocketknife. When he saw her he snapped the knife shut and jammed it in the pocket of his ragged overalls.

He stood when Louise approached. "Heard you was looking for a man."

His teeth were rotten, and his breath stank like raw sewage. "I'm sorry, sir, but I hired a fellow just this morning."

His glare set the hairs on the back of her neck bristling.

"If you say so, ma'am." He snarled the words.

Louise would have taken anyone else seeking work to the kitchen and asked the cook to make a sandwich or two before sending him away. Not Lars.

He left. She watched from the window until he was out of sight.

Chapter 18

June 1905

It was another sultry night, and the canvas walls of the Chautauqua tent in Rapid City, South Dakota, had been rolled up for the health and comfort of the audience. Standing just outside the tent and as close to the stage as possible, Frank and Marie awaited the appearance of Marie's idol who was to be the night's much-anticipated final act. It would be the first appearance for Helen Keller on the Chautauqua stage, she and the former Annie Sullivan having joined the tour after the honeymoon of Annie and John Macy.

Marie whispered. "Have you seen them? Where are they now?"

"Be patient. She's going to tell what it's like to be blind and deaf, and then she'll answer questions from the audience."

"But how can Miss Keller be a presenter if she can't see or hear? Can she speak?"

"Not so you can understand her," Frank said. "Mrs. Macy can understand her, though. She's her translator."

"Who is Mrs. Macy?"

"Anne Sullivan Macy. She's the one who taught Miss Keller how to . . . here they come."

The crowd rose applauding and waving white handkerchiefs in the Chautauqua salute.

"Tell me what she looks like," Marie said.

"Serene and lovely, like an angel. Wearing a smart-looking blouse with a big lace collar, a red hat, and her hair—"

"Tell me about her eyes."

The crowd sat down and grew silent.

"Her eyes are blue," Frank whispered.

Mrs. Macy spoke first, describing her education of Miss Keller. Then she invited the mayor to help demonstrate how Miss Keller could "listen" to someone without an interpreter.

"How are you enjoying your visit to our fair town?" the mayor asked.

"Tell me," Marie said.

Frank whispered. "Miss Keller 'listens' by placing her fingers on the mayor's throat, mouth, and the side of his nose." He placed Marie's hand in this manner on his face. "She feels the words instead of hearing them."

Then Miss Keller spoke. The sound emitted by the lovely young woman only vaguely resembled words. Absent were the vocal changes that give meaning and color to speech. Instead her pitch and volume meandered.

Marie gasped. "I can't understand her."

"Few people can," Frank whispered. "Just listen, and Mrs. Macy will interpret."

* * *

IN THE DAYS LEADING UP to Marie's birthday, Louise's melancholy set in. She rattled around in the afternoon void and would have welcomed hearing the repetitive scales she used to find annoying. And she longed to hear certain musical phrases, especially her favorite in Pachelbel's "Canon."

With her daughter hundreds of miles away, Louise brooded

about life's unfairness. Fueling her bitterness was an item in the *Nonpareil's* social news about Doc having just returned from a European vacation. Knowing as she did that the late Mrs. Foster had suffered from gonorrhea, Louise was certain it was Doc, not Frank, who had caused Marie's blindness. Yet he suffered no consequences. Often as she thought about him, she contemplated revenge. But she could never act on it, never risk hurting Frank and Marie. The telephone rang—the three short rings that identified it as a call for the Morrissey home. She accepted the collect call from Frank. "Hello."

"I'm putting Marie on. She wants to tell you all about her birthday celebration."

"Hello, Mother?"

"Yes, Marie." Already Louise had a lump in her throat.

"We had a party at the ice cream shoppe, and you'll never guess who came." Without waiting for a reply, she went on. "Well, there was Father, of course, Mr. Science, Mr. And Mrs. Ryder—I knew they'd be there. But the big surprise was Miss Keller and Mrs. Macy. And guess what? Miss Keller's birthday is just two weeks after mine, so we celebrated hers, too. She's twenty-five, though, and I'm only ten. Father says we'll notch the doorframe as soon as we get home. It won't show exactly how tall I was on my birthday, but it will have to do. Do you know what else? Miss Keller and I got to fly kites together. And Father says to tell you my piano lessons are going splendidly."

"I'm so lonesome for you," Louise said. "I'm going to buy you a new dress and embroider it for you to wear at the Riverbend Chautauqua."

"I hope it will have lots of flowers. Miss Keller likes to brush my hair. And guess what? She taught me to make little yarn dolls. First you wrap yarn around a piece of cardboard to make the doll's body, then you wrap another piece of yarn the other way for the arms, then you make yarn braids. The hardest part is cutting out a circle of felt for a skirt. Miss Keller showed me how to fold a felt square two times, then cut off the tip to make a hole for the doll's waist and cut an arc through the four layers of fabric to make a circle for the hem. Yesterday I made one without any help. Her name is Sunny because she's yellow, like the sun. She's for you."

Louise wondered if Marie still had the adorable habit of moving her mouth when she cut with scissors. She barely managed to speak without sobbing. "I'm counting the days until I get to see you . . . and Sunny."

Frank's voice could be heard in the background. "Hey, Junior, make it snappy. This call costs money."

"Frank, don't hang up yet." Louise choked back the tears.

"Here's Father."

"Louise?"

"Frank?" Louise wasn't sure when she'd have another chance to talk to Frank about the Inn and hoped that turning the conversation to practical matters would stop the tears.

"Yes, go on."

"There have been some staffing problems that I didn't want to bother you with, but they're resolved now. I had to let Mrs. Jelinek go because she was pilfering food from the kitchen, but I hired a new baker."

"Does she make kolaches?"

"Yes. She's learning Mrs. Jelinek's recipe, and I think she'll get along just fine."

"What else?"

"Buster quit."

"Why? He was a good worker."

"He said he couldn't take orders from a woman. The new man's name is Harley. He just came north from Tennessee."

"How's he working out?"

"He's good, but slow. If you saw him you'd say you have to drive a stake next to him to tell if he's moving. And we need to talk about making some sanitary improvements. Some of our regular guests are starting to complain about germs. Mrs. Hyde says New York passed a law requiring hotels to use nine-foot long sheets."

"What for?" Frank asked. "Nine-foot long beds?"

"Of course not. The top sheet gets folded over the blanket to prevent guests' faces from coming into contact with germs on the blanket."

"That's New York for you," Frank said. "I guarantee you that nonsense won't catch on in Nebraska."

"And that's not all. Up-to-date hotels install window screens in the summer to keep out flies and mosquitoes because of the germs they carry. And wood is no longer acceptable in water closets."

"I suppose it's a haven for germs," Frank said.

"That's right. Mrs. Hyde says she can't stomach a water closet with wood floors."

"Well, Mrs. Hyde would be hard-pressed to find fancy tile in hotels in Nebraska. You know what that would cost? Riverview Inn was fine enough for the King of Prussia, it's fine enough for Mrs. Hyde. You know what I think? You have too much time on your hands without me and Marie to fuss over. One good thing about this 'sanitary revolution,' though—housewives will stand in line to buy the Whirlwind Maid."

Frank was so predictable. He would complain to Bernard about how germ talk had gone too far when lawmakers could tell hotel owners what kind of sheets they could use. Then Bernard would impress upon him the ease with which dreaded diseases are communicated. Frank would ruminate on the matter, and before long he would tell her to make sanitary improvements to the hotel and think it was his own idea.

After the call, Louise went to the kitchen and fingered each of the nine notches on the doorframe. She remembered Marie on her first birthday, wiggling as Frank tried to make the first notch. On her sixth birthday, she tried to trick him by standing on her tiptoes. And on her ninth birthday—the pony cart accident overtook Louise's reminiscence.

She went to the breakfast room and collapsed into a chair, her elbows on the table and her head in her hands. Missing the ritual stirred up the deepest longing for her daughter and something more. It was grief for the baby and child Marie had once been and the ache of not knowing the child she was becoming.

* * *

Ten days after Marie's birthday, Louise picked up her mail at the Inn's desk, and on top of the stack was an envelope addressed in a childish hand. The shape of the letters, flattened at the bottom, suggested the writer had used a ruler as a guide. The envelope was postmarked Valentine, Nebraska. Louise opened it and began to read, "Dear Mother . . ." There must be some mistake.

Surprise. Mrs. Macy is teaching me how to write.
She taught Miss Keller. I miss you. We are in
Valentine. The park has a statue and Father lets me
climb on it. It is fun.
Love,
Marie

Louise clutched the letter to her breast and wept with joy and with longing to wrap her arms around her daughter. Staring at the page with its cockeyed lettering, she could picture Marie biting her lip as she labored over each pencil stroke. It was her nature to practice until she became proficient. Her mother's daughter. Louise's melancholy lifted. Marie had a most promising future.

* * *

FRANK WAS ON A SALESMAN'S high. Not the fleeting high that comes with a big order; that kind of high carries the knowledge that next month you'd have to go out and do it all over again. Not the high that comes from trouncing the competition; that kind of high means some poor sap like yourself is hurting. Not the high that comes when making the big sale rescues you from the brink, the point at which you were about to sell your wife's almost new electric icebox to make ends meet. No, Frank's high was the mountain climber's exhilaration upon nearing the summit, the drowning man's relief upon seeing a rescuer's rope, and getting rip-roaring drunk, all rolled into one.

Frank Morrissey had a salesman's high from being onto a sure thing. Two sure things, in fact. The first was that orders for the Whirlwind Maid exceeded his projections such that Tom even had to hire back two laid-off bicycle mechanics to meet demand.

Marie was his other sure thing. Audiences adored her. She could be the child elocutionist for two, possibly three, years before she would become too mature for the role. By then he would be able to convince Ryder to keep her on as a piano soloist. Her piano teacher, in his broken English, had already called her a "prodigy," and said her beauty, stage presence, and blindness would ensure her future popularity.

In Frank's blueprint the Chautauqua served as the springboard to the concert stage. When Marie became a young woman, he would hire a companion for her, and he would stop traveling. She would have a satisfying life after he and Louise were gone. Louise might scoff at his grandiose plan, but he knew what he was doing.

Chapter 19

It being Friday, Louise totaled the week's receipts, prepared the bank deposit, and placed it in her satchel. She joined Yonder at his table in the Inn's dining room, and when he finished breakfast she picked up the satchel, and they left the Inn by the side door to the porte cochère.

A light breeze carried the fragrance of honeysuckle from the bushes that lined the drive. As they approached the carriage house, it began to sprinkle. Fat drops pelted Louise's face, and she stopped abruptly. "Umbrellas. I'll get them, and you can bring the car around for me."

Yonder continued on to the carriage house, and Louise turned back. As she neared the porte cochère, she glimpsed a flash of movement through the honeysuckle bushes. A man leaped out. She froze, clutched the satchel to her chest. *Lars.* The glint of a blade, hatred in his eyes.

She ran for the door. "Stop! Thief!"

From behind came the foul breath she remembered, then a hand on her arm. His other hand jerked the bag, but she held it tight and wrenched it away, generating forward momentum that caused her to stumble. Her ankle twisted. Holding the bag close to her body, she braced her fall with a hand and landed with the satchel beneath her, striking her forehead on the brick paving. Unable to move, she stiffened, expecting a knife blade in her back, wishing she'd surrendered the satchel. But there was only stillness and no sign of the work boots and pant legs she'd glimpsed when she went down.

Hearing footsteps, she rolled over to one side and raised herself to her elbow. "Don't let him get away," she called to Yonder who was running toward her. "I'm all right."

Yonder spun around and dashed into the woods.

Louise sucked in air, clenched her teeth, and held her breath as though that might stop the pain. Her heart pounding, she clutched the satchel and scooted over to the building and sat with her back to the wall.

Yonder returned minutes later shaking his head. "He must not have followed the path or I'd have seen him."

By now a crowd of Inn guests and staff had gathered.

Yonder, his wrinkled brow expressing his concern, knelt next to Louise. "You're trembling."

"I'm scared. Think what could have happened."

"You're safe now. Don't try to stand. Do you think anything is broken?"

Louise shook her throbbing head. "I think my ankle is just sprained." She noticed the brief shower had passed; there'd have been no need for umbrellas.

A man came towards them. "Can I help?"

"You can hold the door for us." With that, Yonder picked her up. Giving a nod to the man, he carried Louise inside and through the hallway that led to the lobby and stairs.

The people who were gathered in the lobby stopped talking and stared. Mrs. Monfort, working at the front desk, gave a loud gasp.

Louise gave them a wave. "It's nothing serious."

As they went up the stairs, Louise felt the rise and fall of Yonder's chest and found comfort in the warmth of his body and his familiar Ivory-soap scent.

When he got to her front door, he said, "Can you open it?"

She turned the handle, gave the door a shove, and wondered if it occurred to him that one day he would carry Giovanna across a threshold in similar fashion.

When they reached the back parlor, he seated her in her favorite chair. He took the satchel from her and placed it on another chair.

Henryetta rushed to them. "Mercy sakes, what happened to you? Look at that goose egg, will you?"

Louise touched the bump, which felt enormous. "That man who was here looking for work about a couple of weeks ago, he tried to get the satchel, and I fell."

"He'd been here before?" Yonder's concerned look turned to one of surprise. "I only got a glimpse of him when he ran into the woods, but I'm almost sure he was the man sitting on the loafers bench when we went to the bank last week."

Henryetta lifted Louise's feet onto the ottoman, and Louise raised her skirt to expose the swollen ankle.

"I'll get an old sheet," Henryetta said. "Yonder, fetch something nice and cold from the icebox she can hold on her head, maybe the package of bacon."

Yonder left and returned with the bacon, which Louise held to her temple.

Louise smiled. "I'm going to smell like bacon all day."

"Louise, I'm so sorry," Yonder said. "I should never have left your side."

"It's my fault. I wasn't thinking when I told you to go get

the car. I should have kept you close."

Henryetta came back with a sheet, which she began tearing into strips. A knock at the front door interrupted her bandage-making. When she returned from answering the door, she was shaking her head. "Sheriff has the manners of a billy goat. He would have come right on in here except I told him to wait in the front parlor until I wrapped your foot."

Louise pointed to an afghan on another chair. "Cover me up and have him come in. Let's not keep him from going after Lars. You can wrap my ankle later."

While Henryetta went to get Sheriff Andy Maguire, Yonder draped the afghan over Louise's lap and legs. She noted that, being a gentleman, he had averted his eyes from her exposed ankles.

Henryetta escorted the sheriff into the room. The tall, lanky man may have lacked manners, but he never forgot the people he owed favors, and Frank had helped him get elected in a close race. "I'd have gotten here sooner, but I been talking to the folks downstairs who give me a description of the thief. My men been suspicious of him ever since he showed up in town. Probably rides the rails from one place to another, commits a few petty crimes, and moves on. Henryetta here says he come to the Inn about a month ago?"

"He claimed he was looking for work," Louise said. "His name is Lars. I wish I'd learned his last name, but he frightened me. I was so eager to get rid of him I didn't so much as offer him a sandwich."

The sheriff cracked his knuckles, first one hand, then the other. "How'd he know you'd have a satchel full of deposits?"

"Yonder remembered seeing him when we left the bank

last week. He must have seen us and figured it was our regular time to make deposits. But he'd have seen Yonder, too. Why would he risk coming after me if he thought Yonder would be with me?"

The sheriff looked at Yonder. "Where were you when he attacked?"

"I was bringing the car around while Mrs. Morrissey waited under the porte cochère."

The sheriff cracked his knuckles again. "Some things are beyond explaining. Your typical criminal isn't very smart. He might could've thought Mrs. Morrissey would be alone." He turned to Louise with a sympathetic look. "Now, don't you worry. If he's still in the vicinity, we'll get him. But I have a hunch he's moved on."

That night Louise's body and mind conspired against sleep. Her temple throbbed as much as her sprained ankle. Ordinary night sounds—beams creaking, a shutter rattling—jarred her from a light slumber to skin-tingling wakefulness.

But after a time, fear overrode pain. *What if Lars returns? Don't be a fool. The man is miles away by now.* In an effort to still her pounding heart, she took deep breaths and in time fell off to sleep, only to dream of Lars looking up from cleaning his fingernails and lunging at her with his pocketknife. Only it wasn't Lars, it was Pa.

She sat bolt upright and called out, "Yonder!" She awakened, searching for her friend's protection. But of course he wasn't there. Her trembling hand went to the nightstand where the cold metal of the gun's barrel assured her that she could defend herself against Lars. Her mind willed her to rest, and she lay back on the pillow, but her body was still on high alert. Suddenly she was struck with another fear: what would be her defense if she called out Yonder's name with Frank lying next to her?

CHAPTER 20

July 1905

From Valentine, the Chautauqua traveled one hundred sixty miles to Alliance, Nebraska. After the opening night's show there, Frank took Marie for ice cream, then after tucking her in bed in the hotel room went to the saloon to meet Bernard.

Frank spied Bernard, caught the barkeep's eye, and held up two fingers. He sat down, and the barkeep brought two beers.

Frank took a long drink, smacked his lips, and exhaled. "I couldn't get away with that at home. Louise frowns on a man enjoying his beer too much—says it's behavior unbecoming a gentleman." He raised his mug. "Here's to good drinking buddies forever."

Bernard raised his mug. "To good drinking buddies."

The men clinked mugs and drank.

"But not forever," Bernard said. "At least not on the Chautauqua circuit."

"What do you mean? Don't tell me they're putting you out to pasture."

"I told you it was my last season. The wife wants me at home, and I vowed I'd quit while I'm on top and the Chautauqua is on top. "

Frank's stomach felt hollow. He shook his head. "You never told me."

"Did, too. You were too drunk to remember. The motion picture will be the end of the traveling Chautauqua. You watch, pretty soon every town in America will have a Nickleodeon, and the next thing you know they'll have *talking* motion pictures. Then who will come to see the likes of us? I'm going into business with my little brother—Feldman Brothers Enterprises."

Frank could not imagine the Chautauqua without Bernard. "What kind of business?"

"Manufacturing. Ceiling fans to start, then we'll diversify."

"In Omaha?"

Bernard nodded.

Frank shook his head. "Labor costs will kill you. Hope your baby brother knows something about manufacturing. I'll wager *you* don't."

"What he knows is an untapped market when he sees one. Summers are brutal, and folks want comfort. They go to the mercantile and feel that cool air from the circulating fans and they want that same luxurious feeling at home. Not to mention the salutary effects on their health from getting rid of stale air. We'll hire a fellow to run the manufacturing side."

Frank eyed his empty mug. "Think you can win us a round?"

Bernard motioned the barkeep to the table. He took a coin from his pocket and drew around it on a piece of paper. Then he carefully tore out the hole, took a larger coin from his pocket, and challenged the barkeep to put that coin through the hole without tearing the paper.

The befuddled man turned the coin every which way but could not fit it through the hole. He threw up his hands.

Bernard folded and creased the paper so the hole made a half circle, unfolded the paper partway, and slipped the coin through. The flummoxed barkeep shook his head and produced the drinks.

Frank gave the barkeep a sympathetic look. "He never ceases to amaze me with his bag of tricks. He does this every night."

Bernard said, "It's survival. When I was a boy, Mama would give me money to buy a soup bone, I'd go to the butcher shop, make a wager like that with the butcher, and bring home a pot roast."

"The funny thing is," Frank said after the barkeep left, "you don't take advantage of it. You tip like you're the Prince of Siam even though tomorrow night that fellow will rake in the dough making bets he can pass a coin through a little hole in a piece of paper."

Bernard said, "Spread the wealth, I say." He took a deep breath as he always did when he was about to wax philosophical. "I'm getting to be an old man, on the brink of 'second childishness and mere oblivion,' as Shakespeare put it. It's the oblivion that we mortals fear most."

Frank interrupted. "A kindred spirit. You, me, Ozymandias."

Bernard went on. "I spend many an hour contemplating my legacy. The wife and I have everything we need or want, we've invested wisely, and I expect to make a fortune in manufacturing. Philanthropy, that's my ultimate calling, especially children's charities. 'The Feldman Brothers Foundation.' Mark my words, one day the Feldman name will be synonymous with good works."

"So you're really going to do it, you're not coming back,"

Frank said. "Guess I'll have to pay my own bar bill."

"Don't count your chickens 'til they're hatched," Bernard said.

"What do you mean?"

Bernard leaned forward, speaking in a confidential tone. "You see Durfee hanging around the show tonight?"

"Why wouldn't he? He owns the show. I'd expect him to check on how it's doing."

Bernard looked dead serious. "Rumor has it Durfee wants his granddaughter to be child elocutionist for one of his circuits, and it could be ours."

*   *   *

ARRIVING IN SCOTTSBLUFF, NEBRASKA, EARLY in the afternoon a week later, Frank and Marie stopped at the newspaper office before going to the hotel. While the staff gushed over Marie, Frank looked at the paper's front-page announcement of the Chautauqua, gratified to find The Chautauqua Darling prominently featured. He always bought up extra newspapers to pass around to presenters and ordered copies of the next week's paper, which would carry Chautauqua reviews, to be sent to him at the tour's next stop.

Once settled in the hotel room, Frank sat on a bed and opened the cardboard box filled with newspapers, trinkets people gave to Marie, a scrapbook, and a cigar box containing scissors, paste, pencils, pens, ink, and crayons. He carefully clipped the article from *The Scottsbluff Standard* and glued it on a blank page in the scrapbook.

"Read to me." Marie sat down beside him.

"It says, 'Acclaimed Blind Child Elocutionist Marie Alouette

Morrissey will delight Chautauqua audiences with her gifted recitations.'" He flipped back a few pages in the scrapbook. "Here's our favorite review: 'Marie Alouette Morrissey is a *tour de force.* This little charmer declaims with such eloquence that she drives the audience to the depths of despair then lifts them to giddy heights of laughter.'"

Marie squealed her delight.

Whenever Marie became homesick and melancholy, Frank comforted her with the scrapbook and trinkets. He took out her favorite gifts and mementos from the box and described them in detail, and they reminisced about their odyssey.

Frank's collection of reviews had more than sentimental value. It was part of his calculation to win Marie a contract for another year.

* * *

LOOKING IN THE MIRROR LOUISE coaxed curls into a becoming frame of her face under her straw sunbonnet. Then she put on her gardening gloves, picked up her weeding tool, and went to the tulip bed. It wasn't in dire need of weeding, but Yonder would be working nearby on this beautiful summer morning. Lately something was on her mind, a discussion she hoped would satisfy a yearning for a deeper connection with her good friend. But would it be appropriate, given that she was a married woman and he was betrothed? And how obvious would it be, this pretext to be near him?

From the tulip bed, she watched unseen as Yonder carried the new wooden trellis Frank had bought but never gotten around to installing. Her eyes lingered on the graceful movement of his lean body as he gently placed the purple flowering clematis on the ground and dismantled the old flimsy trellis.

He wrestled with the new trellis, and she realized he was trying to set it in wet concrete without trampling the vine it would support. The job required two people, exactly the excuse she needed. She stood and walked toward him, stepping around the scraps of wood he'd tossed aside. "Would you like some help?"

"Thanks. If you'll hold it steady until I get it anchored." He knelt and planted the trellis legs in the wet concrete.

Holding the trellis while he smoothed the concrete, she looked down at his back and drank in his familiar Ivory soap fragrance. She didn't notice that he'd finished anchoring the legs to the last support until she heard, "Louise, you can let go."

He stood.

Trying to hide her embarrassment at getting caught in reverie, she bent down to pull a lone dandelion. Yonder reached for it at the same time. They bumped heads, which set them laughing with the abandon of school children.

"That dandelion deserves to live." Yonder reached up and adjusted her sunbonnet.

The gesture, so casual yet so intimate, made her giddy. "My sentiments exactly." The look they held felt like souls touching, but was the feeling shared? Could she truly talk with him about anything?

She pointed to the wheelbarrow as he tossed in scraps of wood. "This may sound silly, but looking at that old trellis with most of its paint flaked off, it seems something of a metaphor."

Yonder's brow wrinkled. "A metaphor?"

"What I mean is, it was once raw wood before it was made into a trellis and painted."

"And before that it was a tree."

Putting her thoughts into words wasn't working. They wanted to lodge in her throat. "Yes. Well it made me think—in fact, it's something I've thought about for years but I didn't know who else would understand." She took off her gloves and regarded her manicured hands. "I worry about not being authentic. And I wonder," she looked at him, "do you remember where you were and how old you were when you began practicing to be someone you weren't?"

She didn't know what to make of his furrowed brow. At least he wasn't laughing at her. She went on. "For me it was after I started school." Recalling the ragamuffin taunts and Pa's lecherous hands, she crossed her arms and held herself as though against a cold wind. "If I were ever to escape, I had to imitate my teacher—the way she talked and walked and never chewed her fingernails. What about you?"

"It was the same for me. A teacher took me under her wing. That's when I first heard my name pronounced 'Yonder' instead of 'Yon-dare.'"

"I often worry about where the real Louise ends and the artificial, made-up one begins."

"I still grapple with that. I've almost completely given up being Indian."

"Considering what I've learned from you about assimilation, isn't that a matter of survival?"

He turned and tossed his work gloves into the wheelbarrow. When he looked back at her there was resignation in his unsmiling eyes. "As I get older and perhaps wiser, I've come to regret my role in the white man's myth. The boarding schools are just another way to oppress the Indian. Like reservations.

What's lacking is a meaningful, systematic path to acceptance by white society. That's what I've been advocating for too many years without success."

"Oh, Yonder." She placed a hand on his arm. "But look at you." Concerned that her hand lingering on his arm could be construed as a caress, she withdrew it. "You're a respected policymaker. Your fiancée's family accepts you. It may take time, but—"

He shook his head. "I'm the token Indian that people like to show off. I've assimilated, and my children's children won't even know their Santee Sioux heritage."

Yonder, a father and grandfather? Whether he was speaking rhetorically or hopefully, she stiffened with envy that Giovanna might bear his child and know the joy of motherhood without the cloud of an illicit union over her head. If she didn't squelch these thoughts, she feared she might break down. "Frank always says to be an American means letting go of our roots. Tradition is for people who would stop progress. We're a melting pot."

"Not everyone is welcome in that pot," Yonder said. "I should have recognized the goal of assimilation was subjugation of the Indian. Take children far from their homes to boarding schools, punish them if they dare to speak their native language. Mock their *pagan* spirits and teach them to sing 'The Old Rugged Cross' and so they forget the comforting 'Song of the Bear.' And to what end?"

His jaw tensed. "Take Sammy Beddow. Navaho, an excellent student, wanted to be a bookkeeper. He tried to get on at a dozen or more places. Finally the railroad hired him. Not to keep their books. No, an Indian's place is doing back-breaking work for low wages. So he's a gandy dancer."

"I had no idea. It's so unfair. I don't know what to say."

Yonder shook his head as though to absolve her of guilt and placed his tools in the wheelbarrow. He nodded toward the trellis and grinned. "Frank will be pleased that you're no longer nagging him to replace that broken trellis."

Louise was grateful for the change of subject. "He telephoned last night. He says when they return Marie will talk your head off about all she's learned from Mr. Science."

Yonder gripped the handles of the wheelbarrow, which tipped a bit from the uneven load. He set it down and shifted the bag of concrete to the center. "I shall be leaving in September, soon after they return from the Chatauqua tour."

Louise scowled. So soon? "Where will you go?"

"San Diego. I'll start working with Giovanna's father."

She looked at the clematis lying heaped on the ground. It would be Yonder who would pick it up and restore it to the trellis where it would thrive. That's what he was to her, a nurturing friend. Without him there was a part of her that could not thrive. She forced a smile. "Do you have a wedding date?"

He nodded. "March twenty-fourth. She still has this sentimental notion we should get married on her parents' anniversary."

"I'm happy for you, Yonder." She hoped her voice didn't betray her selfish longing to hold onto his comforting presence. "You deserve to have more of a life than is possible here."

In the heat of the late morning sun, she was beginning to perspire. She wiped her forehead with a glove. "I can't bring myself to tell Frank and Marie about your leaving just yet. It will break Marie's heart."

*   *   *

When another letter arrived from Marie, Louise held the envelope and traced its letters with her finger before opening it. She smiled, picturing Marie as she labored to make each letter.

Dear Mother,

Today we went to a park and I climbed on six statues of pioneers and horses and a covered wagon.

Guess what? A boy likes me and I like him. His name is Dan. He sings in the Children's Chorus. I miss you.

Your loving daughter,
Marie

Louise wanted to reach out and hold her daughter and never let go. *She knows nothing about boys. If only I were there. Frank must put a stop to this.*

CHAPTER 21

It had been a hard day's drive to Broken Bow, Nebraska. Rain pelted the truck all day, and the cab's side curtains couldn't begin to keep Frank and Marie dry. He fought to keep the car on the road where a ten-mile stretch had turned the surface to gumbo. On that same stretch he stopped and spent the better part of an hour helping a motorist get his car out of a ditch.

Even so, after arriving in Broken Bow and donning dry clothes, Frank mustered enough enthusiasm to make a sales pitch to the owner of Atlas Hardware that resulted in orders for two Whirlwind Maids. With that sale he had now exceeded his revised projections, which was cause for celebration.

He sat in the Wayfarer Hotel's saloon and quaffed more beers than he could remember, picking at the flaking sunburn on his arm and only half-listening to Bernard gripe about July in Nebraska.

Noticing Marie had fallen asleep in a corner, Frank scooped her up along with her cane. As he carried her through the dingy hotel lobby, two old-timers who were hunched over a game of dominoes turned to watch. Frank took her to the hotel room, awakened her long enough to get her into her nightgown, and tucked her in for the night.

He rejoined Bernard, who was entertaining the barkeep and

several of the dozen or so men in the saloon with yet another trick. This time, Bernard had attached the bowl of a spoon to the tines of a fork, then stuck a toothpick into the joined silverware and rested the toothpick on the rim of a glass. When he let go of the toothpick, the silverware remained suspended.

"There." Bernard grinned.

The barkeep shook his head. "Confound it all."

But Bernard had just begun. With a flourish, he struck a match and lit one end of the toothpick, then the other. The ends burned until they met the glass and the silverware. The fork and spoon stayed suspended. The barkeep's eyes opened wide.

Being Mr. Science, Bernard started to explain away the miracle and educate the barkeep about principles of the center of gravity and torque.

Frank interrupted him. "Two boilermakers."

The barkeep brought the glasses of whiskey and mugs of beer.

Frank patted the table where he wanted them placed. "Thank you, sir. You are a gentleman and a scholar." Then he chuckled over the next thought taking shape. "Just an expression, but take my friend Bernard, here. He really *is* a scholar. Studied science and medicine in England. Has more degrees than a thermometer."

Frank tossed down the whiskey. He let out an "aah," partly to relieve the fire in his throat and partly from satisfaction at the anticipation of alcohol rushing to his brain. "Talked to Ryder today. You were right about Durfee's granddaughter."

"I'm sorry."

"It's okay. She signed with his other circuit. I got Marie a new contract."

Bernard's unruly eyebrows lifted.

"Besides being the child elocutionist she'll be a piano soloist." He grinned.

A bolt of lightning caused the lights to flicker.

"Not a fit night for man nor beast," Frank said.

Thunder cracked and rumbled.

"Marie okay?" Bernard asked.

"She could sleep through Armageddon."

"You still get a kick out of being a nomad?" Bernard asked.

"Not like at first. Novelty wore off. One town's just like another, one hotel room—but it got me away from Riverview Inn. My prison. Promised my father I'd keep it going."

Bernard reached for his beer, but Frank placed a hand on his forearm, leaned forward, and fixed his eyes on his companion's. "Listen to me, Bernard. Never enter into a deathbed promise unless you're the one dying."

Frank released his grip and took a swig of beer. "But I'll tell you, this nomad life will be my claim to fame. The Chautauqua Darling and the Whirlwind Maid. Just in time, too. That Hoover guy, all he's got is a bag-on-a-stick, but one crackerjack marketing scheme. Do you know my own wife got invited to a Hoover party?"

"Did you let her go?"

"Hell, no!" Frank watched Bernard go in and out of focus. He looked away and sighed. "A man's got to have a claim to fame. You show me a man who just says, 'Dear Lord, all I want from life is enough to get by on,' and I'll show you some sorry wretch who just got off the boat and hasn't yet gotten religion American-style. You can't live in these times, in this great nation without getting bit by ambition. Well, I've cast my fortune with my little girl and my grand invention." He raised his mug. "To The Chautauqua Darling and the Whirlwind Maid!" The mugs clinked and beer sloshed. Bernard attempted to mop the table with his handkerchief.

As Frank watched, a sentimental feeling washed over him. He would miss Bernard, as true a friend as there ever was. "Let me tell you something, Bernard. Louise thinks the Whirlwind Maid is a lark. What she doesn't know is I lost my shirt on some risky railroad investments. The Inn provides a decent livelihood but not for much longer. Riverbend is becoming the industrial sister city to Smithville, and Burlington is planning to close our depot. So I'm forced to take the Whirlwind Maid to the cities, challenge Hoover."

"You'll leave Louise running the Inn?"

"She's managed while I've been gone. Haven't told her yet." Frank held up two fingers, and the barkeep brought another round. The two friends sat in silence, looking down at the table.

Frank downed his whiskey. "Not long till we play the hometown, then in a few more weeks the season ends. How about you?"

"Forty-eight more days, to be exact." Bernard grinned. "Mrs. Science can't wait for Mr. Science to come home and work his magic."

Laughing, Frank reared back so far his chair teetered. "You old coot. You're too old to get it up."

"You should be so lucky you get to be my age."

"Bullshit! Don't give me that crap." Frank waved his arm to shoo away the bullshit and knocked over an empty glass. He fumbled, one hand sabotaging the other, until he set it upright.

"Expect me to believe Mrs. Science sits at home waiting for your old pecker?"

Bernard's mood soured. His shoulders rose and fell with heavy drunken breaths. He glared at Frank. "Let me tell you something, my friend. *I* never gave *my wife* the clap."

Frank worked the words around in his head until, in a flash of brilliance that swelled his confidence, said, "She's the one gave *you* the clap." He laughed.

Bernard shook his head and swigged his beer.

Frank mulled over Bernard's words, still unable to make sense of them. "You're drunk. You talk nonsense."

"I'm not drunk," Bernard said. "You're the one who's drunk."

"What'd you say—who has the clap?"

"Never mind," Bernard said. "Got to take a leak."

Bernard left. When he returned he set a worn deck of cards on the table.

"Hey, I've got better cards than that." Frank reached in his pocket and produced a deck of Whirlwind Maid cards. He shuffled, let Bernard cut, and dealt a hand of gin rummy.

Bernard drew a card from the deck.

"What was that about the clap?" Frank asked. "Something about the clap."

Bernard discarded the two of diamonds. "Never mind. Your turn."

"No, I remember. You insulted my wife."

"I said I never gave my wife the clap."

Frank's temper flared. "Yeah? Me neither."

Bernard leaned forward and spoke in a hoarse whisper, "You did, and you know it."

"You're crazy. You old coot. Who listens to a crazy old coot?"

Bernard's nostrils flared, and his bushy eyebrows met over the bridge of his nose. "This close," he said, holding his thumb and index finger less than an inch apart, "this old coot is this close to a medical degree. You infected your missus and your daughter, I hate to say."

"Whoa, whoa, now," Frank said. "Leave Marie out of this."

Pulling his drunken frame upright, his chin jutting like a professor too full of himself, Bernard enunciated: *"Ophthalmia neonatorum."*

"Speak English," Frank said.

"Babies' sore eyes. Marie's blindness."

"Baby's sore eyes?" The words swirled in Frank's brain until they coalesced into a hazy scene of a hot summer afternoon. The nursery, the air thick with baby smells.

Bernard nodded. "From the mother. From her comes *Neisseria gonorrhoeae* bacteria that infects the baby's eyes."

Frank struggled to connect what Bernard was saying with memories of Louise flopping about, delirious, him not knowing if she would live or die. His baby girl's eyes oozing pus. Dr. Foster saying something like "baby has sore eyes." What did all of this have to do with the clap?

"I don't have the clap." Frank pushed against the table to stand. It wobbled, sending glasses crashing to the floor. He gripped Bernard by his jacket lapels and pulled him up out of the chair. He took a swing which barely grazed Bernard's chin.

The men in the saloon stopped what they were doing and edged closer to watch.

Bernard's shove sent Frank reeling back. He landed on

one hip and elbow. When he saw Bernard's extended hand, he took it and rose clumsily to his feet. He looked at the gawkers. "What are you staring at?" He sat down and put his head in his hands.

Clues Frank had been dodging for years had wormed their way deep into his being where they had waited for just this moment to erupt into consciousness: supposedly fathering a baby in spite of a limp dick, Marie's black hair "straight as a little Indian's," and something between Louise and Yonder that he couldn't quite fathom. Anger burst in his gut. It propelled him out of his chair and sent him careening between tables like a man on fire.

"Watch it, fella,'" a man said.

Frank bumped him and sent beer sloshing onto the table.

He got to the wall telephone in the lobby. He steadied himself with one hand on the wall, knocked the receiver off the hook, and let it dangle while he turned the crank. He had to repeat his directions several times to the operator. He waited. "Answer the goddamn phone, Louise."

Upon hearing her voice he shouted over the words of the operator who was trying to ascertain if Mrs. Morrissey would accept charges for the call. "Tell Yonder he's a dead Indian."

"Yes, operator. Frank, you're drunk. It's nearly three o'clock. Where's Marie?"

"I'll blow his brains out."

"You're drunk. Go to bed."

Frank watched Bernard's blurred outline move closer and the domino players advance and recede, their arms suspended in play. Teetering, he leaned against the wall. "Ought to kill you, too. Filthy whore."

"Where's Marie?" Louise's voice became shrill with panic. "Who's looking after Marie?"

"I'm coming home. I'll tear that Indian limb from—"

"Where is Marie?" Louise shouted.

"Sleeping."

"Listen to me, Frank. Are you there? Stay where you are. Yonder already left for San Diego. I didn't have the heart to tell you before now. Now get to bed. You'll see how foolish this is in the morning."

Frank pushed away Bernard's hand reaching for the phone. "I'll hunt him down. He's a dead Indian. I'm coming home."

"You're not going anywhere," Bernard said. "You're going to bed."

Frank shouted, "I'm coming home."

Bernard elbowed Frank in the ribs and seized the receiver. "Don't worry yourself, Louise. I've got him."

"I'm coming to get him!" Frank didn't have the strength to resist Bernard who gripped him by the shoulders.

"Come on," Bernard said. "Sleep it off."

Both men stumbled up the stairs. Inside Frank's room, Bernard turned on the light. Marie was sleeping soundly. Bernard shoved Frank onto the other bed. Frank tried to get up but fell back down and slapped at Bernard's hands removing his shoes. Suddenly everything went black.

*   *   *

THE URGE TO PEE ROUSED Frank well before dawn. With one foot he dragged out the pot from under his bed and relieved himself in a long, satisfying stream. But something gnawed at the edges of his brain. The fight with Bernard. Yonder. *That bastard.*

He put on his shoes, fumbled with the laces, and left them untied. Throwing off Marie's covers, he shook her awake, and yanked her to her feet. "Come on."

"Father, what's wrong?"

Taking her hand he led her down the stairs and past the unattended desk.

"You scare me!" She was crying now.

Frank shouldered the front door, which did not budge. "Goddam son of a bitch!" He jerked the door which yielded and sent him staggering backwards. He recovered and lunged forward, dragging Marie out into the driving rain.

When they reached the gravel drive, Marie cried, "Ouch, my feet!"

Realizing his daughter was barefoot, Frank picked her up and carried her the rest of the way to the truck.

"Where are we going?"

"It's going to be okay." He shoved her into the truck. He climbed in on the driver's side and reached behind the seat until he felt the rifle's cold barrel. From under the seat he retrieved a bottle of whisky. Wet and chilled, he took a long drink and thrust the bottle at Marie. "Hold this."

He put the truck in gear, and it lurched forward. Even hunched over the steering wheel, his face nearly against the windshield, he had difficulty seeing the road through the rain and darkness. A shadowy form did not show itself to be a mailbox until he bore down on it. "Damn!"

His sudden swerves caused Marie to flop against him like a rag doll. He grabbed the bottle. A fence. He slammed on the brakes and instinctively threw his arm across Marie to keep her from hitting the windshield. The truck stopped just short of the fence. He looked at the bottle in his hand, congratulated himself on not having spilled a drop, and took a drink. As he steered the truck back onto the road, he thought to switch on the headlamps.

Marie was still crying. "Where are we going?"

"We're going home, Junior." *Junior.* As soon as he said the word, it struck him that his beloved daughter was not his.

"But we can't, the show. The rain's coming in. I'm cold."

Without slowing down, he wriggled out of his jacket and draped it over Marie. He noticed her straight black hair. *Like a little Indian.* "I'll kill him, so help me, he's a dead Indian."

"Father, you scare me."

"Ioway, my foot."

Marie whimpered. "I want my mother."

Over the next couple of hours, events and snatches of conversation played over and over in Frank's mind. *She tricked me. Yonder, the story about her Ioway great-grandmother, baby's sore eyes, the clap. That whore. I should kill her, too.*

Shortly after dawn the truck engine died. Frank tried to start it again without success. Out of gas. Marie had fallen asleep against him. He propped her up with one hand as he got out of the truck, and while rain pelted his head and back he eased her down onto the seat without awakening her. He retrieved a gas can from the back of the truck. Standing in water that covered his shoes, he emptied the can into the tank.

Marie was still asleep when he got back into the truck. He reeked of gasoline, his wet clothes clung to his body, and he shivered and slapped himself to try to get warm. His hands stiffened on the steering wheel. He tipped the bottle but had long since drained the last drops. Stopping the truck, he got out and stood in the rain as he felt under the seat, hoping against hope to find another bottle. Empty-handed, he climbed back into the truck.

He looked at Marie sleeping peacefully as though she were home in her own bed instead of slumped on the truck seat in her wet nightgown with rain pelting her. *She was my pride and joy, my claim to immortality.* What if Bernard didn't know what he was talking about?

To save time, he turned off the paved road to Lincoln onto the dirt road toward Sprague. It was all he could do to hold the truck on the road as it sashayed in the mud.

Marie awakened. "Where are we? Why is the truck slip-sliding?"

"Going home, Junior, going home."

"Why are we slip-sliding?"

"Mud. Pretend we're in that song." He began to sing, "'She'll be comin' round the mountain when she comes. She'll be comin' round the mountain when she comes.' Come on, sing with me, Junior."

Together they sang, "'She'll be driving six white horses . . .'"

Frank saw the bridge railing and hit the brakes. As the truck veered to the right, he threw his arm across Marie's body.

* * *

WHEN SHE HUNG UP THE phone after talking with Frank, Louise fought the impulse to dash to Yonder's quarters in the carriage house to warn him. She dared not risk being seen by some guest. The warning could wait. It would take maybe six hours for Frank to get home, fewer only if he drove like a madman.

Her overriding concern was Marie's welfare. *Please, Frank, don't drag Marie into this.*

Maybe he would not come at all. Bernard sounded confident he had the situation under control. Maybe Frank had forgotten to take the rifle with him. She checked the closet where he kept it, knowing what she'd find. No rifle. *What to tell Yonder?*

The night grew heavy. Every muscle urged her to action, but there was nothing to do except wait. And wrestle with her thoughts. She prayed out loud, "Please, God, don't let Marie suffer any more for my sin. Don't let her know Frank isn't her father. Don't destroy their precious bond."

Come daylight when Frank sobered up, he would see how ridiculous his assumption was. What ever gave him the idea? Could she convince him he was wrong? She had to.

Sitting on the sofa, she drifted into restless sleep. Her father appeared, brandishing a stick and cursing her, "daughter of the devil." Unbearable heat. Standing at the edge of a pit, the flames of hell lapping closer and closer. Something struck her temple, perhaps her father's stick. The wound opened as a portal through which her trapped secrets escaped, and she floated safely above the flames. She awakened, drenched in perspiration, to sun streaming in her window. Momentarily she felt free. But then she remembered Frank's call.

She swabbed her face and neck with a cool washrag. With any luck, Bernard had put Frank to bed, and he had slept it off and forgotten about Yonder. But if not?

It occurred to her to call the hotel. Without drying off she went to Frank's desk and found his itinerary. She held her breath, lifted the telephone receiver, and asked the long distance operator to connect her with the Wayfarer Hotel. When the clerk answered, Louise said, "This is Mrs. Francis Morrissey. I'm calling to inquire if Mr. Morrissey and our daughter are still guests of the hotel."

"No and good riddance. They hightailed it last night without paying their bill. We'll be holding their things until we collect."

"I understand. Mr. Morrissey and I are in the hotel business, too. Send me the bill, and I shall handle payment promptly."

Louise hung up the telephone. She smoothed her hair and applied powder with a trembling hand, trying to conceal the dark pouches under her eyes. Best not to let her appearance suggest something was wrong. After donning a crisp blue and white dress, she went to the Inn's dining room where she acknowledged breakfast patrons with her most cheerful "Good morning."

In a corner of the Inn's kitchen, out of the cook's way, she fried bacon and eggs to make sandwiches for Yonder to take with him. But no sooner had she put the sandwiches in a bag than she remembered the bacon still on the grill. She remade the sandwiches and placed them in the bag.

Entering the dining room, she saw Yonder eating breakfast at his usual table. The thought of telling him he must leave brought a lump to her throat. She approached him and said, "Come with me."

"What's happening?"

She led him through the kitchen and out the back door. Once outside, she thrust the bag at him. "You'll need these."

He took the bag and looked inside. "I don't understand. Are you all right?"

She struggled to find the words. *How had it come to this?*

How can I banish him from the family that had welcomed him as one of its own? "You have to leave. Hurry so you can make the eight-forty train. I shall send your things later."

The screen door banged. One of the housekeeping girls came out carrying a trash bin. Louise babbled about Yonder needing to check out a noise the car was making. Once the girl was well out of earshot and emptying the trash into the incinerator, Louise took a deep breath. "Your life is in danger. Frank's on his way home. He telephoned last night, drunk, shouting like a madman." She struggled for the right words. "Yonder, it's my fault. . . . He threatened to kill you."

"Frank couldn't—"

She swiped at tears that flowed down her cheeks. "Listen to me. You can't take the chance."

"You're not making sense, Louise."

Her voice became barely audible. "He has this crazy notion you and I . . . he thinks you're Marie's father."

Yonder shifted his gaze. When he faced her, Louise saw a look of estrangement in his eyes reminiscent of the time he told her about getting beaten for courting a white woman.

He thrust the bag at her. "If you'll excuse me, I'm going to go finish my breakfast."

*　　*　　*

Late morning, after several hours of keeping watch, Louise could not force her eyes to stay open against the sun's merciless rays. She stood and turned away from the sun, and as her eyes began to feel better, she realized her mouth was parched. But water would have to wait. She dared not leave the post she had set up on the uncomfortable iron settee next to

Morrissey's folly. She checked her watch again. The truck must have broken down along the way. Frank and Marie should have arrived long ago.

After leaving Yonder in the dining room, Louise had gone to her apartment and picked up the dress she was embroidering for Marie, hoping that busy hands would steady her nerves as she waited. But she'd worked in fits and starts, her concentration broken by thoughts that tumbled over one another. Sorrow for the words that must have wounded Yonder. Anger towards Frank and Bernard. Self-loathing for having been the cause of so much pain. And longing to hold Marie safe in her arms again. *Nothing good can come of this.* Louise recalled the sense of foreboding she'd had on the eve of Frank and Marie's departure for the Chautauqua tour.

Now that her eyes were rested, Louise sat down and picked up the dress again. A light breeze twisted the silk ribbons draped across the arm of the settee.

As she untangled and cut a length of red ribbon, she rehearsed what she had decided to tell Frank. Assuming that sobriety and daylight had brought him to his senses, she would remind him that her maternal grandmother was part Sioux, with hair straight as a stick just like Marie's, a plausible lie since no family photographs or documents existed to disprove it. And point out that Marie had the fair complexion of a Morrissey. Even Frank's cousin had remarked about it once on a visit to Riverbend.

If Frank refused to believe her, then what? She would have no choice. Holding the ribbon, her hands dropped to her lap. To save Yonder she would have to tell Frank about Doc.

The hours passed with hunger pangs that came and went,

relentless thirst, and lips becoming dry and cracked. The sun had moved, putting Louise in the shadow of the Inn. She jumped at the sound of a vehicle downshifting for the steep climb up High Street. She stood halfway, then sat back down. Not the sound of Frank's truck.

When the automobile came into view, she recognized it and wondered what brought the sheriff. Perhaps news about Lars.

The car entered the drive, turned around, and parked facing the street, but it was several minutes before the sheriff opened the door, stood, tossed his hat onto the seat, and strode toward her. In that time, Louise worked her tongue and mouth which had become so dry she couldn't have spoken with slurring.

"Good morning, Mrs. Morrissey." Sheriff Andy Maguire squinted against the sun. He started to crack his knuckles but stopped himself and hooked his thumbs in his belt.

"You caught Lars!"

"No, ma'am." He blinked a few times and shifted his gaze from Louise to the dress she was working on.

She wondered why the sheriff did not get to his point. The law did not come calling for no reason. An uneasy feeling from childhood returned, the occasions she'd watched Pa get arrested. She held up the dress. "For Marie. She likes embroidered things. She can touch them and make out the designs. It's for her Chautauqua appearance in Riverbend."

"It's right pretty, ma'am." The sheriff's voice broke. "I'm afraid. . . I got a call from the sheriff over in Lancaster County. Mr. Morrissey and your little girl . . . there's been an accident."

"Are they hurt?" The way he looked down at the ground and cracked his knuckles alarmed Louise. They must have been badly injured.

"Ma'am, I don't know how to tell you." His voice broke. "They was killed."

Marie's dress fell to the ground. Louise gripped the settee. Nonsensical images careened in her mind . . . a hotel fire, Lars wielding a knife, her father brandishing a stick. The world went dark. If she reached out, her fingers would graze walls closing in. Then an instant of clarity. "No. It can't be. Frank and Marie are on their way home. They'll be here any time."

"No, ma'am. They died when their truck went into a creek."

"No, not my husband and daughter. You're mistaken. Someone else."

"Mr. Morrissey had identification."

"I expect them home any time."

"Yes, ma'am, they was on their way, driving on West Stagecoach Road near Sprague when they run off Olive Branch bridge."

Louise stared at the needle in her hand trailing red ribbon and wondered what it was for. *Oh, yes, Marie's dress.* She shook her head. "What makes you so sure it was them?" The guttural anger in her voice surprised her, a detached voice that seemed to come from someone hovering next to her. "My husband is a good driver."

"If it's any comfort, ma'am, they died instantly. They wasn't in any pain."

Louise was trembling, and her words came out in a shriek. "How can you know they didn't suffer?"

"Their necks was broken, ma'am. Lancaster County sheriff said they died instantly." He picked up Marie's dress and placed it in her hands. "I'm right sorry, ma'am."

PART 3

Chapter 22

July 1905

The bodies of Frank and Marie had been taken to the Lancaster County morgue in Lincoln. Louise would have to arrange for them to be transported to the undertaking parlor in Riverbend, then brought home for the funeral service.

Woozy from the laudanum she had taken to calm her nerves, Louise sat in the back parlor where she felt murmurs around her, J.D.'s voice dominating a conversation that included Yonder and Dovie. She gazed at her hand that stroked the arm of her chair. Stroked it over and over.

Snatches of phrases registered, but mostly Louise drifted somewhere beyond meaning. Dovie had insisted she drink the opiate, reminding her that Elizabeth Barrett Browning had written her best poetry under its influence. Louise wondered how. She could not grasp a thought long enough to string words into a simple sentence.

Other voices, muffled. Yonder got up and closed the pocket doors that divided the back parlor and dining room.

Louise watched Dovie approach and felt her hand on her arm.

Dovie said, "Who do we need to notify out of town?"

"I don't know, Frank's cousin and . . ."

"Where is your address book? We'll go through the names

and make a list."

Louise shrugged and swept her arm in a wide gesture. "I have to see them . . . the bodies. Now."

"Of course." Dovie looked toward her husband. "J.D.?"

Yonder spoke up. "I'll drive you there."

* * *

FOR MOST OF THE TWO-HOUR drive to Lincoln, Yonder and Louise retreated into silence. Louise's eyes took in the sun-washed scenes of people going about their everyday lives—some children playing kick-the-can, older boys and girls detasseling corn, a farm wife weeding her vegetable garden. She strained to remember what an ordinary day was like.

Each time the automobile neared a bridge, Louise held her breath and fought off images of Frank and Marie being crushed or flung into the creek.

The laudanum was wearing off. Regaining control of her faculties was good, but she longed for the narcotic fog, a shroud against the awful reality she held at a distance.

"Alive." She blurted the word without knowing why.

"Beg your pardon?"

"Nothing. I cannot comprehend that they're . . ." She could not bring herself to say the word.

Louise had become all too familiar with death, helping Ma wash and dress the bodies of her baby brothers. She took pains to lay them out as though they were just sleeping. Pa would head for the stables to make coffins but end up going on a bender for days, and Ma would send Louise to the saloon to fetch him, a pointless errand as there was no prying him away from his card game and bottle. Meanwhile the little ones' mouths and eyes would contort in ghoulish ways. And the stench would make Louise gag.

After little Malachi died, Louise searched for just the right stone, one smooth enough to inscribe with a piece of coal.

Malachi Jacob Caldwell
B. 1869   D. 1871
God's Little Messenger

Joshua died not long after he'd learned to walk, a time when the ground was still frozen. His coffin, nailed shut to keep coyotes from the body, sat outside next to the house. It was April before he was laid to rest in the side yard. Weeks later his baby brother was interred next to him. Louise marked their graves as well.

Joshua David Caldwell
D. 3-21-1875
Aged 1 Yr. 28 Ds.
God's Little Jewel

Baby Boy Caldwell
D. 5-12-1875
Aged 3 Ms. 17 Ds.
God Had No Right To Take Him

After the third baby died, Louise decided she hated God. Had Pa been able to read, he would have boxed her ears for the words she put on that stone.

"This must be the morgue," Yonder said as he parked the

automobile.

Louise opened the jar of Vicks VapoRub that Dovie had insisted she bring. She smeared the gel inside her nostrils and winced at its sting, then handed the jar to Yonder. The pungent menthol odor brought back memories of Marie squirming to get away as soon as she smelled it. Now Louise knew she could never again use it as a cold remedy.

She stepped from the automobile. Yonder's firm hand on her arm brought back the old anxiety that Frank would misinterpret his intentions, and with that thought the drunken telephone call played again in her head, rousing the guilt that always lay beneath the surface.

Inside, a frumpy matron grudgingly set aside her knitting. "The bodies was just delivered. Haven't got them cleaned up yet."

Louise and Yonder followed her through a dim corridor to a formaldehyde-smelling, gray room with concrete walls and floor. Sunlight poured through open windows, its shafts like spotlights on an insect drama abuzz with the frantic wings of maybe a hundred flies stuck on flypaper strips hanging from the ceiling.

Louise took a chair across from Yonder at a metal table. She stared at the double doors behind him until a group of flies alighted on the table and busied themselves in a huddle. Louise pressed her palms on the table's cool surface, a contrast to the heat and humidity that sapped her strength and sent rivulets of perspiration trickling between her breasts.

She jumped when the double doors swung open with a loud bang. The end of a sheet-covered gurney appeared. Its wheels squeaked. Pushing the gurney was an attendant wearing a grimy white jacket. A wheel jammed, and he gave it a kick. The figure under the sheet shifted, almost imperceptibly.

"He's alive," Louise cried out. "You've made a terrible mistake."

She lunged for the gurney, but Yonder caught her and pulled her back.

She stared as the attendant removed the sheet. The gray, bloated body scarcely resembled Frank. The forehead was bashed, the nose lay to one side, and shards of glass protruded from several of many cuts.

Louise turned away. The smell overpowered the Vicks and made her retch, body-racking dry heaves. Soon she was looking into a metal wastebasket that Yonder held while she vomited. She sat down and wiped her forehead with her handkerchief.

"These effects was on the body, ma'am." The attendant's words diverted her attention from the body to a tray that held Frank's silver money clip, pocket watch, four rifle shells, and other items.

When the attendant lifted the sheet from Marie, Louise steeled herself. She looked at a bloated face covered with gashes. Gently, so as not to cause any more pain than necessary, she plucked one of a half dozen shards of glass from Marie's face.

The attendant took it from her hand. "They went through the windshield, ma'am."

The candy-striped nightgown, stained with mud and blood, had a gaping tear at the shoulder. Louise brought the torn edges together and attempted to make them stay in place. But as soon as she withdrew her hands the tear gaped again.

Moving the matted hair, she bent to kiss Marie's forehead, but it was crushed. She dropped to her knees, saw the table leg looming large, and felt hands jerking her backward away from the leg. It was Yonder, his eyes filled with alarm at her near miss. He knelt beside her and held her quaking body as she sobbed into his shoulder.

She heard him say they should leave. But leaving her daughter was unconscionable, her daughter who was supposed to come home triumphant. *It was my fault. I should never have wished Marie wouldn't outgrow her nightgown.*

Before they could leave the morgue, Louise signed papers at the front desk while the matronly woman sat knitting what appeared to be a baby's sweater. The woman pointed a knitting needle in the direction of two suitcases along with a small box, which turned out to hold items retrieved from Frank's truck.

Yonder took the box and suitcases out to the car. When he returned he asked the woman, "Are there more boxes?"

Without looking up from her knitting, she said, "Nope."

"There should have been a rifle," Yonder said. "Mr. Morrissey carried it for protection when he traveled."

"Nope."

"You see, Yonder?" Louise said. "The rifle wasn't in the truck. Frank didn't mean what he said."

* * *

Another hour or so of daylight remained, and Louise insisted that Yonder drive her to the bridge where the accident occurred. The site was only about fifteen miles from Lincoln, but it was slow going on the narrow road. The recent heavy rains had turned the road to muck, and deep ruts grabbed the tires, jerking the automobile from side to side.

"I don't reckon we'll ever know why Frank would take this

God-forsaken road when he could have taken the two-lane macadam all the way," he said.

Louise shook her head. What was it after all these years that caused her husband to suspect that she and Yonder were lovers? What would he have done to Yonder? And her? In this moment she saw with clarity the terrible events her infidelity had set in motion. Marie's blindness, now her death and Frank's. She hoped Marie, the little innocent, had died still believing Frank was her father. She looked at Yonder, another innocent ensnared in her deceitful web.

"Olive Branch bridge." He slowed the car and stopped on the side of the road.

Neither moved nor spoke. Louise closed her eyes and held her breath so as not to break the stillness and its momentary sanctuary.

The bridge railing was intact. Deep tire tracks that ended at the creek bank's edge indicated where the truck had been dragged from the creek.

Standing next to the tire tracks, Yonder ran his hand over the end of the steel railing. "Black paint. That's where the truck grazed it. He missed the bridge altogether."

Louise wanted to feel that the place was hallowed, that she could reach out and embrace the spirits of her loved ones. But it was just a bridge. "Did they—"

"Their necks were broken. Both would have died instantly."

Louise shielded her eyes against the glare of the setting sun and scanned the creek. A piece of cloth had snagged on a stick and bobbed, almost lifelike, with the flowing water. She studied it, trying to make out whether it was a fragment of Marie's nightgown. She looked away. "Frank was a good driver.

Sober or drunk. I've seen him when he could hardly stand up, but he could still drive."

Yonder nodded. "Most likely Frank didn't even see the bridge. The mud could have caused him to lose control. It's bad enough now, think what it must have been like in the dark, probably with a blinding rain." He nudged Louise toward the automobile. "We've seen all that we need to."

As they turned to go, Louise could not resist one final backward glance. When she did, something caught her eye, something that whoever recovered the bodies from the rain-swollen creek had overlooked. Yonder turned as well. Hoping to discover that her mind was playing tricks, Louise stepped closer to the creek to study the long object that caused the flowing water to break and ripple over and around it. But there was no mistaking what was visible now, what Yonder had undoubtedly seen as well: the edge of a rifle barrel.

Chapter 23

July 1905

As Louise's trembling hands chain-stitched a blue edge along the collar of Marie's dress, thoughts of the collar gracing her daughter's broken neck set her weeping. Her mind would not let go of that night, the drunken telephone call, the crash that sent them through the windshield, the rifle in the water. Louise reached for the laudanum bottle, unscrewed the cap, and winced as she swallowed the bitter opiate.

Relief. Her breathing slowed, and she lost herself in each languid, deliberate stitch. In, out. In, out. No hurry. She had until September. Marie would not need the dress until her Chautauqua appearance in Riverbend. Marie, beloved by all, The Chautauqua Darling, would hold the adoring audience in the palm of her hand.

* * *

FRANK WOULD HAVE WANTED A service in the parlor. He may have chafed at being tied to the Inn, but it was sentiment more than inertia that held him to his lifelong home. Louise heard herself harping at him—if only she could take back the words. She had called their apartment a *mausoleum*.

Curly Ambrose arrived early to take formal photographs of Louise with the coffins, both of which were closed. Later he would photograph scenes at the hearse and graveside.

Mourners filled the Morrissey parlor and dining room. For the first time in the history of the Durfee Chautauqua Bureau, substitute performers were found and some acts cancelled, thus enabling those close to Frank and Marie to pay their respects. Mr. and Mrs. Ryder attended, as did Miss Keller, Mrs. Macy, Bernard, Giovanna and several crew members.

For Louise, shrouded in a laudanum fog, the day was a blur of disjointed sounds and images. Sitting flanked by Dovie and J.D. on one side and Yonder and Giovanna on the other. Noticing flowers standing stiffly in vases, living things being leeched of their very life essence as she watched. Wincing as Reverend Harper hissed his *s's* whenever he said *Morrissey* or *salvation*. Hearing Yonder eulogize his "best friend" and thinking, *His best friend wanted to kill him.* Trying to silence Frank's last angry words ringing in her head—*I'm coming home.* Knowing her public tears of grief masked secret tears no one else could possibly understand. Weeping openly again when Mercy Maguire, the sheriff's wife, sang "Amazing Grace," a favorite of Frank's, and when Bernard Feldman recited Marie's signature poem, "The Wreck of the Hesperus." Handkerchiefs coming out, reminding her of Frank's pride when he told her about the first time an audience gave Marie the Chautauqua salute.

* * *

Bernard visited Louise the next day. He offered a substantial lump sum for rights to the Whirlwind Maid. Louise would receive fifteen percent of all profits. He would honor Frank's intention to convert Tom's Bicycle Shop to a modern factory. In addition he would locate a second factory in the northeast.

The offer fell on her ears as numbers that evaporated as soon as he spoke them. Recalling that J.D. had advised her to hold off on making any major decisions, she thanked Bernard and agreed to consider it. She tried to think about the Whirlwind Maid, what Frank would want her to do. But her stubborn mind fixed on Bernard as the last man to see Frank and Marie alive. What really happened that night? What does he know?

CHAPTER 24

August 1905

Four weeks after the accident, Louise awakened to the sound of Frank hammering something, then with the dawning of consciousness realized it was a dream's cruel trick and someone was knocking at her kitchen door. After putting on Frank's seersucker robe and her slippers, still half-awake, she shuffled to the door, opened it, and found Yonder standing there.

"I'm sorry, Louise. Where's Henryetta?"

Glad to see him but not in her just-out-of-bed state, she said, "Come in, sit down. I'll make coffee. Henryetta has a new job."

Instead of going to the breakfast room to sit, he followed her to the sink where she started filling the percolator with water. "You look—you don't look well. Have you been ill?

Embarrassed, she tried to push her hair into some semblance of order. "Do I look that bad?" No doubt he'd noticed her sallow complexion, a recent condition she'd been hiding with make-up. "It's my morning look. You got me out of bed."

She spooned coffee into the percolator and set it on the stove, then sat at the breakfast room table. She reached behind her neck and straightened the collar of Frank's robe.

Sitting across from her, Yonder looked at her as though he were about to deliver bad news. "Are you still using laudanum?"

"You think I'm still using laudanum?" The truth was that she had gone four days without the drug. "I know I look a fright, but the last three days I've been working overnight teaching Henryetta to make kolaches. She's my new baker since the other one quit. I figured there wasn't much for her to do now that she doesn't have Frank and Marie to fuss over. I can get one of the hired girls to clean for me, and I can manage meals myself or pick up meals from the dining—Oh—" She slapped her hand on the table. "Now I know why you're here. I was supposed to meet you in the dining room to go to the bank."

They drank coffee while she prepared the bank deposit. Yonder waited while she dressed and put on her face. Then they walked together to the car.

As they turned from the Inn's driveway to the street, Yonder said, "It's a relief to know Lars is in jail,"

"Yes. The sheriff came by yesterday." Louise clutched the satchel in her lap with both hands.

Along the way, a crew of men who were mulching young maple trees stopped what they were doing to look at the Cadillac, still a curiosity as one of the only closed-body cars in town.

As Yonder turned onto Main Street, Louise fixed her eyes on his hands operating the steering wheel and gearshift, not wanting to see what she knew loomed in the distance: the Chautauqua's main tent, which was to have been the scene of Marie's hometown triumph.

"I never had an opportunity to see her on stage," Louise said. "I missed the most important part of her life. She was growing, making friends, becoming a confident performer. Her

Chautauqua family—" Her voice broke, and the tears came. She fumbled in her handbag for a handkerchief and blotted her eyes and nose. "I lost my daughter before the accident. I lost her when she joined the Chautauqua family and no longer needed me."

They were still several blocks from the bank, but Yonder steered the car to the side of the road and stopped. He placed a hand on hers. "Louise, you were always the single most important person in Marie's life. You prepared her to live in the world and then did the hardest thing a mother can do: you allowed her to try her wings."

She shook her head. "But I wanted her to need me. Am I being selfish?"

Yonder patted Louise's hand. "My mother's gone, but I still need her."

Grateful for his touch and words, nevertheless she could not shake the sense of having been displaced by Frank, Bernard, Helen Keller, and the Chautauqua.

Yonder withdrew his hand, shifted gears, and drove forward. With his turn onto Main Street she took a deep breath and regained her composure. She entered the bank wearing the face of the widow who was "missing them terribly but managing to get along, thank you."

* * *

SEPTEMBER CAME, NEARLY TWO MONTHS since the accident, and Louise struggled to bring some order to her days. She could point to little she had accomplished. She'd hired a man to refurbish Morrissey's Folly. And she'd gone out with Yonder for driving lessons, something Frank hadn't had the patience to see through.

Now looking out a window of the Burlington depot, she watched a burly switchman at work in the driving rain. Gripping a long lever that protruded from the ground, he thrust it forward to move a set of tracks. Probably the tracks that would take Yonder away from Riverbend.

At one end of the depot where people waited on wooden benches sat a trio Louise presumed to be a grandmother with her daughter, who was a younger version of herself, and granddaughter. The child and elderly woman, her cane propped beside her, were playing cat's cradle, the little girl patiently waiting for grandma's bent fingers to manipulate the strings.

Louise stood close to the stove, hoping to warm her wet feet. She noted the peeling paint on the walls and buckling floorboards that attested to years of neglect. Wind whistled through poorly sealed windows, an accompaniment to the buzz of conversation.

Yonder returned from the ticket window. He carried just a satchel and overnight bag, having shipped his other belongings earlier in the week. "You needn't wait, you know."

Louise looked past Yonder at the clock on the wall and the relentless movement of the second hand. *I don't want to lose you, too.* She inhaled his Ivory soap scent and gazed at his face with the intention of committing to memory its features, lines, and color. "This is what families do. See their loved ones off with good wishes for a safe journey. You'll always be family no matter where you go."

"Thank you for taking me in."

A polite goodbye. Why could he not have said, "I've changed my mind. I don't want to marry Giovanna. This is my home."

"Marie always had to get French burnt peanuts when we came to the depot." She nodded toward the row of dispensers that held candy and nuts.

"We could sit down," he said.

A train was pulling into the station.

"It won't be long. There's your train."

"You'll be all right?"

"I shall be fine."

He looked down at her figure. "You've lost weight. Promise me you'll eat proper meals?"

His concern came close to bringing tears. "Promise."

"If you ever need anything, you have Giovanna's address."

Louise looked through the window at people departing the train. "Thank you. I appreciate it."

"With this early cold snap, Harley should start putting up storm windows."

Louise considered the meaning of the moment. Together they had been two people who had always been comfortable with periods of silence, but in parting they kept chattering as though a string of words might bind them together. And as though a pause in the conversation might break the bond. "I understand the climate in San Diego is very pleasant year-round."

Passengers from the arriving train entered the depot. Several were met by friends or family with hearty slaps on the back or embraces.

"I didn't have a chance to tell Henryetta good-bye," Yonder said. "Tell her I'll miss her kolaches."

"I know she'll miss you. With both you and Frank gone,

there's no one to tease her about the strings on her fingers."

"If the car needs work, have Tom look at it. He'll take care of you. And I reinforced the trellis just to make sure it can withstand a high wind. Your clematis should thrive this year."

The ticketmaster announced boarding for Yonder's train. About a dozen people shuffled toward the exit to the platform. As they passed through the door, each person in line turned to the one behind and said, "Watch your step." Louise noticed they were referring to a broken floorboard in front of the door.

Yonder inclined his body in the direction of the door but seemed reluctant to leave.

Perhaps he's changed his mind.

He set his bag down, and Louise hoped for an embrace, but instead he simply opened his coat and retrieved his train ticket from the inside pocket. "I can't tell you how much your friendship has meant to me."

"To me, as well," she said.

"The Sioux language has no word for goodbye. So in parting we prefer to say, 'I'll see you again someday.'"

"I like that sentiment." Louise held her hands to her breast. "I'll keep it here."

"Last boarding call," the ticketmaster said.

Yonder picked up his bag, turned, and headed toward the door where the old lady with a cane was preparing to exit. He took her arm. She turned, looked tearfully at her daughter and sobbing granddaughter and blew a kiss. Taking her arm, Yonder guided her over the broken floorboard and through the door.

The mother, tears flowing, picked up her daughter, patted her back, and jostled her in a futile attempt to comfort her. The scene had all the markings of a forever goodbye.

Tears welled in Louise's eyes.

CHAPTER 25

Nothing seemed to matter. Once a paragon of efficiency, Louise now moved as though slogging through quicksand. Each morning began with sincere but vague intentions that by afternoon left her immobilized with indecision.

This morning, she shoved aside the clutter on the breakfast room table to make space for a cup of tea and a slice of toast. She noticed and dismissed stains on the sleeve of her coral chenille robe, the one Frank favored. He had loathed the widow's customary public attire of mauve and black.

She started a list of minor repairs the Inn needed, but then her ragged fingernails caught her attention. She got her manicure set from the bedroom. But in the midst of filing her nails she spied the unfinished stack of "thank-you" notes to people who had helped with the funeral. After writing just one note, it occurred to her she should mend the hem of her robe where the stitching had come loose. She stood up, but stunned by the absurdity of her behavior dropped back into the chair and buried her head in her hands.

* * *

THE FIRST NIGHT THAT HENRYETTA took over the baking alone, Louise could not sleep. Drinking warm milk didn't help. As soon as her head hit the pillow, her mind began playing a continuous litany of sins. She got up. The short distance from her bed to the hall closet was the path of indecision. Opening the closet door and seeing the little brown bottle in its place on the shelf was always the point of no return. But tonight, holding the bottle in her hand conjured horror stories of laudanum fiends, brilliant women like Elizabeth Barrett Browning and Ada Lovelace who succumbed to the bottle and lived in a stupor night and day. She set the bottle down. A nearby shelf held boxes of photographs that needed organizing.

Opening a box, she saw the photographs from Marie's birthday party. Marie in the pony cart before she fell, the children at the table before the cake was cut, Marie feeding a carrot to the pony. She shuffled through the remaining pictures until one caught her eye. Frank was measuring Marie. They stood in front of the kitchen door, and he held the ruler on top of Marie's head. He looked so proud, and Marie stretched to her full height and beamed with expectation. Louise had an idea, one so satisfying that she slept through the night without her bitter medicine.

*   *   *

The following Monday Louise and Dovie took the early train to Omaha to meet with A. B. Fremont, a metal sculptor. A statue would be expensive, but Louise had amassed a sizeable rainy day fund.

A taxi dropped the women off at the studio where bronze gargoyles, children, and animals appeared to be at play behind a tall iron fence. The women went inside the enclosure and inspected the figures.

"Look, Louise." Dovie pointed to a sneering gargoyle. "He looks like . . ."

A squat, big-boned woman wearing a leather apron came out to greet them.

"We're here to see Mr. Fremont," Louise said.

"*Mr.* Fremont was my father." The woman spoke without a smile. "I'm A. B. Fremont." She extended a hand as leathery as her apron and shook hands first with Louise, then Dovie. "I'd be living on canned beans if I'd tried to make a career as Anna Belle Fremont."

They went inside where Louise and Dovie took seats across from Miss Fremont at a small table. Louise took the photograph from her handbag and handed it to the sculptor.

"Don't say anything." Miss Fremont studied the image and inhaled deeply, seeming to draw it in to become part of her. She exhaled audibly and set the picture down. "Bronze, no less than three-quarters life size. That's the only way I'll agree to do it."

Louise hesitated, having a hard time fitting the crusty woman across from her with the joyous sculptures outside. "Those are examples of your work out front?"

"Of course. Now tell me about the photograph."

"That's my husband, Frank, and my daughter, Marie Alouette, on her ninth birthday. They were killed in an automobile accident. This picture was made not long before the happiest time in Marie's life. You see, she was blind and rather lost until her father got her a part as the child elocutionist with the Chautauqua. They were touring—"

"I saw the newspaper item." Miss Fremont appeared to be moved. "I'm very sorry."

"I don't want to tell you how to do your work," Louise said.

"I know you're a great artist, but I have an idea about how this should be interpreted."

"Go on."

"The picture cuts off the doorway just above their heads and shows the kitchen door closed. I envision the statue as the whole doorframe with the door open behind Frank and Marie. The open door suggests the opportunity that awaits her."

"Anything else?"

"Frank's hair is too long. He needed a haircut."

The sculptor pushed her chair away from the table and leaned back. "Mrs. Morrissey, I've earned a reputation that allows me to work primarily on public projects—well-funded, I might add—and I've earned a reputation that, within certain parameters, allows me considerable artistic freedom. I rarely accept private commissions, and I'll tell you why."

Louise felt a nudge from Dovie's knee.

The sculptor went on. "Too much interference. I might have concluded the same thing myself with respect to the doorframe and open door. But I'm an artist, not an order taker. I can't work feeling like you're looking over my shoulder. I'm not the person for this project, but I appreciate your consideration."

Louise stood up and thrust the picture into her handbag. "Well, Dovie, I guess it's time for us to leave. Miss Fremont, I appreciate your candor, but I know what I want. Now, will you please direct me to someone who will welcome the opportunity to work with me?"

"Go see August Potemkin. He's young. Still eating canned beans."

"And where might we find Mr. Potemkin?"

The sculptor pointed. "A couple of miles. The artists colony in back of the Venetian Café."

Once they were in the taxi and headed to the artists' colony, Louise and Dovie looked at one another and laughed until tears made little rivulets in their makeup.

"'I'm not an order taker,'" Dovie mocked.

"I do agree with her on one thing—two, in fact. Bronze, no less than three-quarters life size."

"Be sure to include that in the order you give Mr. Potemkin."

After a successful meeting with the young sculptor, Louise and Dovie went to the Paisley Tea Room, where they enjoyed mint tea and dainty cucumber sandwiches served on plates garnished with tiny, edible flowers.

Dovie asked Louise, "Where do you intend to place the statue? Not in the cemetery I hope."

"No, at the Inn. Morrissey's Folly stands on the south side of the walk, so it will have to go on the north side."

"But it will be dwarfed by that shipwreck."

"The shipwreck stays. I just had her refurbished at considerable expense."

"No offense intended, but she's still no great beauty." Dovie nibbled a flower.

"Give me another idea."

"I know just the thing," Dovie said. "Chautauqua Park."

Louise took a moment to picture the scene. "Here's the edge of the bluff." She placed her palm on the table edge to her right. "And the floor represents the Chautauqua grounds. It could go on the edge of the bluff so that when you look at Frank and Marie at the doorframe you see the Chautauqua grounds below through the door opening. Dovie, you're a genius."

Dovie's eyes misted.

"What's wrong?" Louise asked.

"Nothing's wrong." Dovie sniffed, taking the handkerchief Louise offered. "Do you know what happened today?"

Louise mentally ran through the day's activities.

"Look at you, excited about the future. Don't you see, you have something to live for. You even laughed today!"

* * *

Before going up to her apartment, Louise stopped at the Inn's front desk to collect her mail. A small, flimsy package caught her attention. It was wrapped in wrinkled brown paper and tied with a dirty length of string, actually several pieces of unmatched string tied together. The sender had printed the address in pencil. It looked like a child's hand.

She set the mail on the breakfast room table and removed the string and paper from the strange package. From outside came the clunk-clunk sound of the ladder being moved as Harley, the building superintendent, hung storm windows.

The package held two ugly woven placemats in adversarial shades of orange and green. She checked the postmark. Lincoln. Lars, the thief, captured and imprisoned after attacking her.

She went weak, feeling his putrid breath on her neck again as he reached from the state penitentiary. Was it a warning? Lars was in prison, but his brother lived in town.

That night after finally falling asleep, Louise awakened to a sound like metal striking metal. Instantly alert, she kicked off the bed covers, sat up, and picked up the loaded pistol. That noise again, followed by a hiss. Recognizing the familiar clank and hiss of a radiator, she breathed with relief. On any other night the sound would be a friendly signal of the cozy warmth inside. Tonight it had conspired with the creaking rafters, rattling windowpanes, ticking grandfather clock, and her own breath and heartbeat to torment her. She set down the pistol and lay back down with one ear against her pillow and covered the other with a second pillow. It muffled the noises, but the fear simply changed forms, like a worm to moth. If Lars' brother or someone else wanted to attack her, she would not hear him enter.

Thinking about being in the bedroom with nowhere to escape made her skin prickle. Going to the kitchen to make a cup of tea, she carried the pistol and moved stealthily so she might hear any unusual sound. The noisy act of running water into the kettle seemed both foolhardy and heroic. She took her tea and the pistol into the back parlor but could not make herself sit down. She paced. Glared at the grandfather clock, ticking quietly. Looked outside, but there was nothing but the blackness of night. Finally she sat and tried to read a magazine, but she could read the same paragraph over and over and not grasp the meaning; her mind played tricks so she saw the word *will* as *kill,* and *deal* as *dead.*

She got up, turned on lights and checked the locks on the kitchen and front doors. The balcony! If Lars had been watching her comings and goings before he attacked her, he might have gone behind the Inn and seen her on the balcony. An agile man could scale its support, just as Dovie's son John had done at Marie's birthday party, and breach the flimsy French doors. She went to the French doors, jiggled the key to make sure they were locked, removed it, and set it on a table. Then she turned off the lights and sat stiffly in her chair, all her senses laid raw. Occasionally she would slump drowsily in the comfortable chair for a time but then jerk to attention.

Oh how she missed Frank. She had taken his protection for granted. Was he watching over her now? Why had they never discussed their views on death? They should have come up with signals to try to communicate from the other side. "Frank," she said out loud. "You'd know what to do. Tell me what to do."

Then reality seized her. She remembered the visceral, drunken rage of a madman in the hours before his death. He probably hated her. How could he not? He was wrong about Yonder, but he was right about her infidelity. Was he watching her suffer, glad to see her getting her just reward? Was God still punishing her?

The line she'd carried since childhood came to her: "They enslave their children's children who make compromise with sin." She knew why, of all the lines in the long poem, this one stuck with her. It shrieked a warning. There had been no escaping the curse of Pa's evil. It lived in her.

Chapter 26

November 1905

Was it grief that played tricks with Louise's mind? That disabled her rational brain? She had taken for granted her financial security only to find it a myth. In putting her affairs in order she had discovered that Frank's investments were worthless. Riverview Inn receipts scarcely covered operating and living expenses. She would have to accept Bernard's offer to buy the Whirlwind Maid.

* * *

"Hip, hip, hooray, hip, hip, hooray." Feigning enthusiasm, Louise joined in the cheer that erupted in the Henklemans' dining room after J. D. announced he would be a candidate for state senate.

The Thanksgiving supper ended with fruitcake, coffee, and sherry, and J.D.'s story of a holiday when he traveled home by train from military academy and he and other passengers had to help clear snow from the railroad tracks.

"In his wool uniform he smelled like a wet sheep," his mother said.

They were laughing again, and it grated on Louise. Her hope that sharing the holiday with friends would provide some comfort had been dashed the moment she stepped through the door. The laughter that filled the house left her an outcast.

It seemed to mock her state of bereavement and alienation from family, branding her as that most pitiable of creatures—a woman alone.

Louise almost envied Dovie, who seemed in her element. With Gertrude's help, Dovie orchestrated a memorable meal for extended family, tried to tame her rowdy sons and their cousins, and cajoled J.D. from one of his rants into a grudgingly affable mood—in general, she had taken responsibility for everyone having a pleasant holiday. Dovie's life had purpose.

J.D.'s mother dabbed her mouth with her napkin and set it on the table. "Let's all retire to the parlor for a songfest."

The Henkleman twins pushed past Louise, punching each other on their way to the parlor. Louise feared for Dovie's coveted Wedgwood display.

Dovie must have, too, for she yelled, "Settle down, you hooligans, before you break something!"

The boys ignored her but halted in their tracks when they saw their father.

As the group was taking seats in the parlor, J.D. stopped Louise. "I have something to speak with you about in private."

She followed him out to the hall and heard the strains of "Oh! Susanna" coming from the parlor organ.

"I want to talk to you about the Inn. Operating a hotel is no job for a woman." J.D. tilted his head back so Louise had to look up at him. "Look what happened when Frank left and that gypsy stole your receipts."

The hair on the back of her neck bristled. "He wasn't a gypsy, and I managed to hold onto the satchel."

"I'm only thinking of your welfare. I happen to know that Burlington plans to suspend passenger service to Riverbend—"

It seemed the floor was moving, and Louise had to place a hand on the hall table to steady herself. "What did you say?"

The boisterous singing in the parlor stopped, and Gertrude could be heard saying, "'O God, Our Help in Ages Past,'" followed by a few voices taking up the hymn.

"Burlington will suspend passenger service to Riverbend," J.D. repeated, "leaving the nearest depot in Smithville. It's a grievous state of affairs for our economy, the only salvation being that they'll continue freight service. But this places you in an untenable position. There won't be enough business to support the Inn."

"This is so sudden. I don't know what—" She had sold the Whirlwind Maid to Bernard and would eventually receive a share of its profits, but for now she was still dependent on income from the Inn.

"But to get to the point, you don't need to worry your pretty head. I'll take the Inn off your hands, give you a fair price. Riverbend needs an old folks home. Young people today don't want to take in their elders. I even plan to do some of the renovation myself, get my hands dirty, use some of the skills my grandfather taught me. You can remain in your apartment. Nothing has to change except you won't have the burden of running the Inn. You'll be set for life."

His certainty that he would own the property set her heart racing and riled her to the point she wanted to say, "It's not for sale." But she caught herself and said, "I need time to think."

Another loss. Now that it was in jeopardy, the Inn she had always wanted to escape for a dream house became something dear. But if what J.D. said was true, she had no choice but to accept his offer.

PART 4

Chapter 27

March 1906

Louise closed the breakfast room curtains to block sunlight streaming through the window, but there was nothing she could do to muffle the joyful squeals of children sledding on the hill adjacent to the Inn, now Riverview Old Folks Home. The sounds reminded her of watching a terrified Marie try to hold onto Frank's back the one and only time he took her on the sled he'd owned since he was a boy.

The fall and winter months had become especially bleak after Yonder's departure. Louise noted that if things were going according to Giovanna's plan, today, March twenty-fourth, was their wedding day. Louise tried to brush aside her feelings, tried to be happy for Yonder, but in truth she wanted him for herself.

Two things had sustained her. One was helping to set Henryetta up in business baking kolaches, a project that had occupied her for several months. She had informed J.D. when she accepted his offer to buy the Inn that she owned the kolache recipe, and if he wanted to serve them to residents he should buy them from Henryetta.

The second was Dovie's determination to keep her busy. She was grateful for Dovie's friendship and her "activity plans," because left idle, she often retreated under the covers wanting only to be left alone. On days that they didn't have plans together, Dovie always made it a point to telephone to see how

Louise was doing.

This afternoon as she leafed through her mail, Louise came to a wrinkled envelope with crude lettering that made her skin crawl. *Lars?* On closer examination she noticed the stamps were foreign. Opening the curious envelope, she removed a note and photograph. Mrs. Jelinek, stout and frumpy, stood with a gangly boy, about the same height. There was a vacant look in the eyes of the boy, too tall for the suit that hung on his thin frame.

Louise read the note through tears. "Mrs Morisey. You a good woman. Boy need me. Thank you. Mrs. Jelinek."

Louise went to the den at the sound of the telephone's three short rings. The caller was Dovie.

"Louise, have you been crying?"

Louise wiped her nose with her handkerchief. "Bittersweet tears." She told Dovie about the letter and described the picture.

"Why is she writing to you?"

"You'll think I'm crazy. When her family arrived at Ellis Island, Miklos was sent back to Bohemia for being a mental defective. I caught Mrs. Jelinek pilfering food and petty cash from the Inn, saving up to go back home to him."

"That's why you fired her?"

"I didn't fire her. I gave her the money to make the trip. I said it was payment for her kolache recipe."

"Gave her money. Why?"

Louise smiled at the absurdity. "Your question shines light on my logic and exposes the flaws. I didn't have a good reason. Just an overpowering urge. One mother helping another. Consider what she risked to get home to her son, a boy no one wanted. I was in awe of that mother's love. I could never measure up."

"Now you listen to me," Dovie was sounding like a scolding schoolteacher. "If that had been Marie sent back, you'd have walked on broken glass to get to her. I saw how you sacrificed for that girl. The hours you spent teaching her Braille and helping her with her piano lessons. She was the luckiest blind girl alive." "I mean—"

Dovie's kind, if not well-chosen, words, were intended to comfort but instead aroused guilt which Louise was careful to mask. "I know what you mean. And thank you, Dovie. Your friendship means the world to me."

As much as Louise had wanted to pour out her feelings to her good friend, she could not. How to explain that helping Mrs. Jelinek atoned in some small measure for her own failure as a mother? How to explain that Marie wasn't blinded by accident, but as punishment for her mother's sin? How to explain that she could not look at Marie without feeling rebuked?

But something Dovie had said lightened Louise's burden of self-recrimination: yes, she would have walked across broken glass to get to Marie.

* * *

THE NEXT MORNING LOUISE LANGUISHED in bed, heartsick from a dream in which the little boy at Baby Giveaway Saturday was chasing after the woman taking his "Sissie." When his small hand reached out to grab the woman's skirt, it turned out to be Louise's skirt.

Still in the place between dreaming and awakening, she heard herself say, "Needlessly blind." Those had been Dr. Vandegrift's words the day he had examined Marie. Louise had been so shaken that she could scarcely remember what he said, but a few phrases stuck: "She would not have lost her sight if the doctor had instilled drops when she was born. . . . Doctors fail to act on what they know. . . . Courageous people must educate the public and legislators. Respected people like yourself." Maybe he'd said, "Courageous people," not "Respected."

It would certainly take courage to do what Dr. Vandegrift was suggesting, a willingness to risk respectability. But such courage paled against what Mrs. Jelinek had done. The woman had risked arrest and jail for her cause.

In the kitchen, Louise whisked two eggs in a bowl while butter sizzled in a skillet. Most days she preferred to take breakfast alone, not in the dining room where residents padded around in slippers and robes.

She tried to enjoy her scrambled eggs, but the little boy wouldn't let go. When she could stand it no longer, she cast about in her mind for some action she might take. She wanted to scream at someone who could get results, but who?

The state legislature, of course. Instead of washing up her dishes, she went to the den where she placed a long distance phone call to Lincoln and learned the name of the chairman of the Health and Welfare Committee and how to contact him.

She sat at her secretary to draft a letter, but the words choked in her hand before reaching paper. More formidable than trying to write the perfect letter was knowing that setting herself up as an advocate might bring unwanted consequences. Thinking of something Frank used to say made her smile: "Don't open the can of worms if you think the worms might win." Admitting the worms stood a very good chance, she persisted nevertheless. Finally she wrote:

Dear Sen. Bruegger:

I am writing to you to request that you propose legislation that has been proposed in several other states that would prevent a leading cause of blindness.

Wordy. Too blunt. Don't use "that" three times in the same sentence, and "propose" twice.

Finally satisfied after several attempts, she copied a draft on her embossed linen stationery.

Dear Sen. Bruegger:

I appreciate the efforts of the Health and Welfare Committee on behalf of the citizens of Nebraska. I am writing to bring to your attention a serious problem that afflicts the youngest, most vulnerable Nebraskans. Legislative action can protect them.

This problem is unnecessary blindness caused by a condition known as "babies' sore eyes." It has been estimated that this preventable condition is responsible for one-fourth to one-third of all admissions to state asylums for the blind.

This devastating disease can easily be prevented and completely eradicated with a public health program that requires doctors and midwives to instill dilute silver nitrate drops in all babies' eyes at birth. You see, the condition is not immediately apparent at birth.

The drops have been proven to work in England and France for many years. I beseech you to propose legislation that would prevent this leading cause of blindness. I urge you to act now.

Respectfully yours,
Mrs. Francis J. Morrissey

Nearly two weeks passed before Louise received a reply to her letter. She read hurriedly past the senator's "thank you for writing" paragraph, and as soon as she saw "After serious consideration," she stopped reading and slumped in her chair. *I was a fool to get my hopes up.*

After a time, her agitated heartbeat slowed, and she smoothed the wadded-up page. The letter went on to say that the state fulfills a plethora of obligations to ensure the health and welfare of its citizens, and that the Committee's role is to review and act on public health matters brought to its attention by the state Bureau of Hygiene.

His arrogance made her bristle. Apparently matters raised by mere citizens did not merit the Committee's consideration.

When she had written to him, all her worries had been about how she would present her case to the Legislature and at what risk to her reputation. Now it seemed the challenge was how to get in the door.

After getting the name of the Bureau of Hygiene's director,

Dr. Milton Weil, she wrote another letter. When two weeks passed without a reply, she decided to wait no longer.

CHAPTER **28**

April 1906

On the slow taxi ride from the train depot in Lincoln to the state offices, Louise willed herself to remain calm. But when she held her mirror to check her face and hair, her trembling hand betrayed her anxiety. If she succeeded in seeing Dr. Weil, it would mean having to talk to him face-to-face about an unspeakable disease. If she failed to see him, she would leave behind a letter summarizing her appeal. Then go home and wait. The worst outcome would be to meet with him without gaining his support. In that event, she knew nowhere else to turn.

In the cavernous lobby of the state office building, a receptionist directed her to the office of Dr. Milton Weil. "See his secretary to secure an appointment."

Alone with her echoing footsteps in the long gray hallway, Louise scolded herself for not having made an appointment by phone. She opened the door to a cramped office where a smartly dressed, buxom woman was watering plants. The woman, whose hair was piled high and held by a large daisy-shaped barrette, turned.

At the sight of the unmistakable wide-set eyes, Louise froze. It was none other than Daisy Friend from New Lexington.

"May I help—" The professional tone turned to a shriek. "Lulu?"

The sting of that name took Louise back to the schoolyard taunts of Daisy and the other rich girls.

"Look at you!" Daisy rushed forward and clasped Louise's hand in both of hers.

"Daisy?" Had Daisy forgotten tormenting her? Why was she working for a living? Had she never married? "I go by Louise. Mrs. Francis Morrissey."

Daisy offered her a chair and squinted as though trying to recall something. "Louise Morrissey. I remember, now."

What does she remember? Me wearing her Aunt Mamie's cast-off coat?

"You wrote to Dr. Weil, something about blind babies. I was about to send you a reply, but, oh, I'm so glad I didn't. When he returns from his meeting, I'll get you in to see him. And then, oh, Lulu, you have to promise me you'll join me for lunch in the cafeteria."

"I would like that." Louise said it to be polite, hoping to find an excuse to leave right after meeting with Dr. Weil. Daisy's show of friendliness was not to be trusted. She no doubt intended to pump Louise for information she'd share later in gossiping with her old friends back home.

As Daisy neared the door to the inner office, an attractive man came through it. He had apparently just put on his suit coat and was tugging at his shirt's French cuffs. Without acknowledging Louise's presence, he said to Daisy, "Something has come up. Cancel the rest of my appointments."

"I shall, Dr. Weil, but first I want you to meet my old friend Mrs. Francis Morrissey. We were chums growing up in New Lexington, and I have not seen her in years."

By no stretch of the imagination were we ever chums. Louise wondered when the snide, mocking, rich girl would surface.

"She came from Riverbend for the sole purpose of meeting with you."

He grasped Louise's hand. "Forgive my lack of manners. The morning has been hectic."

"My manners are lacking as well," Louise said. "I should have secured an appointment with you first."

"Dr. Weil, can you spare five minutes to talk to Mrs. Morrissey?"

He hesitated, but the plea in Daisy's eyes seemed to move him, and he gestured toward the inner office. "By all means. Come in, Mrs. Morrissey."

After they were both seated, Dr. Weil leaned forward and rested his arms on his desk. If he still felt harried, it did not show.

Nevertheless, Louise felt her mouth go dry at the prospect of broaching such an indelicate subject. Clutching her purse so tightly in her lap that her knuckles turned white, she managed to say, "I appreciate your time, and I shall get straight to the point. I imagine that being a medical doctor, you are familiar with the condition called 'babies' sore eyes.'"

He nodded.

"You may also know of efforts in some states to get legislation requiring silver nitrate drops in babies' eyes at birth."

"And you want Nebraska to do the same."

"Yes."

He leaned back in his chair, and Louise steeled herself for rejection.

"Allow me to explain the Legislature's priorities. Health and social causes aren't among them. This state spends more money helping farmers keep their livestock healthy than on people. We have pleaded for years for a state sanitarium for consumption patients but can't get it, so these patients stay at home and infect their families. Here is what you're up against."

He ticked off each item on his fingers. "First, legislators won't touch gonorrhea with a ten-foot pole. Second, their constituents already feel there's too much government intrusion in their private lives. Third, who would pay for silver nitrate drops? Fourth, there would be the matter of enforcement. I could go on and on. Your cause is worthy, but to be blunt, it doesn't stand a snowball's chance in hell."

Louise felt her resolve cracking. "I was told that the Legislature acts on bills that come out of the Health and Welfare Committee, which receives guidance from you."

"That's generally what happens."

"So you are my only hope?"

"Not necessarily. The process can begin anywhere. A lone senator might act on pressure from powerful interests back home and use his political clout to create a bill and ramrod it through. Don't count on that happening with babies' sore eyes. I know these senators better than their own mothers do, and there isn't one who would spearhead this. But legislators also respond to a groundswell of public opinion. Mustering that is your only hope. I wish I could give you more encouragement." He placed his hands on the edge of his desk and seemed about to stand.

Acknowledging that the meeting was over would be the polite thing to do. But Louise wasn't ready to give up. "I appreciate your good advice and your time, but I'm at a loss as to what to do next. How does one woman on a mission arouse public opinion?"

He leaned back. "It's a tall order. You would have to educate the public as to what babies' sore eyes is, show how easily it can be prevented, and make them care enough to demand legislation." He thought for a minute, perhaps moved by her obvious distress. "You might start by getting the social workers and nurses involved. They know firsthand about babies' sore eyes. They're overworked and underpaid, but they thrive on causes like yours."

* * *

DAISY INSISTED ON TAKING LOUISE to the Capitol cafeteria, where they waited in a long, slow-moving line. Red-faced cafeteria ladies hunched over a serving table and spooned globs of creamed chicken, scalloped corn, sauerkraut, and apple crisp onto thick pottery plates with chipped rims. Louise wondered at the ease with which her former classmate moved in the spartan setting where the clatter of pots and pans, the screech of chairs being slid, and the noise of dozens of conversations bounced off tile floors and walls, a setting far removed from Waterford crystal, sterling silver, and crisp table linens.

Daisy leaned forward to speak to the worker who was dropping a biscuit on each plate. "So good to see you back, Mrs. Rogers. I hope you're feeling well."

The woman's dour expression softened ever so slightly. "Some better. Thank you, miss."

Daisy led Louise to a table in the crowded dining room. After they were seated, she laid a coarse paper napkin in her lap and lifted her fork. Every move suggested good breeding. An observer might regard both women as born to privilege, but Louise could not ignore the chasm dividing them. Fine manners were the birthright of one, the pretense of the other.

Daisy leaned forward. "Isn't Dr. Weil the nicest man you ever met?"

"A very nice man." Louise's tone was polite without reflecting Daisy's enthusiasm.

"Now then, I'll tell you why I left New Lexington. Remember Clifton Dodge? The class two years ahead of us?"

Louise nodded.

"Well, we ran off and eloped when I was sixteen. He was Roman Catholic, and he got a priest to marry us. Mother and Father had conniption fits. They disowned me, and Clifton's family got the marriage annulled."

With a sweeping gesture she said, "Overnight, no family, no servants, no riding club. I thought the world had ended, but I said to myself, 'Daisy, you can't do anything about the past. Get off the pity pot. Go out and get a job.' So I came to Lincoln, went to secretarial school, and here I am. I still dream of having a husband some day, but I'm almost thankful I had the opportunity, or necessity really, to support myself. It builds character."

At a nearby table, two loutish men talked with their mouths full, one of them stabbing the air with his fork to punctuate his remarks. Daisy seemed not to notice. Louise admired her self-assured manner that perhaps derived from being a woman on her own. If she cursed the fates that had thrust her into this noisy cafeteria it was not evident.

"That's very courageous." Hoping to forestall discussion of her own past, Louise was about to ask Daisy how long she had worked for Dr. Weil, but Daisy spoke first.

"Talk about courageous, what about you? How old were you when you left town?"

"Twelve. I tried passing myself off as fifteen, though I doubt I convinced anyone, and got a job as a housekeeper. Later I worked at a bank where I met my husband. His family owned a hotel in Riverbend. Do you ever get back to New Lexington?"

"No. Burned those bridges. You're no one there without money, as you know. Besides it's too provincial. Tell me, do you have children?"

Louise shifted in her seat, causing her napkin to flutter to the floor. Daisy's question was one she never got used to. She picked up the napkin. "A daughter, Marie. She and my husband were killed in an automobile accident."

"I'm so sorry."

"She was the child elocutionist with the Chautauqua."

Daisy looked away as though searching for what was familiar in Louise's words. "Oh, yes. I remember reading about her. The beautiful blind girl who recited those long poems."

"Yes. Blinded soon after birth by infection from pneumococcus bacteria." Her eyelids fluttered shut. "A remarkable child."

"So now I understand, at least partially, why you contacted Dr. Weil. What is this 'babies' sore eyes'?"

Louise used her fork to nudge sauerkraut away from the apple crisp. She debated whether to mention gonorrhea. "It's a blinding condition that affects newborn babies."

"That's positively awful. What were you expecting from Dr. Weil?"

"The condition is preventable, but it requires that every baby receive dilute silver nitrate drops at birth. State legislation mandating drops is the key to prevention."

"Was Dr. Weil helpful?" Daisy dabbed her lips with the napkin.

"He seemed understanding but not optimistic, at least when it comes to getting the Legislature to act. He advised mobilizing nurses and social workers to build public awareness."

"He's right, you know," Daisy said. "Women are the power behind social reform. Look at Harriet Tubman and Jane Addams. Forget doctors and senators for now. You have groundwork to do."

Inspired by the prospect of women as the moving force, Louise straightened, feeling a burden start to lift. She did not have to be a lone woman trying to influence men. Motivating women came naturally. But hope was tinged with caution. "Daisy, there's something I didn't tell you. You might not be so encouraging if you knew the cause of babies' sore eyes."

Daisy looked puzzled. She set down her fork.

"It's hardly a subject for the dinner table, if at all." Louise folded and unfolded the napkin in her lap.

"Don't leave me in suspense. Go on."

Louise felt Daisy's eyes on her and wondered about the wisdom of continuing. She shifted in her seat. "Babies' eyes can become infected in the birth canal if the mother has . . ." She whispered, ". . . gonorrhea."

Chapter 29

May 1906

As Frank would have said, it was time to take the bull by the horns. Louise would convene a group she'd call The Nebraska Committee to Save Babies' Sight. A core group of a dozen people would be ideal. She wrote letters inviting social workers and nurses from Riverbend and surrounding towns, as well as the superintendent of Smithville State Asylum for the Blind, to an organizational meeting.

Although Louise balked at having to explain babies' sore eyes and its cause, she had to address the matter when she extended invitations to her friends. She hoped they would play key roles on the Committee except for Gertrude, given her belief that children's afflictions were God's punishment for their parents' or ancestors' sins. Louise hoped to find someone as conscientious as Gertrude to handle details.

Alice lacked initiative but thrived on being of service and would wholeheartedly pitch in to carry out any assignment. Perhaps her greatest contribution would be her sweet, affable nature. She could win over people who might otherwise dismiss the campaign as the doing of uppity women who did not know their place. Alice would need continual reassurance that she was doing a good job.

Madge was restless for a new project and would bring superb organizational skills to the campaign. Often she could be the contrary voice, an annoying trait, but one that could prevent the group from adopting an idea before giving it full consideration. But would she ally herself with something so controversial?

Dovie, of course, would be Louise's right hand. She would raise funds and see to it that J.D. provided free printing services and publicity.

Daisy, who stayed in touch with Louise by telephone and letter, had already volunteered assistance in dealing with the Legislature.

When Louise presented her concept for a Committee after a meeting of the Tuesday Bibliophiles, Dovie immediately agreed to help and Alice and Madge followed. Gertrude begged off, saying she was too busy organizing her church's upcoming summer Bible camp.

Louise had no sooner arrived home and put away her hat than the telephone rang. It was Dovie, sobbing.

Louise imagined a terrible accident, probably involving one of the boys. "What's wrong?"

"It's J.D."

"I'll come right over."

"No, no, he's all right. Unless I kill him. I've never been so mad at him." There was a long pause. "Louise, I don't know how to tell you this. He forbade me to join your Committee. He says it wouldn't be fitting for a state senator's wife."

"No! Why?"

"He says a bunch of women stirring up a ruckus over an unspeakable disease will make Riverbend the laughingstock of Nebraska. Those were his exact words. I'm so sorry. I know this means so much to you."

"This cause—" Louise's throat tightened. She could not imagine the campaign without Dovie or even life without Dovie. "I can't lose you, too."

"We're friends forever, Louise, but I just can't be on your Committee."

* * *

Five women, not counting Louise, sat at the library's large reading table on Saturday morning for the organizational meeting of the Nebraska Committee to Save Babies' Sight. Louise watched as they chatted and brushed kolache crumbs from their bosoms. A disappointing turnout, and not a single woman had an important sphere of influence. It would be naive to think this could work.

Before opening the meeting, Louise gave herself a pep talk. These women were special in their willingness to support a controversial cause, and she would act as though this mighty little band could move mountains. "Let's go around the table and each of you tell us your interest in the campaign."

Madge began. "Louise Morrissey brought the problem of babies' sore eyes to my attention. It is positively galling to think that babies are needlessly blinded. It is time for women to challenge the taboo against talking about venereal disease, a taboo that enables philandering husbands to keep their wives in the dark. Only if we are willing to talk about this subject unfit for polite society can we awaken right-thinking men and women to this cause of protecting babies' sight."

The women clapped.

Alice, sitting to the left of Madge, smiled. "I don't really have a speech. I'm here because Louise twisted my arm." She clutched her arm as though injured.

Amid chuckles, Irina Taylor, now a nurse at Riverbend Hospital, nodded and laughed as she pointed to a woman knitting a navy blue scarf. "Bonita twisted my arm."

Irina, the woman with blue-violet eyes. Louise recalled the admiring look Doc had given her the night of The Twister. If only she could forget. Even more, she wished it didn't bother her.

Bonita Hobbs, a visiting nurse, was as plain and stoic as Irina was pretty and engaging. Her knitting needles clicked as she spoke. "Babies' sore eyes hits close to home. Not just in my work. My sister's boy, too." She looked down and bit her lower lip.

Jerrylynn Knudsen, a social worker at Smithville State Asylum for the Blind, spoke in a gravelly voice. "When parents bring their child to the asylum, I witness their last good-byes. It never gets any easier. It infuriates me to see so many cases of preventable blindness." She paused. "If I don't do something constructive with my anger, I'll explode. This Committee has a formidable task, but we can and must succeed."

Louise led the women's applause. "Yes, we can and must succeed. Great things happen when women band together in pursuit of a cause. When you look at social movements like child labor reform and—"

The door opened, and Alice snickered. She looked at Louise. "You were saying?"

Standing in the open door, Doc looked puzzled, obviously aware he was the source of amusement.

Louise said, "I'm sorry, Dr. Foster, the library is closed till eleven."

He addressed Louise. "This is the meeting of the Nebraska Committee to Save Babies' Sight?"

Bristling at his brazen intrusion, Louise said, "It is."

"Do you mind if I join you?"

"Of course," Madge said. "The more support from the medical community the better."

Irina scooted her chair around the corner of the table to make a place at the end. Louise forgot what she planned to say next. She was rattled almost to the point of trembling but sufficiently clear-headed to notice how the mood of the room had shifted. Bonita even stuffed her knitting in her tote bag.

"You all know Dr. Foster?" Louise asked.

The man she had tried to put in the farthest corner of her mind now sat directly across from her at the very table they had occupied the day he abandoned her and walked away scot-free.

"Please, Mrs. Morrissey, don't let me interrupt what you were saying."

She sat as tall as she could. "I was just noting that we were all women . . . and that the great social reform movements have been led by women." Shallow breaths threatened her composure. She forced her voice to remain strong, all the while fearing others could detect her feigned bravado. "That's why we found your entrance amusing."

In spite of being knocked off center by Doc's presence, Louise was determined to stay the course. "Now, it's important that we all understand the problem before we devise a strategy for influencing the state legislature to mandate drops. I would advise taking careful notes."

All except Doc opened tablets and began writing. Louise was reminded he took pride in his "photographic memory."

"Jerrylynn," she asked, "will you describe the impact of babies' sore eyes on admissions to the asylum?"

"It accounts for nearly one-third of our admissions. Usually the parents don't know that gonorrhea caused the blindness, but we can tell by the appearance of the eyes."

Louise took a deep breath. The campaign had yet to begin, and already she would have to defend her reputation. "But there are other bacterial infections that can cause blindness and scar the eyes in a similar fashion." Although she was looking at Jerrylynn, she could feel Doc's eyes. "My daughter, Marie, for example, was blinded by the pneumococcus bacteria."

"Pneumococcus scars the eyes but rarely blinds an infant," Jerrylynn said. "I suppose you've considered that leading this campaign will expose you to a public perception that Marie was blinded by gonorrhea. I hope you're prepared to bear that burden."

"No, I'm not willing to bear that burden." Louise avoided looking at Doc and wished she didn't have to state the lie in the presence of the man she most wanted to acknowledge the truth about Marie's blindness. Her eyelids fluttered as she spoke. "I intend to make it abundantly clear that my daughter was blinded by *pneumococcus,* that my interest in the campaign is that of a concerned mother who wants to prevent babies from being blinded regardless of the cause."

Doc spoke up, almost as though to rescue Louise. "Mrs. Knudsen, do you have statistics on the number of babies blinded by gonorrhea each year?"

"Unfortunately, no," Jerrylynn said. "Last year we admitted seven children so afflicted, but most blind children remain at home. In some cases, there's partial vision or just one eye is affected. A few babies actually die of the infection."

Madge frowned. "How can we arouse public support when so few children are affected? It pales compared to the number of children who die of consumption or get maimed falling into farm machinery."

"A valid question," Doc said. "I think the answer is that babies' sore eyes, unlike consumption and many farm accidents, can be easily eradicated and therefore should be."

Louise said, "There's no question but what we have great obstacles to overcome—social taboos, prejudice, the cost of drops—"

"And folks get their backs up when government sticks its nose in their business," Bonita said. "Some people think laws are meant to be broken. Visiting nurses fight that every day. There's folks that refuse to get their kids vaccinated and some that put their kids to work instead of sending them to school."

The campaign faced more obstacles than Louise had ever imagined. If her own core group had so many doubts, how could it succeed? "This is the place to express our concerns. What I would ask you to do is keep it in this room. Outside that door, we represent ourselves as indomitable champions of a noble cause, that because we are doing the right thing we shall not be deterred. Can we all agree to that?"

The group murmured and nodded.

"Now we have much to do," Louise said. "In New York, the campaign showed a picture of children with the label 'Needlessly Blind.'"

"That reminds me." Bonita fumbled in her handbag until she produced a worn photo which she handed to Louise. "My sister's boy, Vinny."

Louise gasped. "I've seen this child! Baby Giveaway Saturday at Wilson's Department Store." She stared at the picture of a dark-skinned little boy with curly, black hair, about three years old, a Teddy bear dangling from one hand. He was barefoot and wore overalls. One eye was scarred like Marie's, the other clouded. The picture captured a plea in the upward tilt of his head and vacant expression. "Where is he now?"

"My mother took him and his sister after their mother died," Bonita said. "His sister got adopted. Mother has a weak heart, has to take it easy. Keeping Vinny corralled was too much for her. So now he's at the Asylum."

Alice became teary-eyed, the others solemn, as the picture went around the table. The campaign had a face.

In the time left before the library would be open to patrons, the group discussed how they might respond to challenges and divided up responsibility for refining those responses to bring to the next meeting the following Saturday.

Louise closed the meeting. "I would like to paraphrase Daniel Burnham, architect of the great World's Columbian Exposition in Chicago. His formidable task was to mobilize forces to build a veritable city in two years. He said, 'Make no little plans; they have no magic to stir men's blood.' I say, Make magnificent plans; with their magic we shall soar over insurmountable obstacles."

As the meeting was breaking up and library patrons were arriving, Doc approached Louise. His manner was businesslike. "Have you given thought to how your campaign will be funded?"

She made a study of placing papers in her satchel just so. While she might hide from his gaze, there was no hiding from his maple syrup fragrance and velvety smooth voice and the memories they stirred of feeling his touch on her neck and all that it promised. "I didn't raise the issue today because in my experience talking about how to obtain resources too early in the discussion inhibits a group's ability to create a vision."

"You are absolutely right. But I know of two companies that manufacture silver nitrate, and I suspect one of them would be most eager to support this cause as it will open up a new market. Shall I pursue it?"

Louise wished she had thought of it. "By all means."

"I'll attend to it immediately. Meanwhile when it comes to legislative process, I have connections in the Bureau of Hygiene who can help."

Louise said, "So do I."

As she walked home, Louise tried to make sense of the morning's events. Thoughts careened in her head. The little boy from Baby Giveaway Saturday. The awkwardness of having to pretend that Marie was not blinded by gonorrhea, in front of Doc, no less. Doc swooping in without any warning, welcomed like a knight in shining armor. Could she work with him? Did she have a choice? Would anyone else have thought to solicit funding from silver nitrate manufacturers?

With a well-heeled campaign she could pay to have tracts and letters printed. Postage, long distance telephone calls, travel—all would be within reach. She wanted to be hopeful. Instead . . .

*　*　*

At the first Tuesday Bibliophiles' meeting in July, following the book discussion, Gertrude served applesauce cake, smothered in buttery brown sugar frosting and black walnuts.

Dovie licked her fingers. "Gertrude is on her church committee that's trying to persuade Rev. Garnet Horton to bring his revival meeting to Riverbend. If he had a taste of this cake, he wouldn't be able to resist."

Amid a chorus of approval, Gertrude had a satisfied look that relaxed her usual pinched expression. "Not next year—Garnet already has a full revival schedule—but the following year."

Louise decided there was no good time to make her announcement so she might as well get it out of the way. "Changing the subject, I haven't been fair to you with my intermittent attendance and lack of preparation."

Seeming to know what Louise was about to say, Dovie gasped.

Louise could not look at her friend. Her throat was closing around the finality of the words she was about to speak. Her voice quivered. "My duties with the Nebraska Committee to Save Babies' Sight have multiplied, and . . . I regret more than you can know that I must resign from the Tuesday Bibliophiles."

Alice cried and blew her nose. "Louise, you've been our rock."

Louise tried to lighten the moment. "Now don't be crying, Alice, or you'll bring on an asthma attack."

"We'll all miss you," Dovie said. "Maybe you can visit us from time to time."

"Thank you, Dovie. When I founded The Bibliophiles, I thought I never wanted it to end," Louise said. "I feel that sentiment even stronger today. The friendships, the opportunity for self-improvement have made this one of the richest experiences of my life. But I have to respect the demands on my time. This is a very sad day for me."

The handkerchiefs came out amid hugs and promises of continued friendship and regular reunions.

Dovie asked Louise to remain for a few minutes. After the others left, she placed a brown paper bag in Louise's hands as though it were something very fragile. "I want you to have this. For your work."

Louise opened the bag and picked up one of the rubber-banded stacks of currency it held. "Dovie, your rainy day fund?"

"Only part of it. I'd give anything to work on your Committee, Louise, but J.D.—"

Louise embraced Dovie and made a silent promise that nothing could come between them.

CHAPTER 30

August 1906

August brought welcome rain that moved on just before the Chautauqua arrived. Again this year Louise would avoid the shows. The thought of some other girl taking the stage as the child elocutionist trapped Louise in a spiral of grief chasing guilt and guilt chasing grief that left her breathless and sobbing. This year she would leave town.

With her energies focused on a trip that could result in a big boost for the babies' sore eyes movement, she re-opened the suitcase on her bed to pack Marie's Braille slate and stylus. What had set her on this journey was receiving *The Ladies' Home Journal* and a letter from Miss Keller in the mail on the same day. Somehow a thought about the magazine's crusade against venereal disease collided with the notion that readers could hardly get enough of Miss Keller, and from that collision came a "eureka" moment. *What could be more influential than an essay on babies' sore eyes by Helen Keller?*

Better not to risk a written rejection. In spite of her anxiety over traveling alone, Louise decided to go to Chicago where Miss Keller, with help from Anne Sullivan Macy, would be keynote speaker for the annual meeting of the Chicago Federation of Women's Clubs. She telephoned the Palmer House and left a message that Mrs. Francis Morrissey would like to meet with Miss Keller.

Louise was about to close her suitcase when she thought to pack Marie's little doll Sunny for good luck, which she would need if her impromptu scheme was to work. Its boldness made her giddy.

The ringing telephone interrupted.

"I know you're busy so I won't keep you," Dovie said. "But you remember Giovanna planned to retire from the Chautauqua tour? Well she's here now, and Yonder isn't with her."

"What happened?"

"J.D. says she was using Yonder to make her old fiancé jealous, and it worked. She's showing off a ruby engagement ring."

"Where is Yonder?" Please say he's coming home.

"That I don't know. I'll call you if I hear anything more."

* * *

LOUISE BLAMED THE TAXI DRIVER'S surly manner on the heat wave that gripped Chicago. He wasn't the only one in a foul mood. As the taxi approached the Palmer House, Louise saw placard-carrying protesters with signs that read "Unions Against Foreign Scabs" and "Foreigners Go Home." Her concern about traveling as a woman alone was heightened when she got out of the taxi and encountered police with nightsticks shoving the men away from the hotel.

She went to her room to freshen up, then unpacked the Braille slate and stylus and wrote a brief note which she carried to the ballroom where Miss Keller and Mrs. Macy sat with other dignitaries on the podium. Serenely beautiful, Miss Keller seemed so young—indeed, she was merely twenty-six.

Wearing a navy blue suit and ostrich-plumed red hat, she looked as fashionable as any woman in the room.

Louise asked a woman who was handing out programs to deliver the note. The woman looked from the note to Louise's face, which she scrutinized. Louise gave her a congenial smile and only later realized the woman thought she was blind.

When the note was delivered to Mrs. Macy, she looked at it and gave it to Miss Keller.

Seeing Miss Keller's fingertips glide across the page brought a lump to Louise's throat as she remembered the last time she watched Marie doing her lessons.

Miss Keller's placid expression did not change. If she was glad to know of Louise's presence, her face did not register it.

When it was time for Miss Keller's address, Mrs. Macy translated the speech urging women to join the cause of improving the lot of downtrodden workers whether they be American citizens or the despised class of new immigrants. Louise admired Miss Keller's courage in speaking so forthrightly to an audience in which it was likely that a significant number of the upstanding women had husbands who were the very employers she railed against.

Mrs. Macy translated: "Why is it that so many workers live in unspeakable misery? With their hands they have built great cities, and they cannot be sure of a roof over their heads. They have gone into the bowels of the earth for diamonds and gold, and they haggle for a loaf of bread. They plow and sow and fill our hands with flowers while their own hands are filled with dust.

"So long as I confine my activities to social service and the blind, they compliment me extravagantly, calling me 'archpriestess of the sightless,' 'wonder woman,' and 'a modern miracle.' But when it comes to a discussion of poverty, and I maintain that it is the result of wrong economics—that the industrial system under which we live is at the root of much of the physical deafness and blindness in the world—that is a different matter!"

At the end of the program, women rushed to surround Miss Keller. Most merely stared at this remarkable curiosity, made famous by the popular press. Louise imagined them taking in details they could share later with eager listeners and so acquire a modicum of fame themselves. One admirer shook Miss Keller's hand and gushed compliments, then stammered an apology upon seeing her unchanging blank smile.

At one point Miss Keller spoke to Mrs. Macy, who then asked, "Is Mrs. Francis Morrissey present?"

Louise felt a flutter of nerves and exhilaration at the same time. She rushed forward. "Hello, I'm Mrs. Francis Morrissey."

Miss Keller's face brightened as Mrs. Macy signed Louise's words on her palm, and she placed both her hands on Louise's face, tracing her features. A silent crowd watched.

The three adjourned to the hotel suite of Mrs. Macy and Miss Keller, who insisted that because they all shared a bond through Marie they should interact on a first-name basis.

Helen talked about the exploitation of workers and her efforts to bring about labor reform, the abysmal hotel food, her determination to eat a Chicago hot dog before she left town, and Marie. "She became very special to me in the short time I knew her. She was so full of promise. Truly a credit to you and your husband."

As much as she strained to make out Helen's words, Louise

grasped only a few. Upon hearing Annie speak the words, she winced at the praise she didn't merit. Then she wondered if Helen might have extra-sensory perception that would enable her to detect guilt and other emotions. "Thank you. I know she cherished your friendship."

The women talked for another hour or so, with only a short break during which Annie got glasses of water for them all.

Finally Helen said, "You came to see me for a reason."

"I heard you say today that women can accomplish anything they set their minds to. As you know from my letters, I've been speaking to women about babies' sore eyes legislation, trying to convince them that they can move the legislature to act if they will get behind it."

"Good for you. It's a big task you've set for yourself. Don't get discouraged."

"There's are two major obstacles. The women we need to mobilize have never heard of babies' sore eyes, and they're too polite to concern themselves with anything involving gonorrhea."

Helen smiled. "It's a process of education. Getting out leaflets, getting material in libraries, setting up a speakers bureau—"

"There's one thing that will have women all over America, not just in Nebraska, talking. As you know, Edward Bok has been writing editorials warning women about venereal disease in *The Ladies' Home Journal.*"

Helen nodded.

Louise went on. "Women have read with great admiration your articles about your life. You're a hopeful symbol of personal triumph over misfortune. But you are so much more. You are an influential champion of causes you believe in. Do you have any idea how much good might be accomplished if you would write an editorial to educate women and urge them to demand drops?"

Louise held her breath, waiting for Annie to finish signing her request.

Helen spoke, and Mrs. Macy interpreted her words. "Do you know I was studying for exams at Radcliffe College when Mr. Bok asked me to write the story of my life? I was a nervous wreck. I wanted to do both perfectly. The dean made me take my exams in a room all alone to make sure that I didn't get any help from Annie. There were always rumors that she did my work, that a blind and deaf girl could not do what I did, but my exams proved otherwise."

Louise found herself growing impatient for Helen to answer her question. "That's an extraordinary accomplishment for anyone."

"Thank you. Now about babies' sore eyes. You are a good strategist and a persuasive one." Helen smiled. "I am most impressed that you traveled here just to present me your intriguing proposition."

Louise sensed a "however" coming.

"I shall talk to Mr. Bok; however his editorials on venereal disease have cost his magazine upwards of twenty-five thousand subscribers. While I know him to be a man true to his convictions, I cannot promise you his publisher will be keen on printing another controversial article."

* * *

Louise returned to Riverbend and waited, hoping to be

able to bear good news to the Committee. But by the time of the next meeting, Miss Keller had not yet secured the go-ahead to write an article for *The Ladies' Home Journal.*

"I shall help you clean up," Madge said to Louise after the Committee meeting.

Louise handed Madge a dishtowel and filled a basin with water. She considered, then dismissed, the idea of telling Madge about meeting with Helen Keller, something she had not disclosed to the Committee. There was no point in getting hopes up prematurely.

"Did you know Dr. Foster has been working for several years to persuade his medical society colleagues to use drops?" Madge asked.

"I did not."

"He is unduly modest about it; he has not had great success, but these things take time."

"That's admirable."

"It is more than admirable. The man is a leader, Louise, not to disparage your efforts. But he has influence where we need it most, and I am loathe to say it, but he *is* a man . . ."

Louise stopped washing the cup in her hand. "Just what are you getting at?"

"To put it bluntly, our Committee would stand a greater chance of succeeding if Dr. Foster were chairman."

Louise wanted to throw the cup against the wall. "For you of all people to abdicate power to a man—"

"I am being a realist. He is a man and a medical doctor."

Louise tried to interpret the plea in Madge's face and voice. It could have meant she regretted undermining Louise's authority or regretted acknowledging the superiority of men.

Or both.

"Louise, as much as I advocate women taking leadership roles, it is not fair to test it on the backs of innocent children. Ours is a formidable task, and—"

"The others, where do they stand?"

"They hold you in the highest esteem—"

"But want me to step down, even Alice?"

Madge nodded.

"How do you know he'll accept? After all he's very busy."

"It was his idea."

Chapter 31

November 1906

Louise acquiesced to Doc's narrowly focused leadership while her original plans for the Committee smoldered inside her. When Doc assigned yet another letter-writing task, she sensed what was almost a collective sigh from the four women seated at the large reading table. The only one seemingly happy with her duties was Irina, who stood alongside Doc at the end of the table.

"The object of these letters is to reinforce the remarks I shall be making when I speak at the Nebraska Medical Society convention in three weeks." He handed materials to Irina. "Miss Taylor will pass out lists of physicians' names and our new printed letterhead and envelopes. You can see how impressive our letterhead looks. It suggests that our message is one worthy of serious consideration."

Louise set down the list and stationery Irina handed her without looking at them. She bristled. His assumption that printed letterhead would excite the scribes was ludicrous, but if Louise challenged him it would seem like sour grapes.

"Once we get enough physicians on board," Doc said, "we shall work on securing the endorsement of the Medical Society, and that will provide sufficient clout to pressure the legislature."

"How long do you expect it to take, to get the Medical Society's endorsement, that is?" Madge asked.

"It's difficult to say. Perhaps as little as a year with concerted effort."

With the exception of Irina and Alice who were politely attentive, the women seemed less interested in Doc's agenda than in Bonita's argyle-patterned sock taking shape stitch by stitch with the steady click of her knitting needles.

Louise said, "Dr. Foster, you have said yourself that you've been working for ten years to persuade doctors to use drops, and in that time perhaps five percent have gotten on board."

"Yes."

"With all due respect, I believe we would achieve our goal much faster if we broadened our campaign to achieve grassroots support, educate nurses and midwives, and begin making inroads to the legislature."

"I am in agreement," Doc said. "But we should concentrate first on the physicians and adopt a broader campaign as our next phase."

Bonita set down her knitting, and the women looked to Louise who held up the new stationery. "If we are to be nothing more than scribes, this Committee won't exist much longer."

"Just what would you propose?"

"Irina and Bonita can develop a curriculum for midwives and talk to professional nursing and social work organizations. Madge and Alice can create pamphlets to be distributed at every speaking engagement and mailed to women's clubs."

Madge spoke up. "And another set of pamphlets for mothers that could be placed in clinics and distributed by visiting nurses."

"Public pressure," Jerrylynn said. "That's what will move the legislature."

"All good suggestions," Doc said. "But without staging them in phases, we risk spreading ourselves too thin."

Madge said, "Let me give you a bit of advice. We must remember Louise's words at our first meeting: 'Make magnificent plans; with their magic we shall soar over insurmountable obstacles.'"

With the moribund Committee showing signs of life, challenging Doc's plan, Louise anticipated he would dig in.

"I also recall at that meeting," Doc said, "that Mrs. Morrissey extolled the power of women to achieve social reform. I thought of that when I learned the man who was to be keynote speaker for the Women's Auxiliary of the Medical Society had cancelled. Would it not be a coup if Mrs. Morrissey took his place?"

"A speech?" Louise gasped. As the full impact hit her, she said, "In three weeks?" She shook her head. "I'm no speechmaker. Get someone else."

"Come now, Mrs. Morrissey," Doc spread his arms, "you speak so eloquently to this gathering. Just think of this engagement as speaking to a few more people."

Louise suspected now that Doc's idea had been spur-of-the-moment, a way to punish her for questioning his authority. "No. Dr. Foster, you must find someone else."

Alice's face and voice pleaded. "Louise, this is an opportunity we can't pass up." Then she brightened. "I have an idea. Bonita, may we use Vinny's photograph on a big poster?"

"That picture would melt the hardest heart," Madge said.

The women looked toward Bonita, who said, "My sister, God rest her soul, was so ashamed of having gonorrhea, even though she was the innocent victim of a philandering husband.

I'll have to think it over."

The prospect of giving a speech, forgotten, Louise felt a flush rising from her neck and averted her gaze away from Doc. *Did Bonita's words move him? Does he accept that he infected me and blinded Marie?*

* * *

THREE WEEKS LATER, LOUISE AWAKENED from a dream in which she was shackled to a chair. She shuddered free of the restraint. Setting her feet on the floor and yielding to the sensation of its cool surface helped to clear her mind. Now a paralysis of another sort seized her—the thought of giving the speech.

Today she was going to Lincoln to the Nebraska Medical Society convention to speak to the Auxiliary while Doc spoke to their husbands. Louise would have to interact with him only once, at which time he would hand off the poster he carried in a large portfolio. The poster featured Vinny's picture with the heading, "Needlessly Blind."

There was time to rehearse her speech once more before leaving for the train depot. Standing in the kitchen, she went through the motion of removing the watch pinned to her lapel and placing it on an imagined lectern. With this ritual she would mentally shift into her public speaking role which set the words she knew by heart flowing almost automatically. She shut out the annoying drip of the kitchen faucet, figuring she needed the discipline of handling distractions. The speech lasted exactly twenty-one minutes and went according to plan. But she held out hope that the train would be late or that some *deus ex machina* would save her from having to give the speech

On her way out of the Inn—it would always be "the Inn"

even though J.D. had turned it into Riverview Old Folks Home—she stopped at the front desk to report the leaky faucet. Harley would probably have it fixed by the time she got home from Lincoln.

The journey behind her, she met Doc in the hall outside the adjacent ballrooms where they'd be simultaneously presenting their speeches. She squeaked a "hello."

"You look stricken. Stop thinking about all the things that might go wrong. You have rehearsed, you know what you want to say, and you have your notes, right?"

She nodded.

"Good. You have a solid foundation. Now fix your mind on the profound significance of your message. And fix your mind on how important it is that your audience hear that message. Concern yourself *only* with conveying your message to your audience. Hold that thought in your mind from now on until you have finished your speech."

Louise nodded. How could she have allowed herself to get into this situation? Letting this man who should have no place in her life volunteer her to speak and now stand here and lecture her? *Who does he think he is?*

A man approached and said he would be introducing Dr. Foster to the assembled doctors. Doc followed him, leaving Louise to make her way to the North Platte Room. The sight of about one hundred women seated there caused her breaths to become shallow. As she approached the stage she was greeted by an officious-looking woman in a smart black and white suit who directed her to an empty seat.

The women seated on either side of Louise introduced themselves. She instantly forgot their names.

The sound of the gavel caused Louise to look in the direction of the lectern, next to which stood the easel that would hold Vinny's picture. Her hand went to her mouth to stifle a gasp. *Doc has the poster.* Her presentation depended on the picture. How would she manage without it?

There being no choice, she mentally reorganized her speech as the woman in the black and white suit welcomed the guests, made introductions, and launched into a lengthy thank-you to individuals, committees, and companies for all manner of support. Then the business meeting began, with reports from the secretary, treasurer, and committee chairs. Louise checked her watch. She breathed deeply, trying to summon the courage she would need to speak. But another committee chair was called to report. And then another.

When Louise was finally introduced, she was stunned to hear she would be allotted just ten minutes. She carried her notes and a stack of petitions to the lectern and looked around in vain for a friendly face. The audience had grown restless, their scheduled break delayed. Just as rehearsed, she reached for her watch, but the clasp would not budge. Instead of being a graceful, purposeful gesture, it appeared pointless, and she would have to guess at the time.

"Thank you, Madam President." Her voice quivered. She looked down at her notes. "I am honored to address this very august organization. Women today are the vanguard of social change to benefit society's health and welfare, particularly that of its children. I noted your efforts along those lines, such as with your committee to advocate vaccinations for school children. I am here today because I would like to enlist your invaluable support for The Nebraska Committee to Save Babies' Sight."

Watching women squirm and check their watches was leeching the last shred of confidence right out of her body. She was Lulu again, back in New Lexington, stammering through an oral book report. *Concern yourself only with conveying the message to your audience.* She set aside her notes, rendered useless anyway by the severe time constraint. At the heart of her message was Vinny, whose sweet picture the audience would never see. If nothing else she wanted to convey his plight so poignantly they would wish to save others from his fate. "I want to tell you the story of three-year-old Vinny. He is legally blind and has lived at Smithville State Asylum for the Blind since the death of his mother. Vinny and approximately one-third of all children in the state asylum were needlessly blinded.

"*Needlessly blinded,* you ask. Yes, needlessly, because for some thirty years there has been a known preventative for the blinding condition known as *babies' sore eyes.* If all babies received dilute silver nitrate drops at birth, babies' sore eyes, this cause of so much unnecessary blindness, would be wiped out.

"Now I must bring up an indelicate matter. Like all of you I was bred to eschew language unbecoming a lady. I was also bred to do what is right, and I reached a turning point in my life at which I realized that to do right, I must say the unspeakable. For, you see, babies contract the blinding bacteria"—here the breath support for her voice waned—"in the birth canal of mothers who have gonorrhea." Pausing until the murmured reaction of her audience subsided gave her a chance to take some deep breaths.

"Vinny's mother was a good woman. Like many women, she was infected by her husband. Vinny was needlessly blinded because . . ." The well-rehearsed words simply vanished. "Forgive me, but I've lost my train of thought." She paused, trying not to feel the women's impatience. "Vinny was needlessly blinded because society's taboos against talking about venereal disease stood in the way of taking action.

"Discuss this matter with your husbands. They are better qualified to explain the medical side of this issue than I, and they will confirm what I said about the efficacy of prophylaxis. The Nebraska Committee to Save Babies' Sight, which I represent, seeks nothing less than legislation mandating drops in all newborn babies' eyes.

She nodded to the woman who held her petitions. "We shall now pass out petitions which, when signed, will be delivered to the state legislature. I hope you will carry them to your communities. We need influential women such as you to carry our educational message and to mobilize other women to get behind this cause.

"It is too late for Vinny. But let us act today to protect the children of tomorrow. Thank you."

Louise acknowledged polite applause and started to pick up her notes but thought better of it, realizing that holding notes would make the trembling of her hands obvious. She watched the stacks of petitions move from hand to hand like hot potatoes. Perhaps a total of four, maybe five, women took a petition. *Damn Dr. Vandegrift. Damn Doc.*

* * *

DAISY HAD INSISTED LOUISE STAY overnight and get the early train the next morning. "Just let yourself in," Daisy had said. "You'll find the teapot and scones in the kitchenette. Help yourself. I'll be home shortly after you arrive."

The taxi ride took Louise to the Hampton Arms in a seedy part of town. Entering the building, she followed a long, dark hallway where the only ornamentation was a telephone mounted to a wall and telephone numbers scrawled in pencil. She climbed stairs to the third floor where a single bulb lit the narrow hallway. A heavyset man wearing a bathrobe and carrying a towel exited an apartment. His jowls jiggled, set in motion by his lumbering gait.

Louise opened a door to a cramped, windowless parlor. Frank would have said, "It's so small you can't cuss a cat without getting fur in your mouth." Painstaking attempts had been made to brighten it. Daisies abounded—on a decorative quilt hanging on one wall, on the cushions of two white wicker chairs, on a curtain separating the parlor from the kitchenette, and on a hooked rug. A wicker coffee table held a silver vase with cut daisies. On one wall was a Murphy bed, which Louise presumed would be hers.

An open door revealed a bedroom, and as there were no other doors, Louise realized she'd be sharing a toilet and bathtub with the likes of the jowly neighbor. Hard to imagine that Daisy, bred to enjoy finer things, had invited her to stay in such a place, and without apology. *A lesson in acceptance.*

Louise was pouring a cup of tea when Daisy burst in cradling a fat and aging fox terrier.

"Meet Hercules. Hercules, this is my old friend Lulu." Before taking off her coat, Daisy reached for a scone which she broke into tiny bites and coaxed Hercules to eat. "He scarcely has any teeth left." She nuzzled the dog. "Is Mama's baby hungry?" She explained to Louise, "The neighbors watch him while I'm at work. I always worry he doesn't get enough to eat."

Once the two women and Hercules were settled in the wicker chairs, Daisy asked Louise how her presentation was received.

"Worse than I could possibly have imagined." Louise described how she had failed to get Vinny's poster, how her time was cut short, and how the audience was restless for a break. "And they handled the petitions like they carried cholera germs. Afterwards I realized I had failed to explain why *all* newborn babies needed drops even if there was no chance the mother had gonorrhea. And I should have urged them to write to their legislators."

"But look at you, Lulu, you did it. I would simply die if I had to give a speech. You'll bowl them over next time."

"But this was such an important occasion. I should have practiced on an audience less critical to our mission."

Daisy shook her head. "As I recall, you didn't have a choice. That doctor shoved you into the lion's den with almost no time to prepare. Darned inconsiderate, if you ask me."

"I wonder if the audience would have been more sympathetic had I mentioned that many women die of gonorrhea."

"All I know about speechmaking is from comments Dr. Weil makes, but I'm inclined to think that even if everything had gone as planned your speech wouldn't have moved the audience to act. They were probably so stunned to hear the word *gonorrhea* they scarcely heard anything else. An audience should be primed first, know something about the subject and its indelicate nature. Maybe mail them a leaflet. Or place an item in their newsletter. Addressing an audience cold is a recipe for disaster."

"That's why Doc had the Committee send letters to the doctors. We should have sent them to the wives as well."

"How many women took a petition?"

"Five at most." Louise noticed Daisy's smile and raised eyebrows. "Oh, I see what you're getting at. We have five allies we didn't have before."

"Yes." Daisy spoke the word with such gusto that Hercules awoke with a jerk. She stroked his head till he sighed and returned to sleep.

After a light supper, Daisy put on her coat and took Hercules for a quick walk. When she returned, she started toward her bedroom. "Let's get comfortable. I can't stand this corset another minute."

Louise gladly changed into her nightgown, robe, and slippers. When Daisy returned to the living room, she was wearing pajamas and slippers and was carrying crocheted afghans, one of which she handed to Louise. "Here. The landlord is stingy with the heat." Then she poured two snifters of brandy, and the women sat in the wicker chairs.

Louise had noticed the chill but hadn't said anything.

Hercules begged at his mistress' knee, and Daisy scooped him into her lap. He circled and settled, and she tucked the afghan around him.

As they drank their brandy, talk centered on Dr. Weil, namely that Daisy had a crush on him and sometimes noticed signs that he had feelings for her.

It was while drinking their second brandy that the conversation turned to New Lexington, a place both women had permanently left behind. Daisy exhibited a remarkable ability to remember their school days and the names of schoolmates.

"Did you hear what became of your parents after you left?"

Louise shook her head.

"Remember the poor girl they called 'Dumb Sandy'?" Daisy asked.

"Of course. My father worked for her father."

Daisy snickered, and Hercules flinched. "You got in a fist fight with Charles Baumgartner because he and some other boys were teasing her."

"I'd almost forgotten. I got my nose bloodied. You know what he did that made me so mad?"

"Oh, I remember it well," Daisy said.

"He put a live frog in Sandy's lunch pail."

Daisy's expression turned sober. "I envied what you did. Wished I'd had the nerve to beat him up myself."

She envied me?

Daisy shifted the afghan over Hercules' exposed hindquarters. "Be glad you left when you did. Her father caught yours having his way with her in the horse barn . . ."

Louise gasped.

"Horsewhipped him and ran him out of town. Your mother followed."

"My God, Daisy. It's because I left." Louise covered her mouth as she spoke. "He wouldn't have bothered her if I'd stayed. I never considered the consequences of leaving."

"Then that's why *you* left."

Louise nodded. "Poor Sandy."

"It's not your fault."

"You don't understand." Louise heard her volume rising with a brandy-inspired confession. Her mind played its litany of sins: causing Pa to lust after her, failing to protect Ma, committing adultery, deceiving Frank, blinding Marie. And because she'd deceived Frank, causing the worst unintended consequence of all, the accident that killed him and Marie. "It's always my fault."

Daisy reached over and placed her hand on Louise's. "I'm so sorry. I shouldn't have said anything. You mustn't blame yourself." She stood, set Hercules in her chair, and patted Louise's shoulder, then picked up both their snifters. "Another drink would do you good."

That night Louise awakened shaking from a dream. Pa was touching her in places he shouldn't, trying to kiss her, and as she tried to fight him off he shoved her away, saying "Shame on you," and calling her "daughter of the devil."

She lay awake, recalling how she had learned to read his eyes, the shift from indifferent to leering that meant she must run or fight. Over and over she'd uttered silent prayers: "Cleanse the evil in me that makes Pa lust for me. Rescue me from hell on earth. Smite Pa with your sword of righteousness."

At night when sleep would not come, she planned her escape down to the last detail. Only one thing kept her from carrying it out. She had to protect Ma.

But everything changed one day soon after her twelfth birthday. She was bent over next to the rain barrel, dipping a pot in the water to rinse her hair, when Pa grabbed her from behind. In one swift movement, he threw up her skirt and pulled down her drawers. She whirled about to break his grip but her foot caught on the drawers at her ankles. From the corner of her eye, she spied Ma watching from the porch. Pa tripped and fell, giving her time to kick off her drawers and run across the garden, trampling the tender shoots in her path. She could not outrun him. She saw the rake lying in the potato patch. When she turned and raised the rake, Pa stopped. She swung the weapon like a baseball bat, but he ducked. Thrown off balance, she spun around in a full revolution that seemed to last an eternity, a peaceful hiatus from fear and anger that ended with the rake slamming squarely above his ear. Bloodied and screaming, his eyes bulging, he dropped and writhed on the ground. She ran from the garden and saw Ma hobbling down the porch steps. Louise ran for the road and never looked back.

Chapter 32

November 1906

Upon returning from Lincoln, Louise approached the Inn and saw workmen pushing wheelbarrows piled high with boards toward the scrap dealer's horse-drawn wagon. More renovation. The latest, of which J.D. was very proud, was having the shingled exterior painted a hideous burnt orange. Gone was the warmth of brown. J.D. declared it too solemn, but Louise had always found it comforting, the Inn nestled naturally next to the woods. J.D. was even more proud of the elevator which had been installed next to the staircase. Adding to Louise's disquiet, the lobby lacked the vitality of travelers coming and going. Instead there was the monotony of the same people playing cards or working jigsaw puzzles. Even though her apartment remained unchanged, the Inn no longer felt like home.

Nearing the scrap dealer's wagon, Louise was struck by the familiarity of its load of weathered boards. She hastened to bring the scene into full view, hoping to dispel her suspicions. She stopped abruptly. Louise knew those boards. Had tweezed their splinters from Frank's hands, the very hands he had dreamed with, had used to rescue the old ship—and himself—from obscurity. Like the sculptor seeking his own immortality in preserving his subject: *My name is Ozymandias . . .* Now these men were tearing down Morrissey's Folly.

Making her way to the Inn's front door, she avoided residents who sat in the Adirondack chairs watching men jam crowbars into the ship's hull, tear away the boards, and expose the ribs beneath.

Passing through the lobby she held her composure long enough to exchange pleasantries with the three friendly, blue-haired widows who sat working a jigsaw puzzle at their usual table.

Standing outside her apartment, she fumbled for the lock through a blur of tears. Once inside she dropped to a chair and wept. Frank would have had a name for the blue-haired widows.

* * *

It was near sundown when Louise answered a knock on her door. It was J.D. Holding a pipe wrench in one grimy hand, being a man who cultivated calluses and eschewed manicures these days, he looked at her with glazed eyes. His chest heaved with each drunken breath. "At your service, madam." He grinned.

Dovie had confided to Louise that she was worried sick over J.D. Since losing his bid for state senate two weeks earlier he had taken to drinking every day.

He clutched the edge of the sink and lowered himself to his knees. Grunting, he squirmed into position to get at the pipe under the sink. He kept up a running commentary about cheap materials and workmanship and the ruinous effects of immigration.

"There!" He stood up, dropped the pipe wrench, and stumbled but caught himself. When he lunged toward Louise, she thought he had simply lost his balance, but he grabbed her with grimy hands and placed a slobbery kiss on her mouth. She pushed him away and kneed him in the groin.

He yelped and shielded his privates.

She pushed him toward the door. "Shame on you. Now you take your little pipe wrench and get out of here."

She slammed the door. Stepping back, her chest heaving, she stared at the door and reflected on what had just happened. There was more to widowhood than grief and loss. Was merely being a woman alone an invitation to men like J.D.? Sometimes a woman had to take off the kid gloves. It was good she had not been born a lady.

She ran water in the kitchen sink and kneeled down to check the pipe. No leak. She stood, and suddenly the episode with J.D. took on new significance. *What if he carried the scent of my gardenia bath salts? He could tell Dovie I had tried to seduce him.*

*   *   *

BETRAYAL. WHEN HAD LOUISE FIRST felt betrayed? By Pa? Was it betrayal when someone you never trusted proves untrustworthy? Ma! Now, there was betrayal that cut so deep she had buried it for years. Ma, watching her and Pa in the vegetable garden and turning away. *But was I justified in running away, breaking my vow to protect Ma?*

Then betraying Frank. A good provider, and he loved her. *Had I been honest with him, he might even have accepted another man's child.*

Now given a chance, J.D. would betray Dovie, if he hadn't already.

Chapter 33

January 1907

Louise spent a quiet New Year's Day reflecting on the old year, impatient for the new. The following day, she went down to the lobby three times to check for mail. Each time she exchanged pleasantries with the elevator operator who, on the third trip, looked at her askance. When the mail finally arrived, there it was, the January issue of *The Ladies' Home Journal.* Louise entered the elevator, gave the operator a polite nod, then paged through the magazine until she found Helen's article, "I Must Speak: A Plea to the American Woman."

Once inside her apartment, she went to her chair in the back parlor and began reading. Her eyes settled on words intended to elicit the reader's concern. But for her, the words brought back frightful memories: "The symptoms of the disease appear in the infant's eyes soon after birth. The eyelids swell and become red, and about the second day they discharge whitish pus.

"What is the cause of *ophthalmia neonatorum?* It is a specific germ communicated by the mother to the child at birth. Previous to the child's birth she has unconsciously received it through infection from her husband. He has contracted the infection in licentious relations before or since marriage. 'The cruelest link in the chain of consequences,' says Dr. Prince Morrow, 'is the mother's innocent agency. She is made a passive, unconscious medium of instilling into the eyes of her newborn babe a virulent poison which extinguishes its sight.'" Louise gripped the arm of her chair. Feeling anything but innocent, she had to stop reading. When she'd asked Helen to write an article, she hadn't considered how the words might rip open her old wounds. She set down the magazine and went to the kitchen for a glass of water.

Returning to the back parlor, she sat and picked up the magazine. "In mercy let it be remembered, the father does not know that he has so foully destroyed the eyes of his child and handicapped him for life." The old anger welled. "Risk of a medical complication," Doc had said. "We'll dispose of this burden." At the time it seemed a ruse, but he *had* known the risk. The weight of this certainty sat on her chest, constricting her breathing. She stepped out to the balcony to clear her head and regain her composure.

Then she returned to the parlor and continued to read."It is part of the bitter harvest of the wild oats he has sown. Society has smiled upon his 'youthful recklessness' because Society does not know that 'They enslave their children's children who make compromise with sin.'"

Those words again. Her anger toward Doc was displaced by guilt that seized her almost like a living thing. She could go for long stretches seeming to have put it behind her, but it was lurking in the shadows, waiting for her next vulnerable moment. She would have to finish reading the article later.

*   *   *

LOUISE ARRIVED EARLY FOR THE January Committee meeting and found the library door already unlocked. Without thinking, she'd tried the door with her injured left hand. She bit her lip against the pain. She'd punctured that hand several days earlier as she jabbed an icepick at stubborn frost in her electric icebox. What had been a minor wound was now infected and streaked with red.

Upon opening the library door she caught the scent of Doc's pipe tobacco and the silver-bells sound of a woman's laughter.

Doc sat at the reading table tamping tobacco in his pipe, and across from him sat Irina, pen in hand. She was especially attractive today, wearing a peacock print silk scarf that flattered her blue-violet eyes.

It was innocent enough. He was reviewing the curriculum for midwives that Irina and Bonita had drafted.

"Join us," Doc said. "Irina has a superb idea."

Louise hung up her coat and hat, removed her gloves, and took her usual seat at the table. She kept her left hand in her lap, hiding her ugly injury.

As Doc explained, Irina watched him with sparkling eyes. "We'll ask Argent Laboratories to provide silver nitrate for a demonstration project at Riverbend Hospital."

"The hospital has already agreed, contingent on us supplying the drops," Irina said.

"Thanks to Irina," Doc said.

That Doc had said "Irina," not "Miss Taylor" did not escape Louise's notice. Her hands in her lap, she absently twisted her emerald-and-pearl anniversary ring.

"Also, we're going to use some of Argent's funding to provide sandwiches, coffee, and cookies at our midwives' training sessions," Irina said.

"Nothing like free food to boost attendance," Louise said. Since when did the two of them act on their own without bringing matters before the Committee?

She sighed. "I had an incident last week talking to the Midlands Social Workers Society in Omaha. *Social workers*, mind you. A woman stood up and said, 'You can say it's not just immigrants who get the disease, but no one I know ever got it and never will.' Then she pointed to the poster of Vinny on the easel and said, 'There's your typical case. If that boy isn't a Dago, I'm a monkey's uncle.' It was like a knife through my heart, but I remained calm and acknowledged that the incidence is higher in big cities and crowded slums but that no class is spared. Then another woman argued that those numbers only reflected births in hospitals, and everyone knew that immigrants gave birth at home and never even bothered to get birth certificates."

"We could replace Vinny with a little blonde girl," Irina said.

Louise glared at her. "Then replace me, too."

"Surely you don't mean it," Doc said.

The door opened, and Madge and Jerrylynn arrived. Bonita and Alice soon followed, and it wasn't long before Louise's cloudy mood lifted. Doc may have been chairman of the Committee, but at this meeting she was its star. The women gushed over Helen's editorial to such a degree that it almost distracted Louise from throbbing pain.

The Committee was making progress. Louise announced that the Bureau of Hygiene was considering a regulation, which Doc had drafted with Daisy's help, requiring doctors and midwives to report all new cases of babies' sore eyes. Modeled after a Massachusetts regulation, it was designed to identify babies and families in need of follow-up services from social workers and visiting nurses, gather demographic data which was expected to show that babies' sore eyes affected families in all parts of the state and of all social classes, and to serve as a first step toward getting doctors and midwives to comply with drops once they were mandated.

"Lest you think half the battle is won, let me tell you we face strong opposition," Louise said. "One senator actually told Dr. Weil that babies should be allowed to go blind so that they and their mothers will serve as an example of the wages of sin."

"No!" Madge said. "How cruel and ignorant."

Once the Committee members' outrage subsided, Louise said, "I have some good news. Helen Keller will be in Omaha to attend a conference in February, and she has offered to lend support to our Nebraska campaign."

Spirits soared.

After the meeting Doc approached Louise as she was picking up papers. "Congratulations on getting Miss Keller's endorsement."

As she was sliding papers into her satchel, he said, "That's a nasty looking wound. Come to my surgery and I'll lance it."

"It will be fine, thank you."

He exhaled noisily. "I can lance it now or amputate later."

Louise followed Doc into his surgery, a tidy room that reeked of alcohol.

He turned on a lamp at the end of the examining table. "If you don't mind standing, the light is better over here." He washed his hands, then gathered together a scalpel, gauze, and bottles of alcohol and hydrogen peroxide.

When he turned and faced her across the table, she thought she saw a glint of recognition, that this moment evoked the night they stood across from one another treating victims of The Twister. That night Doc had selected her, seemingly at random, to assist him, and in spite of inexperience and self-doubt, she managed to administer morphine, dress mangled limbs, and comfort victims and survivors. She remembered the glow within when, at the end of the long night, Doc said, "You performed your duties as skillfully as a trained nurse." The affair and its life-altering consequences had so eclipsed the memory of that experience, that only now did she recognize the special power of that night, the awakening to possibility, to a sense that within her lay untapped passion not of a carnal nature but something even more profound. She had thrived on becoming so lost in a worthy task that nothing else—appearances, respectability, achievements—mattered.

Doc patted the table indicating where she should place her hand. His gaze suggested a desire for connection and took her back to a moment when she could reach up and touch distant constellations. She had to look away. That feeling, she recalled, was one that both Doc and Frank had once had the ability to arouse. Or had she been so desperate for intimacy she ascribed meaning to a certain look, a meaning that might not have been intended? Had she felt exalted because she imagined it so?

Doc swabbed the wound liberally with alcohol. "I must caution you that this will hurt. If you will recite a forgotten poem in your mind, the mental effort will help to take your mind off the pain."

She could not recall a poem without picturing Marie practicing her elocution lessons. "Just get it over with." She looked away and felt the pressure of Doc's hand gripping hers, then the cut. Pain caused her to grit her teeth and produced an unwanted quiver in her privates. Her free hand gripped the table edge.

"I am sorry." He squeezed the wound to expel the pus and flushed it with hydrogen peroxide. "Puncture wounds are tricky. They want to heal over on the surface before the wound has a chance to heal underneath, so they fester. Do not bandage it. Allow air to get to it, and keep it cleansed with hydrogen peroxide."

She thanked him and picked up her handbag and satchel. He opened the door for her, but she pushed it shut and turned back toward him.

"I shall be blunt," she said. "If there is anything between you and Irina, I plan to tell her you're a carrier . . ."

"Stop, now, Louise. My intentions are nothing but honorable. I made it clear to her the loss of my wife had rendered me unable to love another woman."

"I don't remember you being especially fond . . ."

Scalpel in hand, he puffed up like a cornered animal, chest heaving and eyes flashing. "Do not presume to know my feelings for my late wife."

As though embarrassed by his menacing stance, he turned, picked up a towel, and wiped the scalpel in a slow, deliberate manner, placed it in a tray, and dropped the towel in a hamper. "My wife was an extraordinary woman once. It was my fault we became estranged. I infected her, just as I infected you. I have been celibate since I first saw Marie. I vowed I would never endanger another woman . . . or blind another child."

"Tell me something." Louise tried in vain to steady her

trembling voice. "I have to know. Why did you fail to inform me that you had gonorrhea and fail to treat Marie?"

His face sagged. "I did treat Marie, but—"

"Don't weasel out of this. It was too late. Her eyes were already infected."

"I had a bout of it once—"

Louise slammed her handbag on the examining table. "But you're a doctor! You knew you might still be a carrier. I want to know why a doctor, one who prides himself on being progressive, would knowingly expose women to gonorrhea."

"It's *because* I am a doctor. I convinced myself I could manage the risks. I knew that once infected there was a possibility, not a certainty, mind you, that I would continue to carry the germ. It was not until my wife became ill that I knew I was a carrier. I begged her to have surgery, but she refused. Scar tissue from the disease made her infertile, and she suffered chronic pain. She hated me for infecting her. She felt cheated by not having children and eventually gave up on life."

"And you infected me."

"I loved you." His usually resonant voice became thin and nasal, the sound of a man desperate to defend the indefensible. "The truth is I wanted you so badly. The risk—the day your husband summoned me, when I saw Marie's eyes, I knew you were infected. That is why I wanted you to get under a doctor's care right away."

Louise resented his trying to shift blame to her. "Why would I? For the longest time I had no idea I was sick until I started having unbearable pain. I ended up having surgery for pelvic inflammatory disease. Even then I didn't know the cause. It wasn't until I learned the cause of Marie's blindness that—"

Doc frowned and shook his head. "Before I left your home that day, I talked to your housekeeper. I told her to give you a message, that you must see a woman's doctor in Omaha as soon as you were fit to travel. I tried to impress upon her that it was very important."

"Henryetta?" Louise recalled the days after Marie's birth, drifting in and out of a fog. She had not even been aware that Doc had examined her and Marie until Frank told her later. No one had given her a message from Doc.

He looked away as though scanning his memory. "A little, stout woman with strings on her fingers."

"Henryetta. What did she do when you told her?"

"She said she would tell you."

"Did she tie a string on another finger?"

"No."

"Are you certain? You didn't see her reach in her apron pocket for a string?"

"No. I remember the scene as though it were yesterday. When I entered the kitchen, she was putting a handful of meat through the grinder, she picked up another handful and scarcely looked up. She was so intent on grinding that meat, looked like she planned to make hash, that I thought she might have been too distracted to apprehend my words so I repeated myself."

"She forgot. That's why she didn't tell me."

Doc's face contorted in anguish. "Louise, I am truly sorry. I should have made certain you saw a specialist. I loved you, yet I acted the coward at your expense."

"You loved me? You made me believe we would go away together and start a new life—"

"Which I wanted more than you will ever know."

"Then why did you abandon me?"

"Not because I wanted to. I had a duty to care for my wife. You did not need me. She did."

"What about Marie? Had you informed me of the danger, had you instilled drops when she was born instead of waiting—"

"I was like everyone else in my profession, which I know is not an excuse. We knew the efficacy of prophylaxis, but we failed to act on what we knew. I am ashamed to say it, but I gambled with your life and Marie's sight."

"You knew and you gambled. How could you?"

Doc slumped, and his head turned from side to side. "I meant to end our liaison after our first encounter, but I lacked the will." Seeming to realize his admissions were out of character, he snapped to a confident pose. His voice took on a defensive tone. "You know yourself that even though a woman may have gonorrhea, it does not inevitably blind her newborn baby. Quite the contrary. Infection develops in just a small percentage of cases. I have witnessed just two in the last ten years, yet the number of women in Riverbend with active or latent gonorrhea is legion. When I told you there might be a medical complication, I was being selfish. To be honest, I considered your having a baby a personal complication for me. My words were intended to get you to abort. I didn't think for one minute that the baby would be infected. Now you no doubt wonder why I support the campaign. It's because of Marie. She taught me humility."

He reached for her hand, but she withdrew it.

"Louise, I cannot be so bold as to ask your forgiveness."

"Marie taught you humility? You saw this pathetic little

baby lying in her crib, her eyes oozing pus, and you went away with a lesson in humility. Do you know what Marie taught me? I lived with her every day and witnessed her valiant attempts to thrive in a sighted world to which she would never belong, and I got a daily lesson in God's wrath, that I had betrayed my husband and blinded my precious daughter. Marie taught me that every day was God's punishment for loving you."

Hearing her own shrill voice, bent on bludgeoning Doc with words, Louise felt possessed. Rarely had she expressed herself without regard for behavior unbecoming a lady, and it left her raw and exposed.

As she reached for her handbag, her injured hand struck the counter. She ignored the pain. "Don't fool yourself into thinking that I still love you. The campaign needs you."

CHAPTER 34

February 1907

In Omaha for a labor reform meeting, Helen Keller committed two days to the Nebraska campaign. People who had closed their doors to Louise opened them wide for the chance to meet Helen. With interpreting assistance from Annie, the women addressed a meeting of the Visiting Nurses Association, met with the executive board of the Federation of Women's Clubs, and received a most encouraging response from the dean and faculty of the School of Nursing at the University of Nebraska Medical School.

Now, at the end of a long day, Louise sat with Helen in the parlor of the Victoria Hotel suite Helen shared with Annie, who was napping. Louise had thought Helen must be wealthy until learning that the luxurious accommodations were provided by her sometimes benefactor, Andrew Carnegie, whose admiration for Helen exceeded his loathing of her socialist ideals.

The parlor was two different worlds. One belonged to Louise for whom it held sensual pleasures: marble fireplace, polished brass lamps, crystal chandelier, damask wall covering in ruby red and forest green, gold brocade draperies, and overstuffed mahogany furniture. The crackle of the fire, the bump of logs, and the chatter of sleet on the windowpanes. In Helen's presence Louise's senses became more acute, not to be taken for granted, a guilty indulgence.

The other world belonged to Helen for whom it parceled out minimal sensual cues to differentiate it from any other place: the fragrance of flowers; the feel of crushed velvet upholstery; the warmth from the fireplace on her hands and face in contrast to the chilly draft on her neck; the vibrations of footsteps, bumping logs, or closing doors. Helen was trapped in a world she called her "prison of darkness and silence."

The friendship that began after Marie's death had deepened with Louise's determination to bridge the chasm of Helen's deafness and blindness. Few people could understand Helen's slurred speech, and even fewer bothered to learn her tactile sign language.

Helen spoke, breaking Louise's reverie. "Annie tells me that when you were asked the cause of Marie's blindness by a board member of the Federation of Women's Clubs, you said it was a *pnuemococcal* infection."

Whether expressing delight or anger, Helen's voice was an undulating falsetto, hard to read. But now everything in her posture and demeanor said "judgmental." "But it wasn't *pneumococcus.*"

Louise signed into Helen's hand. "What are you getting at?"

"Marie's eyes were once described to me. I understand your wanting to protect your reputation, but honesty and trust are cornerstones of friendship. I regard your stubborn insistence that Marie was not blinded by gonorrhea as an impediment to our friendship. Come now, Louise, there's no shame in having been the innocent agent who carried the blinding infection."

Louise resented the invasion of privacy and had no intention of setting the record straight. There were things a woman should keep to herself that Helen did not seem to appreciate. Helen was fifteen years younger, and moreover emboldened by the influence of Annie and her husband, John, and their freethinking intellectual friends. Her hand shook as she signed, "How would you like it if I pried into your private life?"

"There's precious little left of my private life," Helen said. "Rumors about my shared living arrangement with the Macys. The press report when Peter Fagan and I secured a marriage license last year."

"Yes. I knew, of course. I'm so sorry. I read that your family intervened." Louise was being tactful. In fact, Helen's brother-in-law ran Fagan off with a shotgun, and on another occasion Helen's mother abducted her to keep her from meeting him.

"What the press didn't know is that Peter and I continued to communicate. We had a secret place where we left notes. We planned to elope. I sneaked down to the porch during the night and sat until morning with my packed bag. He never arrived, and I never heard from him again."

Louise's throat tightened. Of all the stories of love pursued and lost—the Indian maiden leaping from a cliff to join her beloved brave in death, lovers separated by race or religion or oceans—the pathos they aroused paled against the image Louise held of this young deaf and blind woman sitting on a porch throughout the night with her packed suitcase. Waiting with just a few material possessions, willing to break with her family and Annie, intoxicated with the anticipation of being spirited away by her lover. Time passes. Doubt creeps in. Then dread, as it becomes certain he will never appear.

Louise tried to steady her hand as she signed in Helen's palm, "Do you know what happened?"

"No. Perhaps he recognized the burden of caring for a deaf and blind wife. And I came to regret the pain I caused my mother. I cannot account for my behavior. I seem to have acted exactly opposite to my nature."

Louise squeezed Helen's hand before responding. "You are not alone. I was so in love once that I became a person I scarcely recognized. Do you regret the romance?"

"I am glad that I have had the experience of being loved and desired. The fault was not in the loving but in the circumstances. But we digress. Why will you not state the obvious?"

"Where I come from, masking one's true nature is a virtue."

A knock on the door saved Louise. She signed, "Room service is here."

* * *

A TAXI RIDE THROUGH HEAVY sleet took Louise and Helen to their last appointment, a meeting with Sen. Mortimer Phillips of Omaha, chairman of the legislature's powerful Ways and Means Committee. Nearly a year had passed since Louise had first attempted to get the attention of the legislature with her letter to Sen. Adolph Bruegger, and subsequent letters and petitions had brought only terse replies. Doc had once had a meeting with some senators, set up by an influential medical colleague. It resulted in a polite brush-off. But with the mention of Helen's name, Louise found Sen. Phillips eager to meet.

He greeted them in the sparsely furnished office of his company, which manufactured farm implements. At first he mistook Louise for Annie. Louise explained that Mrs. Macy was in the hotel room getting some much-needed rest.

He pumped Helen's hand. "My stock went up with my

wife and daughter when I told them I was meeting with you today."

He beckoned them to join him at a window that overlooked the manufacturing floor.

As they approached the window, Helen became visibly distressed. Being extremely sensitive to vibrations, she flinched at all the factory noises. Louise began to think it had been a mistake coming here. She took Helen's hand and signed a description of workers carrying materials to men who stood at giant saws and presses turning out parts that all came together to make plows and harvesters. After a bit, Helen seemed to grow accustomed to the commotion and calmed down.

Louise continued to sign, interpreting the Senator's words. "What you're witnessing is not merely a manufacturing operation." Sen. Phillips' big voice carried over the rumbling from the plant below. "What you're seeing is the marriage of two great industries, agriculture and manufacturing, the industries that are building America. Mark my words, one day this upstart country will be the envy of the world."

He dragged two straight-back chairs toward his metal desk, a catch-all for papers, a camera, lunchpail, and greasy machine parts. "Please have a seat, ladies."

Sen. Phillips talked at length about important matters facing the Ways and Means Committee and the various interests competing for limited resources. Almost without taking a breath, he launched into a rant about the demands of serving the citizens of Nebraska and their lack of appreciation. When he griped that he received a mere pittance for his efforts, that he served out of a selfless sense of duty, Louise nudged Helen with her knee as she signed, "It's an effort not to laugh."

Helen smiled.

He boasted that the Nebraska Legislature prided itself on keeping a balanced budget. He said the legislature's commitment to agricultural and industrial growth would bring prosperity to all Nebraskans, including the blind. "Rising waters lift all ships."

Finally he gave Louise and Helen an opportunity to speak. Louise interpreted for Helen, who laid out the need for state-mandated drops to protect all newborn babies. "Senator Phillips," Helen said, "do you insure your factory against possible destruction by fire or some other catastrophic event?"

"Yes, of course. I'm a prudent man."

"You would say it is prudent to pay a minuscule fraction of the property's worth to protect yourself against the cost of replacing it even though the risk of catastrophe is slight. What we're proposing is a plan to protect the state's coffers by making a small investment against the known risk of blindness. If a tithe of the money we now spend to support unnecessary blindness were spent to prevent it, the state would be the gainer in terms of cold economy, not to speak of considerations of happiness and humanity. The citizens of Nebraska are fortunate to have your stewardship of their hard-earned tax dollars. They will see the wisdom of investing in prevention to save money over the long term."

Louise was impressed with Helen's carefully targeted message. If anything could move this man, it was an appeal to his thrifty nature.

The senator looked at his pocket watch. "I assure you that at such time a bill would come before the Ways and Means Committee, it would be given full consideration." He stood.

The women remained seated. Louise said, "With all due respect, Senator, it was our hope that you would sponsor a bill."

"Sen. Adolph Bruegger. He's your man."

"Anyone else?"

"A bill of that nature requires Bruegger's blessing."

Louise signed, "I've come full circle. He advises talking to the chairman of the Health and Welfare Committee who has already turned down several requests. I apologize for wasting your time."

Sen. Phillips took the camera from his desk and handed it to Louise. "Do you know how to use a Kodak?"

"Yes."

"Good. We'll go down to the loading dock where there's ample light. I have a favor to ask of Miss Keller." He opened a desk drawer and produced a copy of Helen's book, The Story of My Life. "My daughter wrote a book report and got the highest mark of anyone in her class. Would you ask Miss Keller if she would be so kind as to autograph this?"

CHAPTER 35

After meeting with women in eight rural communities during a whistle-stop tour of Nebraska, Louise arrived in Kearney, her last stop. There she had been aided in setting up a speaking engagement by a doctor's wife, one of the few who had taken a petition the day of Louise's first speech. The setting was the Kearney Public Library, decorated for the season with cornstalks and pumpkins inside and out.

Attendance in Kearney, as in other communities, was high, no doubt due to Helen's article. As usual, Louise's strategy was to speak briefly, touching on the same points highlighted in Helen's article. Then she invited the audience to express their concerns.

"It's an outrage that legislators just dig in and refuse to consider a bill," a woman said.

Louise had learned that if she didn't say everything she knew in her speech, chances were the opportunity to make her points would come up during the question-and-answer period. She responded to the sympathetic woman's comment. "Telling them the human stories of children like Vinny who are needlessly blind hasn't moved them. But we expect to make progress as we compile statistics about the cost of educating a child in the Smithville Asylum versus the cost of prevention. We believe the state could provide silver nitrate for every hospital, every doctor, and every midwife at a cost less than keeping one child in the Asylum."

After the program, Louise comforted a tearful mother who said her child's sightless but normal-looking eyes brought stares and gossip which she blamed on the campaign. "I can sympathize," Louise said. "I've been the target of vicious tongues as well. Be strong, and know in your heart that you are pure."

It wasn't the first time she'd met a mother who felt she and her child were maligned, that the campaign planted false assumptions. Louise always encouraged those mothers to tell her their stories. The poor women needed someone who would listen and understand. It was in these moments that the campaign's failure to win legislation weighed most heavily. She pitied the blind children who suffered ridicule and vowed it must not be for naught.

* * *

ARRIVING HOME EXHAUSTED FROM KEARNEY, Louise was nevertheless buoyed by the number of women who were receptive to her message. She passed through the lobby and acknowledged the three blue-haired widows who sat at their regular table working a jigsaw puzzle. They smiled and returned the greeting. After collecting her mail and newspaper from the front desk, she was looking forward to a steaming hot bath with no end of hot water.

She summoned the elevator, and when its doors opened one of the housekeeping girls got off pushing a Whirlwind Maid. It was a familiar sight, yet it always aroused a touch of nostalgia.

Shortly after she entered her apartment, a porter delivered her bags. Louise first opened the one that held Sunny. Clutching the doll to her breast, she pictured Marie cutting out the felt skirt, the movement of her mouth synchronized with the scissors. She returned Sunny to her special place and decided the rest of the unpacking could wait.

After drawing a bath, she eased into the tub, enjoying the sensation of water so hot it stung her legs. She closed her eyes. Relaxation set in. Resting her head on the tub, she let idle thoughts go where they would. Twirling a finger in the water caused whorls to appear and vanish, like thoughts that flowed easily and gently without leaving a trace of their existence on her mind. She reveled in the forgetting, the emptiness, a welcome contrast to the campaign's intensity.

She stepped from her bath, put on her nightgown and Frank's robe, and made a pot of tea. Seated at the breakfast room table with her tea, the mail, and the newspaper, she sighed, so grateful to be home.

One item in her mail was an envelope with Bernard Feldman's return address, different from the envelopes in which he sent checks for her share of the Whirlwind Maid profits. It was a short ink-smudged note.

Dear Mrs. Morrissey,

I write to you with a heavy heart, as though I carry the weight of a giant boulder. I cannot bear to live with myself since the passing of Frank and Marie for I failed them and you. I was with Frank that fateful night at the hotel. We were in our cups, and I said something that hit him wrong. I should have done everything in my power to prevent him from driving. I went to bed thinking he would sleep it off. I should have done more to stop him.

My sin of omission leaves me with as much guilt as if I had been driving that truck. I wish G-d had taken me instead of them. I am not asking your forgiveness, for my actions were unforgivable. If there is ever anything I can do for you, do not hesitate to ask.

I trust this finds you well.

Yours truly,
Bernard Feldman

Louise remembered having felt unnerved when Bernard looked at Marie's eyes. In the course of his medical studies had he learned to recognize the characteristic scarring from gonorrhea? Did Bernard say something to Frank about gonorrhea in a drunken argument? Something happened that night to make Frank think Yonder was Marie's father. She had no idea what to make of this letter, much less how to respond to it.

Chapter 36

January 1908

Louise left the January meeting worried about the morale of the dedicated Committee, which, following a couple of disheartening announcements, had dissolved into petty bickering. Doc announced that after a year of providing silver nitrate for midwives and Riverbend Hospital, Argent Laboratories was withdrawing its financial support due to "dismal prospects for passage of legislation in Nebraska." Bonita was taking a leave of absence from the Committee. A state senator wrote a letter about his own child, blinded in an accident, who he feared would become an object of ridicule if the public suspected gonorrhea had caused the blindness.

Louise thought about her sphere of influence. Helen had played her part magnificently. Daisy would continue to help her understand the workings of the legislature and Bureau of Hygiene. Jerrylynn was compiling statistics on the economics of providing drops versus the cost of housing a blind child in the Asylum. Doc worked doggedly to win over doctors. Perhaps he should turn his attention to hospitals. Alice was busily writing to clubs to arrange speaking engagements and petition drives. Irina was doing a creditable job with the midwives. Madge helped Louise reach nurses and state senators. She also relentlessly corresponded with the press but to little avail. Newspapers remained in the dark ages regarding matters of sex.

What the Committee needed was a major donor whose funds would provide silver nitrate for multiple hospitals and midwives. *Of course. Bernard Feldman. His letter has been nagging me for months. He would do anything to assuage his guilt.*

* * *

BERNARD'S SPACIOUS OFFICE IN THE Feldman Building in Omaha housed a veritable Chautauqua museum. A blackboard with diagrams from a "germ" chalk talk sat on an easel, and photographs covered an entire wall.

Louise found Bernard even more exuberant than usual. He almost bounced when he walked. She displayed polite interest in the memorabilia, but she was on edge. She'd intended her visit to be about soliciting funds for a demonstration project at Riverbend Hospital, but on the train to Omaha she'd agonized over the meaning of Bernard's letter. She would have to get at the truth.

Bernard directed Louise to a group of pictures. "I'll never forget this day." He pointed to a photograph of Frank and himself helping Marie and Helen fly kites. "Look at those faces, will you?"

"Tell me the truth, Bernard, was Marie happy?"

"We all adored her—Frank, Miss Keller, Mrs. Macy, Mrs. Ryder—everyone in the Chautauqua family. We smothered her with love." His face and voice filled with sadness. "Oh, but I have pictures in my mind of her when she got homesick and missed her mama. When I was a lad I loved my mama so much I got lonesome for her at school every day and couldn't wait to get home to see her." He brightened. "But I tell you Marie was as happy as any sighted child."

Louise then noticed a picture of Marie straddling one end of a seesaw at its peak, laughing, her head thrown back. The girl on the other end obviously shared her delight.

"When people come to my office and look at this wall, I watch for their reaction. It happens without fail, when they come to that picture, their faces light up. The joy of those youngsters is positively infectious."

Louise could not speak, caught in a bittersweet emotion, seeing the companionship shared by Marie and another child and having never witnessed such a moment.

Bernard grabbed the picture off the wall and thrust it at Louise. "You must have it. Take it, it's yours."

He placed the picture in her hand and clasped her other hand in both of his. His eyes glistened with tears, and his voice broke. "I am so sorry. I'm to blame for Marie and Frank not being here today. I should have stopped him."

"I don't blame you. But what did you say that angered him so?"

He looked away. "I don't remember." He removed a wadded up handkerchief from his pocket and wiped first one eye, then the other. "I was too drunk—as drunk as Frank."

He folded the white square so the corners met perfectly, aligned the edges just so, and returned it to his pocket. "We were quarreling, the way men do, trying to outdo the other guy. It's that dumb animal instinct that comes out after men have a few drinks. I haven't had a drop to drink since that night."

"And you don't remember what you said?"

Bernard took a step back and shook his head. "Like a shot he charges off to the telephone, I go after him, and I hear him threaten to kill Yonder."

Louise sighed. *He can remember Frank's threat but not his own words.* "I don't blame you for the accident. You put Frank to bed for the night. You did what you could. But in your letter you referred to a burden of guilt. Is it due to not stopping Frank or to saying something that made him so angry he wanted to kill Yonder?"

Bernard shrugged, a move that left his body slumped.

"I have to know. Did you say something about Marie's blindness being caused by gonorrhea?"

He looked at her, tears welling in his eyes. "Forgive me, Louise. Yes, I accused Frank of having gonorrhea. I had no idea—"

"It wasn't Yonder."

Bernard looked puzzled.

"And it wasn't Frank." The confession, which she had not divulged to another living soul, left her feeling weak. "I need to sit down."

Bernard took her elbow and guided her to an armchair. Then he pulled up another chair and sat across from her.

"My burden is this," she said. "If I had been truthful with Frank, I don't know what would have happened to me. But I know that he and Marie would still be alive." She sobbed and reached into her handbag for a handkerchief.

The photograph slipped from her lap. Bernard reached down, picked it up, and handed it to her. He, too, was crying. She propped one elbow on the chair's arm and dropped her head in her hand.

When she was able to speak, she looked up but away from Bernard. "I do know this. We human beings are very complicated creatures. We cannot begin to fathom our capacity to do harm and, by the same token, we cannot fathom our capacity to do good."

She heard herself spewing platitudes. In that moment, truth found her, not the truth of what sent Frank into a rage, but a liberating truth about herself. She stopped in the midst of a vacuous sentence. "What I am trying to say in a roundabout way is that having come to grips with *my own* capacity to do great harm and to do great good, I cannot judge you."

"Thank you." Bernard took her hands in his and gave her a look that told her he grasped the significance of her words, that she was sharing an excruciatingly private part of herself. "Now, you came to ask for help from the Feldman Brothers Foundation."

Louise sat facing the easel with the germ talk diagram on a blackboard several feet away. She described the Committee's work and its ultimate goal of preventing blindness which she felt would square beautifully with the mission of Bernard's foundation. She described the interim steps toward the goal. Specifically she addressed the demonstration project at Riverbend Hospital, the training of midwives, and attempts to mobilize doctors and citizens. "We're at an impasse. Argent Laboratories was supplying silver nitrate for the hospital and midwives and funding for some of our administrative costs. But just as we were planning to expand our demonstration to six other hospitals around the state, Argent pulled out, citing our slow progress. It's going to take a grassroots demand for legislation, but most Nebraskans have never heard of babies' sore eyes."

Bernard looked inspired. "Newspaper advertising, have you tried it?"

"I'm not sure what we'd advertise. Our cause doesn't meet their standards of decency."

"Advertise announcements of your meetings. 'Come learn how you can protect the health of your family and community. Free refreshments.'" Bernard's voice rose and his eyes flashed as he talked through his idea. Louise was reminded of how Frank used to relate new schemes at breakfast.

Bernard continued, "Feldman Enterprises advertises in newspapers all over Nebraska. If the Feldman Brothers Foundation sponsored your advertisements, I assure you that our dollars would trump their editorial policy."

Had she been too subtle in stating the need to fund drops? "Your support and influence would mean a great deal." She hoped he hadn't detected disappointment in her voice.

"I can almost see what you're thinking, Louise. How many children have to go blind before the state will take action?" Bernard stood up. He slapped his hand on the table. "Since when does charity begin with the state? What ever happened to people taking care of their families and neighbors? When I was growing up, it was the synagogues and churches that gave food and shelter to the poor. If you ask me, we have too much government meddling in our lives as it is."

Louise wanted the meeting to be over. Bernard would not be the ally she had hoped for.

"On the other hand," he said, "I stand for public health. Germs would be the end of us all if we didn't have public education and programs to prevent disease and epidemics. So I applaud government programs that promote vaccinations for children, and isolation of consumption patients, and the like.

"But I digress. Bear with me. I'm thinking out loud. What

if you put together some numbers, tell me what it would cost to get a dozen demonstration programs like Riverbend Hospital? I can't imagine a better cause for the Feldman Brothers Foundation."

Louise gasped.

"Of course I'll have to talk it over with my brother first."

* * *

THE DAY AFTER VISITING BERNARD, Louise was surprised by a telephone call from Dr. Vandegrift all the way from Philadelphia. Static on the line interfered with their conversation, and she wasn't certain she understood, but it sounded as though he was inviting her to be one of ten charter members of the National Society to Save Babies' Sight. When the static stopped, she clearly understood. He wanted her to attend the Society's organizational meeting in Washington, D.C., in September.

It seems she had made a name for herself, first by enlisting Helen Keller to write her piece in *The Ladies' Home Journal,* and then by running a top-notch hospital demonstration program and midwives' training program, both of which were characterized by rigorous documentation and regular audits that made them models for programs in other states.

She remembered the days when her loftiest goal was to be recognized as a civic leader in Riverbend. She smiled to herself, thinking of the epitaph that came to her in the stairwell the afternoon The Twister struck: *Devoted Wife and Civic Leader.* Now she was a woman with national influence.

Sometimes she felt something deeper, not the drive for recognition, but the spirit of the girl in the schoolyard who beat up Charles Baumgartner for teasing Sandy. And the spirit of the woman aiding victims of The Twister.

But, if anything, the recognition brought her more pain than joy. *I am not the virtuous woman they think I am.*

Chapter 37

The Independence Day celebration was held on a picture-perfect afternoon in Chautauqua Park with a tolerable performance by the high school band and only occasional swarming gnats. Louise stood with Dovie and the sculptor, August Potemkin, waiting through reminiscences by Riverbend's veterans of war for her statue's dedication. The unveiling, scheduled to occur in full sunlight, was delayed by the long-winded veterans. So when the time came, the sun dropped behind trees, putting Marie in shadow.

The statue had cost Louise a fortune but was worth every penny. August had captured the expectant moment when Frank held the ruler atop Marie's head as she stood with her back against the doorframe. From the statue's position on the edge of the bluff was a view through its doorway of the Chautauqua grounds below. This was its rightful place.

After the ceremony, children climbed up on the pedestal or scrambled through the doorway. Marie would have explored every inch, jumping up to touch the doorframe, gliding her fingers over her own bronze face, and climbing up to find the perfect niche in which to curl up, then begging for just a few more minutes when it came time to go home.

The youngsters scampering on the statue watched a girl about Marie's age limp towards them and try without success to pull herself up onto the pedestal. Louise noticed her withered right leg. The child almost made it, but a boy hanging from the doorframe jumped to within inches of her fingers and laughed when she lost her grip.

Children can be so cruel. Louise was about to go over and give her a boost when another boy on the pedestal reached for the girl's hand.

"Here." He pulled her up. "Come on. I'll show you the best place to climb."

* * *

WALKING THROUGH WET GRASS EARLY the next morning, Louise felt her chilled feet squishing in her shoes by the time she reached the statue. Dewdrops on Marie's bronze cheeks too closely resembled tears, which Louise brushed away with her fingers. The image took Louise from the sweet memory of Frank measuring Marie on her ninth birthday to what followed, the disastrous party and ill-fated pony cart ride. Her "little chums," Frank had called them. Marie had no little chums. *I should have helped her cultivate friendships, but I failed her.*

Once her mind took this dark direction, it was as though floodgates had opened, spewing forth all her sins of commission and omission. Placing her hand on the cool forearm, she heard an echo from the past, the day Marie wanted her to touch the cold silver bowl, reached for her hand, and said, "Don't cry, Mother. It's not your fault."

A lump in her throat, she stepped back, looked at the faces of Marie and Frank, and summoned the will to say to them aloud, "It *was* my fault." The tears flowed in cathartic abundance.

*　　*　　*

On a mid-July afternoon with storm clouds moving in from the west, Louise made her usual trip down to the lobby to collect her mail and the weekly newspaper. The only sound was wind rattling the windows. Sensing she was being watched, she turned in time to see the blue-haired ladies lose themselves in their puzzle.

Upon returning to her apartment she dropped the mail and newspaper on the breakfast room table, made a cup of tea, and carried it to the table. She sat and wrapped her hands around the cup, enjoying its warmth. Leafing through the mail, she set it aside and picked up the newspaper. Not much was happening in Riverbend. The town council voted to pave High School Road as development was moving in that direction. The Riverbend Garden Club donated another bench to be placed downtown for the comfort of older folks who get weary as they go about their errands.

Louise folded back the newspaper to read the inside pages and smiled to see an advertisement for the Whirlwind Maid. Frank would be proud.

She looked at J.D.'s editorial, wondering what had stuck in his craw lately. She did not have to read far before discovering she was it. Without naming her or the Nebraska Committee to Save Babies' Sight, J.D. wrote about how a tiny minority of citizens had sullied the town's wholesome reputation.

Riverbend is home to upstanding, God-fearing citizens. Look upon Riverbend, and you will see seven steeples, each representative of a flourishing congregation. Look upon Riverbend, and you will see honest, hard-working shopkeepers who provide all that one could need and want, and at a fair price. Look upon Riverbend, and you will see neighbors helping neighbors without expectation of anything in return. I dare any man to show me a more salubrious town in which to rear his family.

But who outside our fair city knows the Riverbend I describe? Riverbend is becoming known, all right, not for its plethora of virtues, but for a band of once-righteous citizens whose do-good impulses have led them to rabble rousing. They speak the unspeakable and challenge our sense of moral decency, all in the name of a cause that is a condition of the lowest classes, most of whom live in squalid city slums, and bring it on themselves with their filth and immorality.

The consequences for Riverbend are grave. The Reverend Garnet Horton has announced that he will not appear in this 'den of iniquity,' thus the Great Revival of 1909 will be relocated from Riverbend across the river to Glendale Junction. Not only are we inflicted with the knowledge that souls who might have been saved remain lost, but we are also burdened with the loss of a stellar opportunity to bolster the local economy. This is a blight on Riverbend's reputation.

* * *

THE NEXT DAY LOUISE ENTERED the library at closing time. Dovie, who was dusting a windowsill, turned, saw Louise, and set down her feather duster. Against the window's backlighting she appeared in silhouette, her features obscured. Her voice was somber. "The editorial."

Louise nodded.

Dovie came over to the reading table where Louise was standing. She was wearing a most becoming gray and violet tweed suit with a crisp, white blouse ruffled at the cuffs. Attire that was most impractical for a dusty library. But more fitting than bloomers for a woman whose husband planned another bid for state senate.

The newspaper, the issue with the offensive editorial inside, lay folded on the table. Dovie swept it aside as though it was of little consequence.

"I don't understand. Why?" Louise grabbed the newspaper and shook it at Dovie. "Why would J.D. want to ruin me?"

"It's not you. It's complicated. Do you know what it will cost Riverbend to lose the revival meeting? And poor Gertrude, she put her heart and soul into it. She almost single-handedly convinced Rev. Horton to come to Riverbend. J.D. can't bear to see his little sister hurt."

"But you find it acceptable for him to destroy me." Louise's voice trembled. "I give people a friendly greeting and they look away or whisper to one another. It's all I can do to hold my head up."

"And whose fault is that?" Dovie yanked the newspaper from Louise's hand and slammed it on the table. "Don't blame J.D. You go around talking in public about things you and I don't even discuss—"

"But *should* discuss. Dovie, gonorrhea is rampant. It's not a respecter of class. Every woman should consider the possibility her husband could infect her, even you."

Dovie's face bore the unmistakable look of a wife who knows her husband. "What are you trying to imply?"

"No more than what I stated."

"You've let your cause corrupt your sense of decency. For your own sake, for the sake of Riverbend, quit this campaign."

"I came here hoping J.D. wrote his editorial without your blessing. Now it seems . . . what's really going on?"

"Riverbend is my home, Louise. We suffered a blow when we lost rail passenger service, and the prospect of the revival meeting helped restore our pride, but now it won't happen because of your campaign. You've embarrassed us. That's hard to swallow."

"You know what I think? I think J.D. is scapegoating the Committee. I think your Rev. Horton figured his revival could draw more people in a town that has passenger train service. This is about money, not morality. And J.D.'s political ambitions. And yours."

"I care about you, but for your own good I have to tell you that you're alienating everyone."

"So be it. So we become outcasts. If nothing else, it will strengthen the Committee's determination."

"Not the Committee. You. You're the easy target, the voice and face of the campaign, the reason for Riverbend's notoriety. And Louise, it's hard for me to tell you this, but people are starting to talk . . . about Marie's blindness."

A flush crept up from Louise's neck to her cheeks. "Marie's blindness was caused by *pneumococcus*. It's bacteria a woman's body can harbor without any symptoms. Had her blindness been caused by gonorrhea, do you really think I'd risk public exposure?" It was the rehearsed explanation Louise used whenever an audience member asked the cause of her daughter's blindness. But face-to-face with her friend—or rather the woman who was withdrawing her friendship as they spoke—she could not keep her eyelids from fluttering shut.

"Don't lie to me. Your secret is safe."

"My secret?"

"I overheard you and Doc."

"You overheard what?"

"Here in the library. One cold winter day years ago. I knew you'd be working in the library so I stopped by to drop off some books and take you down to Rich's for hot chocolate. But I left when I heard Doc call you a terrible name."

Dovie was the one who left books outside the library. The room was closing in. Louise's body stiffened and she practically snarled her next words. "Whatever you think you heard, I resent the inference." She strode toward the door. Resolute. Eyes straight ahead. Determined not to see the sofa. Which meant it intruded anyway, large and green in her mind's eye.

Chapter 38

By now a seasoned speaker, Louise nevertheless couldn't ignore a queasy feeling as she sat amid a dozen charter members at the organizational meeting of the National Society to Save Babies' Sight in Washington, D.C. Being surrounded by doctors, professors, and big-city society matrons made her acutely aware she was merely Louise Elizabeth Caldwell Morrissey of Riverbend, Nebraska.

But what mostly agitated the butterflies was her embarrassment at having to report the Nebraska campaign's slow progress to this august body assembled around a table in a meeting room of the Corinthian Hotel. The only solid efforts Louise could point to were the Riverbend Hospital demonstration project and training program for nurses and midwives. She had hoped to report that the Health and Welfare Committee would hear a bill before the Christmas recess requiring doctors, midwives, and hospitals to report all cases of babies' sore eyes. But in talking with Dr. Weil before she left home, she learned that Senator Nordstrom had not yet agreed to sponsor the bill.

Smoke hung heavily, the most noxious wafting toward Louise from a cigar smoker seated across the table. An elderly woman wearing a handsome pin-stripe suit and heirloom jewelry sat at Louise's left and chatted with a woman similarly bejeweled next to her. At Louise's right was Helen, who was inclined toward Annie signing in her hand. With nothing else to do, Louise opened her new leather portfolio, which she'd bought for the occasion, and perused her notes as the people around her engaged in chit-chat.

At the end of the table, Dr. Vandegrift stubbed out his cigarette in an ashtray, stood, and welcomed the group. He had dark circles under his eyes and looked to Louise to be ten years older than when she and Marie had visited him four years earlier.

He thanked everyone for their dedication to the cause, then took a few minutes to introduce each member, after which he said, "I have sobering news. Your attendance here might be in vain. Our fledgling organization may not get off the ground."

People looked at one another and frowned, as though they didn't want to be alone when the bad news came down.

Dr. Vandegrift continued, "When we determined the time was right to begin our campaign, we knew there would be obstacles. We identified three obstacles: one, society's taboo against speaking of venereal disease; two, prejudice against our poor and immigrant populations, erroneously believed to be the only groups carrying gonorrhea; and three, an entrenched culture in the medical community reluctant to recognize the value of preventing disease. Formidable obstacles, to be sure. What we did not anticipate was that another obstacle—perhaps the greatest—would come from our own ranks." His voice grew thin and bordered on trembling. "It has been reported to us that in three of our hospital demonstration programs—in New York City, Baltimore, and in Philadelphia, the latter being under my own watch—careless nurses accidentally administered insufficiently dilute silver nitrate, resulting in blinding of otherwise healthy babies."

Louise gasped, as did others. She gripped Helen's left hand while Annie, her face contorted in anguish, continued signing in her right. Helen shrieked, and the room went silent. Louise squeezed her hand and fought back tears.

Finally the man with the cigar said, "Were these babies blinded in both eyes?"

"Yes," Dr. Vandegrift said.

"Wouldn't a baby's reaction to drops in the first eye alert the nurse that something was wrong?"

"Your point is well taken," Dr. Vandegrift said, "but even properly diluted drops are caustic, such that a healthy baby lets out a cry that usually alarms the mother."

"Those poor little darlings," a woman said.

"We must look at this statistically," a man said. "How many babies are saved from blindness versus how many might be accidentally blinded?"

Amid the uproar that followed, a woman said, "That's an outrage. One simply can't let accidents occur on the basis of statistics."

There was much nodding in agreement.

"She is right," Dr. Vandegrift said. "To put healthy babies in jeopardy of being blinded is unconscionable. Besides we'll never get the public support we need to bring about legislation when word gets out. We must figure out how to prevent accidental blinding."

Louise spoke up. "We have developed a training program in Nebraska for nurses and midwives. In our demonstration programs, we provide silver nitrate only to be administered by personnel who have completed our training. Granted our program is relatively new, but we conduct stringent audits, and we've had no accidents or close calls."

There was some agreement, although no consensus, that training was the key to preventing accidents. The meeting that had begun with lively chatter ended with funereal murmurs.

* * *

WHEN LOUISE ARRIVED HOME FROM Washington, she took off her coat and went straight to the den to place a phone call to Dr. Weil's office to find out if Senator Nordstrom had agreed to sponsor the bill requiring reporting of babies' sore eyes. Given what had transpired at the meeting, that some programs had lax safety practices that allowed healthy babies to be accidentally blinded, Louise found it most urgent to move the bill forward. Daisy answered her call.

"Daisy, I've just arrived home, and I'm so eager to find out about the bill that I haven't even removed my coat yet."

"Dr. Weil is gone for the day." Daisy's matter-of-fact voice suggested she was speaking to a stranger.

"What can you tell me?"

"Louise, I think Dr. Weil should tell you himself."

The frost in Daisy's voice, the fact that she said "Louise," not "Lulu," alarmed Louise. *Have I played the fool thinking my childhood nemesis had become a true friend?* "Senator Nordstrom has refused to sponsor the bill, hasn't he?"

"Oh, Lulu." Daisy's voice cracked. "No one will support a bill now."

"Why? I don't understand."

"There's been a tragic accident at Riverbend Hospital. A

baby was accidentally blinded by drops."

Louise dropped into Frank's chair. "Oh, no."

"The nurse was Irina Taylor."

After hanging up the phone, Louise sobbed, horrified to think of the poor baby, the caustic solution searing its eyes, needlessly blinded. She would notify Bernard, but not yet. It would surely be the end of the Feldman Brothers Foundation's support. She would learn the details of the accident, and maybe given a little time she could think of a way to put a better face on it. She felt an old, self-protective reflex surfacing, the one that had led her to lie and manipulate. *And look where that got me.* No, she would call and tell him the truth.

But he called her first. "Mrs. Morrissey, did you know a baby in Riverbend was blinded by silver nitrate?"

Now her failure to call him felt worse than being irresponsible and instead smacked of cowardice. "I know. I—"

"Why did I have to hear it from the Argent Labs salesman?"

"I just arrived home, just found out about it myself. I planned to call you later."

"How could that nurse have been so careless?"

"Fatigue. The hospital was short of staff because of a flu outbreak, and Miss Taylor had been on duty nearly twenty-four hours. She got distracted. It's tragic—the baby, the poor mother."

"It tears my heart out to tell you this, but under the circumstances . . . this accident isn't an isolated incident. Human beings make mistakes. It will happen again. We can't continue to support drops. My brother never was keen on it, did it for me. Now we have a customer who's been after us to sponsor a summer camp for crippled children. We can't do it all. But if there's anything else I can do for you . . ."

Louise hung up the phone and stood staring at it. Should she press forward with the campaign? Abandon it? Irina, of all people, a woman who taught nurses and midwives how to administer drops. No one was more conscientious about safety. Bernard was right. Human beings make mistakes. It would happen again.

In the month that followed the accident, Irina did not formally resign from the Committee. She simply vanished from Riverbend. Madge resigned. She had re-evaluated the Committee's purpose in light of having a married step-daughter of child-bearing age. "She isn't going to contract gonorrhea, Louise. I can no longer advocate a program in which a perfectly healthy baby might be blinded."

That left Doc, Jerrylyn, Alice, and herself. Louise wondered if the little Committee had the will to carry on. *Do I have the will to carry on?*

CHAPTER 39

"Whirlwind Maid" read the block lettering on the pick-up truck that made a wide right turn from the road and proceeded through the iron gate toward the imposing, vine-covered Smithville State Asylum for the Blind. Louise had borrowed the truck from Tom's factory so she could deliver Christmas presents the Committee had gathered and take groups of children shopping downtown. Tom's business was thriving, thanks to a contract with Feldman Enterprises to manufacture the Whirlwind Maid's rolling carts, and he was happy to loan Louise the truck.

She desperately needed today's outing. Irina's accidental blinding of a baby had shaken her commitment to the campaign. Seeing the asylum's children, especially those blinded by babies' sore eyes, might restore her sense of purpose. And she anticipated the children's delight on the shopping excursion she would help chaperone.

Louise neared the asylum and remembered she'd always thought it looked like a poorhouse in a Charles Dickens novel. A parking area lay between the building and a playground, or what looked more like the ghost of a playground: a slide with missing steps, a little wooden glider covered in leaves, swings and a seesaw. No sign of children.

When she reached the stone steps leading to tall, double

doors, the past dropped over her like a shroud. She and Frank had climbed these steps, Marie between them, each holding a hand. Her chest tightened.

She opened the front door and was assailed by the reeking smell of pine disinfectant. In the silent, high-ceilinged foyer, Jerrylynn was buttoning the coat of a girl who sat on a bench with other children bundled against the cold.

Jerrylynn looked up. "Welcome. Did the odor about knock you down? Happens all the time. I'm sending two boys to unload your truck. We can't thank you enough for the presents. You're early, but the children are ready. They can scarcely contain themselves."

Of about a dozen children, five had the characteristic look of babies' sore eyes. Louise scanned their faces until she recognized Vinny, a seven-year-old version of the Baby Giveaway Saturday child, the poster child whose story she knew so well.

Jerrylynn took Vinny's hand. "Mrs. Morrissey is a friend of your Aunt Bonita. Can you say 'hello?'"

In a small, muffled voice he said, "Hello, Mrs. Morrissey."

Another boy nudged him and whispered. "Ask her, go ahead, now."

Vinny said, "You ask."

The boy spoke up. "Vinny wants to know if we get to ride in a truck."

"You certainly do. Let's go." Louise took Vinny's mittened hand, the hand that in her disturbing dream had clutched at her elusive skirt. Her heart lodged in her throat. She longed to sweep him into her arms and spirit him away, give him hot chocolate every day if he wanted. But her best intentions . . . would it be a storybook resolution to her dream or another nightmare?

The older boys climbed into the pickup bed unaided while Jerrylynn and Louise assisted the girls and lifted the younger children. Jerrylynn passed around blankets.

Once they were all unloaded outside Perkins Mercantile, Louise handed a quarter to each child and received "thank you's" in return

Jerrylynn said, "Mind your manners. It's okay to touch the toys, but don't pick up anything unless you intend to buy it. And thank Mr. and Mrs. Perkins for letting us shop here. And if you have to cough, cover your mouth."

Jerrylynn led the girls to the dolls, and Louise took the boys to the trucks and soldiers.

"Do I have enough money for this tractor?" a boy asked her.

She looked at the price. "Yes. And you'll have money left over for candy."

"Goody."

Another boy asked, "Will you please take me over to the dolls?"

The other boys snickered.

"Not for me, you dopes," he said. "I'm getting one for Elaine. Hers broke."

His generosity brought tears to Louise's eyes. She led him to the dolls and helped him select one.

When she rejoined the other boys, a horse-drawn fire wagon caught her attention. She held it up and admired the sturdy construction and the clean-sounding snap as she removed the ladder from the brackets.

As the last child finalized her purchase at the counter,

Louise said to Jerrylynn, "I want Santa to bring this to Vinny. I'd give anything to see his face on Christmas morning."

"It's a beauty," Jerrylynn said.

Louise held the door for the children and Jerrylynn to file out. She noticed two lanky boys approach, kicking rocks along the boardwalk. The older one took a long, cocky drag from a cigarette which he then passed to the other.

The boy with the cigarette pointed at Vinny. "Get a look at them eyes."

He started a slow, deliberate clapping, and the older boy joined in.

Jerrylynn marched toward the clapping boys. "Shut up before I tell your Ma, both of you."

She jabbed at each boy's chest, and as they backed away they bumped into one another.

"We didn't mean nothing, Mrs. Knudsen," the older boy said.

She kept jabbing hard, jabbing past the druggist's shop, jabbing until first one boy and then the other jumped off the boardwalk, dashed across the street, and slipped into the pool hall, as though that was where they intended to go all along.

Louise was shaking as she set the fire truck on the boardwalk, led the children to the truck, and boosted them into its bed. Then she returned to the boardwalk and asked Jerrylynn, "Did that mean what I think it did?"

Jerrylynn nodded. "'The clap.' Wish you hadn't seen it."

"Oh, my God. My worst fear was Marie would be taunted . . . now seeing it firsthand . . . the cruelty is beyond belief."

Jerrlynn gestured toward the truck. "They're too young to understand."

Louise appreciated Jerrylynn's attempt to placate her. All it would take was one older child to corrupt the younger ones with the sordid truth.

"In some twisted way," Jerrylynn said, "this is a sign of our campaign's success. When we started, no one knew what we were talking about. Now even young bullies know."

Louise picked up the fire truck, now just a hunk of red metal. "Those bullies . . . my efforts created those bullies. *I* created those bullies."

* * *

LOUISE DROVE TOWARD HOME IN the stingy light of the setting winter sun. On either side of the road were fields scraped nearly bare, pocked with spent cornstalks.

She had expected to drive home with a renewed sense of purpose and the satisfaction of having spread Christmas cheer to blind children. But all she could think was, what price progress?

Louise sensed what Yonder must have felt that led him to quit the assimilation movement. If she'd known his whereabouts, she would have reached out to him, to seek his comfort and wisdom.

She could hear the boys clapping. *Progress on the backs of children already afflicted.*

She could feel the suffering of the little babies whose eyes were seared by silver nitrate. *Progress at the risk of blinding healthy babies.*

I can't go on.

CHAPTER 40

At the sound of the telephone's three short rings, Louise stopped cutting up beef for stew and wiped her hands on her apron. Alice's words came in short bursts riding on wheezing breaths. "My cousin in Glendale Junction just called me. . . . She never calls anyone long distance . . . so it had to be bad news. . . . She went outside to hang clothes this morning . . . and she noticed at the Bartons' house next door . . . no one had let the chickens out of the coop yet. . . . In the fourteen years she's lived there . . . the chickens have always been out in the yard at the crack of dawn."

Louise thought Alice would never get to the point.

"And the children should have been outside . . . doing chores."

"What happened?"

"I do declare, Louise, it gives me goosebumps all over. . . . That whole family and the two Chamberlain girls who spent the night . . . were axed to death in their sleep."

Louise gasped. "In Glendale Junction?"

"On a quiet, residential street. . . . the parents, their four children, and the Chamberlain girls. . . . My cousin had just seen them all the night before . . . at church for the Children's Day program. . . . They think the killer let himself in the house . . . while everyone was at church and hid in a closet."

"What kind of monster could do such a thing?"

"There's talk it was Mr. Barton's ne'er-do-well brother-in law . . . or a man who used to work for him. . . . or the dark-skinned stranger who knocked on my cousin's door yesterday . . . looking for odd jobs . . . a scruffy man with long gray hair . . . I wanted her to bring the children and come stay with me till they catch him . . . but she said he's probably riding the rails and could even be in Riverbend by now. . . .. Keep your doors locked."

If the killer were dark skinned, Louise thought, that could be a setback for the campaign, given that many people thought only immigrants got gonorrhea. *Good lord, when I should be feeling sorry for the victims, I'm seeing this tragedy in terms of the campaign.*

*   *   *

IN THE WEEKS SINCE HER visit to the Asylum, Louise had decided to quit the campaign and devote herself to helping children at the Asylum. She had already informed Jerrylynn of her intentions, and today she would disclose them to Doc and Alice.

Doc arrived at the library before Alice. He and Louise took seats across from each other at the large reading table, the way they had sat fifteen years earlier when he told her there was a risk of a medical complication and wanted to terminate her pregnancy.

"I have wrestled day and night with a moral dilemma," Louise said. "I wanted this meeting because I've arrived at a decision. I intend to devote myself to helping the Asylum children. They need a music program with a real music teacher and decent instruments, and they most desperately need preparation for jobs and help with job placement."

Doc scowled. "You're not abandoning the campaign, I hope."

"I am."

Doc stood and paced. "We have to stay the course." He poked the air to emphasize each word.

"You, perhaps. Not me. Not if it means healthy babies can get blinded by drops, and blind children get bullied for no fault of their own."

"I'm as concerned about safety as you are." His voice was pleading. "But there's no turning back. It's unfortunate that blind children get taunted by bullies, but the cat's out of the bag."

Louise looked out the window at the grey sky. "Do you know what this campaign has done to me?"

"You've been shunned, even scorned by your best friend's husband. That must be terrible."

"Yes, but that's only part of it. This campaign has warped me. When Alice told me about the axe murders, as soon as she mentioned a dark-skinned man was possibly the killer, all I could think about was what a setback that would be for us, what with the prejudice that it's only immigrants who get gonorrhea. I see everything in light of 'is this good for the campaign or is this bad for the campaign.' I've lost my humanity. That's what this campaign has done to me."

The door opened, and Alice entered, wheezing. Louise and Doc helped her to the wingback chair. She fumbled in her bag and retrieved a pack of asthma cigarettes. Doc helped her light one, and Louise placed an ashtray on the end table.

When Alice was able to speak, she said, "Did you read . . . J.D.'s editorial?"

Neither Louise nor Doc had seen it.

Alice stubbed out her cigarette and gestured toward a newspaper lying in the chair next to her. Doc picked it up, his eyes quickly scanning the editorial.

"He's riled up . . . about what he calls . . . 'the catastrophic consequences of unfettered immigration.'"

Doc said, "He reminds readers that a dark-skinned killer may be on the prowl."

"The axe murderer?" Louise asked. "But there are half a dozen suspects with light skin."

"Well," Doc said, "J.D. seems to prefer the 'swarthy man' theory," Doc said. "Here's his conclusion: 'Granted, certain business interests benefit by importing cheap, unskilled labor. But those people bring loathsome diseases, moral laxity, and criminal activity, which is bad enough when confined to particular ghettos, but eventually these ills will spread like contagion to respectable quarters of our society. And if that isn't reason enough to keep these people out, mark my words, they will marry your daughters and bring about the mongrelization of the Anglo-Saxon race.'"

"That man has lost his moral compass," Louise said. "Exploiting the axe murders for his own gain."

"He knows his voters," Doc said.

"It's bad enough to malign immigrants," Louise said, "but to play on the fears and sympathies of . . . Hand me the newspaper."

She plucked out the page with J.D.'s editorial and spread it on the table, then picked up Alice's ashtray and emptied it onto the newspaper. She strode to the wastebasket and ceremoniously deposited the little bundle.

"Madam Librarian, don't tell me you've sunk to practicing censorship." Doc grinned. "That's the spirit."

Louise sat down, and Doc gazed at her with the seductive look she remembered too well. The first time she had seen it was the night of The Twister, only it wasn't directed at her but at Irina when he handed her an ampoule of morphine.

Louise gasped, the image of that night seizing her in a fit of inspiration. The ampoule that Doc had passed to Irina held an individual dose of morphine. "Remember the night of The Twister you gave Irina and me glass ampoules of morphine? Would it be possible to package silver nitrate already diluted in individual . . ."

Doc's eyes brightened, and he practically shouted, "Brilliant!"

Alice looked thoughtful. "I'm surprised no one . . . has thought of that . . . before now."

"All the attention has been on procedure," Louise said, "how to ensure that nurses administer the drops correctly."

"And there's always been a premium placed on keeping the cost down," Doc said. "No one has dared to consider individual doses. It would be as though you expected a man who needed a new horse would consider buying a car." Doc looked pleased with his analogy until he glimpsed Louise's frown. "Don't get me wrong. Your solution is brilliant, but it will be very costly."

"But worth it if we could guarantee that no baby would ever be blinded by silver nitrate." Louise realized as she spoke that assuring safety of the eyedrops was paramount, that it overrode her other reasons for wanting to resign.

"I gather you've changed your mind," Doc said.

"Yes, I'll carry on with the campaign. And I appreciate your steadfastness. Both of you."

* * *

LOUISE TALKED WITH A REPRESENTATIVE at Argent Laboratories who suggested that packaging dilute silver nitrate in wax ampoules instead of glass would be more economical, but would nevertheless triple the cost over the bulk product.

She telephoned Bernard, explained the strategy, and begged him to reconsider giving up the cause. "It's asking a great deal, especially with the added expense." She considered reminding him of his debt to her, that he said he would do anything, but thought better of it. The wisdom of her decision became evident with Bernard's answer.

"I should have thought of that myself," he said. "I haven't been able to sleep, I'm a man of my word and withdrawing our support . . . If you can guarantee the safety of drops, I shall guarantee you the Feldman Brothers Foundation will continue to finance them."

PART 5

Chapter 41

"**N**o!" Louise instantly grasped the futility of shouting at someone who is deaf and blind. She took Helen's hand and signed, "Never. You only *think* you know—"

Helen jerked away her hand. "I know enough. You value your precious reputation more than our cause." The slurred angry falsetto vaguely resembled the whine of a small engine laboring at capacity. "Speaking the truth would do so much good. The public wants to believe that only depraved immigrant women are afflicted. I can do only so much to dispel the myth. What do I know? But you . . . you're a paragon of virtue." Helen turned her back to Louise and clasped her hands in her lap.

Helen was nothing if not persistent. Louise had hoped the subject would not come up tonight. Since arriving in Washington, D.C., earlier in the day, they had enjoyed catching up on news and gossip, and taking advantage of the Corinthian Hotel's amenities. Tomorrow night the two women would be corseted, coiffed, and formally attired for a banquet at which both would be honored. But tonight was theirs to do as they pleased, so after a swim in the hotel's indoor pool they lounged in robes and slippers in front of the fireplace, their hair still damp, a shared afghan around their shoulders, the fragrance of congratulatory flowers in the air.

Now Louise's stomach roiled with words unspoken, and she anticipated a night of fitful sleep. There was no resolving their argument. She would do what she had intended before Helen confronted her.

She touched her friend's arm, but Helen's clasped hands refused to yield. Louise picked up the tissue-wrapped doll from the end table. Her constant companion, it had inspired her, when all else failed, to endure another trip, deliver another speech, or fend off another adversary. She unwrapped it, brushed its yarn braids against Helen's hands, and placed it in her lap.

Helen's face brightened. She brought the doll to her cheek as though to take in its essence. "This must be Sunny." Holding the doll made Helen smile, but it was a wistful rather than happy smile. "I recall that her body is yellow, her braids are red, and her felt skirt and hat are purple."

Louise could almost have anticipated Helen's description, being familiar with her friend's curious fascination with color. Marie had loved color, too. "You recall correctly."

Helen sat quietly with the doll in her lap. Her smile faded to a pensive look. "I am touched to think you would part with Sunny. I remember how proud Marie was when she made her."

"If it hadn't been for Marie, I wouldn't know you. I'm giving you Sunny to express how much I treasure our friendship."

"I treasure it as well," Helen said. "But it troubles me that you continue to hide under a pretense of perfection. I'm always waiting to see the genuine Louise. Had I been blessed with your faculties, I would indulge in communion with my fellow human beings, seeking to know them and to be known. You squander abilities to develop intimate friendships I might only dream of possessing. By hiding your true nature, expressing only what you want others to see, you hold even those you love at a distance."

Shifting logs and flying sparks startled Louise almost as much as the realization of what she was about to say next. She signed into Helen's hand, "When you quoted the phrase 'They enslave their children's children who make compromise with sin,' you were writing about me."

"But you must not blame yourself. I made it clear in my article that the wife is merely an innocent agent."

Shivering, Louise lifted damp curls off her neck and turned up the collar of her robe.

Helen reached behind her, placed a hand on her neck, and massaged vigorously. "You carry a great deal of tension. I feel it when we embrace and in your hands when we talk."

The deep circles Helen's thumbs made on Louise's neck produced an uncomfortable, popping sensation that made her shoulders hunch.

"That's where your secrets reside," Helen said. "Stop using your gift of speech to conceal who you really are. Tomorrow night, I beg you, speak the truth."

Louise took Helen's hand. "No."

Helen's jaw tensed and her voice became shrill. "You would let your stubborn pride—"

Louise yanked Helen's hand. "Stop it. Now." The words she wanted to shout had to be spelled methodically in Helen's hand, and the necessity for restraint added resentment to her anger. But it was irrational to blame Helen. "I'm sorry. It's not about stubborn pride. My reputation back home is already ruined. I couldn't care less what the rest of the world thinks. Yes, I had gonorrhea. What you don't understand is I contracted it from illicit relations . . . with Dr. Foster."

Helen gasped. A long silence followed before she spoke. "I would never have suspected that Frank wasn't Marie's father. He doted on her so."

Little could be inferred from the singsong voice, but the words were not condemning.

"Now you understand why I cannot make a public confession. To tell the whole truth would defeat our purpose. Resepectable wives would not see themselves in my story. And to admit to having gonorrhea without exonerating Frank would be unfair to him. He was such a good man. I can't ruin his good name. I couldn't tell you before because I feared it would ruin our friendship."

"Never. Louise, my dear friend, you're only human. I can't begin to fathom what you've suffered all these years."

Helen's hand brushed the floor in search of the yarn doll that had fallen from her lap. Finding it, she sat up and sighed.

Louise offered more details about the affair—her expectation that she and Doc would have a life together, Doc's rejection and insistence that she abort.

"Did he ever tell you the medical reason for wanting you to abort?"

"No, and because he didn't I was convinced there was no medical reason, that it was merely a ruse. It wasn't until years later when I met Dr. Vandegrift that I realized his warning might have had merit and that I should have listened to him."

"You wish you had aborted Marie because she was blind?"

Louise's breath caught in her throat. If only she could

take back her words. How would she justify her position to a woman who was both blind and deaf?

"The truth is, many times I thought I should have aborted. When I first saw the baby with Doc's black hair, I knew she would be an ever-present reminder of my sin. To look on her would always arouse fear of being found out. And had she not been born, she would not have come to such a tragic end."

"You haven't answered my question. Did you wish you had aborted because she was blind?"

"It's very hard to talk to you on this subject. But I won't sugarcoat it. I couldn't imagine life without Marie. But, yes, when I saw her struggle to do the simplest tasks and saw how lonely she was, and especially when I considered what would become of her after Frank and I were gone, it seemed abortion might have been the wiser choice. That was before I knew you and witnessed your meaningful life."

A knock at the door relieved Louise of further discussion. Another bouquet. Louise had already received flowers from Doc; from Dr. Weil and Daisy, now happily married; and from Bernard. No doubt this delivery was for Helen, whose other bouquets had come from John D. Rockefeller, Mark Twain, and Alexander Graham Bell, as well as from lesser-known admirers.

Louise set down the vase of red carnations accented with evergreen. When she pulled out the card from the cluster of blooms, she was shocked to read: "Louise, Congratulations. You have enriched the lives of so many people. I count myself as one. Your friend, Yonder."

Louise held the card and wondered what was coming over her. It was that moment in Pachelbel's "Canon" when the music rises to a point that holds the soaring spirit breathless in anticipation. *Yonder. Where is he? How did he know?*

CHAPTER 42

November 1909

Waiters pushing dessert carts glided among the tables where some one hundred people were seated at the Founders Day banquet of the National Society to Save Babies' Sight.

Louise made mental notes of the women's fashions, floral arrangements, food, and topics of conversation, because back home in Riverbend, Alice would demand a detailed account. But mostly she did it to quiet her thoughts. Her mind wanted to dart about, from Helen's challenge to reveal the truth to memories of her infidelity. It didn't help that she was wearing her aqua dress from The Twister Tenth Anniversary Observance. The diaphanous fabric was out of season, but it was a beautiful gown, and leaving it in the closet was silly. She made it do by adding a ready-made brocade jacket.

A flash caught Louise's eye and gave her a start. Suddenly it was like watching fireflies as waiters bathed servings of baked Alaska, the Corinthian Hotel's signature dessert, in flaming liqueur. Louise found herself back at her Chautauqua eve supper and what she'd come to think of as her "peach melba revelation," the realization that a dessert had eclipsed her reputation as a civic leader. That experience had re-kindled her desire to do good, but never would she have believed it would lead to this moment.

The past had dogged her all day, especially after spending the afternoon with Helen and Annie in the hotel's beauty salon. The beauty operator had applied a pomade to manage her wayward locks, and its lavender fragrance took her briefly back to another life-changing day and the comfort station above Anderson's Seed and Feed.

Louise sat at the head table between Helen and Dr. Vandegrift, who looked handsome in his tuxedo. But for his having the audacity to tell her the truth about Marie's blindness, she would not be sitting here tonight. For all her efforts to earn respect and recognition, it had not been virtue that brought her to this moment.

Dr. Vandegrift gestured toward Louise's dessert. "Eat, my dear." His voice was pleading. "You need nourishment to sustain you through a night of long-winded speeches. You've scarcely touched your entrée."

Suddenly Louise wanted to cry. Here she was, Louise Elizabeth Caldwell Morrissey, the ragamuffin from New Lexington, Nebraska, seated between Helen Keller and one of America's pre-eminent ophthalmologists, and he had noticed her untouched plate and cared enough to say something. Such a little thing, but it touched off a wave of gratitude.

So much to be grateful for. She looked out at the table where Dr. Weil and Bernard engaged in animated conversation, and Edward Bok offered a cigarette to Daisy Weil who declined with a smile and a little wave. Next to Daisy was Doc. The man Louise had loved and despised had become a tireless champion of the cause.

Louise turned her attention to the first in a series of speakers and tried to ignore the large mother-of-pearl buttons digging into her back.

Finally Helen and Annie were introduced and approached the lectern. Dr. Vandegrift, on behalf of the National Society, honored Helen for her role as national spokesman for the babies' sore eyes campaign. He presented her a framed certificate to which was attached a duplicate certificate embossed in Braille.

"Thank you, Dr. Vandegrift and everyone here tonight." Helen spoke the words which Annie interpreted. "Although I can neither see nor hear you, I can tell you what I feel. I feel your courage, and I commend you. With a plethora of worthy causes in which you might invest your time, talent, and money, you exhibit courage in supporting one that will more often bring you derision than praise.

"The time for hinting at unpleasant truths is past. Let us insist that the states put into practice every known and approved method of prevention, and that physicians and teachers open wide the doors of knowledge for the people to enter in. The facts are not pleasant. Often they are revolting. But it is better that our sensibilities should be shocked than that we should be ignorant of facts on which rest sight, hearing, intelligence, morals, and the lives of children. Let us do our best to rend the thick curtain with which society is hiding its eyes from the unpleasant but needful truths."

When Helen returned to her seat after a long, standing ovation, Louise squeezed her hand.

Dr. Vandegrift addressed the audience. "We all regret the occasional instances in which a healthy baby was accidentally blinded by insufficiently diluted silver nitrate. If we could not guarantee the safety of all babies, we could not justify our movement. But thanks to the ingenuity and initiative of one extraordinary woman, packaging dilute silver nitrate in safe, individual doses is now standard practice. Allow me to present Mrs. Francis Morrissey."

Dr. Vandegrift held up a plaque and gestured for Louise to join him at the lectern. "It is my privilege to present you with the first Visionary Award from the National Society to Save Babies' Sight."

Louise accepted the plaque and thanked Dr. Vandegrift, who sat down. As the audience applauded, she surveyed the crowd, silently thanked them for supporting the cause, and set her prepared notes on the lectern. Her eyes stopped on a man who had just entered the ballroom and was taking a seat at a table in back. *It can't be.* Her breath caught in her throat. *But, yes, it's Yonder.*

With a hand on her neck she caught herself in time to stop a gasp. In the awkward silence, she struggled to think of her opening words but finally had to resort to looking at her notes. "I am grateful to the National Society for recognizing my accomplishments, which would not have been possible without the support of Dr. Vandegrift, as well as nurses, social workers, doctors, public health workers, civic leaders, philanthropists, and others back in Nebraska."

She paused and looked about the room and let her eyes rest briefly on Yonder. "Any good that I do is to honor my late daughter, Marie Alouette Morrissey. It occurred to me that tonight it might be snowing back in Riverbend, my home, as it is here. Had Marie not been blind, had a tragic accident not taken the lives of her and my husband, tonight I might be home in Nebraska, sitting with my husband and fourteen-year-old sighted daughter in our darkened back parlor watching the magical first snowfall of the season out the window. As important as tonight's event is in the movement to prevent babies' sore eyes, I must tell you honestly that parlor is where I would rather be."

A hush came over the room.

"As Miss Keller pointed out, advocating this cause is more likely to bring you derision than praise. If you ever find yourself wavering, I want you to remember what I experienced as the mother of a blind child. Imagine trying to comfort your daughter when sighted children exclude her from play. Imagine trying to explain to your daughter that she cannot attend school like other children. Imagine trying to answer your daughter's question, 'I shall never marry, will I?'"

Louise looked toward the table where Yonder sat. When he raised a handkerchief to his eyes, she had to look away.

"Marie was, of course, the inspiration for me to champion the cause to end babies' sore eyes. More than that, she met life with more courage than I shall ever have, and I draw on her courage daily to face the biggest obstacles."

She looked down at her notes and hesitated. Gripping the lectern to still her trembling hands, she tried to censor herself, but a force within drove her to say, "But I shrank from one obstacle, one that existed within myself." She picked up the pages, tore them in half, and set them aside. "I could not bring myself to tell the truth. I always maintained that Marie was blinded by *pneumococcus.*"

She felt partitioned. One side of herself watched helplessly as the other side gathered speed. She recalled Marie wondering what kept the elevator from rising through the roof. At this moment, nothing. With no thought as to what happens beyond the roof, the practiced speech forgotten, any fear of exposure dismissed, she yielded to the momentum. "I had planned to go to my grave with this secret. But now I find myself compelled to speak. I had gonorrhea, and I caused my daughter's blindness."

The room seemed frozen in time, figures as still as those caught in Pompeii. People held poses as if for a photograph. Even smoke from cigars and cigarettes seemed to hang suspended in mid-air. Except for Edward Bok, taking notes, and Annie, spelling words into Helen's hand, everything stopped.

"In fairness to my late husband," her voice cracked and grew faint, "I must acknowledge that he did not have gonorrhea. He was not Marie's father."

She noticed Edward Bok, and her face burned. "Mr. Bok, I see you are writing. Tell readers of *The Ladies' Home Journal* I speak out to expose the false pride that would suppress this movement. In her speech earlier tonight Miss Keller told you of 'the shame that shelters evil.' Shame follows anyone who has gonorrhea, whether the disease was contracted in the bordello or in the marriage bed. Pity the poor woman who must watch the germ ravage the eyes of her precious baby. I ask you, which is the greater shame for a woman—having gonorrhea or letting false pride lest she be suspected of having the disease prevent her from demanding eyedrops for her newborn baby? When women have the courage to tell their doctors, 'Put drops in my newborn baby's eyes,' and when women and men band together to tell their legislators, 'Put drops in the eyes of every newborn baby,' this dreaded disease will no longer be the leading cause of blindness in children. It will be eradicated forever."

In the audience women wept openly and men looked down at the floor.

"If my speech wanders, just know I speak from my heart. I cannot leave here without pointing out that we stand on the shoulders of those who are already blind. We owe them a debt of gratitude, for too often they and their parents are condemned by ignorant people. I used to ask myself, 'How will I know when our campaign is making progress, that we're reaching the public with our message?' Sadly I saw the answer on a small town Main Street. I was accompanying children from Smithville Asylum for the Blind on a holiday shopping excursion when some young rowdies spotted one of our youngsters and . . . they began clapping."

Louise paused to collect herself and to wait for the murmurs to die down. She remembered the conclusion she had prepared.

"I stand here tonight so that no mother or father will have to carry in their hearts the knowledge that they caused their child's blindness. I stand here tonight so that no mother or father will suffer the anguish of their child asking, 'Did you make me go blind?' But most of all I stand here tonight for the children, so that no child will be needlessly condemned to a prison of darkness or bullied as the result of a parent's transgressions."

Louise's heart swelled to the applause. Seeing Bernard stand and wave a handkerchief, she fought back tears. Soon she was looking at a field of handkerchiefs waving because somehow she had pushed aside the fear and revealed her truth. She wanted to hold onto this moment forever. For she faced the vanguard and saw the promise of the future.

Louise noticed Helen's extended hand and gripped it tightly.

During the standing ovation, Louise looked to Yonder. She

returned his intense gaze, and in a trick of vision he came so close it seemed she could reach out and touch him.

After the applause had died, Louise was surrounded by well-wishers. "Thank you," she said, looking past them to seek Yonder's face in the departing crowd. When she spotted him, he was leaving the ballroom. Struggling to hide her disappointment, she continued to acknowledge the people around her.

The bejeweled society matron from the National Committee meeting took Louise's hand and gushed, "My dear, you have done wonders to advance our cause."

"Thank you, but it takes all of us working together," Louise said. Suddenly she realized Yonder was walking toward her, looking handsome in his Western-style tuxedo and holding a black Stetson in his hand. She was momentarily stunned by his smiling eyes that could soften the edge of her hardest mood. How should she greet him? But hesitation gave way to her longing to embrace him and hold on longer than might be proper.

She stepped back and brushed his collar. "I'm so sorry. I left face powder on your beautiful tuxedo."

"I remember your gown. You still do it justice." He caught himself. "Not that you wouldn't. It's been, what, five years since The Twister anniversary?"

"I shall take that as a compliment."

"You were magnificent tonight," he said. "You're one of the bravest people I know." He took her hand and led her to the nearest table. "Come, let's sit down."

He held a chair for her, then sat to her left, placing his Stetson on the empty chair next to him.

Louise turned toward him so she could look in his eyes. "I hadn't planned to speak so candidly. Seeing you in the audience gave me courage."

His expression didn't change. If he was pleased to know how important he was to her, it didn't show on his face. Had she gotten too close? She had no way to fathom what the intervening years had done to their friendship. And now after confessing to having contracted gonorrhea in an illicit relationship, she had bared the worst of herself. "Of course, the consequences of my candor remain to be seen." Her words were crisp. "It's probably best that I leave Riverbend."

"Wherever you go, go with all your heart."

"That's lovely. An Indian blessing?"

His smiling eyes brightened with mischief. "Confucius."

At the moment, the intervening years didn't matter. The bond she and Yonder had shared endured.

From the corner of her eye, Louise glimpsed Daisy and Dr. Weil approaching. Louise glanced at Daisy, then shifted her gaze back to Yonder, and Daisy steered her husband away.

"I brought you something." Yonder reached in his pocket and brought out a miniature cut-glass jar with a cloissonné lid.

Her treasured friend, whom she had assumed was out of her life forever, was presenting her with a gift. Louise fingered the lid, puzzled by its image of a red carnation, wishing she knew the language of flowers. Did he? Most likely the jar held a solid fragrance.

"Go ahead, open it." His eyes gleamed with expectation.

Now catching his contagious anticipation, she was more than curious as she removed the lid and lifted the jar with its whitish contents to her nose. It looked and smelled familiar but not fragrant.

He laughed. "You don't know what it is, do you?"

She inhaled the jar's contents again and shook her head. "I give up."

"I've been following your campaign. J.D.'s editorials have been positively brutal. I figured you might be bruised after . . ."

"Lard and salt? Like I mixed for your bruises."

He grinned. "Even though you wanted me to go away."

She laughed and cried and then reached out and hugged him. She mouthed an inaudible plea, *Oh, Yonder, please don't go away again.*

CHAPTER 43

Marie's birthday. She would have been seventeen. Almost seven years since the accident that took her life. Fluttering leaves on cottonwoods filtered the rays of the sunrise, causing the statue to shimmer in the dappled light. The brisk morning, the breeze carrying cotton tufts shed by the trees, and hazy light were reminiscent of several of Louise's annual pilgrimages to Chautauqua Park.

Louise ran a hand along the statue's doorframe, touching each notch beginning with Marie's first birthday, pausing to remember what was special about each year. She tried to bring back the exact moment that was the subject of the statue, the moment when Frank measured nine-year-old Marie standing tall against the ruler in his hand, the fragrance of birthday cake wafting from the oven. What silly thing had he called her? Something about growing from a little sprite to a budding neophyte?

Louise toweled off dew and cotton wisps from Marie's head and recalled braiding her daughter's hair before the measuring ritual. Her hand moved over a shoulder and brow and then the eyes. They were partially closed in an expression of delight. This was where Louise willed her thoughts to linger. Ever since her first visit to the statue, when she had confessed to Marie and Frank—"It *was* my fault"—she had discovered the statue's ability to inspire comfort, not self-recrimination.

The breeze shifted, and the aroma from the new Heart of the Plains bread factory caught her attention, an aroma that hadn't existed the last time she stood on this spot. That had been with Yonder, a year earlier. He had wanted to visit the graves and see the statue. She complied, although she ached with the memory that Frank had wanted to kill him. Anticipating that the awful subject might come up, she had met it head on. "There are some things I must explain to you. You were innocent, a victim—"

He had interrupted her. "I know everything I need to know."

Now she turned toward the sound of his voice.

"Can you smell the bread?" Yonder approached and handed her the shawl she'd asked him to retrieve from the car.

With his help, Louise drew the shawl around her shoulders. A thought made her smile, and having Yonder to share it with heightened her amusement. She closed her eyes and inhaled deeply. "The smell of progress. So much for my rabble-rousing stifling Riverbend's growth."

They lived in Omaha now. Yonder owned a construction business that employed Indian workers whom he groomed for success in a white man's world. Several of them had been hired by Bernard to work for Feldman Brothers Enterprises. Louise continued to press for legislation, but progress was slow, not just in Nebraska but elsewhere, with only two more states having mandated drops in the last three years. If all went well, the Nebraska Legislature should approve the printing and distribution of informational pamphlets in its next session. Meanwhile, Bernard influenced other philanthropists to provide drops for more and more hospitals. Louise kept up a full speaking schedule and remained active with the National Society to Save Babies' Sight.

She had become passionate about serving blind people, especially the children at Smithville Asylum. Jerrylynn had retired, and together they advocated for educational reform and career placement. Vinny was learning to tune pianos and spent his vacations with Aunt Bonita.

Riverbend was mostly a memory, save for the annual visit to the cemetery and statue. Madge and Mrs. Henkleman, Marie's piano teacher, had passed. Doc worked tirelessly with a Nebraska Medical Society committee he'd established to promote drops. Dovie was Dolores Henkleman now, the state senator's wife. She had passed the reins of the Riverbend Ladies Lending Library to Alice who declared the demands on her time prohibited continued involvement with Louise's campaign. Gertrude had surprised everyone by running off with Rev. Garnet Horton to live in a Utopian community in Texas. Irina's whereabouts were unknown, but it was rumored that she was the inspiration for a scandalous novel penned by her twin sister. Henryetta had expanded her kolache business to include distribution in Omaha and Lincoln. Tom's Whirlwind Maid factory was thriving.

As for those people who didn't live in Riverbend, Louise and Helen kept up a lively correspondence, and Daisy and Dr. Weil continued to promote legislation and were among Louise and Yonder's closest friends, along with Bernard and Miriam Feldman.

There was much Yonder never said. Never asked why Frank had wanted to kill him. Never asked how she got gonorrhea, simply trusting that she no longer had it. Never needed to know who Marie's father was. Never talked about Giovanna.

"You were running in your sleep again last night," Yonder said, "and pleading with someone to stop."

That was another thing he'd never asked about, until now. If she cried out during the night and awoke out of breath from trying to escape Pa's groping hands, Yonder simply held her until it was safe enough to close her eyes and rest her head on the pillow.

Yonder adjusted Louise's shawl, turned to face her, and held her hand. "Would it help to talk about it?"

His eyes beseeched her to share her burden. She looked at the ground and her voice was weak as she began to tell him about Pa's advances, about hitting him with a rake, and running away while Ma watched. "He used to call me 'daughter of the devil.'"

"He blamed you for his lust?"

She nodded and looked toward the statue, almost fully lit by the rising sun.

"And you believed you were responsible?"

She looked at him with disbelief. "That's what I was taught, what every girl was taught."

Yonder shook his head. "You told me once about beating up a boy at school because he played mean pranks on a girl."

She nodded. "They called her Dumb Sandy."

"Do you think Sandy was in any way responsible for the bullying she got?"

"Of course not."

"Then why do you think you caused your father to molest you?"

"That lesson was engrained. As long as I can remember

I've known that girls and women were the source of men's lust." *"Jezebel," Doc had called me.* She adjusted her shawl over her bosom.

He looked stricken. "When you cry out in your sleep . . . I'm helpless. All I can do is hold you and try to comfort you. If I could, I would banish your demons forever." He gripped her arms just below her shoulders and looked determined to make her understand his words. "I can't help you, Louise. Only you can. You must rid yourself of this false, and I daresay ignorant, assumption. Yes, men—and women—lust. But you are not responsible for the vile actions of your father." His voice rose, and his eyes flashed. "He forced himself on you, the child he was supposed to protect."

Louise tried to choke back tears, but when he pulled her to him she buried her head in his shoulder and wept. His words were meant to absolve her of guilt she'd held for most of her life, guilt that she could not readily let go of. But safe in his arms, nurtured by his acceptance, she felt lighter, her spirits lifted. The tears stopped flowing with a series of sighs. Finally calm again, she stepped back. "Thank you."

Picking up the peonies she had cut at home earlier, she unwrapped them and arranged them on the pedestal. "One time the Garden Society tried to plant flowers here, but the children trampled them. So then they posted 'Keep Off' signs to no avail. I think that was a victory for Marie."

The rumble of a passing train set Louise to thinking. "I just realized that had the Burlington not eliminated Riverbend's passenger service, I might still be the respected proprietor of Riverview Inn instead of the woman who spoke out about venereal disease and brought ignominy to Riverbend."

"That would have been a shame," Yonder said. "On the other hand, I saw you growing restless long before the accident. Your spirit is such that you'd have found an important calling."

Yonder took the towel and wiped the parts of the statue she couldn't reach. As he toweled off Frank's shoulders, he said, "Frank was a good father, a protective father. It was the drink that made him crazy."

"Yes."

He wiped off the ruler. "The statue is a fine tribute to their bond. I always envied him." He turned toward Louise and touched her cheek. "In more ways than one."

Married close to a year now, and I'm blushing. Louise stepped around the statue and stood past its open door. "Remember our visit here last year? I was standing in this very spot."

Yonder dropped the towel and joined her. "I got down on one knee, and when I stood up, my pant leg was wet from dew."

Louise smiled. "Until that moment, I was afraid you might never propose."

"I was terrified you wouldn't accept."

"Remember our kiss?"

"Refresh my memory."

Her eyes beckoned while his gaze shuddered through her body. Then his lips met hers, and his tongue played around her mouth, teasing it open. His hands on the small of her back pulled her into him, against his manhood.

They parted, and she asked, "Did we get it right?"

"I believe more practice is called for. What are your plans for the afternoon?"

"I'm ready for the Feldmans' visit tonight except for making corn pudding. Other than that, I'm all yours."

Yonder smiled, the wrinkling at the corner of his eyes reminding Louise of what had first endeared him to her so long ago. "Let's go home."

# # #

Acknowledgments

If I wanted to wrap myself in mystique, I'd tell you how I toiled alone in a drafty garret, sometimes forgetting to eat and sleep, a slave to a master that commanded me to forsake all else in pursuit of the writing. It didn't happen that way. This novel came about in fits and starts and with help all along the way, notably from the following:

My husband, Timothy, who only thought he knew what he was signing up for when he married me six years ago.

My children, Steve and Cindy, who would have been conscripted to read my work-in-progress if they hadn't volunteered.

Ramon Carver, who adapted scenes from my novel for the Salado (Texas) Living Room Theatre; my granddaughter, Quinn, who played the part of Marie; and Tim, who played Doc.

My writing critique group in Austin, Novel in Progress, where I proudly hold a self-appointed position as Name Sheriff.

Many friends and family members who read and critiqued my work and offered encouragement.

Professional sources, namely American Academy of Ophthalmology, Sherwin Isenberg, M.D., Jane Kivlin, M.D., Ivan Schwab, M.D., and Prevent Blindness America.

Discussion Questions

Louise can be cunning and manipulative. To what extent is she a product of her time and circumstances? To what extent is she simply self-serving?

What is the significance of Louise's fluttering eyelids?

Louise blames herself and Doc for Marie's blindness. Who or what else might be at fault?

What did Louise learn about herself from the night spent caring for victims of The Twister? How did it influence her later on?

Why does Louise risk her hard-earned reputation to champion the babies' sore eyes cause? What price does she pay for her role? What does she gain from her role?

Louise and Dovie's friendship seems rock solid. What drives them apart?

Louise's childhood nemesis, Daisy, greets Louise like a long lost friend. Why does Louise so quickly trust that Daisy has changed?

What do you think of Louise's approach vs. Frank's when it comes to preparing Marie to succeed in a sighted world?

At the Chautauqua supper party, what was it about Giovanna's presence and guests' praise of Louise's peach melba, that awakened Louise to a lost part of herself?

Doc says it was because he was a doctor that he didn't think Louise would become infected. What does he mean?

What were the prejudices that impeded the babies' sore eyes movement and subsequent legislation? What else stood in the way?

What makes Frank ill-suited to innkeeping? Did he find his calling with the Whirlwind Maid & Marie's Chautauqua career?

Often what Louise fears doesn't materialize. When she fears that the child who leaves for the Chautauqua won't be the one who comes home, what is she anticipating?

What do you think Marie's prospects were had she lived?

Was Frank capable of killing Yonder?

Helen Keller's romance was sabotaged in large part because of a bias against people with handicaps marrying. Does this bias exist today?

How does Louise's understanding of her "compromise with sin" change over time? Does she ever come to grips with it? Can she forgive herself?

What are some erroneous beliefs Louise and others have

regarding sex? What is the impact of these beliefs on her?

Betrayal is one of the themes of the novel. Which characters betray or are betrayed?
What enables Louise to forgive her mother's betrayal?

Although Helen Keller is presented in a fictionalized friendship with Louise, the representation is true to her character. What surprises you most about her abilities and views?

When Bernard accuses Frank of giving Louise the "clap," Frank immediately suspects Yonder is Marie's father. What are the clues throughout the novel that cause him to jump to that conclusion?

How do you think Yonder feels about the assimilation movement and his role in it?

Why does Louise consider abandoning the campaign for drops?

Discuss any of these themes explored in the novel: shame and redemption, artifice vs. authenticity, friendship, and false pride.

Afterword: What's Real and What's Not

"Babies' sore eyes" is real. Minutes after you were born, it's almost certain that, by state law, a prophylactic agent was instilled in your eyes. The practice was, and still is, mandated by state law.

The purpose is to prevent *ophthalmia neonatorum,* or "babies' sore eyes," an infection caused by *gonococcus* bacteria transmitted when the baby passes through the birth canal of a mother who has gonorrhea. Infection can also occur when the highly contagious germ is picked up from a towel, blanket, or hands.

Gonorrhea raged unchecked in the early twentieth century. A man could be treated for symptoms yet remain a carrier and infect his wife, who might not know she had the disease until serious complications developed.

* * *

The grassroots movement to get states to mandate drops in babies' eyes stands as one of the great public health triumphs of the twentieth century. An unsung triumph, to be sure. It took many years, from about 1910 until 1940, for all states to adopt this legislation. Today's preferred prophylactic is erythromycin ointment.

Sadly it is true that some healthy babies were accidentally blinded when they were given silver nitrate drops that hadn't been sufficiently diluted. Eventually it became the practice to package dilute silver nitrate in individual doses in wax ampoules.

As the public became aware that blindness could be caused by gonorrhea, some blind people and their families were stigmatized. To my knowledge, however, there was never a "clapping" incident.

* * *

With the exception of Helen Keller, the real heroes in the eradication of "babies' sore eyes" do not show up in the pages of *Compromise With Sin*. They're worth noting:

Karl Sigmund Franz Credé, Director of the Lying-in Hospital in Leipzig, Germany, in 1882 published results of his experiments showing that instilling dilute silver nitrate drops into newborn babies' eyes would prevent blinding from *ophthalmia neonatorum*.

Dr. Lucien Howe, an American who led the movement for state laws, has been called "the father of *ophthalmia neonatorum* legislation."

Dr. Prince Morrow and Dr. Park Lewis were prominent figures on the Commission to Investigate the Conditions of the Blind in New York State, which published a report that influenced establishment of the National Society for the Prevention of Blindness.

Louisa Lee Schuyler, a prominent philanthropist and civic leader, read the report of the New York Commission and was struck by a photo of blind children captioned "Needlessly blind." She instigated a movement that became the National Society for the Prevention of Blindness. Schuyler, the granddaughter of General Philip Schuyler and Alexander Hamilton, was seventy-one years old at the time. I named my protagonist "Louise" as an homage, but the only resemblance to Schuyler is her courage in tackling the taboo subject of venereal disease in order to save babies' sight.

* * *

Ignorance and injustice flourished in this time of strict taboos regarding sex. Some examples:

The wedding night came as a shock to many an unsuspecting bride.

Topics considered improper included sex, pregnancy, and venereal disease.

Many people believed women were responsible for a man's lust and/or impotence.

A proper woman went into her "confinement" once her pregnant condition showed.

An unmarried woman who got pregnant could expect that she and her "bastard" child would be shunned by the community and even her own family.

* * *

Helen Keller, Anne Sullivan Macy, Peter Fagan, Edward Bok, Rev. Russell Conwell, and Andrew Carnegie are actual historical figures. I have fictionalized them but with a keen sense that I wanted to remain true to who they were.

Yes, Helen Keller did write an opinion piece (actually two) in *The Ladies' Home Journal* warning mothers about babies' sore eyes. I changed the date of the article I quoted. It actually appeared in January 1909. She also served on the National Committee for the Prevention of Blindness, which became the National Society for the Prevention of Blindness, today known as Prevent Blindness America.

Keller was such a tireless reformer, however, that in retrospect her labor reform, anti-war, and other activities to aid blind people must have eclipsed her role in the babies' sore eyes movement. In her autobiography *Midstream,* published in 1929, Helen devotes just three pages to the subject where she says prevention is near to her heart and she wishes she could devote more time to it.

Helen and Peter's romance was real, but I've changed her age. You can read more in her autobiography *Midstream: My Later Life* and the biography, *Helen Keller: a Life,* by Dorothy Herrmann.

Helen and Annie did tour with the tent Chautauqua and even went to Nebraska, but not when I said they did. There was no Durfee Chautuaqua Bureau, and most of the acts I describe were made up.

The Ladies' Home Journal did in fact lose 25,000 subscribers after Bok's editorial on venereal disease.

Baby Giveaway Saturday was a real event held at Burgess-Nash Company, "Everybody's Store," in Omaha, Nebraska. The event was called Adopt a Baby Saturday, and the orphans came from Child Saving Institute. You can see a copy of a 1916 newspaper ad on my blog.

Many of the towns in my novel are fictional, but St. DeRoin was a real town devoured by the Missouri River as it changed course. The town sat on the edge of the vanishing Halfbreed Tract.

I based my novel's axe murders on an unsolved crime committed in Villisca, Iowa, in 1912.

The early twentieth century saw protests to halt immigration from Eastern and Southern Europe.

* * *

"They enslave their children's children who make compromise with sin" wrote Helen Keller in her essay for *The Ladies' Home Journal.* Keller took the phrase from the poem, "The Present Crisis," by James Russell Lowell.

"The Wreck of the Hesperus," written by Henry Wadsworth Longfellow, challenged many an elocution student. "Little Flo's Letter" is usually attributed to Anonymous but was actually written by Eben E. Rexford. I have fond memories of sitting with family at the kitchen table of my late mother-in-law, Clesta Gabrial, while she recited this and other poems she'd learned as a girl.

Please sit back and forgive—or enjoy catching--the anachronisms. There are quite a few. For example, the Cadillac Osceola that Frank bought in 1905? Well I needed a closed-body car, and although it was invented that year it wasn't put into production until 1910. Also the story demanded that I get some Nebraska towns prematurely wired for electricity and phone service.

You'll find an abundance of background material on my blog

NovelWords.Cafe

Looking for More?

Go to my blog, NovelWords.Cafe for more of the story behind the story. There you'll find, among other things, Helen Keller's complete *Ladies' Home Journal* essay, pictures of cars, a link to a video about lighting a Coleman iron, and an Editor's Cut: scenes that didn't make the book.

Maybe *Compromise With Sin* left you wanting to know more about certain characters. Irina Taylor, the nurse with the blue-violet eyes and silver-bells laughter, intrigued me. Why did she disappear from Riverbend? Watch for publication of her story. Its working title is *You Knew I Was a Writer.*

One More Thing

With this novel, I set out to write a book I'd want to read. I hope it's one you enjoyed reading. What do you think? I'd appreciate your comments on Amazon or Goodreads or my blog, NovelWords.Cafe.

About the Author

I stumbled into writing *Compromise With Sin* when life handed me something I couldn't resist. While serving on the board of the Nebraska chapter of the National Society To Prevent Blindness, I was intrigued to learn that the organization was founded in 1908 to promote passage of legislation to prevent a blinding condition known as 'babies' sore eyes.' That term grabbed me. My initial research revealed a disease caused by gonorrhea and responsible for one-fourth to one-third of all admissions to asylums for the blind. If that wasn't enough of a hook, discovering that Helen Keller played an important role clinched it. From there I started to wonder what might happen to a family whose child was blinded by babies' sore eyes.

Causes on behalf of preventing blindness and serving blind

people have been a lifelong interest. I once belonged to a little band of volunteers who transcribed print books into Braille. Years later, I had an opportunity to use my ability to read Braille (by sight, not by touch) and write it when I taught the first blind student mainstreamed into an Omaha, Nebraska, high school.

I now live with my husband, Timothy, in Austin, Texas, where we volunteer as narrators for the Texas Talking Book Program. Inline skating and polymer clay are favorite activities, along with anything that involves my two children, grandtwins, and extended family.

Leanna Englert